TRAITORS
OF ROME

SIMON SCARROW

EAGLES · OF · THE · EMPIRE

TRAITORS OF ROME

HEADLINE

First published in Great Britain in 2019
by HEADLINE PUBLISHING GROUP

1

Cataloguing in Publication Data is available from the British Library

ISBN 978 1 4722 5840 3 (Hardback)
ISBN 978 1 4722 5839 7 (Trade paperback)

Typeset in Bembo by Avon DataSet Ltd, Bidford-on-Avon, Warwickshire

Printed and bound in Great Britain by Clays Ltd, Elcograf S.p.A.

MIX
Paper from
responsible sources
FSC
www.fsc.org   FSC® C104740

Headline's policy is to use papers that are natural, renewable and recyclable
products and made from wood grown in well-managed forests and other
controlled sources. The logging and manufacturing processes are expected
to conform to the environmental regulations of the country of origin.

Traitors of Rome is dedicated to Anne and Mel Richmond, my beloved parents-in-law. Sadly, we lost Mel during the months this novel was being written. We miss his humour and hearty enjoyment of every day that life gave him . . .

THE FRONTIER BETWEEN
ROME AND PARTHIA
IN THE FIRST CENTURY

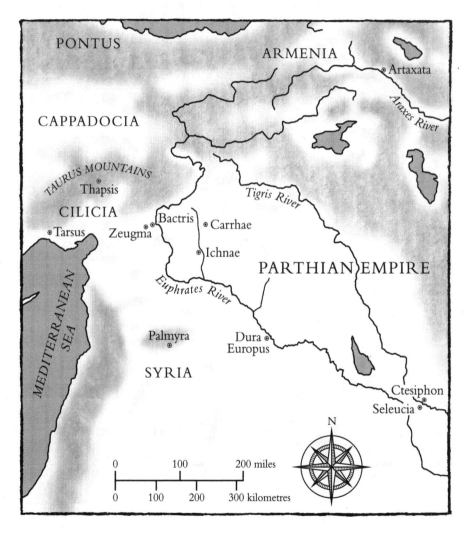

CAST LIST

Quintus Licinius Cato: Tribune in command of the Second Cohort of the Praetorian Guard

Lucius Cornelius Macro: Senior centurion of the Second Cohort of the Praetorian Guard, a tough veteran

General Gnaeus Domitius Corbulo: Commander of the armies of the eastern Empire and tasked with the challenge of taming Parthia, while not being given the necessary resources to do so

Apollonius of Perga: an agent of General Corbulo, and aide to Cato. Transparently a shrewd and devious man, with an opaque past

Lucius: son of Cato, a delightful young boy raised amongst soldiers and picking up some of their language, alas . . .

Licinia Petronella: bride-to-be of Macro, formerly Cato's slave. A stongly built woman with equally strong opinions

Cassius: a feral dog rescued from the wild in Armenia, now devoted to Cato and prone to terrifying those who are taken in by his fearsome appearance

Second Praetorian Cohort

Centurions: Ignatius, Nicolis, Placinus, Porcino, Metellus

Optios: Pantellus, Pelius, Marcellus

Fourth Syrian Cohort

Prefect Paccius Orfitus: recently promoted commander of the unit. A thrusting glory hunter

Centurion: Mardonius

Optios: Phochus, Laecinus

Macedonian Cavalry Cohort

Decurion: Spathos

Sixth Legion

Centurions: Pullinus, Piso

Optio/Acting Centurion: Martinus

Legionary: Pindarus

Legionary Selenus: an unfortunately hungry veteran

Others

Prefect Clodius: the edgy commander of the First Dacian Auxiliary Cohort watching over the frontier at Bactris

Graniculus: Quartermaster at Bactris. A content horticulturalist hoping for peace

King Vologases: King of Parthia, the 'King of Kings' and keen to impress on his subjects that the price of treachery is an agonising death.

Haghrar, of the House of Attaran: A prince of Ichnae, also known as Desert Hawk, treading delicately in the lethal world of court politics

Ramalanes: a captain of the Royal Palace Guard

Democles: a river boat captain who always has an eye open to fiscal advancement

Patrakis: river boat crewman

Pericles: an innkeeper who wishes that his customers always settled their bills in full

Ordones: spokesman for the people of Thapsis

Centurion Munius: Centurion in charge of the engineering detachment, with the thankless task of building a bridge over a raging torrent

Mendacem Pharageus: a professional rabble rouser

Legionary Borenus: another rabble rouser who may not be all that he seems

CHAPTER ONE

Autumn AD 56

'Here they come,' Centurion Macro muttered as he gazed towards the far side of the training ground, where a small cloud of dust indicated the approach of a column of soldiers. He finished chewing the end of an aniseed twig and tossed the frayed length aside, then spat to clear the fibrous pulp from his mouth. He turned to see his superior leaning back against the trunk of a nearby cedar tree, dozing in the shade. Tribune Cato was a slender man in his late twenties. His dark hair had been cropped short the day before and the stubble made him look like a recruit. In slumber, his face would have looked serene and youthful were it not for the white scar tissue scoring a ragged diagonal line from his forehead across his brow and down his right cheek. He was a veteran of many campaigns and he looked the part. Beside him lay his dog, Cassius, a large, wild-looking beast with wiry brown fur. One of its ears had been mauled at some point before Cato had taken the animal on a year before, when they had been campaigning in Armenia. It rested its head in Cato's lap, and every so often its tail swished a little in contentment.

Macro regarded Cato in silence for a moment. Although he had served for twice as long as the younger man, he had come to recognise that experience was not everything. A good officer had to have brains as well. And brawn, he added to his shortlist. The latter Cato may have lacked, but he made up for it with courage and resilience. As for himself, Macro readily accepted that experience and brawn were his main qualities. He smiled as he reflected on the reasons why he and Cato had been close friends as long as they had. They each made up for the one quality the other was deficient in. It had served them well for nearly fifteen years, as they had fought through campaigns across the Roman Empire, from the freezing banks of the Rhine to the baking deserts of the eastern frontier. The two officers had an enviable record, and the scars to show that they had shed blood for Rome.

However, Macro had begun to wonder how much longer he could tempt the Fates. They had spared him thus far, but there must come a time when even their indulgence would be exhausted. Whether his death was dealt by an enemy's sword, spear or arrow, or by something inglorious like a fall from a horse or sickness, he could sense the moment drawing closer. What he feared even more was a crippling injury that would leave him less than a man for the rest of his years.

He frowned at such morose thoughts. Five years ago he would never have entertained them. But now he was conscious that his muscles felt stiff in the morning, and there was a painful twinge in his knees at the end of a hard day's marching. Worse still, he no longer moved as swiftly as he did in his prime. That should come as no surprise. After all, he reminded himself, he had already served with the army for over twenty-six years. He was entitled to request his discharge and take his bounty and the grant of a small plot of land, as was his due, and settle into retirement. That he had chosen not to do so was simply because he had not been able to imagine a life outside of the army. It was his home, and Cato and the others were his family.

But now he had a woman in his life.

He smiled as his mind filled with the image of Petronella; bold, brassy and beautiful in precisely the way that Macro valued beauty. She was well-built, with dark eyes set in a round face, and while her tongue could be sharp, her hearty laugh warmed his heart through and through. It was partly because of her, and partly because of the burden of his years, that Macro was now giving more and more thought to the notion of retiring from the army. And yet he felt guilty when he caught himself contemplating applying for a discharge. It was as if he was betraying the men under his command and, more importantly, letting down his friend, Tribune Cato.

He would have brooded on this more, but there was no time for that now. There was work to be done.

Macro cleared his throat as he approached the tribune. 'Sir, the Syrian lads have arrived.'

Cato opened his eyes, then blinked at the bright sunlight just beyond the boughs of the cedar tree. The dog raised its head and looked up questioningly. Cato gave it a brief pat on its neck, then eased himself up onto his feet and stretched his shoulders as he made a quick mental calculation. 'They've taken their time. They were supposed to be here at noon. That was at least an hour ago.'

The two officers squinted across the expanse of dry ground stretching out from the treeline. The auxiliaries of the Fourth Syrian Cohort were tramping along the track that led from the city of Tarsus to the training area. They were just one of the units from the army that was being assembled by General Corbulo to wage war on Rome's long-standing eastern enemy, Parthia. Several auxiliary cohorts and two legions were in camp outside Tarsus, over twenty thousand men in all. It would have been an impressive figure, Cato reflected, were it not for the poor quality of most of the men and their equipment. Consequently there was no question of the campaign beginning until spring, at the earliest. In the meantime, Corbulo had given instructions for his men to train hard while equipment and stocks of food were gathered in to supply the army.

For its part, the Syrian cohort had been ordered to make a ten-mile route march in the country surrounding the city before heading to the training ground to carry out a mock attack on a stretch of defences that Cato's men had erected a short distance to his right. It measured a hundred paces end to end, with a gate halfway along its length. Already the men of the Second Praetorian Cohort were emerging from the shade to take their positions along the packed earth rampart that ran behind the timber palisade. In front of them was a ditch that completed the defences.

Cato looked over his men with an experienced eye and felt a familiar surge of pride swell in his heart. These soldiers, in their off-white tunics and segmented armour, were without doubt the finest men serving in General Corbulo's army. They had already proved their worth fighting in Spain, and in the previous year's campaign in Armenia. The thought of the latter caused Cato's pride to subside as he recalled the men he had lost in a bid to place a Roman sympathiser on the Armenian throne. The three hundred survivors represented just over half the number that had marched out of their barracks on the edge of Rome when the cohort had been sent east to act as Corbulo's bodyguard. When they eventually returned to the city, there would be much grieving for their families, as well as the need to find replacements for training.

Hopefully, Cato reflected, that training would proceed more swiftly than was the case with the units of the Eastern Empire. For too long they had served as garrison troops, keeping order amongst the local people and ensuring that taxes were collected. Very few of them had ever been on campaign, and they lacked fitness and experience of battle. Corbulo had spent the last year gathering his forces for the coming invasion of Parthia, and many of the men were ill-equipped and un-ready for war. The Syrian auxiliaries tramping towards the Praetorians were typical of the poor calibre of men under the general's command.

The dog nuzzled Cato's hand and then jumped up, resting its long forelegs against his chest as it tried to lick his face.

'Down, Cassius!' Cato pushed it away. 'Sit!'

At once the animal went down on its haunches, the tip of its tail still wagging.

'At least someone can be trained,' said Macro. 'I'm starting to wonder if we'd be better off with a pack of dogs rather than those layabouts.'

There was a shout from the officer riding at the head of the Syrian column as he raised his arm, and the soldiers sham-bled to a halt. Without waiting for permission, some of the men lowered their spears and shields and bent over, gasping for breath. The commanding officer wheeled his mount and rode back down the column, berating his subordinates and gesturing furiously.

Macro shook his head and spat to one side. 'Just as well today's drill ain't an ambush, eh?'

Cato nodded. It was easy enough to imagine the chaos that would have caused amongst the exhausted auxiliaries. 'Get our men ready. I want them to go in hard when the Syrians make their attack. They need to understand that we're not playing at war. Better a few bruises and broken bones now than have them thinking it's going to be a gentle stroll into Parthia.'

Macro grinned and saluted before striding out in front of the length of rampart. He halted near the middle and turned to face the Praetorians. They had been issued with training weapons: wicker shields, wooden swords and javelins with blunt wooden heads. Though designed to cause less damage than the real thing, such weapons could still deliver painful blows and injuries. He raised his centurion's vine cane and patted the head of the gnarled length of wood in the palm of his spare hand as he addressed the men in the clear, loud voice he had perfected over the years for training soldiers and commanding them in battle.

'Time for a little exercise, lads! There's nearly six hundred auxiliaries over there. Twice as many as us. And that's bad odds for them.' He paused to allow the men to smile and chuckle. 'That said, if even one of those idle bastards gets over the rampart, I'll have every last man of the century manning that stretch on latrine duties for a month. And since the remaining men will be fed a diet of prunes, you will be so deep in the shit that you will be dreaming of fresh air!'

There was a chorus of laughter from the Praetorians, and Macro indulged them a moment before he raised his cane to command their silence. 'Never forget, we are the Second Praetorian Cohort, the finest body of men in the entire Imperial Guard. Now let's show these Syrian layabouts why!'

He punched his stick into the air with a savage roar, and the Praetorians followed suit, stabbing the rounded tips of their training javelins towards the heavens as they shouted their battle cries. Macro encouraged them for a moment longer before he turned away and strode back to join Cato and his dog. Cassius's remaining ear had pricked up at the sound of the cheering, and now he rose back onto four feet, his hindquarters swaying as his bushy tail swept from side to side. Cato took a sturdy leather leash from his belt and tied it to the dog's iron-studded collar as he muttered, 'Can't be having you eat any of the Syrians . . . Bad for morale.'

Taking a firm hold on the leash, he straightened up and looked out over the open ground towards the Syrians. The centurions and optios were busy marshalling their men into a battle line opposite the rampart. Cato saw that the lines were poorly dressed even as the officers pushed and shoved the auxiliaries into position.

Macro stood with the top of his cane resting against his shoulders and let out a long sigh. 'Sweet fucking Mars, have you ever seen such a shower of shite? I wouldn't bet on that lot being able to fight their way out of a roll of wet papyrus. If they ever go up against the Parthians, they'd better pray that the enemy kill themselves laughing, or they haven't got a hope.'

A glint on the track behind the Syrians drew Cato's eye, and he saw several riders approaching. They were bareheaded, but wearing gleaming breastplates. 'Looks like Corbulo has taken an interest in today's drill.'

Macro sucked his teeth. 'Then he's in for a bit of a disappointment, sir.'

They watched the general and his staff officers ride round the far flank of the Syrian cohort before drawing up a short distance beyond to observe. Cato glanced at the prefect in command of the auxiliaries and felt a brief twinge of pity for the heavy-set and balding man. Paccius Orfitus was a decent enough officer. He had served as a legionary centurion on the Rhine frontier before being promoted to command the Syrian cohort barely a month before, and had only just begun training his men for the coming campaign. And now he had the additional burden of carrying out an attack drill under the scrutiny of his commanding general.

With the cohort formed up in two lines of three centuries, Orfitus dismounted, took his shield and helmet down from the saddle horns and armed himself to lead the formation. Like the Praetorians, the auxiliaries had been issued with training equipment that was heavier than their field kit, and no doubt added to their evident exhaustion. Orfitus waited until the colour party took their place between the two lines, then paced to the front of his cohort and gave the order to advance. The glint of the sun on their helmets shimmered as the formation rippled forward.

Macro watched for a moment before he commented grudgingly, 'At least they can keep in step. That's something for the prefect to be thankful for.'

Cato nodded and then jerked his thumb towards the rampart. 'Better get yourself up there with the lads.'

'You not joining in the fun, sir?'

'No. Just observing.'

Macro shrugged, then saluted before jogging off behind the rampart to pick up his kit and join his men. Cato was left alone with the dog. Sometimes, he reflected, it was best to stand apart from such drills to get an overview; it was easy to miss important details from the heart of the action. He wanted to see how his own cohort performed during the exercise.

The Syrian auxiliaries steadily closed the distance, and then, just out of arrowshot, Orfitus gave the order to halt. His men drew up and there was a moment of shuffling amid the shouting of the officers to dress the line, before the formation stood still and awaited his next command.

'Second Century! Prepare to form testudo!'

Cassius pulled on his lead and Cato tugged him back as he watched the auxiliaries in the centre of the front line form into a column. When they were ready, their commander moved into the front rank and shouted the order. 'Form testudo!'

What followed was every bit as bad as Cato had anticipated. Those in the front rank were supposed to present their shields to the enemy before the second rank raised theirs overhead, followed by each rank in turn. Instead, many men moved to lift their shields as soon as the order was given, causing chaos as they knocked into the men around them and clashed shields with the surrounding ranks. Once again the air filled with the curses and bellowed instructions of the junior officers as they struggled to restore order. In the end, Orfitus was obliged to make his way down the column, overseeing each rank's efforts to adopt the formation. From the rampart came a ragged chorus of jeers and laughter as the Praetorians looked on.

When at last the century was ready, Orfitus returned to his position and gave the order for the cohort to advance. The men of the two flanking centuries began to open their ranks as they prepared to hurl their training javelins. At the same time, they raised their shields until the rims covered most of their faces. Glancing back towards the rampart, Cato could make out the crest of Macro's helmet as the centurion hefted his own javelin and waited for the Syrians to come within easy range. The mockery and taunts faded, and a relative quiet fell over the training ground as the men on both sides prepared to engage. Cato looked on with professional approval. This was as it should be. Training was a serious matter. It was the quality of their training that allowed the armies of Rome to dominate a vast empire and defeat the barbarians who regarded its riches with envious eyes.

'Prepare javelins!' Macro bellowed.

The men along the rampart eased back their throwing arms

and widened their stance before bracing themselves. Then they stood still, like sculptures of athletes, thought Cato, as the Syrians tramped closer, sheltering warily behind their wicker training shields.

'Loose javelins!' Macro ordered.

The Praetorians stretched back their throwing arms and then hurled the weapons into the air with a ragged chorus of grunts. Cato watched the shafts, dark against the clear sky, as they arced towards the auxiliaries. The men of the front rank stopped in their tracks, causing disruption as those behind were forced to draw up. Even so, there was just time to duck behind their shields as the training javelins pelted down. Their light construction and blunted tips meant that there would be few injuries, but the auxiliaries' instincts made them hesitate and take cover, just as they would in a real battle. It was up to their officers to keep driving them forward.

'Don't stop!' Orfitus bellowed. 'Keep moving! Advance!'

He called the pace as the testudo edged forward, with the flanking centuries keeping up on either side. On the rampart, fresh javelins were being passed forward to the men along the palisade, and the Praetorians were hefting them as they prepared to unleash another volley. But the attackers got in first, the centurion on the right of the line raising his sword and calling out to his men.

'First Century! Halt! Ready javelins! Loose!'

The rushed sequence of orders led to a ragged response from the Syrians. Already tired from their forced march, many of the men were unable to throw the training javelins far enough, and the shafts plucked handfuls of soil from the foot of the rampart or fell into the ditch. Less than half, Cato judged, struck at the palisade and the men standing behind it. The Praetorians had raised their shields, and the shafts clattered aside, save for one lucky shot that caught one of the men on the shoulder. He stumbled back a pace before losing his balance and rolling down the rear of the rampart in a cloud of dust and loose soil.

As soon as the men on the other flank realised that their comrades had unleashed their volley, they followed suit, with just as little effect. By contrast, the Praetorians' second throw was well ordered, and the javelins clattered down on the auxiliaries' shields with a brief rattling staccato, causing some of the more nervous men to lose grip of their shields.

Orfitus continued to count the pace as he led the testudo towards the narrow causeway in front of the gate, where Macro was positioned. On either side individuals snatched up the training javelins from the exchange of volleys and hurled them back at the opposition in a steady flow of shafts to and fro. As the testudo reached the causeway, Orfitus ordered his men to halt. And Cato wondered what the prefect was planning to do next. The assault ladders were in the rear with the three centuries of the reserve line. There was a brief pause as they were brought forward and fed through the testudo, ready to be thrown up against the rampart for the assault to begin. Then it would be man on man between the auxiliaries and the Praetorians, and he had little doubt that his cohort, though outnumbered, would be able to hold the rampart.

'Form pontus!' Orfitus called out. At once the leading ranks of the testudo ran across the causeway and raised their shields, bracing their spare arms against the timbers of the gate. As the following ranks moved up, adding their shields and each assuming a lower posture, the bridge of overlapping shields began to form a ramp leading up to the palisade.

Cato tensed in surprise, and then smiled grudgingly. He had not expected this bold manoeuvre, particularly from a unit he had been ready to dismiss as third rate. 'Well, well,'

11

he mused quietly, realising how well this must have been rehearsed.

Some of the Praetorians along the palisade were equally surprised, and leaned forward to observe Orfitus and his men, until their officers bawled at them to face the front.

'Seems like our friend Orfitus is more than a little resourceful . . .' Cato clicked his tongue and fondled Cassius's ears.

The dog twitched its head to one side and gave its master's fingers a quick lick, then gently eased forward until restrained by the taut leash.

'Keen to get stuck in, eh? Not this time. Those men are on our side, boy.'

Cato focused his attention back towards the causeway. The new formation was almost complete, and the century that had been following the testudo was trotting forward to advance over the makeshift assault ramp. Ahead of them the Praetorians stood waiting, training swords levelled at the edge of the wicker shields, ready to strike. But there was no sign of Macro's crested helmet amongst them. Cato frowned, wondering what had become of his friend in the moment the dog had distracted him. Had he been knocked down? Or slipped back off the rampart? That was hard to believe, as Macro had the veteran's keen awareness of danger, as well as sure-footedness in the heat of battle. So what had happened?

He noticed a party of men gathering behind the gate, a half-century or so, in tight formation. Above them their comrades were duelling with the first of the auxiliaries to reach the palisade, wooden swords striking at wicker shields, helmets and exposed limbs with the flat of their weapons. Already, one of the Syrians was attempting to climb over the palisade to gain a foothold on the walkway above the gate.

Just then there was a roar as Macro and the Praetorians

opened the gates and bellowed their war cries as they surged forward. A tremor went through the auxiliaries who formed the assault ramp. A handful of the men making their way up to the fight toppled off and rolled into the ditch on either side before the formation crumbled into a confused mass of men struggling to stay on their feet. Then Cato saw that the gate had been opened, and there was Macro's crest bobbing above the fray as he and his men drove forward, thrusting the attackers back and causing yet more men to tumble into the ditch. Prefect Orfitus tried to rally his men at the end of the causeway, but there was no time to steady them before the Praetorians charged on into their disordered ranks. Cato caught one last glimpse of Orfitus before he was knocked down, then his men turned and fell back before Macro's onslaught.

Cassius tugged at the leash again. He strained and looked up at Cato plaintively.

'You want to play?'

The dog wagged its tail and Cato loosened his grip. At once Cassius bounded forward, the leash whipping from side to side behind him.

Cato shrugged. 'Whoops . . .'

More of the Praetorians clambered down inside the defences and poured out of the gate in pursuit of the retreating Syrians, roughly knocking them down or tripping them over. Cassius raced in amongst them, jumping up at men from both sides as he weaved through the mayhem. Cato watched for a moment longer before strolling forward, cupping his hands to his mouth as he drew a deep breath.

'Second Praetorian! Halt! That's enough, boys!'

The nearest of his men turned and drew up obediently. Those further off had one last go at their opponents before following suit as the officers relayed the command. Macro gave the order for the centuries to form up, then watched with an amused grin as the downed auxiliaries struggled to their feet, retrieved their equipment and stumbled back across the training ground to where the rest of their comrades stood, catching their breath as they regarded the Praetorians warily. Cato caught sight of the crest of the prefect's helmet as Orfitus sat up and shook his head. He made his way across, bending down and holding out his hand. Orfitus blinked and squinted up at the shape looming over him before he realised that it was Cato.

'Your men don't seem inclined to take prisoners, Tribune Cato,' he gasped, then coughed to clear his throat.

Cato chuckled. 'Oh, they're happy enough to take prisoners as spoils of war. But there was no profit in sparing your lads, I'm afraid.'

They grasped forearms and Cato hauled the other officer to his feet. Orfitus briefly dusted himself down as he scanned the training ground and saw the last of his men limping over to rejoin the rest of their comrades. Then he glanced towards Corbulo and saw the general sitting stiffly in his saddle, his amused-looking officers exchanging comments to one side.

'I don't think the general is pleased with the way that went.'

'Don't take it too badly,' Cato responded. 'It was a neat move to use the pontus. I didn't see that coming.'

'Didn't do us much good though, did it?'

'Not this time,' Cato admitted. 'But you were up against my Praetorians. And men like Macro know just about every trick in the book, and how to counter them too.'

There was a chorus of angry shouting from across the training ground, and the officers looked round to see that Cassius had herded several men off to one side and was racing around them, nipping at anyone who tried to break away.

'Would you mind calling off your cavalry, Tribune? I think he's caused enough mayhem.'

Cato stuck two fingers in his mouth and gave a piercing whistle. Cassius stopped in his tracks and looked back. Cato whistled again, and the dog gave a last longing look at its prey before turning sharply and bounding back towards its master.

'I owe you a drink when I next see you in the officers' mess,' said Orfitus. 'You and that bloody wildman, Centurion Macro.'

They exchanged a nod before Orfitus marched stiffly to take command of his cohort, trying to preserve as much dignity as he could. Cassius ran up and skittered to a stop, flanks heaving as his long tongue lolled out of his panting jaws. Cato took up the leash and made his way over to where Macro was standing in front of the Praetorians drawn up before the rampart. The men stood at ease, wicker shields grounded as they laughed and joked.

'Good work, Centurion. That was quick thinking.'

Macro grinned. 'Coming from you, that's praise indeed, sir. Of course, me and the boys had some help.' He patted Cassius on the head and was rewarded with a lick.

'Any injuries?'

'A few bruises. Nothing to worry about.'

Cato nodded with satisfaction. 'Good.'

They were interrupted by the thud of horses' hoofs as the general and his staff rode up and turned to face the disordered ranks of the auxiliaries. Corbulo looked older than his forty-nine years; grey-haired, with a deeply lined face and a wide downturned mouth that made his expression appear sour and severe.

'Prefect Orfitus!' he bellowed. 'Get your bloody men

15

formed up! I'll not have them milling around like a bunch of wasters on a public holiday!'

The hapless prefect saluted, then gave orders for his officers to have the men fall in. With much shouting, liberal use of vine canes and optios' staffs, and shuffling boots, the six centuries of the Syrian cohort took their places and stood to attention under the glowering stare of their general. When at last they were formed up, Corbulo flicked his reins and walked his mount along the front of the unit. There was no mistaking the contempt in his expression as he regarded them. He returned to his former position in front of the centre of the cohort to address them.

'That was the most ludicrous display I have ever seen from any unit in the entire Roman army,' he announced in a harsh, strident tone. 'Not only did you fail to keep up anything like a decent pace on the march, you failed to remain in formation. Ye gods! A band of one-legged vagrants could have turned in a better performance. If that was not bad enough, you shambled onto the training ground like a bunch of first-day recruits. From what I can see of your kit, it is poorly maintained, and some of you don't even have the full issue. Centurions! I want you to take the name of every man here who has failed to turn up in full regulation kit. No exceptions. Officers included. Those who don't come ready for war get to sleep in the open for the rest of the month, and will be issued nothing but barley gruel to eat.' He twisted in his saddle to indicate the rampart. 'As for what might laughingly be referred to as your attack on prepared defences, I swear before Jupiter, Best and Greatest, that a gaggle of vestal virgins would have presented a more fearsome prospect to the enemy.'

There was some laughter from the Praetorian ranks before a sharp curse from an optio silenced the men.

16

Corbulo glared at the Syrians for a moment before he continued his dressing-down. 'If that's how you perform when you go up against the Parthians, I promise that not one in ten of you will survive the experience. You may have amused our Praetorian friends, but I can assure you that the Parthians will not be laughing when they come for you. You and all the other men in the eastern army who have spent their lives sitting on their fat arses in comfortable garrison postings.

'Life has been far too easy for you, but that has now changed, gentlemen. When spring comes, we will be invading the Parthian empire. It will be the greatest test of Roman military might in the east since the days of Marcus Antonius. For those who live to see the final victory, there will be enough booty to make us all wealthy beyond measure. For those who fall along the way, there will only be an unmarked grave at the side of a dusty road, soon to be lost to memory. That is the fate that awaits if you cannot perform far better than you just did.

'Too long you have merely played at being soldiers. Now you must earn the coin of Rome. You must earn it through shedding sweat and blood. You must strengthen your hearts, thicken your muscles and harden your resolve. You must look after your kit. If your armour is weak and worn, it will not save you. If your blade is rusty and blunt, it will not kill for you. If your boots are worn out, they will not carry you far, and you will fall behind to be picked off and butchered by the enemy. And the enemy we face is perhaps the most formidable foe that Rome has ever encountered. Oh, I know there are some who say the Parthians are corrupt and weak, flouncing around in their flowing robes and kohl eye make-up like women, but those who dismiss them as such are fools, and make themselves easy prey for the enemy. Be not mistaken: the Parthian is a skilled warrior. He rides as if he was born in the saddle. He can shoot arrows from atop his mount just as steadily and accurately as if he was standing on the ground. The Parthian cavalry is as the flow of a river. It sweeps round obstacles and moves on unhindered, until its way is blocked by a dam. We will be that dam. We will be the line of rocks the enemy cannot pass. Not even the mailed might of their cataphracts will break us. On our shields and on our spears and swords they will dash themselves to pieces. And then we will have victory.'

Corbulo paused to let his words sink in before he continued in a sombre tone. 'But that will never happen while you shame the reputation of Rome as you do now. I see no soldiers before me worthy of the name. I see only the lazy detritus of a once proud cohort whose men did honour to their standard and their emperor. That must change. If it doesn't, you will all end up carrion for the buzzards of Parthia. Prefect Orfitus!'

The cohort's commander stepped forward. 'Sir!'

'These are your men. You set the standard. If they fail from now on, it is because *you* have failed. And if you fail, then I will show you no pity. I demand the best from my officers. If they can't give their best, then they have no place in my army. Is that clear?'

'Yes, sir.'

'Then you will see to it that these men are trained properly. Those who fail to meet the required standard will be discharged without the usual gratuity. That goes for every other unit under my command. Including the legions.' He jerked his thumb back over his shoulder. 'And the Praetorians.'

Cato and Macro exchanged a quick look.

'That's taking things a bit too far,' Macro said quietly. 'It won't go down well in the ranks.'

'Nor in Rome, once Nero hears about it,' Cato added. 'If there's one lesson every emperor has learned, it's that you

18

don't mess about with the privileges of the Praetorian Guard.'

'Quite right too,' Macro responded with feeling.

Corbulo gave the cohort one last look of withering contempt before he snapped at Orfitus, 'Dismissed!' Then, wheeling his horse around, he spurred it into a canter and led his staff officers back in the direction of the main gate of Tarsus in a swirl of dust.

Cato regarded him for a moment before he glanced towards the Syrians. 'Not quite the inspiring address those men needed from their general.'

'It's exactly what they needed,' Macro responded. 'They're a pile of shit, and they know it. The sooner Orfitus whips 'em into shape, the better.'

Cato nodded. 'Corbulo was right about one thing. If they're not ready when the time comes to face the Parthians, then they're as good as dead.'

Macro grunted. 'On that cheery note – what are your orders, sir?'

Cato thought briefly. 'The men could use some exercise. March them around the city a couple of times before dismissing them.'

'Yes, sir.'

'I'll see you when you're done. Push 'em hard, Centurion.'

'Is there any other way?'

Cato nodded, tugged at Cassius's leash and set off towards the city gate with the dog trotting at his side.

Macro turned to the Praetorians, many of whom were still grinning at the discomfort of the Syrians. It was a fact of life that the units of any army had a competitive rivalry. The legionaries felt superior to the auxiliaries, the auxiliaries resented the legionaries' arrogance, and both groups of soldiers hated the Praetorians. If any of the Syrians ran into Macro's men in the city's drinking holes that night, there was bound to be trouble. In that case, the only thing that concerned Macro was that the Praetorians gave the other side a bloody good kicking.

He sucked in a deep breath as he looked over the depleted ranks of the Praetorian cohort and affected a dark frown as he bellowed, 'What in Hades are you bastards grinning at? You won't be laughing when you know what's in store for you! Stand to! Shields up! Prepare to march!'

CHAPTER TWO

While the rest of the army lived in tents in their camps outside Tarsus, Cato and his men were billeted in the city, as the Praetorians had been assigned to serve as the general's bodyguard. Corbulo's decision to send them into action the previous year had been a calculated political risk as well as a military one, since the emperor would have taken a very dim view of the loss of one of his prized guard units. At the time, though, the general had had so few reliable men at his disposal that his hand had been forced. The Second Cohort had suffered many losses, and there had been no way of replacing them with fresh recruits, as far from Rome as they were. It was small comfort to know that there were too few men left for Corbulo to send them into the field again. They would serve out the campaign at the side of the general and his staff, away from the battle line. That might well frustrate Centurion Macro, but it was a source of profound relief to his woman, Petronella. Especially as she was about to become his wife.

Cato smiled in anticipation of the next day's wedding celebrations. It would be a small enough affair. Besides himself and the other officers of the cohort, there were a few men from other units that Macro had befriended, as well as a handful of the local people and Cato's five-year-old son, Lucius.

It was because of Lucius that Macro had come to meet his bride-to-be. Petronella had been the boy's nurse, bought from the slave market in Rome for the purpose. Fierce and intelligent, she was exactly the kind of woman Macro needed, thought Cato. Moreover, she doted on Lucius, and he in turn loved her. His mother had died shortly after he had been born, and since Cato had been away on campaign for most of the youngster's life, a powerful bond had grown between Lucius and his nurse. Not that she was a slave any longer. Cato had granted her her freedom a year ago, and she and Macro had been living together with him in the house he rented in Tarsus. And now the centurion had decided to make their relationship legal.

Over the last month, Petronella had been joyfully pre-occupied with making the arrangements while Macro looked on in a state of bemusement that turned to concern as soon as he took stock of the money she was spending. But, she explained, such things as a silk stola for the day, flowers, the feast, entertainers and the blessing from the priest of the imperial cult in Tarsus did not come cheap, still less free. Cato had watched in wonder as his friend, the fearless veteran of so many battles, shrugged meekly and surrendered to her wishes. It seemed that love had been able to achieve what no enemy weapon, nor any barbarian warrior, ever had.

Cato turned into a street leading out of the forum towards the Jewish quarter and the comfortable house in which his small household rented rooms. The afternoon heat was even more cloying in the confines of the city, and sweat trickled from his brow as he strode along, avoiding the small heaps of refuse and sewage that had collected in the street. He exchanged a salute with a party of legionaries, who stepped warily aside as Cassius strained towards them. Passing through an arch with a menorah carved into the facing of the keystone, he entered a small square.

The house of the silversmith, Yusef, was on the far side, the entrance flanked by a bakery and a shop selling pottery. As he approached, he saw Petronella sitting on a step a short distance from the door, trying to cool herself with a straw fan. In front of her, Lucius played with some of his wooden soldiers. A small, dark-haired girl in a plain tunic sat beside him. Cato recognised her as the daughter of one of the neighbours; the girl Lucius often spoke of as his friend, before he became self-conscious and denied that he had chosen to play with a girl and that she just tagged along.

Petronella stood up as she caught sight of her former master and waved a greeting. 'Look who's here, Lucius!'

The boy looked up and smiled brightly as he sprang to his feet. 'Cassius!'

Cassius tugged at the leash, but Cato held him back firmly as he drew up outside the silversmith's house. Lucius rushed forward to hug the dog, Cassius's long tongue playing over his face, but the girl flinched away. Cato could well understand her nervousness, given the size and wild appearance of the beast.

'Cassius, eh?' He sighed theatrically. 'No greeting for your father?'

He hunched down and ruffled Lucius's dark curls. His son gave him a perfunctory hug and then continued patting the dog's flank. Cato glanced towards the girl. 'And how is little Junilla today?'

She smiled back shyly, then abruptly turned and scurried away, darting into a passage a little further down the street.

'What did I say?' Cato frowned.

Petronella laughed. 'It's not you, master. Just the dog. He looks like a wolf to most of the townsfolk. If I didn't know him better, I'd be the same. Come now, Lucius, pick up your toys. It's time to go inside.'

The boy gave the dog a last pat on the head, and then recoiled as the long tongue flickered towards his face again. Scooping up his wooden figures, he followed the others up the steps to the front door and into the silversmith's house.

Inside, there was a short corridor leading to the simple atrium, where a shallow basin reflected some of the light coming from the opening above. Arranged around the four sides were the owner's office and living quarters and the kitchen. The rooms that Cato and Macro rented overlooked the small courtyard garden at the rear. The faint tinkle of the fountain greeted Cato's ears as he led the way into the garden and down the gravel path to the pool where the water splashed. He untied the dog's leash and then eased himself down onto one of the benches shaded by the vine-covered trellis that surrounded the pool.

Lucius set his toy soldiers down beside his father and then sat on the pool's marble edge and swung his bare feet over into the water, kicking gently to cool his toes. Glancing round with a hopeful wag of his tail, Cassius waited a moment for someone to play with him. When no one responded, he sat heavily at his master's feet before lowering his head between his paws and letting out a deep sigh.

'How are preparations going for the big day?' asked Cato.

Petronella settled on the neighbouring bench and smiled happily. 'I think everything is ready, master.'

'You think?' Cato arched an eyebrow and smiled. 'Best to be sure, before the centurion gets back. He's a stickler for details, as you know. I wouldn't want to get on the wrong side of Macro.'

'Oh, he's a pussycat, if you know where to tickle him. Besides, I think I've made it clear to him who wears the breeches.'

'Are you sure you weren't a centurion yourself in a previous life? That or a camp prefect. For a fine-looking woman, and wife-to-be, you seem to have the bearing and demeanour of a hardened veteran.'

Petronella's expression became strained. 'Spending most of your life as a slave will do that to a person, master.'

'But you are no longer a slave. You are free. I am no longer your master.'

'Force of habit, sir.'

They exchanged a slight smile. Although she was no longer Cato's property, Petronella, like any person who had been freed, was obliged to regard him as her patron for the rest of her life. In exchange for her loyalty and occasional services, it would be his duty to ensure her welfare. Of course, he reflected, that was the guiding principle. Many failed to honour it. Some masters treated former slaves as but one step removed from their previous status. And many slaves repaid their former owner's kindness with cold contempt once they were freed. In a few instances, freedmen proved themselves so successful in their endeavours that they amassed vast fortunes and became far wealthier than their former owners. Nevertheless, slaves they had once been, and no amount of fine clothes or expensive perfume would ever change their place close to the bottom of Rome's social hierarchy.

But for the imperial preference enjoyed by his father, Cato too would have suffered the fate of a freedman. As it was, he had been granted citizenship, on condition that he served in the army. But even now, he wondered how many of the officers knew of his humble origins and mocked him behind his back, despite his elevation to equestrian rank. Not that he had much cause to care what they thought of him. He had won his reputation the hard way, unlike those who had acquired prestige by mere accident of birth. He had a degree of wealth too, having inherited the estate of his father-in-law, Senator Sempronius. There was a house in Rome, a farming estate in Campania, and rental income from an apartment block on the Aventine Hill, for as long as the building remained standing.

And yet despite such riches, Cato was not content to live a life of comparative luxury in Rome. Although born and raised in the capital, he had found it overwhelming after returning from years campaigning on the empire's frontiers. The stench of a million people and animals living in such close proximity was unbearable, and he had been astonished at himself for not being aware of it earlier. Moreover, the teeming streets made him feel hemmed in, like a sack of grain tightly packed into the fetid hold of an old cargo ship. And then there was the need to cautiously pick his way through the maze of Rome's social and political life. An unintended slight might unwittingly make him an enemy for life. Given the right connections at the palace, or with the criminal underworld of the Subura, such an enemy could prove deadly indeed. Cato might be stabbed in a crowded thoroughfare, or poisoned at a banquet, without ever knowing the reason why.

For all these reasons he preferred life in the army, where a man knew who his enemies were and could count on his comrades. For the most part, he conceded. The influence of Rome could stretch to the furthest corners of the empire for those whose influence was deemed a threat by the emperor and his advisers. For now, though, Cato felt confident that he was too insignificant to be at risk from such attention. The same could not be said for General Corbulo. He might well be a fine soldier who had served Rome well and won the respect of those he commanded. He might even be utterly loyal to whichever emperor sat on the throne, but that would not save him if he was deemed to be too successful.

Cato smiled bitterly to himself. Such was the paradox of empire. Good generals were necessary to defend Rome from its enemies, but if such men were too good they could easily come to be regarded as just another enemy. In which case they would be stripped of their command and spend the rest of their days in Italia, under the scrutiny of the imperial spies. If they were less fortunate, they would be accused of some capital crime and executed, or offered the honourable way out by taking their own life.

'Is anything worrying you, sir?'

Cato looked up and saw Petronella watching him closely. He forced a smile and shrugged. 'Nothing more than the usual burdens of command. Is there anything more I can do to help you prepare for tomorrow?'

'You've already done more than enough. Without your loan, it wouldn't be much of a celebration. Not that Macro would mind. You know what he's like, doesn't appreciate all the fuss. It's just that I wanted to give him a day to remember, sir. Just like your late wife wanted you to have, I imagine.'

Cato's lips pressed together as he stared past Petronella at the hunting scene painted on the plaster of the wall behind her. He recalled his own wedding day clearly enough. It had been a simple affair, but it had seemed perfect at the time. Only later had he discovered that Julia had been unfaithful to him while he had been away fighting in Britannia. Now the memory of his wedding mocked him.

Petronella leaned forward earnestly, misreading the change in his expression. 'Don't worry, sir. I am sure Macro and I will be able to repay you soon enough. He says he's got plenty saved with a banker in Rome.'

Cato chuckled. 'Don't worry about that. The loan is the very least I could do to help. I offered the money as a gift, but Macro insisted that it be a loan. I owe you both more than any man can ever repay. You for raising Lucius, after his mother died. And Macro for . . . well, making me what I am today. I owe him my life. He's got me out of more difficult situations than I care to remember. So don't worry about paying back the money in a hurry. I can survive without it.'

'That's as maybe, sir. But we'll do right by you, and your son.'

'I know you will. Just tell me that you haven't been too caught up in preparing for tomorrow to forsake making us something good for dinner.' Cato rubbed his hands together. 'It'll be Macro's last feast as a single man after all.'

Petronella rolled her eyes. 'Don't remind me! I keep getting those comments about surrendering his freedom, being manacled, giving up on other women . . .'

'Trust me, there are no other women in his eyes. Not now that he has you.'

'Oh . . .' She blushed slightly and flapped her hands. 'Anyway. Dinner. Yes, I'll prepare something special.'

'Bloody delicious!' Macro announced as he pushed his samianware dish away and wiped his mouth on the back of his hand. He looked across the garden dining table at Petronella with admiration. They were eating in the coolness of twilight as swifts darted through the air feasting on insects. 'Well now, that's sealed the deal for me. I'm definitely marrying you.'

'As if there was ever any doubt,' she sniffed.

'Seriously,' Macro continued, 'if you can produce a meal like that . . .'

'I had some help,' Petronella admitted. 'One of your

men, Hirtius. He used to be a cook in a senator's household, he tells me.'

Macro's eyes narrowed fractionally. 'Oh? And since when did you swap cooking tips with the rankers?'

'Tarsus isn't that big a city. I ran into him when I was buying herbs in the market. You don't often see a soldier buying cooking ingredients, so we got talking. He told me there was a dish you liked on campaign last year, so I got him to share the recipe.'

'Last year?' Macro frowned.

'The goat dish,' Cato prompted. 'The night there was a fight between one of our men and the Armenian.'

'I remember . . . Poor Glabius. He deserved a better death.'

'Yes.' Cato nodded sadly.

There was a brief silence as they recalled the man Cato had been forced to execute for killing one of their allies.

Petronella cleared her throat and waved her spoon at Lucius. 'I saw that, young man!'

Lucius started, and then affected a wide-eyed look of innocence. 'What did I do?'

'I told you before, no feeding that mangy beast at the table. I saw you slip it your last piece of meat.'

'I didn't!'

She gestured towards the dog sitting on its haunches at the boy's side. Cassius's pink tongue swept round his muzzle before he used it to give Lucius a nudge.

'He's hungry,' said Lucius.

'He's always hungry. He's a dog. Eating's the only thing he ever thinks about.' Petronella gave an exasperated sigh and shook her head. 'Surrounded by men and beasts, not that there's much difference. What's a poor girl to do? Anyway, it's time for you to go to bed, my boy. It's going to be a busy day

29

tomorrow, and you'll need your sleep. More to the point, I need you to sleep. Say goodnight.'

'But it's early!' Lucius protested. 'And I'm five years old. Let me stay up. Please.'

'No. But if you're good and do as you are told, I'll tell you a story after I've tucked you in.'

Lucius swung his legs over the bench and hurried round to Macro, giving him a hug. 'Goodnight, Uncle Macro.'

'Sleep well, soldier!' Macro beamed as he ruffled the boy's hair.

Lucius wriggled free and went to his father. Cato smiled fondly, even though there was already no mistaking the curve of the jaw his son had inherited from his mother. It made Cato's heart ache with longing, laced with bitter betrayal. He leaned forward to kiss Lucius on the crown of his head. 'Off to bed with you. Be good for Petronella, or I'll have Macro place you on fatigues for the rest of the month.'

Lucius laughed with delight at being treated like one of his father's soldiers. He stamped his feet together and saluted. 'Yes, sir.'

Cato struggled to keep a stern expression as he returned the salute. 'Dismissed!'

Once Petronella had ushered the boy away from the table and the two officers were alone in the garden, Macro grinned. 'He's a fine boy. And he'll be a fine man one day, I'm sure of it.'

'I hope so. It's been good to be able to spend this last year with him. Once Corbulo leads us into Parthia, I won't see Lucius again for a while. Same goes for you and Petronella.' Cato reached for the wine jug and topped up their cups. 'She can't be happy about that.'

'She's not,' Macro responded. 'If she'd had her way, I'd have taken my discharge by now. So I've told her this is my last campaign.' He raised his cup and took a sip. 'Once it's over, I'm leaving the army.'

'I wondered if that was what would happen,' said Cato. 'The lads and I will miss you, of course.'

'Bollocks they will. They'll be pleased as fuck to have me off their backs.'

'Ah, you're a stickler for a good turnout on parade, and you don't miss a detail, it's true. But they respect you. I know they do. And why wouldn't they? Can't be many centurions in the army who have a record like yours. Gives the lads confidence to follow a man into battle who they know will be the first into the fight and the last out.'

Macro shrugged. 'There are plenty of good centurions around. You'll find someone to replace me easily enough, lad.'

'I doubt it. I've served long enough to know that the likes of you are a very rare breed indeed, brother. Truly, it'll be a sad day when you take your discharge.'

They sat quietly for a moment as the last of the light began to fade and the sky above the roof tiles took on a maroon hue. One star already gleamed overhead. The sounds of voices and the rumble of a cart in the street outside carried on the air.

'Have you given any thought to what you and Petronella will do when you leave the army?'

Macro nodded. 'We've talked about it. There's no way I'm settling down as a farmer on whatever patch of swamp some clerk at the palace allocates me. I'll take money instead. Then we'll make for Britannia.'

'I thought you hated the place.'

'I hate campaigning there. Freezing in winter, and wet in what passes for summer. And the natives are an ugly bunch who I wouldn't trust any further than I could spit. As for those

31

crazy Druid bastards . . . fanatics, the lot of them. You'd think they'd have appreciated the benefits of being part of the Empire by now.'

Cato clicked his tongue. 'You're not selling me on the notion of Britannia as a choice place to retire and enjoy the rest of your life with your bride.'

'Oh, it's peaceful enough where we've managed to subdue the buggers and make them realise that we're there to stay. As long as we have loyal tribes like the Atrebates, the Trinovantes and the Iceni at our backs, we're safe enough. And there's still good money to be made in Londinium if we get in quick. My mother's doing well out of that inn we bought together, so we'll join her in the business and make a go of it. As long as I get the chance to sample the wares and spend time swapping stories with passing soldiers, I'll be happy enough.'

'You really think so?'

Macro considered his prospects for a moment and then drained his cup. 'Yes, I do. I love the army. It's been my life. But a man can't stay a soldier for ever. Not if he's going to do the job properly. I can feel my limbs stiffening, lad. I'm not as fast or as strong as I once was, and it will only get worse from now on. Better I quit before I let myself or the men down. I'd rather be remembered the way I am now, not as some wizened old crock who can't even keep up with the bloody stragglers. So one last campaign and then I'm done, and me and the wife will make a new life for ourselves in Londinium. Assuming she and my mother can see eye to eye.'

Cato had met Macro's mother some years before. A formidable woman indeed. He smiled wryly. Now that he thought about it, there were many qualities she and Petronella shared. That might work well for Macro's dreams of domestic bliss, or it might equally be the cause of bitter conflict. It would be fascinating to hear how the two women in his life got on. Or didn't.

'Well, Centurion, I truly hope you find the peace and happiness you and Petronella deserve. Of course, she's going to have to break the news to Lucius.'

'Not for a year or two yet, I expect. By which time he'll be old enough to cope.'

'I imagine so,' Cato replied doubtfully. Petronella had served as the boy's nurse from his earliest months. She was more like a mother to him, in truth. It would be a hard parting for his son.

'Besides,' Macro continued, 'you'll find another woman for yourself soon enough. You're a good prospect.'

He picked up the wine jug and gave it a slight swirl. It was almost empty. He shared what was left between them and raised his cup.

'A toast to our final campaign together. May Mars crush our enemies and may Fortuna fill our coffers with loot.'

'I'll drink to that.'

They drained their cups, but Cato felt little cheer at the prospect of the end of the coming campaign. Lucius might be losing someone he had come to regard as a mother, but Cato was losing someone who had been as a brother and father to him. And when the moment came, it would be impossible not to grieve. He tried to shake off the morose thought. He had no right to begrudge Macro the happiness that Petronella had brought to his life. It was an unworthy sentiment, and he resolved to share his friend's joy in full measure when the pair were married the next day.

CHAPTER THREE

From first light the household was consumed by frenzied activity. Petronella was awake and dressed as a pink hue stretched across the eastern horizon. A quick dig in the ribs was enough to stir Macro into wakefulness, though not without some surly grumbling and rubbing of eyes.

'Up you get, lover,' she greeted him cheerfully. 'There's some barley gruel in the kitchen to set you up for the day. First thing, go down to the forum and get your hair cut, and then pick up the tunic and toga from the fuller opposite the bathhouse. Make sure he's done a good job and pay him four sestertians, and not an as more. You can order the bread on the way back to the house. Tell the baker I want it here no later than noon. Oh, and don't forget the sow.'

'Sow?' Macro looked bewildered.

'For the sacrifice. It's on the list.' She handed him a waxed tablet with her clumsy writing detailing the loaves and pastries required, as well as the ceremonial spelt cake. She arched an eyebrow. 'Any questions?'

Macro stretched his shoulders and winced as a joint cracked. 'Fuck, I thought I was supposed to be the one giving orders.' He coughed to clear the phlegm at the back of his throat, then stood up and saluted. 'No, sir. Anything else, sir?'

Petronella cocked her head to one side and wagged a finger. 'Less of your cheek, my man. Or you'll be remembering your wedding night for all the wrong reasons.' She made an underhand clenching gesture.

'Ouch.' Macro winced. 'As you command, my lady love.'

'That's more like it.' She bent over him and kissed him on the forehead. Macro made a quick fumble for her backside and she retreated and slapped his hand away. 'No time for that. There's work to be done. On your feet, soldier!'

Macro swung his feet down onto the floor and yawned. 'And what will my beloved be doing while I am attending to her list, I wonder?'

She stood in the doorway, her hands on her hips, and frowned. 'Your beloved will be feeding Master Lucius, getting him scrubbed, combed and dressed. She will then be arranging the tables and benches in the garden, baking pies, pastries and honeyed rolls, roasting a dozen chickens and several joints of lamb, and frying sausages. Then she will be cutting up all the cooked meat and arranging it in trays and dishes. After that, she'll be setting up the flowers and wreaths around the trellises, sweeping the flagstones and scrubbing the bird shit off the rim of the fountain. And once that's done, she might take a short breather before she bathes, has her hair dressed for the wedding and makes herself smile sweetly when the guests start to arrive. Satisfied?' Without waiting for a response, she turned and stalked out of the room, slamming the door behind her.

Macro arched an eyebrow. 'Sweet Jupiter, Best and Greatest, I only asked . . .'

When Cato rose a little later on, the silversmith's house was filled with the clatter of dishes, the scrape of furniture being moved, and chatter and laughter, intercut with Petronella's loud voice giving instructions and answering questions. There was something in her tone that indicated it might be best if Cato avoided his usual routine of ambling into the kitchen to request his breakfast and a freshly cleaned tunic.

Instead, he put on his clothes from the previous day and warily made his way past the kitchen and into the atrium. There he found Lucius sitting on the edge of the impluvium, kicking his feet in the shallow water. He was dressed in his best tunic, a finely spun cotton garment dyed a deep blue. His hair was neatly combed and oiled, with ringlets arranged around the fringe. He raised a hand to scratch his head and then pulled it away sharply as he heard his father's footsteps.

'Under orders not to touch your hair, eh?' Cato grinned.

Lucius nodded indignantly. 'Petronella said there would be blood if I messed it up. I don't like her when she's like this.'

'It'll pass. She has a lot to organise today. Once it's all ready, she'll be nice Petronella again, I promise.'

Lucius looked doubtful. 'She's like a Fury, Father. You know, those ladies from the story you told me.'

'I shall have to be careful what stories I tell you in future.' Cato shot him a quick look. 'You didn't say that to her, did you?'

Lucius shook his head, and Cato sighed in relief.

'I'm hungry, Father.'

'Hungry? Haven't you had any breakfast?'

The boy shook his head and his little shoulders slumped. 'She forgot. And when I started to ask, she got cross and told me to wait here. That was ages ago. So I'm hungry.'

'Me too.' Cato glanced round. Petronella's voice had risen to a shriek as she berated one of the women she had hired to help her for the day.

He crouched down on his haunches in front of Lucius and

spoke quietly. 'I think it might be best if we went out and got our own breakfast. How does that sound?'

Lucius looked up, his dark eyes bright with pleasure. 'Can we go to the Cup of Croesus, Father?'

Cato was taken aback at the suggestion. The chop house was a favourite amongst the soldiers billeted in Tarsus, thanks to its cheap food and wine, cheaper women and raucous atmosphere. 'How do you know about that place?'

'Uncle Macro and Petronella took me.'

'Really?'

The boy nodded. 'It was fun.'

'I bet.'

'Please, Father!' Lucius rubbed his stomach. 'I am so hungry.'

'Oh, very well then. Let's go.'

They left the house and closed the door quietly behind them. The street was already busy with people mostly heading towards the city's main market. A few mule-drawn carts rattled in amongst the pedestrians, and Cato took his son's hand to make sure he could guide him safely and not lose him in the crowd. Fortunately Lucius was young enough not to be self-conscious, and Cato felt the boy's grip tighten on his hand as they set off. He smiled, paternal affection swelling in his heart.

On either side of the street hawkers cried out, advertising their wares and trying to lure customers into their shops. The sour tang of humanity mingled with the comforting aroma of bakeries and the sensual lure of scents and spices. Lucius stared around in fascination at the myriad colours of clothing, his gaze lingering on the more exotic people who passed by either way; mostly easterners clad in bright robes.

As the two of them emerged from the shaded street into the market square, they were struck by the full glare of the sun and the swell of noise from the lines of traders' stalls. Closest to them was a low stage on which the auctioneer's servants were arranging the human stock for the first round of sales. There were two groups: the first comprised several well-built men wearing simple tunics and sandals. The second was made up of neatly dressed men and women destined for the wealthy households of Tarsus. As he and Lucius passed by, Cato glanced at the first group. Two of them were young and muscular and might well be spared the endless toil in a fullery or some chain gang on a farm if they were fortunate enough to be bought by one of the owners of the local gladiator schools. He was about to pass on when the last man in the line caught his eye.

He was perhaps as old as fifty, with curly silver hair and lined features. He had a wiry build and stood with his shoulders back and chest out, chin jutting proudly as he regarded the people in the street with a haughty expression. He had the tell-tale tattoo of a small helmet on his right forearm. The sign of an initiate of the third grade in the cult of Mithras was common enough in the legions, and the man certainly had the bearing of a soldier.

Cato stopped in front of him and looked him up and down. As soon as the auctioneer spotted a Roman examining his wares, he scurried over and bowed his head in greeting before speaking in accented Latin.

'I see Flaminius has caught your eye, my dear sir. Clearly you are a man of excellent and discerning judgement. He is a bond slave. He may be old, but he is tough and has many years of good service still in him.' He leaned towards the slave and patted his firm shoulder. The man did not flinch or react in any way; just as a soldier might standing to attention on the parade ground, thought Cato. The auctioneer gestured towards the slave's legs. 'As you can see, my dear sir, he is in fine shape and would make an excellent field hand. Or perhaps a stevedore or porter. Yes, perhaps that, since I imagine you are one of the fine Roman soldiers gracing our city with their presence . . . Or perhaps a bodyguard for your dear little boy there.' He beamed at Lucius and reached out a hand to ruffle his hair, but the boy pulled back out of reach, anxious to avoid Petronella's sharp tongue if her careful arrangement was disturbed.

'What's your story?' Cato addressed the slave directly.

Before he could respond, the auctioneer quickly interposed himself between them. 'Flaminius was landed with the rest of the shipment from Bithynia, sir.'

'I'll speak to him myself,' Cato interrupted tersely.

The auctioneer paused a moment and then nodded his head. 'If you need any further information about this man, or any of the others, I would be honoured to help you, my dear sir.'

He backed away two steps, bowed his head again, and then crossed the stage to his stool a short distance from the auction block.

'Who are you, Flaminius?' asked Cato. 'You have the bearing of a soldier, I think.'

The slave returned his gaze unflinchingly, and Cato sensed that the man was weighing him up before he responded. 'I was a soldier. Twenty-six years with the Fourth Scythica before I was discharged. Honourably.'

'So how did you end up as a slave for auction?'

'Because some bastard senator took a fancy to my farm. I wouldn't sell, so he made sure business went badly for me. I got into debt and my family was ruined. I sold myself to settle the debt, so at least my wife and kids are free. As far as I know. That's my story, sir. That's all there is to it,' he concluded with understandable bitterness.

Cato shook his head. 'That's a sorry tale, brother.'

'You're a soldier, then?'

'My father's a Praetorian!' Lucius chirped up. 'And a tribune.'

39

Flaminius instinctively tried to stand to attention, and the manacles clattered together and pressed into his chafed ankles, causing him to wince. 'Sorry, sir. I didn't realise. Thought you was a civvie.'

Cato shook his head sorrowfully. 'This is no way for an ex-legionary to end his days.'

Flaminius shrugged. 'Fortuna plays her games, sir. I had some good years in the ranks. Just my bad luck coming across some stuck-up cunt who wanted to add my land to his park.'

Lucius tugged his father's hand. 'What's a stuck up—'

'Someone who should know better than to cheat an old soldier out of what he's earned,' Cato said hurriedly. He stood for a moment, deploring the old soldier's bad luck. And Flaminius's fortune was more than likely about to take an even worse turn. He was too old to be bought by a lanista or to be much good as a bodyguard. There were few prospects for such a slave. He would end his days being worked steadily to death. Unless his fortune changed . . .

Cato turned abruptly towards the auctioneer.

'You! Come here!'

The auctioneer had been munching on a seeded roll. He quickly put it on his stool and brushed the crumbs from the front of his tunic as he hurried across the stage. 'My dear sir, how can I assist?'

'This man. What price will he fetch?'

The auctioneer pursed his lips and cocked an eyebrow. 'Who can say, sir? It is an auction after all. Who can put a price on such a man in such a situation on any given day, my dear sir?'

Cato frowned. 'Spare me the sales pitch. How much?'

The other man hesitated momentarily as he sized up the Roman and attempted to work out how much he could

40

afford. 'Four hundred denarians would be a fair price for Flaminius, sir.'

Cato made himself snort with derision. 'Bollocks. He isn't worth half that. A few more years and this man will be good for nothing. He'll be just another mouth to feed for twice as long before he's finally done. I'll give you a hundred and fifty for him. That's more than he'll fetch at auction, and you know it.'

The auctioneer's obsequious expression faded. 'Two hundred and fifty and he's yours.'

Cato grunted and turned to hoist Lucius onto his shoulders. 'Come on, son. This fat fool is wasting our time. Let's go.'

'Two hundred and twenty-five, sir!'

Cato hesitated. 'One hundred and eighty. Not a denarius more.'

'Oh, come now, sir! He's worth more than that. Two hundred at the very least.'

'Done!' Cato thrust out his hand and took that of the auctioneer firmly. 'Two hundred it is.'

The auctioneer gritted his teeth and nodded. 'You can pay my cashier. Over there, behind the stage.'

'No. I want him delivered to my billet. You know Yusef the silversmith?' Cato gestured towards the street leading to the house.

'I know him.'

'Have the slave brought there tomorrow morning. I'll have the money ready then.'

The auctioneer rubbed his hands together. 'A deposit is customary, my dear sir.'

'I am the commander of General Corbulo's Praetorian cohort. You have my word the money will be paid to you.' Cato stared at the man, daring the auctioneer to challenge him. The other man swallowed and nodded reluctantly.

'The word of a Roman gentleman is priceless, dear sir. As you wish.'

Cato looked up at Flaminius and caught a flicker of feeling in the man's face. It might have signified gratitude, he thought. Or resentment. It was impossible to tell. He cleared his throat and nodded at the slave. 'I'll see you tomorrow.'

'Yes, sir.'

As the auctioneer steered Flaminius to the holding pens behind the stage, Cato turned away and resumed his progress along the edge of the market, making his way towards the Cup of Croesus at the crossroads on the far side. He held on firmly to Lucius's ankles as his son clasped his little hands over the crown of Cato's head to hold on.

'Why did you buy that man, Father?'

Cato thought for a moment. The truth of it was that he felt offended by the prospect of a veteran being sold into slavery. He had served long enough to know many men who had put their lives at risk for Rome, and for their comrades. It was the latter that meant most to him. Soldiers looked out for each other. That was the most sacred bond of all. Better that Flaminius was taken into Cato's service than that he was worked to death in the fields or mines. Lucius was too young to understand all that.

'I need someone to replace Petronella now that she's marrying Macro.'

'Is she leaving us?' Lucius asked anxiously.

'No,' Cato reassured him. 'But we'll need someone to look after you and teach you how to get fit and fight. An old soldier is the best person for that job.'

'What about Uncle Macro? He's old.'

Cato laughed. 'I wouldn't tell him that to his face if I were you.'

42

'Would it make him cross, Father?'

'You can't imagine . . .'

Cato stepped in behind a narrow mule cart and followed it through the crowd until they reached the arched entrance to the Cup of Croesus. An artfully painted image of a smiling man raising a huge golden cup adorned the wall beside the arch. On the far side was a large yard filled with tables and benches. Servants hurried to and fro with jugs of wine and clusters of cheap cups, or trays laden with bowls of stew and loaves of bread.

Most of the early customers had already had their breakfast, and there were plenty of spaces at the tables. Cato slid Lucius down from his shoulders and looked round, smiling knowingly as he caught sight of a familiar figure sitting in the corner furthest from the entrance. A neatly tied bundle of cloth rested on his table beside a large jug of wine. Cato saw that the man's hair had been cut and styled as neatly as Lucius's, the refined appearance completed by a freshly shaven jaw. Beside him, tethered to the leg of the table, was a pig, squatting on its haunches as it surveyed the people in the yard with what looked very much like a bored expression.

'Let's join Uncle Macro, shall we?'

As they made their way across the yard, Macro continued to stare down into his cup, which he was gently swilling.

'Is that a pet, Uncle Macro?'

The centurion gave a start and looked up guiltily to see the boy pointing at the pig.

'Pet?' He glanced at the sow, which looked up at him and gave a grunt. 'Er, no. Not a pet.'

Lucius pulled his hand from his father's grasp and leaned towards the pig, giving it a pat between the ears. The sow rubbed its snout against the underside of the boy's arm.

'He likes me!'

'He's a she,' said Macro. 'And I wouldn't get too friendly with her. She won't be around for long.'

'Oh.' Lucius responded with disappointment. 'Can't we keep her?'

'I think that's a question for Petronella. Anyway, what are you two doing here?'

'Breakfast,' said Cato. He glanced towards the counter at the rear of the yard and gestured to one of the serving girls to come over. 'There's not much hope of getting fed back at the house right now. Mind if we join you?'

'Please do.'

Cato sat on the bench opposite Macro while Lucius perched on the edge and continued to make a fuss of the pig.

When the serving girl arrived, Cato ordered bread and lamb chops, and some watered-down wine. He gestured towards Macro's wine jar. 'Have another?'

'Better not. If she thinks I'm drunk, there'll be blood.'

As the girl hurried back to the counter, Cato regarded his friend for a moment. 'Having second thoughts?'

Macro frowned. 'No. None. She's the girl of my dreams. It's just that . . . well, it's a big change in my life. I'm not sure what to think.'

'For what it's worth, I think Petronella is perfect for you. You're a lucky man, my friend.'

'I know.'

There was a brief silence before Cato leaned forward on his elbows and folded his hands. 'So what's the problem? There's obviously something troubling you.'

Macro sighed. 'Can you see me as a married man? Honestly? I'm a soldier. That's all I've ever really known. It's almost like I can't remember being anything else. And now I'm about to fight my last campaign, then give it all up to go and run that inn in Londinium. It's a fucking big change in my life, is what it is.'

'You'll be fine. I'm sure of it. Besides, you can't be a soldier for ever. Best to make the most of it while you're still fit and have most of your teeth . . . which you may not have if you skulk here rather than getting back to the house to help with the preparations.'

'I'm helping with the preparations by keeping out of the way.' Macro smiled. 'No point in giving my girl one more person to shout at.'

They shared a laugh before the serving girl returned holding a tray above her head, doing her best to avoid being groped by customers on the way. She set it down on the table to reveal a wooden platter piled with roasted cuts of mutton, and a basket of small loaves. There was a jar of watered wine and three cups. Cato reached for his purse and paid for the order; since it was a day of celebration, he added a denarius for her tip. Her eyes widened and she muttered her thanks before glancing round and tucking the silver coin into the small purse hanging round her neck. As she hurried away, Macro clicked his tongue.

'Generous of you . . . You've been generous all round lately. Me and Petronella haven't really thanked you enough for the loan.'

'My pleasure,' Cato replied, and realised he meant it. He had no yearning to live a life of useless luxury, and it suited his principles to use his new-found wealth to help others from time to time.

He poured himself and Macro full cups of wine, then put a dash in Lucius's cup before handing it to his son. 'Make sure you sip it,' he instructed. 'A toast, then. To Centurion Macro, finest soldier in the Roman army; and to Petronella, the best

45

wife a soldier could wish for. May they share a long and happy life together!'

All three raised their cups and drank. Then they set about the meal, in that happy mood of light-hearted conspiracy men share when they know they should be doing domestic chores instead. When the food had been eaten and Lucius had used the last hunk of bread to mop up the juices on the platter, Cato sat back with a contented expression.

'Time to go, I think. Before Petronella sends someone to look for us.'

They rose from the table and Macro untied the pig before leading the small party out of the yard. Then with Lucius in the middle, clutching their hands, and Macro holding the pig's leash, the happy trio ambled back to the silversmith's house.

CHAPTER FOUR

The high priest from the temple of the imperial cult turned away from the small torch he had lit on the household altar and raised his hands. 'If the couple would kneel, I will beseech the gods for their blessing . . .'

Macro lowered himself onto the small cushion in front of the priest while Petronella lifted the hem of her stola enough so that it would not catch uncomfortably around her knees as she knelt. When both were settled in position, the priest placed his hands on top of their heads and waited until all the guests were quite still and the only noise came from the faint sounds of the street outside and the contented snuffling of the sow, which was quite oblivious to the fact that it was enjoying its very last few moments.

'Mighty Jupiter, Best and Greatest,' the priest began in a rich tone and easy cadence, 'we are gathered here on this day to witness the marriage of Centurion Lucius Cornelius Macro and Licinia Petronella. Both have freely consented to be married, and Petronella's patron has given his permission for her to wed. We ask that this union be happy and enduring and, in the name of Ceres – for whom we have lit this torch – fertile.'

It was routine to invoke Ceres's blessing thus, but Petronella had not had any children so far, and there was no reason to believe that might change now. It was a pity, Cato reflected sadly, as he was certain that nothing would have delighted Macro more than becoming a father. He had doted on Lucius and been a favourite of the boy from infancy. Still, Ceres might yet surprise them all and give the centurion what he wanted.

'May Fortuna treat them generously, and Minerva bestow her wisdom upon them. May Venus grant them love . . .'

The priest continued with invocations to one god after another, and soon Cato was no longer listening as his gaze wandered around the garden. Under Petronella's keen eye, garlands had been neatly arranged around the trellises that surrounded the open space in front of the small pool, where Cassius had been chained so that he could drink the water. Despite the arrival of the guests, the dog was curled up and dozing contentedly. In the shade beneath the trellises several tables had been set out, with benches on either side. There was not enough room for more than a handful of couches, and these had been reserved for Macro, Petronella and their most honoured guests: namely Cato and Lucius.

The centurions and optios from the Praetorian cohort were arrayed to the left, behind Macro. Petronella's guests were fewer: Yusef and the handful of female friends she had made in the year she had been living in Tarsus. These included two women from the neighbourhood and their husbands, both of whom owned bakeries and who were rivals rather than friends. There was also the Greek wine merchant from the market, whom she had befriended and with whom she had negotiated a very generous discount for the wine supplied for the modest banquet to follow the ceremony.

As Petronella's patron, Cato stood with the civilians and Lucius. He felt a little disappointed that the invitation that had been sent to General Corbulo had not been acknowledged. Macro had felt duty-bound to seek his general's blessing, and it would have been decent of the old man to respond. Of course, the invitation might never have reached Corbulo himself, having been dealt with by one of his clerks or staff officers, who had not deemed it worthy of his attention. It was a shame nonetheless, even though this was not a society wedding.

It was a small affair, Cato conceded, but all the better for consisting only of those whom Macro and Petronella had chosen to invite, rather than all the gate-crashing familial freeloaders who were inclined to invite themselves, as tended to happen back in Rome. In any case, he reflected, there were few enough family members who *could* have been invited. Macro's mother was living in Britannia. His father had died many years before, and Macro was their only child. His sole uncle had been murdered by the leader of a criminal gang when Macro was a youth. As for Petronella, she had only a sister, who lived on her husband's farm not far from Rome. Cato's own parents were long since dead, and with the loss of his wife, there was only Lucius. As he considered this, it occurred to him that Macro and Petronella were the only real family he had. Perhaps that was why they all felt as close to each other as they did. It would be a hard parting when the campaign was over and Macro applied for his discharge and left for Britannia with his wife.

He felt a sharp pang of regret, and grief, at the prospect and tried to push the thought from his mind as he forced himself to focus his attention back on the words of the priest, who had finished invoking the gods and now turned to retrieve a small spelt loaf from the altar.

'With the sharing of this bread, blessed in the temple of our divine emperor, Macro and Petronella signify before their guests and witnesses that they swear to share all that they possess, and swear to each other that they will keep with each other.'

The priest solemnly passed the bread to Macro, who broke the loaf in two and gave half to Petronella. Then they each tore off a small hunk, placed them in their mouths and began to chew. Once the priest had seen that they had both swallowed, he raised his hands and addressed everyone in the garden.

'With the sharing of bread, it only remains for me to present the sacrifice to Jupiter, Best and Greatest, to affirm the gratitude that Macro and Petronella express to the gods in the hope that they will continue to bless this marriage.'

He turned to his two assistants, who had been standing off to one side with the pig. Taking a firm hold of the leash, one of them stepped towards the portable altar that had been set up beyond the fountain. A large copper bowl sat below it, ready to catch the blood, and to one side the glowing embers of a fire that had been lit hours before wavered. Soon the flames would consume the flesh of the sacrifice and the smoke would carry the offering up to the heavens.

But the pig had different ideas, refusing to move and continuing to sit on its haunches. The assistant braced himself, gritted his teeth and tugged hard. The pig squealed and suddenly set off at an angle, trotting the other side of the priest, who had to leap nimbly to avoid being tipped over. Before the beast could reach the married couple, the assistant threw all his weight into the struggle and the pig skittered to a stop. At once the other assistant rushed forward and bent low to grasp its hind trotters. He clearly knew his stuff, and with a powerful wrench, he whipped the animal's legs out, flipped the pig over onto its back and pinned it down as it squealed in panic.

The two men kept a tight hold on the wriggling victim as they carried it over to the wooden top of the portable altar and laid it on its side. The priest was similarly adroit, obviously used to dealing with sacrificial animals that had resolved not to meekly play along with their allotted role. He drew the thin curved knife from the scabbard on his belt and with a deft stroke cut through the beast's throat. A welter of blood splashed across the top of the altar and spilled into the bowl below as the animal spasmed wildly. For an instant Cato feared the assistants might lose their grip, and he had a vision of the pig racing amongst the guests, spraying blood all over them. But the two men held on as their victim's strength faded and life deserted the body.

'Poor pig,' Lucius muttered sadly.

'Yes,' Cato agreed, and tried hurriedly to think of some words of comfort for his little son. 'Poor pig. But lucky gods, eh? I bet they love the smell of roasting pork.'

Lucius looked up at him, his chin quivering. 'She would have been a good pet, Father. I'd have looked after her. Did she have to die?'

'I'm afraid so. We want Macro and Petronella to be happy, don't we? We want the gods to look after them.'

'Yes . . . But—'

'Then there had to be an offering made to the gods. That's how it works. Do you see?'

Lucius sighed unhappily but made no further protest.

As the assistants heaved the dead pig onto the fire with as much decorum as the task permitted, the priest threw his head back and extended his arms towards the skies in a dramatic gesture.

'The sacrifice is made. The gods are content. We celebrate the marriage of Macro and Petronella!'

A ragged chorus of cheers rose from the small band of officers, and Cato joined in heartily as Macro helped his wife to her feet and then threw his arms around her and kissed her hard. She was taken by surprise and resisted for an instant, before grabbing the back of his head in both hands and pressing him closer still.

'Easy there, Petronella!' Centurion Porcino laughed. 'You don't want to break him on the first night!'

Cato felt his hand being tugged and looked down at his son.

'Father, are they going to wrestle again?'

'It looks that way. Let's just hope they manage to wait till later on. Much later on.'

Macro took his wife's arms and eased her back, and they broke off from the kiss, grinning like youngsters. Then Petronella blushed self-consciously and broke free, turning to face the guests.

'It's time to feast. Please take your seats while food and drink is brought to you.' She glanced past them to where Yusef's steward was waiting beside the entrance to the house, and signalled to him.

A moment later, the notes of a pipe accompanied by a harp reached the ears of those in the garden, and two musicians wandered down the path and took up their assigned place behind the couches. The officers arranged themselves at the table on Macro's side, while the other guests sat opposite. When all were in place, the first of the servants emerged from the kitchen carrying trays laden with dishes of dates and figs. More followed with jars of wine, platters of roast meat, pastries, cheeses and bread. Macro sniffed the aromas with delight.

'A proper banquet and no mistake, my love.'

Petronella beamed with pleasure and quickly slipped a large helping of glazed lamb chops into a bowl for Lucius.

'Eat up, young man, and you'll grow up to be a fine strong soldier like Macro!'

While the music played softly in the background, the guests ate and drank their fill and the soldiers exchanged ribald comments with Macro and Cato. Petronella affected to look shocked at the more salacious banter, partly out of deference to her own guests, who weren't quite sure how to react to what passed for table talk amongst Roman soldiers. She tried to make subtle gestures to her husband to be aware of the sensitivities of young Lucius, but the conversation floated over the boy's head as he finished eating and then fetched his toy soldiers to play with on the floor.

Halfway through the afternoon, the steward came hurrying out of the house and approached those lying on the couches. Bending forward, he spoke softly to Macro. 'Centurion, there is a visitor in the hall. He claims to be General Corbulo, and he wishes to speak to you.'

'Me?' Macro raised an eyebrow in surprise. 'Surely you mean the tribune.'

'No, sir. It is you he asked for.'

Macro took a deep breath. 'What in Hades can Corbulo want with me?'

'Only one way to find out,' Cato responded.

Macro swung his legs off the couch and kissed Petronella on the forehead. Then he stood up, brushed the crumbs from the front of his best tunic and followed the steward towards the house. When he had disappeared from view, Petronella shuffled closer to Cato.

'What's Corbulo doing here?'

'Well, you invited him, didn't you?'

'Yes, but he didn't respond. I assumed he wasn't coming. By the gods, I hope Macro's not in any trouble, this day of all days . . .'

* * *

After the bright sunlight in the garden, the atrium of the silver-smith's house was gloomy, and it wasn't until General Corbulo emerged from the shadows by the front door that Macro saw that he was alone. He was wearing a plain cotton tunic and military boots, and he carried a small chest under his left arm, not much larger than a mess tin. Macro snapped to attention in front of him.

'You sent for me, sir?'

A look of embarrassment crossed the general's face. 'Actually, it was you who sent for me, Centurion Macro. You and your wife-to-be. I was only notified of your invitation at noon by one of my clerks, who is even now starting a month on latrine duty. I most humbly apologise and I hope I have not arrived too late to share your celebration.'

Macro shifted uneasily. 'Ah, the thing is, sir, the ceremony is over. But you are welcome to join us for the remainder of the feast, if you are willing.'

It was an awkward situation, and Macro hoped that the general would politely decline the offer rather than upset the warm ambience that had embraced the wedding party, as late-arriving guests of high rank were wont to do.

'Centurion, if the offer still stands, I would be deeply honoured to join you.'

'Yes, sir,' Macro said automatically, then paused briefly before turning and gesturing towards the garden. 'Please follow me.'

With a heart weighed down by misgiving, he led the aristocrat out into the sunshine that filled the garden along with the music and the happy sound of light conversation and laughter. The latter died away as the guests became aware of Corbulo's presence. Cato and the other officers immediately made to rise from their places, while the civilian guests stirred uneasily, not quite certain what they should do.

'Please, gentlemen, do resume your seats.' Corbulo waved them back. 'Today I am just another guest at the wedding of our comrade.'

The benches scraped on the flagstones as the officers sat back down, though none spoke as they regarded their general warily. Corbulo advanced towards the couches, where Petronella hurriedly scrambled up and bowed her head.

'There's no need for that, my dear. Please, just treat me as you would anyone else who is honoured to be here to celebrate your wedding.' A smile creased Corbulo's craggy features. 'But first, I have a gift for you and your husband.'

He held out the small chest and Macro received it with a nod. 'Thank you, sir.'

Unsure what to do with it, he gestured towards the couches. 'If you please, sir, take my place.'

'I will do no such thing. I will join these gentlemen.' Corbulo nodded to the table where the centurions were sitting. As was the convention, the senior of their number sat closest to the head table, while the others were arranged in descending order of status, with the optios at the end. Now they all shuffled along to make room for the general. Once he was seated, he glanced up sharply at Macro and Petronella. 'Well, aren't you going to open it?'

'What? Oh, yes. Of course, sir.'

Macro slipped the catch and lifted the lid. Inside was a large leather bag, bulging with coins. Petronella leaned over to look and gave a light gasp. Working the tie loose, she saw that the coins were silver.

'Two thousand denarians.' Corbulo smiled. 'Enough to give you a decent start to married life, I should think.'

Macro puffed his cheeks. The sum was nearly half a year's

pay for a centurion. 'That's very generous of you, sir. I . . . I don't know what to say.'

'Your simple thanks is enough. Besides, Rome owes you far more than mere silver can ever repay. You have shed blood for the Empire on many occasions. When lesser men would have turned and run to save their lives, you stood firm and fought on. I am well aware of your record, Centurion Macro. Accept this as a token of respect from one who knows your quality and values it highly.' He looked round at the other officers, who still had plenty of food in front of them. 'Now, if it's not too much trouble, what can a hungry man get to eat in this house? I'll have my fill, since there won't be much chance of finding such a feast when the campaign begins in earnest.'

Petronella bustled towards the kitchen, while Cato filled a cup from the wine jug on the top table and set it down in front of the general.

'I imagine the official toasts have been done,' said Corbulo as Petronella returned and stood beside Macro, taking his arm. 'So this is my personal toast to you.'

He raised his cup. 'To Centurion Macro and his lovely wife. May the gods watch over you both; may Mars guard you, Macro, through the coming conflict with Parthia and see you returned home safely to Petronella's arms. May you return weighed down with such spoils of war that you will live a wealthy man in your retirement.'

Macro laughed and picked up his own cup. 'I'll drink to that right enough, sir!'

Once the general had made his toast, the atmosphere eased, and soon the party was feasting happily, with Corbulo joining in the frequently ribald exchanges between the officers. Cato, who was not a hard drinker in any case, made sure that he

56

drank from Lucius's heavily watered-down jug. He was of the view that senior officers were never quite as off-duty as they sometimes gave the impression of being. Words and faces would be remembered. Anything taken as a slight on Corbulo's character could well be used against the officer concerned at some point in the future. In Cato's experience, the bonhomie of senior officers – even those he respected – was to be welcomed, but dealt with warily. Generals were always watchful, always considering the merits or otherwise of those who served under them. The divide between them and their men was necessary and all but unbridgeable. They stood apart from others, and only the words of the most trusted of subordinates carried any weight with them. So it was with Corbulo, and Cato was guarded in what he said as the afternoon wore on.

At length, when all had eaten their fill, and most were happily drunk, the general drained his cup and announced, 'It's been a fine feast, and a privilege to share your celebration, but now I'm afraid I must return to headquarters.'

'Already?' Petronella did not hide her disappointment. 'But I've hired a juggler for the evening. He performs tricks, too.'

'I'm sure he will be very entertaining, my lady, but sadly, my duties demand my attention. So it remains to thank you and your husband for your kindness in inviting me.'

'It is for us to thank you, General,' said Macro, his speech slurred. 'You honour us. And your gift was most . . . most generous.'

'No more than you deserve, Centurion.' Corbulo stood up, and the other officers struggled to their feet too, save Centurion Nicolis, who had passed out and was slumped over the table snoring. Porcino gave him a nudge.

'Stand up, you fool,' he hissed.

Corbulo laughed. 'Oh, leave him be. I apologise for going so soon. Tribune Cato, if you would be kind enough to see me out.'

'Yes, sir. Of course.'

The general nodded his farewells and strode away from the party, back through the house to the atrium, with Cato on his heels. He paused by the front door and regarded Cato for a moment before he spoke. 'I'm afraid there's another reason for my presence here today.'

Cato smiled faintly. 'I wondered.'

'Not that I needed another reason, you understand. Centurion Macro is one of the best, with a long career behind him. That alone warrants recognition and reward.'

'Macro is indeed one of the best, sir. Which is why I will miss him when the time comes for him to apply for a discharge.'

Corbulo's eyebrow rose slightly. 'He's thinking of leaving the army? Not just now, I trust. Not when I have most need of men of his calibre if we're to have any hope of defeating the Parthians.'

'He says he wants to see the campaign out, sir.'

'Good. What does his new wife say about that?'

'She's not as pleased as she might be. But she accepts Macro for what he is. She knows she is marrying into the army.'

Corbulo nodded wistfully. 'For some of us, the army is all we know. It is our entire life. I hope the centurion manages to make the transition to civilian life – if he survives the campaign. Given what I have seen of the quality of most of the units under my command, I fear that I wouldn't give good odds on our defeating the Parthians as things stand.'

Cato was surprised by the general's downbeat tone. But there was no escaping the truth about the poor state of the army, even now, nearly a year after Corbulo had taken up his command and started to prepare his forces. Supplies of equipment had been slow to arrive in Tarsus, and less than half of the replacements needed to bring the legions and auxiliary units up to full strength had been recruited. Even then, those who had enlisted needed to complete their training before they could be led into battle. Cato could see where his superior's line of thinking might be heading, and he cleared his throat.

'I imagine you're concerned about the army being ready to campaign when spring comes, sir.'

Corbulo stared at him for a moment, then shook his head. 'How could I not be concerned? Only a rash fool would take the risk as things stand. I need time to find more men and get them ready to fight. Time is the issue, Tribune Cato. I need more of it.' He paused briefly. 'And you're the man who has to buy it for me.'

'Me?' Cato frowned. 'How exactly?'

'You'll find out soon enough. Be at headquarters no later than the first hour tomorrow. I'll explain then. Meanwhile, enjoy what's left of the party.'

Before Cato could question him further, the general turned, opened the door and stepped down into the street. The door closed behind him.

Cato raised his head and stared up at the heavens through the small opening above the atrium. As the sound of cheery voices and laughter came from the garden, he wondered what Corbulo had in mind for him.

CHAPTER FIVE

There was little sign of life anywhere in the house as Cato slipped out of the door just after dawn. After Corbulo had left, the drinking had continued well into the night, with most of the guests joining in a dice game that Macro had insisted on, now that the general had provided him with a handsome fortune to stake. Fortunately, Petronella had taken the box from him and counted out sufficient coins to let her husband enjoy himself without risking profligate foolishness. Fortuna had decided to bless the newly-wed, and Macro made handsome returns on his betting all night, emptying the purses of most of the other officers until Cato called an end to the game before anyone was tempted to make any wagers based on promises. He knew from experience that that sort of debt between soldiers created bad will and lingering resentment, something he would not tolerate in his cohort. And so, with Centurion Nicolis slung over the burly shoulder of his optio, the officers had noisily made their farewells before stumbling outside and weaving their way down the street back to their billets by the light of the stars. The last of the civilian guests followed in their wake, the wives clucking irritably at their husbands' drunken state and light purses.

Cato, still sober enough to take charge, closed the door

behind them before returning to the garden to find Macro fast asleep on his couch, one arm curled around the bowl containing his winnings. Fetching his cloak from its peg in his room, he covered his friend up and looked down on him with a smile.

'It's been quite a day, hasn't it?'

Turning, Cato made out Petronella standing at the opening to the corridor that led back into the house. He nodded. 'So it has. You want me to move Macro into your room?'

She came forward, and he saw that she had removed the tie from her stola so that it hung straight down from her shoulders. She stopped at his side and gazed at her husband for a moment until Macro suddenly snorted and smacked his lips before rolling onto his back. A moment later, he was snoring; a deep, steady nasal rumble.

'No, I think he can stay here for the night, the state he's in.'

'Not quite the wedding night you imagined, eh?'

She chuckled good-naturedly. 'It's exactly the wedding night I imagined, knowing him as I do. He'll make up for it, if he knows what's good for him.'

Given what the general had said, Cato was not sure how much of a chance his friend was going to have to placate his new wife before duty called him away. He decided it might be best not to say anything until he had spoken to Corbulo. Let them enjoy what time they had together while they could, without the moment being clouded by anxiety over their separation.

'He knows how good you are for him, Petronella. Trust me. Once you settle down in Britannia, I'm sure you'll not find a better man to be with.' Cato clicked his tongue. 'His mother, on the other hand . . .'

Petronella shot him a sharp look. 'I think I can handle her.'

'I'm sure you can.' He laughed. 'I can picture Macro now, caught between the two of you. He'll be running off to the nearest recruiting officer first chance he gets. Better a barbarian horde than the barbed tongues of the two women dearest to his heart.'

Petronella did not share his humour. 'Do you really think so? Would he really prefer to stay in the army?'

'I was joking. He wants to be with you more than anything.'

'And what about you? He'll miss you, I know it.'

Cato's first response was to make some dismissive remark, but then he thought better of it. He owed Petronella the truth. He cleared his throat softly before he responded. 'To be honest, there is no soldier I'd rather have guarding my back. Macro's been there from the moment I first joined up. If it wasn't for him, I'd have been dead long ago. He taught me almost everything I know about soldiering. But I'll cope without him. And I wish you both all the happiness you can find.'

'Thank you, master.'

They exchanged a quick look at her use of the term, and then she shook her head. 'I'm still not used to it. And it'll be hard to leave young Lucius as well.'

'He'll miss you.'

'I hope you're not angry with me . . .'

'Angry?' Cato shook his head. 'Why would I be angry?'

Petronella looked down at Macro again. 'I feel like I'm taking him away from you, and from Lucius. Taking him away from where he belongs.'

'He belongs with you now.' Cato reached out and gave her shoulder an affectionate squeeze. 'Look after him, eh?'

They shared a smile, and then Cato turned and walked away.

As he reached the door to his room, he paused to look back and saw that Petronella had sat down on the couch and was gently stroking Macro's brow. He felt a pang of guilt as he wondered what General Corbulo might have in store for them come the morning.

There were few clerks and staff officers about at the merchant's house that Corbulo used as his headquarters. The duty Praetorians from Porcino's century snapped smartly to attention at Cato's approach, and they exchanged a salute as he entered the building.

The general's office was on the second floor, overlooking the formal gardens at the rear of the house. Cato was asked to wait outside while Corbulo's secretary announced his arrival. There was one other man in the anteroom: a wiry-looking individual, completely bald, dressed in a simple black tunic, who was leaning against the wall next to the window, examining a flute. Cato took him for some kind of entertainer. The man glanced up and looked Cato over briefly before they exchanged a nod.

The secretary emerged from the general's office and stood to one side. 'Gnaeus Domitius Corbulo will see you now, sir.'

The general was sitting at his desk reading a scroll. 'A moment, please.' He raised a finger as he quickly finished the document, and then sat back in his chair, sliding the scroll to one side. 'Good morning to you, Tribune. Take a seat. I trust you are not feeling the effects of last night's drinking.'

'I'm fine, sir.'

'Then you have a firmer constitution than I.' Corbulo smiled. 'But then, you have youth on your side.'

Cato nodded briefly, not willing to admit that he had not had much to drink. He disliked being drunk and losing control of his faculties. He disliked hangovers even more. But he was aware that such notions might be regarded as unmanly by most hardened veterans. Such as the man sitting at the desk.

'You'll recall what I said last night about needing to buy myself some more time.'

'Yes, sir.'

'The army is not ready to invade Parthia, Tribune. Not nearly ready enough. Discipline is poor in some units. Many of the men are not fit enough for hard campaigning.' Corbulo sighed. 'It seems that when the winter comes, I may have to take them into the mountains once again to toughen them up. I'd hoped the last time would be enough to make them ready. Clearly, I was mistaken. This time I will make sure they are pushed hard to weed out the weaklings and ensure that discipline is enforced with an iron will.' He folded his fingers together and cracked his knuckles. 'I'll not spare them any hardship. I want to know that the men I lead to war will be as tough and ruthless as the general who commands them.'

He stared hard at Cato. 'Which brings me onto your mission.'

He reached out and tapped the scroll. 'There have been sightings of bands of Parthians moving up the far bank of the Euphrates. I fear they mean to mass their forces and attack us before the army is ready to meet them in battle. I need time to prepare my men. It would be better still if war could be avoided, even at this late stage. So I have decided to send an embassy to King Vologases and present him with one last chance to prevent war between Parthia and Rome. You, Tribune Cato, will lead that embassy.'

'Me?' Cato shook his head. 'But I'm no diplomat, sir. I'm just a soldier.'

'I have come to realise that you are rather more than that.

You have quick wits and an eye for detail, and I can't think of a better man for the task I have in mind. I need you to buy me some time to prepare the army.'

'If the Parthians suspect the embassy is merely being used as an attempt to win Rome breathing space, then I dare say they'll not be inclined to treat my reason for being in Parthia as diplomatic, sir. I could lose my head. Me and the men I take with me.'

'Then you'd better make sure you go about your business effectively. The main purpose of your being sent to Vologases is to try and prevent a war that will not profit either side, even if it appeals to hotheads who clamour for glory. I need you to try and convince him it is not in Parthia's interests to wage war with Rome. Given that he is already fighting a war on his eastern frontier, he may desire peace with Rome in order to turn his forces against Hyrcania.'

'If I recall, the Hyrcanians are being led by Vologases' son, Vardanes.'

'That's right.' Corbulo nodded. 'And Vardanes and his followers are being funded by Roman gold. We don't expect him to defeat his father, although that would be welcomed, but he and his friends are a most useful distraction for Vologases to have to deal with as far as Rome is concerned.'

Cato thought for a moment before he spoke. 'What would I be authorised to offer Vologases in order to provide Rome with the peace we need, sir? And in whose name should I speak? Yours, or the emperor's?'

Corbulo's lips pressed together in a thin line as he glared back. Then he took a long, deep breath. 'You will be acting on my authority, but you will tell the Parthians that you speak for Rome and the emperor. I cannot afford to let months pass while I ask Nero for permission to send an embassy. Besides, those advisers he chooses to surround himself with have no grasp of the situation I am facing. So I am giving you the order and I will be the one held responsible for the consequences. If Vologases opts for peace, we will be spared a costly war, even if it disappoints those in Rome who want conflict.'

'It seems that I may be held responsible for the consequences too, sir.'

'I see . . . Would you like me to put my orders to you in writing and set my seal on it. Is that what you are after, Tribune?'

Cato shook his head. 'What would be the point? If Nero wants heads to roll, I doubt any document is going to save me.'

'Quite. If it's any comfort, then know that if I fall from favour, I will do all I can to shield you from the repercussions.'

Corbulo rose from his chair and stepped over to the window overlooking the garden. He continued to speak with his back to Cato. 'In order not to dishonour the prestige of Rome, you are instructed to negotiate with Parthia within the following strictures. First, we will not pay them any gold or silver as the price of peace. Second, we will not give up our claim to Armenia. Third, and most important of all, Rome must not be seen to offer peace before the Parthians do. You will emphasise that while we will be content with peace between our two empires, we threaten war and destruction on a scale they have never witnessed before.'

'That might be difficult, sir. I imagine they will not have forgotten their victory over Crassus at Carrhae. Any threats I make might ring a little hollow given that the Parthians all but annihilated eight of our legions and took the head of our general as a trophy.'

'I dare say you are right. One tends not to forget such matters. Nevertheless, it is vital for the honour of Rome, and my survival, that it is the Parthians who sue for peace. And if they do, you must insist on them making an unmistakable act of obeisance. Rome will want hostages and tribute, even if it is little more than a token offering. Appearances are everything as far as the emperor and the Senate are concerned.'

'That is true, sir. And I imagine the same may be said of Vologases and his nobles. They will not be willing to look weak.'

'I can't help that,' Corbulo responded tersely. 'You will have to do what you can. If they will not meet my official demands, you have my permission to make it clear to the Parthians that our requests are a matter of form, to satisfy the emperor and his lackeys. What matters is that we get a peace that is acceptable to Nero. That's what you tell Vologases. He may be prepared to agree to it on those terms. More likely, he will not. Either way, anything that gives me time to prepare the army for the coming campaign will be of advantage to Rome.'

'Then the true object of the embassy is as much to win a delay as to achieve peace.'

The dryness in Cato's tone was not missed by the army's commander. 'A general is forced to use the men, weapons and strategies available to him, Tribune Cato. If I can exploit an embassy as a ruse to gain an advantage over the enemy, then I will.' He paused and regarded Cato closely for a beat before he continued. 'No doubt you are questioning the integrity of offering to make peace while at the same time preparing to wage war.'

'Something like that, yes, sir.'

Corbulo shrugged. 'What can I say, Tribune? We live in difficult times. The Republic is no more than a distant memory. Any sense of honour that may have existed in some golden age is long since dead and buried. What matters now is victory, however that is achieved. With victory comes the prize of writing the history of how that victory was won. Do you really think that, if we are forced to fight, anyone in Rome will give a damn about how we defeated Parthia when the triumphal procession winds its way through the capital? No. The only thing that will matter to the mob, the Senate and Nero is the spectacle of the carts carrying the spoils of war, the sight of prisoners in chains and the garlanded standards of our soldiers being held high for all to see. So spare yourself your piety. You will sleep better as a result. I do. Any questions?'

'I think you have made the purpose of my mission clear, sir.' Cato thought for a moment. An embassy, particularly one sent out by Rome, was usually conducted on a scale sufficient to impress the other side. But the task that Corbulo had handed him was fraught with perils. The general could hardly fail to know that. It would be better, then, to ensure that the price that might have to be paid was as limited as possible. 'Sir, given the circumstances, I think it would be best if I was accompanied by only a small escort. No sense in you losing more men than you can afford.'

Corbulo stroked his jaw for a moment and nodded. 'Much as I would like to impress our Parthian friends with a display of pomp, I agree. Who knows, it might even play out well for us. They are familiar with the austerity of the Greeks. Let's give them more of the same. Let's show that Rome is not concerned with frippery. We are to the point. Try and impress that upon them, Tribune.'

'I will do my best, sir.'

'I don't doubt it.' Corbulo paused a beat before he continued. 'You'll take one of my best men with you as an adviser. Apollonius of Perga. Have you met him?'

Cato shook his head. 'Not that I recall.'

'A pity. He's a man of considerable ability. Fluent in many tongues of the east and knows the region well. Just the kind of man to have at your side for the task at hand. I've already briefed him about the mission. In fact, he's waiting outside. I think it's time you two were acquainted.' Corbulo crossed to the door and opened it. 'Apollonius, in here, if you please.'

The man Cato had seen earlier entered the room and pulled up a stool to one side of the desk without being asked. He set his flute down carefully.

'I thank you for this. It's just what I needed.'

'I'm glad,' Corbulo replied. 'Look after it well.'

'I'll do my best to return it to you one day.' Apollonius smiled. 'You may need it.'

The general did not seem to take any offence at the man's informal attitude as he returned to his own chair.

Cato hesitated. He felt a surge of irritation that this man, Apollonius, should be treated with such familiarity. It was as if he was the general's agent and Cato his aide, rather than the other way round.

Corbulo eased himself back into his chair as he began. 'May I introduce Apollonius, son of Demippos of Perga. You may have heard of his father.'

The name stirred a distant memory. 'The philosopher? A follower of the Cynic school, if I recall.'

'Indeed he was.' Corbulo nodded approvingly.

Cato raised an eyebrow. 'Was?'

Apollonius sat forward and rested his elbows on his knees, clasping his hands together as he scrutinised Cato. 'My father died in exile some years ago. I am surprised you know of him. I had thought his reputation was confined to a small circle of savants here in the Eastern Empire.'

Although his voice was deep, with a rich timbre, Apollonius spoke softly, and there was a pleasing melody and rhythm to his speech that Cato instantly warmed to, before his natural caution intruded.

'His works are not easy to come by in Rome, I admit,' the tribune replied. 'The Cynics fell out of fashion during the reign of Augustus, but I found his *Aesthetics of Being* in the library of Tiberius when I was a youth.'

'And?' Apollonius tilted his head slightly to one side as his dark eyes remained fixed on Cato.

'I was impressed by much of what he wrote.'

'But . . .'

It annoyed Cato that the other man had discerned his reservations about the work so readily. He composed his reply carefully. 'While I admired his style and the lucidity with which he conveyed his meaning, most of his ideas were derived from the work of earlier philosophers. Zeno in particular. Not that there is anything wrong with taking the work of earlier thinkers a stage further through applying dialectics.' He paused. 'But I found his reliance on *epicheirema* unconvincing. However, I am merely a soldier. And a Roman soldier at that.'

There was silence as Apollonius stared straight at him, as if daring him to continue. Then he suddenly shook his head and laughed as he turned to Corbulo. 'He's good! I like this one.'

'I told you he had the makings of a diplomat.'

'Oh, he's more than a diplomat,' Apollonius continued. 'He's a reluctant intellectual, the best kind. My old man may have pulled the wool over the eyes of most of his followers, but the tribune saw right through him.' He turned back to Cato. 'For what it's worth, my father was a plagiarist. It's why I refused to take after him and deployed my talents elsewhere.' He gave a brief, knowing smile before he addressed the general

70

once more. 'He'll do nicely. Just the kind of informed wit that Vologases appreciates. More importantly, he knows when to rein it in. Where did you find such an officer? I was under the impression that nearly all those Roman aristocrats who put on soldier's garb quietly throttled whatever intellectual passions they had previously entertained.'

'They generally do,' Corbulo agreed. 'But our friend Tribune Cato is different. Do not be fooled by the quality of his attire and the cultivation of his mind. He is no aristocrat. He rose through the ranks and married into wealth and position.'

'That does not surprise me in the slightest. I have yet to meet a traditional Roman aristocrat who does not feel the urge to reach for a sword whenever someone mentions culture.' Apollonius opened his hands apologetically. 'Present company excepted, naturally.'

'Naturally,' Corbulo responded coolly. His cordial manner disappeared and his expression took on the hard veneer of an army commander once more. 'You have your orders, gentlemen. May the gods look favourably on your mission. Tribune, pick ten good men to serve as your escort. They'll need to be accomplished riders, mind.'

'Ten men?' Cato sucked in a breath. Barely more than a section of Praetorians to lead into the heart of the Parthian empire. It was an ominous prospect indeed. 'I can find ten good men easily enough, sir.'

'Good. Then have them ready to leave Tarsus the day after tomorrow, at dawn. It's short notice, I know. It's nearly October now. If all goes well, you should be back before the end of the year. However, it would be wise to ensure your will is up to date and that you say your farewells. There's nothing more to add. You are dismissed.'

Cato rose smartly from the stool and exchanged a salute with the general before turning to Apollonius. 'I dare say you already know where I am billeted.'

'Of course.'

'Then I'll see you outside my house, two days from now.'

'As you wish.'

He strode towards the door and left the room. Outside, he let out a long hiss of anger and frustration as he contemplated his mission. The prospect of riding to the heart of Parthia and negotiating a peace between the two empires was daunting. But orders were orders and he would have to carry them out. One particular aspect concerned him more than most: he had no idea if the Greek agent's goals were the same as his own. If they were not, then only the gods knew what lay in store for him.

CHAPTER SIX

'What do you mean, I'm not coming with you?' Macro demanded as they sat at the table in the kitchen. 'Fuck that. If you're marching into danger, my place is at your side.'

'Not this time,' Cato replied firmly as he petted Cassius's head. The dog was leaning against his thigh, head resting happily on its master's lap. 'There should be no danger. It's an embassy, that's all. Diplomatic work. All talk and no action. It's not proper soldiering and you'd be bored witless if you came.'

Macro clicked his tongue. 'Who do you think you're fooling, my lad? You'll be crossing the frontier into enemy territory. Then it'll be who knows how many hundreds of miles to ride before you reach the Parthian capital. You'll be fair game for any bands of brigands or local warlords who decide to take a nice set of Roman heads for their collection. You'll need a small army just to get through the journey alive. Even with me and the rest of the cohort behind you, I wouldn't give good odds for us making it.'

He paused to take a spoonful of the porridge Petronella had made after she'd turfed him off the couch in the garden. No endearments had been exchanged. Macro's surly growl had given way to a grin as he'd reached out to catch her hand, but Petronella, unburdened by a hangover, had stepped nimbly aside and slapped him hard on the cheek.

'None of that, and there'll be nothing to eat until you've washed, shaved and changed out of those filthy rags.'

'What?' Macro had looked down and seen the splashes of dried vomit on the front of his tunic. 'Jupiter's balls! Some bastard has puked on me!'

'Ha!' sniffed Petronella, turning away and striding back towards the house, Macro staring at her gently swaying backside with a lascivious grin.

He smiled now at the memory before his thoughts returned to his conversation with Cato.

'How many men do you think you'll need for the job, sir?'

Cato sighed. 'I'd be happier if I did have a small army at my back. As it is, there'll be twelve of us, including the general's agent.'

'Twelve?' Macro's eyes widened and his spoon sagged back into the bowl. 'Twelve? Are you fucking mad?'

'Not my decision. Those were Corbulo's orders.'

'Then he's the bloody madman. Sending a handful of Romans into Parthia like that. Sending you to your deaths more like.' Macro released the spoon and ran his fingers through his thinning hair. There were pronounced streaks of grey there, Cato noticed as his friend cleared his throat and continued. 'Don't do it, sir. It's a fool's errand. The Parthians will take his terms as an insult, and by way of reply they'll cut you and the others into little pieces and send them back to him. Tell him you refuse to go.'

'I can't. I didn't volunteer for this. It was an order.'

'An order?' Macro sniffed derisively. 'It's a suicide order. That's what it is.'

'Let's hope not. As an embassy, we should be accorded

74

protection at least as far as Ctesiphon. After that, our fate will be in the hands of Vologases.'

'And what about this other character? Corbulo's man.'

'Apollonius?'

'What do you make of him? Can he be trusted?'

Cato thought for a moment, then shrugged. 'I don't know yet. He is clearly Corbulo's creature and accounts to the general before he is answerable to me, even though he is supposed to be my aide. I'll have to watch him closely.'

'All the more reason to make sure I come along,' Macro insisted. 'You need me to watch your back.'

Cato was touched by his friend's genuine concern, and in truth, nothing would please him more than to have the tough centurion join the embassy. But he was already putting his own life at risk, and those of his escort. Macro's presence would make little difference. And if things went badly, then at least he would have the comfort of knowing Macro had been spared. Particularly now that he had found Petronella. To take him away after barely two days of marriage might just occasion a titanic outburst of rage from his wife. That clinched the argument for Cato.

'Listen, Macro. I need you to remain here. The cohort must have a good man to take command while I am gone. You're the senior centurion, so that's your duty. The general also needs you and the rest of the officers to train the recruits joining the ranks of the other units. So take care of the lads. Take care of your wife, and look after Lucius for me. I won't be gone for long, but I'll take comfort from knowing you're running things here in Tarsus. Besides,' he forced a grin, 'rank has its privileges. Corbulo ordered me to go, and now I'm ordering you to stay, and that's the end of the matter.'

Macro made to protest, but knew better than to challenge

an order given by a superior. Instead he sucked air through his teeth. 'I hope you know what you're doing. Keep your eyes open, lad, and watch out for that Apollonius. I don't like the sound of him.'

'I will. I've every intention of coming back in one piece.' Cato coughed and craned his neck towards the pot on the stove. 'Any of that porridge left?'

'You'd better get some in before Lucius wakes up. That boy's got an appetite on him. Eats like a bloody wolf. He's going to be a strapping lad when he grows up. A fine soldier, just like his father.'

'I'll let him decide what he wants to do when the time comes.'

'Ah, come on!' Macro slapped a hand on his thigh. 'Ain't nothing better than a life in the army. You've done well enough out of it.'

Cato was not so sure. Yes, he had won promotion, and come by riches thanks to his service, but he carried numerous scars on his body, and would never be able to forget the dark despair that had almost consumed him during their last campaign, in Armenia. The memories of that bleak time haunted him. If he could spare his son that, he would. At the same time, he was determined that Lucius would be the master of his own fate, whether he chose a military career or not.

They were interrupted by Petronella as she entered the kitchen leading Lucius by the hand. The boy was yawning and looked drowsy. Cassius stirred and trotted over to give him a lick.

'And here's the man himself!' Macro grinned as he reached out and ruffled the child's hair before looking up at his wife. 'How's my lady love feeling now? Am I forgiven for failing to fulfil your deepest desires last night?'

'No,' she said curtly, and then turned to Cato. 'There's a man at the door. He says you bought yourself a slave.'

Cato nodded. 'That'll be Flaminius.'

'He doesn't look up to much. Scrawny and surly.'

'But he served in the legions. He would have ended up in the mines or fields if I hadn't bought him. No veteran who falls on hard times deserves that.'

'But other people do, eh?' Petronella challenged him. 'It's your money, Master Cato.'

'Yes, it is.' He nodded towards the pot on the stove. 'Save me some of that.'

Cato went to his room and pulled the strongbox out from under his bed. Taking the key from the chain around his neck, he unlocked the box and took out a large leather purse, heavy with gold and silver coins. He made his way to the front door and opened it. At once, light and noise from the street spilled into the hall. The slave dealer stood on the bottom step and bowed his head in greeting.

'Tribune Cato, I bid you a good morning, sir. As arranged, I have your purchase from yesterday.' He turned aside and indicated Flaminius standing behind him in the street, arms crossed and a stern expression on his face.

'Good, inside with you then.'

The dealer edged back between them. 'There is the small matter of payment, sir. Two hundred denarians, and five sestertians for the delivery charge.'

'Delivery charge?'

'Indeed, my dear sir. It's a service I conduct myself for minimal cost, since I am giving up my time.'

'But the slave market is just round the corner from here,' Cato protested.

'True indeed, my dear sir. I find my customers appreciate

77

the personal touch of having me bring their merchandise to the door and offer any tips concerning the ownership of the individual in question.'

'Such as?'

The dealer thought quickly. 'Any special attributes not discussed at the time of sale. Or any issues relating to the slave's attitude or health that might need attending to.'

'I would hope you would not attempt to sell me a sick slave.'

The dealer raised his hands. 'Oh, dear sir, I would not dream of doing so. But sickness comes unexpectedly. Or it may have been hidden from me by the trader I bought my stock from. And as I am sure you are aware, the legal situation in such circumstances is let the buyer beware.'

'If you've sold me a sick slave, I can assure you the situation will become let the seller beware . . . my dear friend. Now, the money.'

The dealer opened the flap of a sturdy leather pouch that hung around his neck and Cato counted out the coins to the amount of the agreed price. As he pulled the thongs to close the purse, the dealer coughed lightly.

'And the delivery charge, if you please, my dear sir.'

'It seems I may not have mentioned my reception fee,' Cato responded. 'I find that the merchants who deliver goods to my house appreciate the personal gesture of me giving up my time in order to be in when they choose to deliver the goods. Five sestertians.'

The slave dealer laughed; when Cato's expression remained fixed, he huffed and made to speak, changed his mind, then waved a hand in farewell and turned and stepped down into the street before hurrying off without a backward glance.

Cato smiled with satisfaction and beckoned Flaminius to enter the house. Once the door was closed, he examined his slave by the opening in the atrium. The former soldier was streaked with grime. He had been stripped of the tunic he had worn on the slave market stage and given a ragged garment from the slave dealer's slop chest instead. Even the sandals he had been wearing the day before had been taken from him by the sestertian-pinching dealer.

'Are you hungry?' asked Cato.

Flaminius nodded. 'Haven't had a scrap for nearly two days . . . master.'

The resentful tone of his final word was not missed by Cato, nor was it meant to be, he realised. It would be best if the man was put in his place from the outset.

'Listen to me, Flaminius. It is not my fault that you were reduced to your present status. But I'll not see a soldier who has served Rome end his days being worked to death in the mines or the fields. You deserve something better than that, and that is why I bought you. You are part of my household now, and you will be looked after and treated fairly. In return, I expect the same obedience and loyalty from you that I would expect from every man under my command. Serve me well and one day you will surely earn your freedom. But if you treat me with resentment, I will sell you back to someone like that dealer and wash my hands of you.' He stared at Flaminius for a moment to let his words sink in. 'Are we clear?'

'Yes, master.'

'That's better. Now let's get you something to eat, and then find you something better to wear. You'll need travel clothes and a good pair of boots. Come.'

He returned his purse to the chest and then led the way back to the kitchen, where Macro and the others looked up from the table to scrutinise the new arrival. Cassius let out a soft growl until Macro took his collar and pulled him gently back. Lucius smiled a greeting and Flaminius nodded back before turning his attention to Macro and Petronella.

'This is Flaminius,' said Cato. 'He will serve as my body slave from now on. This is my son, Lucius, who you will recall from the market; Centurion Macro, the senior officer in my cohort, and Petronella, his wife. The dog is mine. He's been tamed, after a fashion. You can sit at the end of the table. Petronella, this man needs some food. Would you see to it, please?'

She rose from the bench next to Lucius and went to the store cupboard. While she searched the shelves, Macro turned to Flaminius.

'I hear you're a veteran of the Fourth Scythica.'

'Yes, sir. Served twenty-six years.'

'I see.' Macro nodded. 'Can't say I know much about the Fourth, except that they've been a garrison unit for quite a while. I guess you didn't get to see much action.'

'We had some trouble from time to time with the brigands in the hills, sir. We didn't spend all our time drinking and whoring.'

Petronella returned from the storeroom with bread, cheese and some cuts of meat left over from the wedding feast. Cassius sat up expectantly and then let out a soft whine as the food passed by him. The veteran's eyes widened as the fare was set down in front of him. He began to eat at once, his jaw working furiously as he chewed on a hunk of bread. Cato made do with what was left of the porridge. He was not feeling hungry. His mind was consumed by thoughts of the embassy to Parthia: the preparations he would need to make for the journey and the arrangements in case he did not return.

Once Flaminius had finished eating, Cato sent him to the slave quarters at the rear of the house, where he could wash himself at the water trough. Meanwhile Cato found some old clothes from his chest, together with a worn but serviceable pair of army boots. After he had handed them over, he found Macro waiting for him in the garden.

'What's the matter, brother?'

'I take it your new slave will be joining you for your little jaunt through Parthia.'

'He will. He might be of some use.'

'So might I.'

Cato sighed. 'Macro, my mind is made up. I'd be a damn sight happier knowing that you're around to take care of the cohort, and my son, if the embassy goes badly. There's no one else I'd trust to bring the boy up if I am lost. Apart from me, Lucius has no family. You are close to him, and I'm sure you and Petronella will do him proud. And there's the dog.'

'You're not taking Cassius with you?'

'It's an embassy, Macro, not a hunting party. I don't want him causing a diplomatic incident by biting some Parthian noble, or trying to hump their leg. Cassius stays here, out of trouble.'

'I'm not so sure he'll manage that. But my lass will keep him in line.'

Cato smiled. It was true that the beast doted on Petronella and, for some reason, obeyed her as if she was Jupiter himself. Then again, so did Macro most of the time.

'Macro, don't worry about me. I've been in worse places before and survived to share the tale.'

'I know. But Parthia's different. They've been the most bitter of our enemies since the time of Sulla. I doubt they'll be interested in peace. And certainly not on the terms Corbulo is offering.'

'Maybe, but if I can't get them to agree to peace, then I

hope I can at least buy the general time to ready the army for war. Anything's possible, Macro.'

'But not everything is probable, lad.'

Cato laughed and shook his head. 'You have me there! Ah well, I need to pack my kit, and write my orders for you while I'm gone.' His mirth faded and he was silent for a moment before he continued in a serious tone. 'Look after my son for me, brother. And take good care of the cohort.'

CHAPTER SEVEN

The sun had not yet risen as Cato and Macro emerged from the eastern gate of Tarsus. The mountains were still wreathed in shadows against the pink sky. The river that gave the city access to sea trade was hidden by mist, and only the tops of the reeds growing on the banks and the masts of moored merchant vessels indicated its course. They had left the house without waking Lucius, as Cato had wanted to avoid an emotional scene. Petronella had risen with Macro and embraced Cato before tucking a neat bundle of cloth into his sidebag.

'Strips of dried beef, master,' she explained. 'Just in case.'

Cato had nodded his thanks before he and Macro slipped out of the house, Petronella closing the door quietly behind them.

The air felt cool outside the city, and Cato was grateful for his cloak. A short distance away on the road, the escort stood by their mounts, along with Apollonius and Flaminius. The letter had been sent ahead with the horses allocated from the army's reserve of remounts, and Cato's baggage. The men chosen for the escort had proven themselves fine soldiers since Cato had taken command of the cohort two years earlier. If it came to a fight, there was no better body of men to have at his back.

Cato stopped and turned to Macro. 'I'll say farewell here, brother.'

Macro nodded, and they clasped each other by the forearm. 'May the gods watch over and protect you, sir.'

Cato relaxed his grip, then slipped his hand into his sidebag and took out a scroll sealed with wax and marked with his equestrian ring. 'If anything happens to me, this tells you the name of my banker in Rome, and how much he is holding for me. There's also the house. You're welcome to live there with Petronella if you choose not to go to Londinium, until Lucius is old enough to make good use of his inheritance. I've had my new will placed in the cohort's strongbox, if it's needed.'

'Let's hope it won't be.'

'Indeed.' Cato smiled grimly and turned towards the waiting men. He refastened the buckle of the sidebag, then took the reins that Flaminius offered him and swung himself up into the saddle of his mount, a chestnut mare, adjusting his position to be comfortable for the ride ahead. When he was ready, he turned to the others and saw that Apollonius had already mounted without waiting for any order. He hesitated, sorely tempted to dress the man down, but feared that it might look petty and get the mission off to a bad start. Where they were headed, he could not afford for the small party to be riven by rivalry and resentment. Instead, he took a calming breath.

'Embassy escort, mount!'

The men climbed into their saddles, settled themselves quickly and took up their reins. Each carried personal kit and marching rations in sturdy packs slung across the backs of their cavalry horses. They wore mail vests over their tunics, and their helmets, shields and canteens hung from the saddle horns. They were armed with swords and daggers. One of the men carried General Corbulo's standard with its depiction of a charging bull. Cato had been reluctant to take the standard with them for fear it might end up as a trophy for King Vologases, but Corbulo had insisted, arguing that it would indicate his good faith as well as proving that Cato was acting on the general's behalf.

A quick glance over the men and their mounts revealed that they were ready, and Cato waved his hand at the road ahead.

'Advance!'

He nudged his knees into the horse's flank and the mare walked forward. Apollonius edged his mount forward alongside Cato, then came Flaminius, followed by the escort, riding in pairs. Turning in the saddle, Cato saw Macro just outside the gate, and raised his hand in salute. Macro returned the gesture. Cato turned back to face ahead and forced himself not to think of those he was leaving behind.

'Are you ready for this, Tribune?' Apollonius asked.

Cato glanced at him and saw the calculating look in the other man's eyes. 'I am always ready to carry out my orders to the best of my ability.'

The Greek looked at him and smiled cynically. 'A stock answer if ever I heard one. You'll have to do better than that when we address the Parthians. I would advise you to answer honestly in such matters, and save the careful responses for times that matter. It will help you to appear to be a man of integrity.'

'Appear? What makes you think I am not a man of integrity?'

'I didn't say you weren't. But it's what you appear to be that counts when you are negotiating with the Parthians. It is better to be a schemer and to appear honest than to be an honest man who might be taken for a schemer.'

'And you think that's how I seem?'

Apollonius thought for a moment before he responded. 'I am told you are a good officer, and that you are as sharp-witted as you are brave. However, I barely know you, so I will reserve judgement for now.'

'And how about you, Apollonius? What manner of man are you? A schemer? A spy? Or a diplomat?'

Apollonius chuckled. 'I am all those things, Tribune. And more. Just be thankful that I am on your side. For now,' he added with an amused expression.

Cato leaned slightly closer and lowered his voice so that they would not be overheard above the steady clop of hoofs. 'I will say this now, Greek. If I ever think you are playing the rest of us falsely, and leading us into danger for whatever purpose of your own, I will cut your throat myself.'

'You could certainly try . . . But come now, let us not start off badly. I work for Rome and your general. Corbulo trusts my judgement and abilities completely, and so should you.'

'If there's one thing I have learned in life, it's that trust has to be earned.'

'A valuable lesson, to be sure. And given your previous experience with your late wife, I can understand why you are so reluctant to trust people.'

Cato felt a chill in his heart. How in Hades did this man come to know about Julia's betrayal? He sensed that he was being watched closely as he formed his reply. This might well be another test of his capacity to deal with surprises. Or perhaps the Greek was just goading him for his own pleasure, though that was unlikely. Apollonius seemed far too self-assured and intelligent to derive satisfaction from such cheap stratagems.

'You could not possibly know enough about her to pass judgement on her character,' Cato said with menacing emphasis. 'You will not talk of her again. And spare me any further conversation. We've a long journey ahead of us. It would be best if we focused on what lies ahead.'

Apollonius nodded. 'As you wish.'

Cato urged his horse forward and opened a gap some two lengths ahead of the others. Apollonius made no attempt to keep up, and dropped back slightly to ride alongside Flaminius.

'You're the tribune's servant, I take it,' Cato heard him say.

'I'm his slave,' Flaminius replied flatly.

'How long have you served him?'

'He's been my owner for two days.'

'Two days? Then you hardly know him. And more to the point, he hardly knows you. Nor do I. But I am sure we'll all have the pleasure of each other's company in the days to come.'

'I doubt it'll be much of a pleasure,' Flaminius replied, and spat to the side.

'If you'll take some advice, it might be better if you adopted an appropriately servile demeanour when addressing a free man, my friend.'

Cato quickened the pace of his horse until he was out of earshot, and then slowed to a comfortable walk again. He reflected that whatever purpose Apollonius's presence served on the embassy, one thing seemed certain: he was going to be a thorough pain in the arse if he continued in this vein. Were it not for Cato's concern for Macro's safety, he would have had his friend riding at his side. He was sure to miss Macro's companionship in the days ahead.

Apollonius suddenly laughed, but Cato refused to look back to see why. Instead he focused on the road ahead, as the pointed ears of his mount rocked gently from side to side with every pace the mare took. The journey to Ctesiphon seemed longer than ever, he decided ruefully.

The embassy followed the road east towards the Euphrates river, which marked the frontier between the Roman Empire and Parthia. They covered some thirty miles a day, stopping each night in the nearest village or town along the road that offered shelter. Cato made little attempt to engage Apollonius in discussion of anything that had no bearing on their mission. He was suspicious of the man's intentions, as it was clear that General Corbulo's agent knew far more than he was prepared to share with Cato. For his part, Apollonius seemed content to keep to himself, and rarely spoke to the men of the escort or Flaminius. The veteran fell easily into the routine of tending to Cato's horse and kit, and ensuring that his new master had no cause for complaint.

At dusk on the fourth day after leaving Tarsus, they entered the town of Doliche, where the road crossed the main trade route that linked Syria and Cappadocia. There they took over one of the barrack blocks belonging to the auxiliary unit that garrisoned the town. The Fourth Cilician cohort had been maintained at less than half-strength for a number of years due to the parsimony of the imperial purse. The barracks that were not inhabited were used for storage and had fallen into disrepair. They were infested by rats, and Cato ordered the escort to find staves to use on the vermin.

While Flaminius unpacked his kit, Cato made his way over to Apollonius, who had managed to sling a hammock in a corner of one of the stalls at the end of the building.

'I imagine you'll want to come with me to speak with the prefect.'

Apollonius shook his head. 'I'll leave that to you. If he has any news of interest, I'm sure you'll share it with me. I'll be gathering my own information. I've found that with sufficient application of wine and a certain charm, one can get a good deal out of merchants and traders.'

'Fair enough.'

Cato paused to inspect the hammock. So far he had not been aware of the Greek's sleeping arrangements, as he kept himself apart from the man.

'Is this what you usually sleep in?'

'When I am travelling, yes.' Apollonius gave it a gentle push to set it swinging and make sure that it did not come up against the wall. 'It keeps me off the ground and away from the vermin and the lice. I picked up the habit of using one when I was at sea in my youth.'

This was the first revelation of the agent's origins, and Cato was keen to discover more without pressing the man too obviously. 'You were a sailor, then?'

Apollonius looked at him for a moment before he spoke in a genial tone. 'Indeed. Five years on cargo ships working the sea routes from Hispania to Alexandria and up as far as Bithynia. That's how I speak as many languages as I do. The gods have given me a gift for mastering tongues. There is no better place to learn such things than on the deck of a cargo ship, and in the streets and inns of seaports. And that is how I came to serve Rome, and General Corbulo in particular, these last few years.'

'I see.'

'Do you?' He tilted his head to one side and smiled slyly. 'What makes you think any of that is true, Tribune? Because I have not said anything about my past these last few days, you have an appetite to know more. And that appetite tends to feed a man's credulity somewhat. Why should you believe what I say?'

Cato indicated the hammock. 'That would seem to bear out your story about being a sailor.'

'Really?' The Greek smiled again. 'The truth is, I won it off a sailor one night in Alexandria.'

'And how do you explain your facility for languages?'

'Through many years of hard work at the library in Alexandria.'

They stared at each other for a moment before Cato asked, 'Is *that* true?'

'It might well be.'

He sighed in frustration. 'For Jupiter's sake, man! Stop playing your bloody games, or so help me I'll give you a kicking you won't forget in a hurry.'

Apollonius's amused expression faded. 'You might want to think again about that, Tribune. Learning languages, however I may have achieved that, is only one of the skills I acquired in my youth.' He paused and looked round for a moment before he pointed. 'Over there. You see that rat?'

Cato glanced over his shoulder and saw a large black rodent sitting in the corner of the opposite stall. The animal rose up on its hind legs and sniffed the air. The next second, it was snatched off its feet and slapped against the wall behind it, the shaft of a slender dagger piercing its body. One of the Praetorians who was grooming his mount nearby whistled in admiration as Apollonius crossed over and retrieved the knife, wiping the blood from the blade using a strip of sacking that lay near the rat's body. Satisfied that he had cleaned off all the gore, he slipped the blade back into a scabbard strapped underneath his left forearm and returned to the stall. As he lifted his saddlebags into the hammock, he spoke without meeting Cato's eyes.

'I'd think very carefully about threatening me again if I were you, Tribune.'

Cato felt distinctly uncomfortable, and vulnerable too. He did not like the undertone of menace in the agent's voice, and the demonstration of his lethal potential was thoroughly unnerving. If he had the choice, he would send the man back to Tarsus, but he could not countermand the general's orders.

Although Apollonius was supposed to serve as his aide, Cato could not help suspecting that he was with the embassy for some other purpose. It crossed his mind to have him arrested on some pretext and held here in Zeugma while the embassy continued into Parthia. However, he feared that Apollonius was resourceful enough to effect his own release and either return to Corbulo to denounce Cato, or come after him to rejoin the embassy. In which case they would be burdened by mutual recrimination and suspicion as they attempted to negotiate with the Parthians. Perhaps, he mused, it would be better to injure Apollonius and leave him behind. It was an unworthy thought; and besides, the agent might well wound Cato and some of his men in the process. He concluded bitterly that he was stuck with the man.

He coughed and cleared his throat. 'Hmm. Report to me after you get back from speaking to those merchants of yours.'

'Of course, Tribune.'

Cato nodded and turned away, striding towards the other end of the barrack block, where Flaminius was preparing a place for him to sleep. He approached the veteran and glanced over his shoulder before he spoke in an undertone. 'Flaminius.'

'Sir?'

'I want you to keep an eye on our friend there.' He nodded in the direction of Apollonius. 'He's shortly going to leave the barracks and head into the town. Follow him. See who he meets. If you can, get close enough to overhear them. Make sure you are not spotted, though. Think you can manage that?'

Flaminius nodded.

'Good. I want you to do the same wherever we stop for the night. And if you can, try and engage him in conversation when we're on the road, or camping beside it. I need to find out everything I can about him.'

'Yes, sir.' Flaminius paused briefly before he continued. 'There is another way. I was trained as an interrogator. If you let me have a few hours with him, he'll tell you everything you want to know. I guarantee it. I was good at my job.'

Cato considered the offer briefly. 'No. It hasn't come to that yet. Let's use subtler methods for now. Just do as I say and report back to me anything you discover.'

Flaminius raised his hand to salute, and stopped. Instead he bowed his head in obeisance. 'Sorry, master. I forgot I am no longer a soldier.'

'Never mind. As it happens, I've decided to arm you in case your combat skills are needed. Once you've attended to the business with Apollonius, find the garrison's quartermaster and tell him I have authorised you to be issued with sword, dagger and mail vest. Tell him to bill General Corbulo's headquarters for the cost.'

The old soldier's expression creased into a smile for the first time since Cato had met him. 'Thank you, sir . . . I mean, master.'

'You can call me sir from now on. Let's keep things as military as possible. I think that will make life easier for both of us. Carry on, Flaminius.'

CHAPTER EIGHT

Cato left the barracks to find the commander of the Cilician cohort. The sun had already set and the sentries were lighting the braziers on top of the four gatehouses of the garrison's enclosure. Above, the sky ranged seamlessly from a thin strip of red on the western horizon to a deep violet away to the east. The tiny dark forms of swifts darted through the gloom, and mules brayed from a pen at the end of one of the other barrack blocks. Despite the fort being built up from the remains of an older military structure that preceded the arrival of the Roman garrison, the engineers responsible for the work had endeavoured to follow the standard layout, and the commander's quarters were located in the middle of the fort beside the intersection of the main thoroughfares.

There was only one auxiliary on guard at the entrance to the building, and though his salute was smartly executed, his helmet was rusty and the leather of his belt and baldric was dull and badly chafed. Macro would never have tolerated such slovenliness, Cato mused as he passed through the arch into the modest courtyard beyond. There were storerooms to his right and cells to the left, while ahead lay the two-storey building that served as headquarters and the accommodation of the commanding officer.

A clerk, the same man to whom Cato had reported on arrival, was working by the light of a pair of oil lamps. He stood as Cato entered, and smiled.

'I trust the barracks are to your satisfaction, sir.'

'The block is filthy and infested with rats. I dare say you could have provided something better, but it will have to do. The men'll need food. I want you to report to the leader of the escort party, Optio Pelius. Take him to the stores and give him everything he requires.'

The clerk, a stout man in his forties with thinning hair, raised his eyebrows uncertainly. 'I'll need the permission of the quartermaster before I can issue rations, sir.'

'As a tribune in the Praetorian Guard, I outrank any officer in the garrison,' Cato responded impatiently. 'Get it done, and settle the matter with the quartermaster in your own time. Where is the commander of the cohort? I need to speak to him.'

'Prefect Sextilius usually takes a bath at this time of day, sir.'

'Does he now?' Cato said through gritted teeth. 'Where?'

'The bathhouse is outside the main gate, sir. Turn right and it's about fifty paces down the street. Can't miss it, sir.'

'I'd better not.' Cato turned and took a few paces towards the door, then stopped to look back. 'Well, what are you bloody waiting for? I told you to report to Pelius. At the double!'

The clerk scurried out from behind his table and bustled past Cato, who followed him to the arch before turning away towards the main gate of the fort. He passed between two occupied barracks blocks, where wavering light illuminated the frames of windows and doors and the figures of auxiliaries sitting outside as they relaxed in the cool evening air. None seemed to pay him any attention, but Cato was too weary to make an issue of it with men who were not under his command. He had seen many similar examples of laxity in garrison units across the Empire. Even if he took them to task and gave them a bollocking, they would revert to their usual ways the moment Cato and his party left the town.

The optio of the watch casually waved him through the gate and into the street, and Cato turned in the direction described by the clerk. From the width of the street and the ruts worn into the cobbled surface, it was clear that it was one of the main thoroughfares of Doliche, and there were still some shops open along the route. The scent of baked bread gave way to a mixture of spices, and then the sharp tang of urine as he passed a fuller's premises. He saw the sign for the bathhouse hanging from an iron bracket outside its entrance. It was illuminated by small braziers on either side and he could easily make out the name in Greek: *The Palace of Dionysius — baths, gymnasium, good food and good women available. Pleasures for all budgets lie within!*

Sounds good to me, he thought with a smile.

He climbed the steps between the pillars of the entrance and entered the hall. A surly-looking man sat picking his nose behind a red-painted counter. Two women with lurid make-up, wearing only loincloths, sat on stools at the end of a corridor with curtained cubicles on either side. On the opposite side of the entrance was another corridor lined with pegs and shelves where customers had left their belongings while they experienced whatever pleasures suited their budgets. A slave sat on another stool beside the pegs, a short club hanging from his belt to deter thieves. Despite the name on the sign outside, the initial impression was more than a little disappointing, Cato decided, as the man behind the counter sized him up.

'Can I help you, sir?'

'I'm looking for a man.'

'We cater for all tastes here. What kind of man do you desire?'

'One who doesn't jump to conclusions,' Cato growled. 'I'm looking for Prefect Sextilius. I was told this was the place to find him.'

'Depends what you want to find him for. We take our customers' privacy very seriously, sir.'

'I'm here on imperial business. Tell me where I can find him before I order my soldiers to come in here and tear the place apart.' Cato tapped his fingers against the hilt of his sword. 'If I were you, I'd be a little bit more cooperative and a little less of a jobsworth.'

The man raised his hands, palms out. 'No offence meant, sir. You'll find the prefect in the caldarium. You can leave your clothes and weapons in the changing room.'

Cato had not considered that his need to confer with Sextilius might happily coincide with the chance to take advantage of the facilities at the Palace of Dionysius. 'What's the charge?'

'For you, sir, nothing. We are honoured by your presence. Please make use of all that you need, or desire.' The man nodded meaningfully towards the two prostitutes. Cato followed his gesture and saw that the women looked bored and tired.

'Perhaps another time.'

He divested himself of his weapons, tunic and boots and took the linen sheet that the man guarding the changing room held out to him. Wrapping it around his waist, he made his way through the opening at the end of the room into the humid atmosphere of the tepidarium. To one side a man was rubbing oil onto his skin while another was being attended to by a slave, who carefully scraped away the oil and the dirt it had loosened with a bronze strigil. They glanced up briefly as Cato passed by and pulled aside the thick linen curtain separating the room from the caldarium. Steam swirled out and he blinked at the wave of heat that struck his face and body, then stepped inside and let the curtain fall back into place.

The caldarium was a smaller room, perhaps twenty feet across. Stone benches lined the walls, and in one corner there was a large iron bowl set into a marble base. Steam curled from within as the fireplace under the floor heated the water. In the other corner, opposite the entrance, was a brazier that provided illumination. By the dim light Cato could make out two other occupants of the small chamber: a slender youth with dark features and a rotund man of middle age. Both were naked and the latter was stroking the youth's back. They looked up at Cato as he crossed the room and sat close by, his sheet draped across his shoulders.

'Prefect Sextilius?'

'Yes,' the older man replied warily as he slipped his arm away from the youth. 'Who wants to know?'

'I am Tribune Quintus Licinius Cato.' Cato glanced towards the youth and spoke in Greek. 'Leave us.'

The youth stared back briefly before turning to Sextilius, who nodded and patted the boy's leg as he muttered, 'Wait for me outside.'

Once they were alone, the prefect shifted round, his pot belly resting on his flabby thighs. He wagged a finger at Cato. 'What is this about? I've already had one imperial bean-counter go through the cohort's books, a month back. He found nothing. Don't tell me this is another investigation?'

'No. Nothing like that. I'm not interested in your accounts.' Cato paused. There was nothing to be lost in telling the truth. 'I'm on the road to Zeugma, and then heading across into Parthia.'

'What in Hades do you want to do that for? The bloody Parthians are threatening to wage war on us.'

'That's what I aim to prevent,' Cato replied. 'I'm leading an embassy. General Corbulo wants to offer King Vologases the opportunity of making peace.'

Sextilius snorted. 'Some hope of that! Those bastards are already crossing the border and attacking our trade routes, and even some of our outposts. I doubt that's going to play well in Rome when the emperor gets to hear about it. Even if you, by some miracle, get the Parthians to accept peace, I'll wager good money that peace will be the last thing on Nero's mind. You're wasting your time, Tribune. And you're putting your head on the block, as well as those of the rest of your men.'

Perspiration was already pricking on Cato's forehead and he dabbed it with the corner of his sheet before he responded. 'Maybe, but I will carry out my orders.'

'Then you're a fool.'

He ignored the insult. There was no point in creating any further tension between them when he needed information. 'So what exactly have you heard about Parthian attacks?'

Sextilius leaned back against the wall and folded his arms. 'I don't know the full details, only what I've heard from the soldiers passing through the town. They say there's some warlord operating out of Carrhae. He's sending mounted columns to attack across the frontier, from Samosata nearly all the way to Sura. After Corbulo pulled his army back to Tarsus to train the men, it was only a matter of time before the enemy realised the frontier was weakly defended.'

'Do you have any idea what the purpose of these raids is?'

'From what I've heard, they seem to be after loot. Aside from the attacks on our outposts, there's been no attempt to take any towns. As for the size of the columns, who can say?

You know how it is. One man will swear there are thousands of them, another will report a fraction of that number. Either way, they're terrifying the locals. The caravans coming from Nabatea have stopped and turned back, and many of the villagers are fleeing to the towns. As far as the military goes, we're no longer patrolling the west bank of the Euphrates, since that's too dangerous. Word has been sent to Quadratus, the governor of Syria, but so far we've heard nothing back.'

Cato wiped his face again and thought over what he had heard. Quadratus would be warned of the attacks first, and might not pass the news on to General Corbulo. The two men were bitter rivals, as a result of which it was possible that Quadratus would delay sending a message to Tarsus for as long as possible. In the meantime, those living on the frontier would have to look to Syria for reinforcements to drive off the Parthians. Given that the governor's best units had been transferred to Corbulo, any reinforcements that did reach the frontier would be too weak to do much good.

'What do you know about the Parthian warlord?' he asked.

'Not much. The word is that his men call him the Desert Hawk.' Sextilius yawned and stretched his arms out, then folded his hands behind his head. 'Sounds to me like the kind of name a man might choose if he was trying to build a reputation for himself. You know the sort of thing – he strikes his prey out of the blue. Nonsense like that.'

'Except that it's not nonsense, though he's striking from the desert rather than the skies.'

'Well, he's hardly going to call himself something like the Desert Camel, is he?'

Cato glanced at him. 'Fair point.'

'Now, is there anything else you need?' the prefect said testily.

Cato thought about mentioning the rations and equipment he had demanded from the garrison's stores, but Sextilius seemed like the kind of officer who would deny him what he needed unless he could provide written authority from Governor Quadratus, which Cato did not have. In any case, by the time the prefect discovered what had been taken from his stores, Cato and his party would be well down the road to Zeugma.

'No. That's all.' He smiled. 'Thanks all the same.'

Sextilius narrowed his eyes, no doubt suspecting that he was being mocked, and responded tonelessly, 'You're welcome. Will you be staying a while to enjoy the baths?'

'No. I'll clean up in the frigidarium, then I have to get back to my men.' Cato eased himself up from the bench. 'We'll be leaving at first light.'

'What a pity. While you're on your way out, please tell my young companion to rejoin me.'

By the time he had completed his ablutions, dressed and returned to the barrack block assigned to the embassy, most of the men were already asleep, and the sound of snoring mingled with the faint sounds of rats scurrying along the roof beams. Flaminius had packed some feed nets under Cato's bedroll to make it more comfortable for his master, and Cato sank down gratefully and took off his boots. He sat for a moment, hunched forward, resting his chin in his cupped hands, and let his thoughts turn to Lucius and the others back in Tarsus. He realised that his greatest fear was not for himself, but his son, and there was guilt that he might not live to protect and raise the boy in a world replete with danger and treachery. No man, woman or child was safe, no matter how far they tried to remove themselves from the politics of the capital. Even if one chose to live outside of the Empire, that would only mean exchanging one set of dangers for another. Cato offered a prayer to Minerva that Lucius would be granted the wisdom to survive should anything happen to him.

His prayer was interrupted by the rusty squeal of hinges as the door at the end of the block opened. A slender figure was discernible against the faint glow cast by the stars, and then the door closed again and footsteps shuffled in the darkness.

Cato called out softly. 'Apollonius?'

'It's me,' the agent replied quietly as he approached. He paused at the end of Cato's stall, barely visible. 'How did you get on with the commander of the garrison?'

Cato briefly recounted his earlier conversation. 'How about you? Did your merchants have anything to add?'

'Plenty, once I had plied them with sufficient drink. They told me that the name of our Desert Hawk is Haghrar, of the House of Attaran. He's the ruler of Ichnae and the surrounding territory, and seems keen to win influence at the court of Vologases.'

'The same as most nobles, then.'

'Quite. But is he carrying out his raids on the say-so of the king, or is he working to another agenda?'

'What difference does that make as far as Rome is concerned? Nero's advisers will attribute the attacks to Vologases and persuade him to go to war.'

'It makes a lot of difference, Tribune. Let's try and think through the possibilities. It might be that Haghrar is acting on orders from his ruler. If so, what is Vologases trying to achieve? The raids will disrupt trade for a while, but the booty to be had will be insignificant compared to the treasure he already possesses. Is he trying to provoke Rome into premature retaliation? If so, does he have intelligence about the weak state

101

of Corbulo's army? And who is providing that intelligence?'

'That can be dealt with later. Let's just hope your master doesn't take the bait if you're right about the raids.'

Apollonius stirred and was then still again, and silent for a moment. 'No man is my master. I choose who I work for. From what I know of Corbulo, he won't act until he is certain his army is ready for the campaign.'

'I agree. You suggested other possibilities,' Cato prompted.

'Indeed. There is something else. What if Haghrar is carrying out these raids in order to provoke his king?'

Cato frowned. 'What do you mean?'

'Suppose for a moment that Vologases is predisposed towards peace with Rome. We know that he is engaged in a war with his son, Vardanes, and the Hyrcanian rebels on the eastern frontier of Parthia.'

'The same rebels being supported with Roman gold,' Cato pointed out.

'That's true,' Apollonius conceded in the patient tone of one confirming the obvious. 'So it follows that Vologases will not be keen to wage two wars at the same time. But what if there's a faction in his court determined to attack Rome? What if Haghrar is attempting to force the issue? If Corbulo was ordered to act immediately, then Vologases would have to come to the aid of the House of Attaran, and the pro-war faction would have the clash they desire.'

'Interesting.' Cato reflected. 'There's another possibility as well. What if the real purpose of this faction is not just to provoke a war, but to bring down King Vologases?'

'How so?'

'Think about it. The king is already fighting one war, against the Hyrcanians. What if he is threatened with another? If he refuses to back up the House of Attaran in a fight against Rome,

102

the nearest kingdoms to Carrhae will feel abandoned and betrayed and may well rise up against him. However, if he does choose to lead the struggle against Rome, he leaves himself open to an attack by Vardanes and the Hyrcanians from the east. In short, Vologases loses his crown either way.'

'As long as there is a war with Rome.'

'Exactly.' Cato yawned. He was tired, and it was an effort to think clearly. 'The question then is what outcome benefits Rome most. If there is a war between Rome and Parthia and Vologases falls, then there will be a struggle to replace him and Parthia will be weakened. But if we avoid a costly war and he remains in power, he will be able to gather his forces for future hostilities against us, if he chooses that path.'

'Or if Nero decides to wage war . . . An interesting conundrum, wouldn't you say?' Apollonius took a step closer. 'What would you do if you were in Corbulo's place, Tribune?'

Cato tried to think it through, weighing up all he knew of the state of the general's army and the terrain over which it must fight if it was to invade Parthian territory.

'In his place I would want to negotiate a peace treaty with Vologases more than ever.'

'Why?'

'Our army will be in no condition to fight for the best part of a year. If we are forced to fight now, it could go either way. Better we concentrate on holding the frontier until we are ready to strike and not allow ourselves to be drawn into an invasion before we are prepared. Better still if we can get a treaty that puts a stop to Haghrar's raids. And without an external enemy to occupy their thoughts, the Parthians may well turn on each other. In the meantime, Vologases has the war against the Hyrcanians to worry about. And all of that suits Rome's interests nicely.'

There was a pause before Apollonius spoke. 'Good. You have grasped the nuances of the situation precisely. Peace it is then. Of course, all of this depends on the war against the Hyrcanians. If it ends too soon, Vologases will be able to turn his entire might against us before we are ready to fight. We'd best hope the Hyrcanians can hold out as long as possible, with whatever assistance we can provide them.'

Cato gritted his teeth at the implication that Apollonius had thought it all through well before him.

'It's late, and I'm tired, Apollonius. I need to sleep. I dare say you do too.'

'As it happens, I can get by with little sleep.'

'Then you have the advantage over me. I bid you goodnight.'

Cato lay down on his side facing the open side of the stall. He watched as Apollonius's shadowy figure remained still for a moment and then moved away in the direction of his hammock. Cato kept his eyes open a while longer, and strained his ears, but there was no further sound of movement, apart from the shuffling of the sleeping men and the rustling of rats above. At length he let his eyes close. It felt uncomfortable to be in the presence of a man who was a step ahead of him, he mused. Apollonius's intelligence was as formidable as his skill with a blade, and Cato fervently hoped that the agent would be on his side rather than fighting against him, or worse, stabbing him in the back. He was not yet sure if such a man was an ally to be prized, or an enemy to be feared.

CHAPTER NINE

Cato had been gone some four days. In his absence, Macro was obliged to take on the cohort commander's duties as well as his own. He was not enjoying the experience, he reflected grumpily as he spent yet another morning at head-quarters. Besides drilling the men, he was now required to deal with the pay and savings records, since Cato insisted on checking the calculations of his senior clerk. Working with figures had always been something of a trial for Macro, and he had to apply himself diligently as he balanced the payments and withdrawals from the cohort's treasure chest. Moreover, there were other records that also had to be kept an eye on: the quartermaster's inventory, requests for leave, the daily strength returns and the tally of those fit for duty, those being treated for sickness or injury and those who were on temporary duties away from Tarsus, such as the six men under Centurion Ignatius who had been sent to Antiochia to fetch a batch of new recruits for the Praetorian cohort.

The latter were extremely fortunate young men, Macro reflected as he sat behind the desk in the tribune's office. Normally the cohorts were stationed at the camp on the edge of Rome, and there was much competition for any vacancies in the guard units. But since the Second Cohort had been sent on active service under General Corbulo it had lost nearly half its men and was now obliged to make the numbers up from those Roman citizens in the eastern provinces eligible to join the legions and the Praetorian cohort. When the unit was eventually recalled to Rome, these men would enjoy all the privileges heaped on the elite corps of soldiers entrusted with the safety of the emperor, without having to compete for places against candidates who had influential sponsors.

All the same, the recruits would need months of training before they could be trusted to fight alongside the rest of the Praetorians. It took time to prepare men for war, and they would have to remain in Tarsus to complete their training if any conflict began before spring. Macro recalled the day when Cato had turned up at the fortress of the Second Legion on the Rhine. Back then the tribune had been a pasty streak of piss, soaked through and shivering as he clutched his meagre belongings amongst the other recruits who had been marched up from Rome. The intelligence that made him such an effective commander now had been a positive burden back then, when the other recruits and the veterans had mercilessly mocked what they saw as his pretensions and his clumsiness. On one occasion he had nearly managed to skewer Macro with a poorly aimed javelin. The centurion smiled as he recalled the moment. And yet, from such an unpromising start, Cato had proved himself a fine soldier and officer, and Macro felt a fierce pride at the way his protégé had turned out. He wondered if any of the new intake would make such a success of themselves. You could never tell, he mused. The tough-looking men sometimes proved to be cowards when they fought their first battle, and the ones you thought were timid had the hearts of lions.

The sound of laughter, hurriedly suppressed, came from the corridor outside. With a frustrated sigh, he rose to his feet and crossed to the window, turning his back on the heap of waxed slates he was working through. There were several disciplinary charges he had to deal with before he could knock the day's record-keeping on the head and get back to training the men of the garrison units that had been called up to form Corbulo's army. The room assigned to Cato to serve as his office overlooked the great market of Tarsus, and Macro leaned his hands on the wooden window frame and leaned forward slightly for a better view over the city. Below, the stalls stretched out under rows of brightly coloured awnings with people and a few mules threading between them like ants, weaving from side to side as they hunted for bargains. In amongst them he saw the tunics of off-duty soldiers, and he longed once again to get out of the stuffy atmosphere of the office.

He took in the view for a moment longer. If anyone in Tarsus was anxious about the prospect of a war between Rome and Parthia, they weren't making their fears apparent. The inhabitants of the city and the merchants passing through seemed oblivious to any danger, carrying on with their routines with an untroubled air. No doubt they looked to the swaggering confidence of the Roman soldiers who were camped outside the city for their cue. If the army's training achieved one thing, it was to give its men the belief that Romans were the finest soldiers in the world. Macro clicked his tongue. While he tended to share that view most of the time, he was well aware that such confidence could prove brittle when tested under the harsh conditions of a campaign, especially in the tough terrain the other side of the frontier. The only solution was good training, and plenty of it. Which was why he was frustrated at not being able to do more of it.

'Shit,' he muttered bitterly as he turned away from the window. 'Bloody stylus-pushing bollocks is driving me mad.'

He strode to the door and wrenched it open. Three Praetorians were leaning against the wall on the opposite side of the corridor and hurriedly stood to attention. Macro glared at them one at a time, noting the bruises on their faces.

'Are you the lairy bastards who started the fight with those auxiliary layabouts from the Syrian cohort? Well?'

He stood in front of them, hands on hips. The three men continued to stare straight ahead, but none spoke, so Macro picked on the man in the middle.

'Guardsman Sulpicius, what do you have to say for yourself?'

Sulpicius was the oldest of them by several years, and his face bore scars on the cheek and jaw. He was well built, with creases about his steely eyes.

'Begging your pardon, sir, but it wasn't us who started the fight.'

'That's not what Prefect Orfitus says in his report. He claims his men were sitting at a table minding their business and having a quiet drink when you three rolled up at the inn. You were drunk, insults were exchanged and then you waded into them. The result of which is that two of them are in the army hospital and the innkeeper is demanding that you compensate him to the tune of two hundred sestertians for breakages. If the provosts hadn't arrived to save your arses, the three of you would have ended up in hospital as well, no doubt. What do you say to that?'

Sulpicius's lips curled in contempt. 'Well, sir, it's like this. First, if the oily little shit who owns the inn reckons his rickety tables and benches are worth half what he says, then I'm the emperor's fucking uncle. Second, we were not drunk. We'd barely had two jars of wine by that stage.' He paused and glanced towards the man on his left. 'Isn't that right, mate?'

His comrade gave a slight nod, not wanting to commit himself to supporting a bald lie.

'Eyes front!' Macro snapped. 'I'm speaking to you, Guardsman Sulpicius. Not your pet fucking monkey.'

Sulpicius faced forward instantly. 'Yes, sir.'

'Continue.'

'Yes, sir. Third, we did not start the fight. We said our hellos and one of the bastards blew a raspberry. So I gave him the benefit of the doubt and told him not to talk out of his arse, sir. Then he said that the Praetorians were a bunch of overpaid, toga-lifting freeloaders who served as the emperor's ponces . . . or some such. Well, I thought I must have misheard him, so I went over and asked him to repeat what he'd said, loudly, so there would be no danger of misunderstanding him. And, er, that's when I busted him over the head with his jar of wine, sir. Can't recall much after that. Harsh words were exchanged. Blows were struck. That kind of thing. Until the provosts broke it up.'

Macro nodded. 'I see. As it happens, I also have their report. According to them, the three of you were backed into a corner and being given a good hiding when they entered the inn.'

'We were outnumbered three to one, sir,' the man to Sulpicius's right protested.

Macro rounded on him. 'Who the fuck said you could speak?'

The Praetorian froze under his superior's ferocious glare. Macro gave him the evil eye for a moment longer before he took a step back to address all three.

'The Second Praetorian is the best cohort in the Imperial Guard. We pride ourselves on our turnout. There is no body of soldiers smarter than us. We pride ourselves on our discipline. There is no order we will not see through until the bitter end.

But most of all we pride ourselves on being the toughest bastards in the entire army. And you three allowed yourselves to be beaten up by a bunch of Syrian auxiliaries? I don't care how many of 'em there were. You are a fucking disgrace.' He took a deep breath and exhaled through clenched teeth. 'Since I am the acting commander, your punishment is for me to determine. So, for damage caused to the premises, you will pay one hundred sestertians. The innkeeper can chase the Syrians for the balance. As for brawling and injuries caused to other soldiers, that is not an offence in my book. Kicking others' heads in, and being the best at it is what the Praetorians are there for.'

The three men struggled to contain their grins, but Macro's expression remained hard and uncompromising as he continued. 'The real offence, as far as I am concerned, is that you let a bunch of bandy-legged auxiliaries get the better of you. For that you will each be fined a month's pay and a month's fatigues cleaning out the headquarters stables. That's all. Dismissed.'

They exchanged a salute before the three guardsmen turned and marched off down the corridor towards the staircase. One of the orderlies from Corbulo's staff came hurrying in the other direction and quickened his pace as he caught sight of Macro as the latter made for the door to his office.

'Centurion, sir! A moment!'

Macro paused and looked round irritably. 'Whatever it is, keep it brief. I'm a busy man.'

The man pulled up in front of him and saluted. 'General Corbulo's compliments, sir. He wants all the unit commanders to report to him at once.'

'Oh?' Macro arched an eyebrow. 'What's up?'

'Not quite sure, sir. But a messenger rode in from the north about an hour ago. Looks like trouble to me.'

★ ★ ★

110

The assembled officers rose to their feet as Corbulo entered the large hall outside his suite of offices. He halted, then swiftly ran his eyes over his subordinates before he spoke. 'Be seated, gentlemen.'

Macro and the others eased themselves back onto their benches and stools. Besides the two legates, and the tribunes and senior centurions from the Third and the Sixth legions, the commanders of the auxiliary units were also present, some fifty men in all.

Corbulo turned to his secretary who had entered the room in his wake. 'Who is absent?'

The man consulted his wax tablet. 'Tribune Maxentius is in hospital with a fever, and Tribune Lucullus and Centurion Laminius are away on a hunting trip, sir.'

'Send someone to find them as soon as we are finished here. I want all my officers back in Tarsus as soon as possible.'

'Yes, sir.'

Corbulo clasped his hands behind his back as he collected his thoughts, and then began to address his officers. 'Earlier this morning, a messenger arrived from an outpost on the road to Thapsis. For those who've just arrived in the province, that's one of our smaller allied kingdoms in the mountains to the north, a small city state no more than a hundred miles from where you are sitting. The commander of the outpost reports that the king and his court were murdered by a faction of his nobles, backed by Parthia. Thapsis is now in their hands and they have proclaimed their loyalty to King Vologases.'

He paused, and there were anxious murmurs from some of the officers around Macro until Corbulo raised a hand to silence them.

'On its own, Thapsis is of little consequence. It does not sit astride any important trade routes, or cut across any lines of communication. It generates very little revenue to the imperial treasury and it has no military value to either side. And yet we cannot ignore this development, nor allow it to stand. The king of Thapsis was an ally of Rome, and as such, our reputation is at stake. There is no question of us standing by and doing nothing, or even letting this little uprising run its course. Our authority must be re-established. We must put down the revolt, punish the rebels and ensure that all our other allied kingdoms, large and small, understand what being an ally of Rome entails, and what the consequences are for upsetting that arrangement.

'Parthia too needs to be taught a lesson. Consequently, I will be leading an expedition to Thapsis to put down the rebellion. A modest force should suffice. I will be taking five cohorts of the Sixth Legion, the Syrian auxiliaries and the Third Cohort of Macedonian cavalry. In addition, engineers and crews for a battery of siege catapults in case the rebels oblige us to lay siege to the city. Some four thousand men in all.'

Corbulo paused to indicate an officer sitting in the front row, and Macro craned his neck so that he could see the individual better: a tall, grey-haired officer whom he recognised as the legate of the Third Legion.

'Gnaeus Pomptilius will take command in my absence and has orders to continue the training and provisioning of the rest of the army. Any questions?'

Macro stood up. 'What about the Praetorians, sir? Are they remaining in Tarsus?'

Corbulo smiled. 'I don't think I can afford to leave your gang of drunken thugs out of my sight for a moment, Centurion Macro. A bit of hard marching in the fresh mountain air will do wonders for their pent-up energy. From what I hear, it may also be something of a relief for certain innkeepers of Tarsus.'

'Yes, sir.' Macro grinned as he sat down. He felt a familiar surge of excitement at the prospect of marching to war, but it was overwhelmed almost immediately by guilt at having to leave Petronella behind. And not a little anxiety over how she might take the news.

'Anyone else?' asked Corbulo.

Prefect Orfitus, the commander of the Syrian cohort, rose and cleared his throat. 'Sir, will four thousand men be enough for the job?'

'Absolutely. More than enough of a show of strength to scare the rebels and their Parthian friends into surrendering. It will be a good chance to put the auxiliary units through their paces if nothing else. They've grown far too used to sitting on their arses in comfortable postings these last few years. Your cohort is no exception, Orfitus. You and your men could use some campaign experience.'

'Yes, sir.' Orfitus remained on his feet.

'Is there anything else you wish to ask, Prefect?'

He shifted. 'Do we have any idea of the enemy's strength, or the composition of their forces, sir?'

'Indeed we do,' Corbulo replied confidently. 'One of the tax farmers here in Tarsus visited Thapsis only a month ago. I've already spoken to the man and he reckons the city has no more than ten thousand inhabitants. The militia, assuming it has gone over to the rebels, numbers no more than five hundred. Plus any Parthians who may have reinforced them. Given that the only reports we have of enemy forces crossing the frontier relate to small raiding parties, I doubt we are talking about more than a few hundred Parthians at most. Nor are the city's defences likely to cause us much of a problem. I'm told the walls are most old and in a poor state. No match for our siege weapons.' He paused for a beat. 'Does that put your mind at rest?'

113

'Yes, sir,' Orfitus replied self-consciously.

'Then do sit down. Anyone else? No? Very well. Those of you involved in the operation will receive your orders later today. The column will leave Tarsus the day after tomorrow. The rest of you will continue your training, but for the sake of caution, have your men ready to march at a day's notice in case I need to call for reinforcements. It's unlikely, but we'd be foolish not to be prepared for any eventuality. That's all, gentlemen. Dismissed.'

'So soon?' Petronella said tonelessly. 'But we've only been married a few days.'

'It can't be helped, my love,' Macro sighed. 'Orders are orders. There's a small rebellion to put down in the mountains. Should all be over before you know it, and I'll be back here in your arms.'

He reached out to enfold her, but she quickly darted back and raised a finger, her eyes narrowing suspiciously. 'You didn't volunteer for this, did you? I bet you did, you bastard.'

Macro affected a hurt look. 'My love, why would I do such a thing? Believe me, I'd rather be here with you every night than shivering under some goatskin tent up in the bloody mountains. I need you to keep me warm.'

Her lips pressed together in a thin, bitter look of contempt for a moment before she continued. 'You're a soldier, Macro, first and foremost, and you just love marching off on some wretched campaign. I know that; I know it will always be your calling, and I know there's nothing I can do about it.'

She shook her head and stood looking at him, inviting him to explain himself. But Macro could not think of anything to say. Petronella was right. He was a soldier before he was anything else, even her husband and lover. He desperately tried to think of something that might comfort her, or at the very least assuage the anger that was swelling up inside her. He had known her long enough to recognise the danger signs: a softening of her voice – the calm before the storm – a slight forward tilt of the head and a tightening of the lips that was more unnerving than a lion coiling to spring on its prey. But no inspired thought came to his rescue and he was reduced to offering her the kind of imploring look that a dog offers its master after having enacted some mischief it knows it will be punished for. It seemed to work well enough for Cassius, thought Macro.

'Oh, for Jupiter's sake! Stop looking at me that way!' She balled her fist and struck him on the chest, hard enough for Macro to think fleetingly about the generous odds he might give her as a gladiatrix.

'Go then. See if I care,' she added defiantly, though he could detect a slight quiver in her bottom lip. 'Bugger off with your soldiers and win yourself a little more glory. With my luck you'll be given another of those bloody medallions for your harness that it'll be up to me to keep clean.'

He went to hug her again, but she pushed him away firmly with both hands. 'Don't you dare!'

Macro stepped back with a hurt look, and at once Petronella lurched forward, threw her arms around him and drew him in, crushing his face into her cleavage as she let out a deep moan of frustration and grief. 'Oh Macro, my love. Promise me – swear to me by all you hold sacred – that you will come back to me unharmed.'

Now that's just unfair, Macro thought. How was a soldier expected to make such a commitment? Did she really expect that in the heat of battle he would suddenly recall the promise and politely decline to continue fighting on the grounds that he had given an undertaking to his wife not to come to any harm? If experience had taught him anything, it was that barbarians tended to pay scant attention to such domestic niceties. All the same, he must offer her some crumb of comfort, before he suffocated between her breasts. As delightful a demise as that might be.

'I will do everything I can to come back to you alive and well, I swear,' came the muffled reply.

She released him and raised his face to hers, and as she kissed him on the lips, he felt the warm wetness of her tears on his cheek. Then she pulled away and wiped her eyes quickly with her fingertips. 'Just make sure that you do. Now, there's a lot for me to do if I'm going to have your kit ready in time. You'll need warm clothes for the mountains, mittens and plenty of spare socks, and I'll prepare a small hamper of treats to take with you. Oh, and the dog needs a walk. Better take Lucius with you to tire him out, or he'll be impossible to get to bed at a sensible hour.' She stopped and looked at him. 'What am I thinking? You must have plenty of preparations to make, and here I am keeping you from your duties like some blubbing old fishwife. You'd better get back to it.'

He nodded gratefully and responded with the two wisest words ever uttered by married men: 'Yes, dear.'

They kissed, and Macro left the house to return to headquarters, pleased with himself for having mollified Petronella. With that deed out of the way, all that remained was the slightly less daunting task of preparing the Second Praetorian Cohort for war.

CHAPTER TEN

There was a palpable atmosphere of fear as Cato and his men passed through the city of Zeugma, less than a day's ride from the frontier. A steady stream of carts and people and animals was leaving by the western gate to escape the threat of a Parthian invasion. As they rode by the civilians, Cato saw the mixture of anxiety and hostility on their faces. One man, carrying a small girl on his shoulders, stopped and took a step towards them, jabbing the finger of his spare hand accusingly as he shouted in Greek.

'Rome is supposed to protect us! That's what we pay our taxes for, but the Parthians are crossing the frontier without any attempt to stop them! And look.' He waved his arm towards the column fleeing the city. 'We are forced to leave our land and homes in order to save our lives. When is Rome going to help us? When?'

'Want me to deal with him, master?' asked Flaminius. 'That's no way to address a tribune. Bastard should keep a civil tongue in his head.'

'No,' Cato replied quietly. 'He has a point. Leave him be.'

The man continued to shout as the small group of soldiers rode by without Cato or any of the others responding to his accusations. Then he spat in the dust and turned to rejoin the column.

Apollonius clicked his tongue and edged his mount alongside Cato as they approached the twin arches of the city gate. 'I wouldn't take it to heart, Tribune. That man's a fool. He'd be far safer if he remained in Zeugma. I doubt the Parthians have any siege equipment, and in any case, they're carrying out raids, not an invasion.'

'That's as maybe,' Cato replied. 'But these people don't know that. They hear stories of the attacks, which become exaggerated in the retelling and no doubt gilded with tales of atrocities, and the result is panic. I've seen it before and there is no reasoning with it. Besides, he's right. We make them pay taxes in exchange for protection, and we're failing to keep our side of the bargain as far as they are concerned. They shout their outrage now, but in a year or two's time they will be cheering us wildly once we have defeated the Parthians. People are fickle. It's the same all over the Empire.'

'Then let's hope we can give them peace now, or a swift victory if Vologases insists on war,' said Apollonius.

They stopped to make themselves known to the optio commanding the sentries at the gate and then entered the city. The same tense atmosphere filled the streets like a foul odour, as those passing by glanced at them resentfully. Many of the shops in the forum were shut, and Cato noted that there were large open spaces between the clusters of stalls that remained. They halted and dismounted at a stable on the edge of the market to rest and water the horses. Some of the men crossed the street to an inn to top up their wineskins and buy hot food, while Apollonius wandered into the market to gather information from the locals and traders passing through. Once the agent was out of earshot, Cato turned to Flaminius.

'Have you found out anything more about him?'

The veteran tilted his head slightly to one side. 'I'm not sure, master.'

'What do you mean, you're not sure? Either you have or you haven't.'

'It's not so easy to tell. For example, this morning, as I was packing our kit and loading it onto the horses, we exchanged a few words about our backgrounds. He asked me where I was from, what my family were like and so forth. I answered him, then asked the same. He said his father was a peasant, a shepherd from Creta, and that his mother had died giving birth to his little sister, who was then sold to a pimp when the father could no longer afford to feed her.'

'Oh really?' Cato smiled cynically.

'Yes, master. And then he said something odd. He told me that he doesn't say any of that to the Roman officers or aristocrats he meets. Instead he tells them that his father was a philosopher, so that they will find him more acceptable, and more inclined to listen to and believe what he says to them.'

Cato sucked in a quick breath. 'Is that so? How interesting . . .'

He was starting to feel like a fool. Apollonius had played him, and possibly General Corbulo as well, unless the latter was in on the truth of his agent's origins. Or maybe he was just having fun at Flaminius's expense. He stared hard at the veteran.

'Do you think he was telling you the truth?'

Flaminius thought for a moment and sighed. 'I don't know, master. He seems convincing enough, and then you catch a look on his face and you just don't know. Either way, I think he's a slippery bastard and I don't trust him any further than I could shit him.'

Cato raised an eyebrow. 'As far as that? All right then, keep at it. But don't make it too obvious, and let me know if he reveals anything else.'

'Yes, master.'

Cato took a sestertian out of his purse and flipped it to Flaminius. 'Go and buy yourself something to eat.'

Flaminius nodded his thanks and hurried over to join the Praetorians crowding the counter at the inn.

Cato stood still, gently scratching the bristles on his neck as he thought over what the veteran had told him. While it was impossible to say which account of Apollonius's origins was true, that ambiguity alone predisposed him to place even less trust in General Corbulo's agent. Cursing under his breath, he walked over to the market and looked down the row of stalls in the direction that Apollonius had taken. He was just in time to see the agent disappear round the end of the last stall.

Cato increased his pace as he moved between the lines of stalls, many of which had been abandoned by their owners. Halfway along the row, he turned aside and slipped between two cloth merchants, whose wares hung from lines stretched around the rear and sides, providing good cover from which to observe Apollonius as he made his way along the second row. Cautiously, he peered round the edge of a large sheet of linen decorated with bright zigzags and looked in the direction he expected to see the agent. But there was no sign of him amongst the crowds milling around the stalls that were still trading. Cato waited a moment longer, until he was certain that Apollonius was not in the second row, then he stepped out from between the cloth stalls and craned his neck, but there was still no sign of the man and he cursed himself for losing track of the agent so easily. Apollonius could be speaking to anyone. Who knew what he was scheming? Or even if he truly served Rome at all.

'Tribune Cato, looking for something in particular?'

The voice came from directly behind him, and Cato spun round, reaching instinctively for the handle of his sword. Apollonius stood no more than four feet away, smiling mockingly.

'I apologise if I alarmed you. I just happened to see you admiring the wares of this stall and wondered if I might be of assistance. I am an experienced haggler.'

Cato took a calming breath and eased his hand away from the sword, tucking his thumb into the top of his belt. 'Is there no end to your talents, or your secrets?'

Apollonius affected a modest smile and reached up to run his fingers over the linen sheet. 'It's a nice piece. Fine workmanship. Far better than you find anywhere in Rome. I can see why it caught your attention. Is it for you, or perhaps your son, Lucius?'

The familiarity with the details of his life felt faintly menacing, and Cato shook his head. 'No. Not for either of us.'

'Who then, I wonder? Is there some fine lady in your life that you have not mentioned to me yet?'

'No . . . I was thinking of it as a present for my friend's wife.'

'Ah yes. The fair, though some might say robust, Petronella. The boldness of the design suits her well.'

Cato had had enough. He turned to the stallholder, who had been watching the exchange and who now edged forward with a welcoming smile. 'How much for this one?'

'Oh sir, you have a fine eye for quality. That is the very best of my wares, and were it not for the need to feed my children, I would save it for my poor sick mother, who—'

'I didn't ask for your bloody life story. I asked how much this was.'

121

'The price, sir, is fifty sestertians.'

Cato made to protest, but Apollonius gently took his arm and led him off a short distance. 'Sir, the game is generally played by offering him no more than half of what he asks and then splitting the difference. But I am sure I can do even better.'

'I am quite aware of how it works,' Cato responded irritably. He returned to the stall and examined the sheet again. 'Twenty sestertians.'

'Sir, that would be an insult to the craftsmen who created this fine piece of work. I can, however, offer you a very special price of forty sestertians, since you are clearly a great Roman noble who honours me with his custom.'

'Thirty,' Cato countered.

'Thirty-five.'

'Done.'

The trader took down the cloth and folded it carefully as Cato took out his purse and counted out the coins, somewhat surprised and angry that he had put himself in the position of adding an expensive item to his baggage when he had only intended to follow and watch Corbulo's agent. Once he had the bound sheet tucked under his arm, he turned to Apollonius. 'It's time for us to get back on the road. I want to reach Bactris by nightfall.'

'That would be best,' Apollonius agreed. 'This close to the border, it would be unwise to camp for the night in the open. Besides, it is uncomfortable.'

'I would have thought the son of a shepherd would be used to sleeping in the open.'

Apollonius clicked his tongue. 'I see that you have set Flaminius to spy on me. I wondered how long that would take. He seemed wholly convinced by the scenes of rural tragedy I

122

made up for him. In fact, if I may sing my own praises for a moment, I was so adept at it that I almost convinced myself.'

Cato's expression remained deadpan. 'I do not trust a man I do not know. And you in particular. I would be happier if you convinced me you were on my side.'

'General Corbulo trusts me, and that should be good enough for you, Tribune.'

Cato ground his teeth. 'It will have to do for the present, at least . . .'

Night had fallen by the time they came in sight of the frontier outpost of Bactris, a small town built on a low bluff overlooking a stretch of shingle banks that served as a ford across the Euphrates. A small cluster of flickering torches and braziers marked out the line of the town's walls and, a short distance away, the fortified camp of an auxiliary cohort against the dark sprawl of the shadowy landscape. Overhead, the velvet blackness was sprinkled with stars, and thin skeins of silvery cloud crawled across the face of the heavens as the party descended from a low ridge and approached the town gate warily. In the present dangerous atmosphere, a jumpy sentry might well loose an arrow or javelin at riders approaching the city in the darkness before they thought to issue a challenge.

Cato cupped a hand to his mouth and called out, 'Roman column approaching!'

A moment later came the response: 'Advance and be recognised!'

They continued towards the town, while dark figures peered down from the battlements above the gatehouse.

'Halt! Wait there.'

There was a delay before the riders heard the rumble of the locking bar being eased from its brackets.

'Is this really necessary,' Apollonius asked in a droll tone. 'It's hardly as if our little party is going to storm the town and reduce it to a smoking ruin.'

'The lads are just obeying orders,' Flaminius explained. 'You should be glad they're alert. Means we'll be able to get a peaceful night's sleep.'

'I'm not worried. Not with you and these fine Praetorians to protect me.'

'That's enough,' growled Cato, then raised his voice. 'Dismount!'

The men slipped down from their saddles, some groaning as they stretched and rubbed their backsides. One of the gates opened with a dull squeal from the iron hinges, and a score of soldiers marched out and advanced their javelins.

An officer stepped ahead of his men. 'Who are you?'

'Tribune Quintus Licinius Cato, Second Cohort of the Praetorian Guard, commanding a detachment under the orders of General Corbulo. I need shelter for the night for me and my men.'

The officer saluted. 'Yes, sir. A moment.'

He looked back over his shoulder and ordered his men to stand down and make way for the riders. Cato handed his reins to Flaminius and stood aside to let his party enter ahead of him as he spoke to the officer.

'What's your name?'

'Optio Albanus, sir. First Dacian.'

'First Dacian?' Cato mused. 'I've not heard of you before.'

'We'd only just arrived in Judaea when Governor Quadratus sent us up here to bolster the garrison, sir. Been here less than a month.

'Can't say I'm happy to be here, sir. All alone on the frontier, with the enemy just the other side of the river.'

'You're safe enough,' said Cato. 'Bactris may be a small town, but it has strong defences.'

'I hope so, sir.'

The last of the riders passed through the gate, and the optio ordered his men to follow them inside before he and Cato entered. The gates were closed behind them and the locking bar replaced.

'Have you seen any Parthians yet?' asked Cato.

'Not many,' the optio admitted. 'And not up close. Just a few scouting parties. They appear on the far bank once in a while. Keeping an eye on us, I suppose.'

'Nothing more than that?'

'No, sir.'

'Hmm. Very well. I need stabling for the horses, and feed. Then food for me and my men and a place to sleep.'

The optio pointed up the street towards the heart of the town. 'Headquarters is up that way, sir. The prefect has taken over the town council's hall and most of the forum. There'll be someone there who can sort out your needs. Do you want one of my men to show you the way?'

'No need. I've been here before, a year ago.'

Cato nodded his thanks, and then ordered his men to follow him as they made their way along the dark thoroughfare. There was little sign of life. The dull gleam of light cast by candles and lamps showed along the edges of some doors and windows. Few of the town's inhabitants were abroad, and they passed only one inn that was open, serving a handful of customers, most of whom were soldiers. Flaminius cast a longing look towards the counter before he moved out of the pool of light cast through the doorway and back into the shadows.

When they reached the town's modest forum, they saw that

most of the marketplace was taken up with carts and equipment being stockpiled for the coming campaign. The auction yard had been converted into stables, and Cato left the others to see to the mounts while he entered the headquarters to find the garrison commander. A clerk showed him through to a large room with stone benches lining the walls either side of the entrance. Two campaign tables, pushed together, stood at the far end of the room, and a man dressed in an unbelted tunic was leaning over them looking at an open tablet while he tore a strip of meat from a chicken leg and chewed.

'Sir,' the clerk announced. 'Tribune Cato, from Tarsus.'

The prefect hurriedly swallowed and laid the half-eaten leg on the tablet before he wiped his hand on his tunic and held it out. 'Prefect Clodius, First Dacian Cohort.'

Cato strode forward, and they briefly clasped forearms in greeting. He was conscious of the grime on his tunic and armour and streaked on his exposed skin. Clodius looked him over and nodded. 'I expect you could use something to eat and drink. If you need it, there's a bathhouse behind the forum. It's still open, even though hardly any of the locals use it.'

'Sounds good. Later, maybe. And yes, some food would be welcome.'

Clodius issued orders to his clerk and then stretched his shoulders before picking up the chicken leg and taking another bite. 'So, what brings you to this charming little bolthole at the arse end of the Empire?'

'General Corbulo has ordered me to lead an embassy to Parthia to make peace.'

Clodius stared at him for a moment, then suddenly roared with laughter, spluttering fragments of chicken before he doubled over and choked. Cato hesitated, wondering if he should slap the prefect on the back, hard, but Clodius coughed to clear his throat, then straightened up, grinning. His expression faded as he saw the serious look on Cato's face.

'You're not joking, are you?'

'Deadly serious,' Cato responded. 'I need to draw rations and feed from Bactris. We'll be crossing the Euphrates at first light and then making for Ctesiphon.'

The prefect shook his head. 'You really aren't joking. You might as well not bother with the rations, brother. The Parthians will find you and you'll all be dead by noon and left out for the buzzards to pick over.'

'Well, that's not my plan exactly.' Cato made his way to the side of the chamber and sat down. 'Peace would be best for both Parthia and Rome.'

'Of course. But do you think for a moment that either will accept it? There's too much at stake. Neither side will back down. You've been sent on a fool's errand, if you don't mind me saying.'

Cato was too tired to care much about what Clodius said. His orders were clear, and he had sworn an oath to obey those who were appointed to command him. Come dawn, he would lead his men over the ford and into enemy territory. Nothing would change that.

'It would help if you had intelligence about the situation on the other side of the frontier.'

'Intelligence? That's rich.' Clodius laughed again. 'Since I relieved the last garrison commander a month back, not one traveller has crossed the river. I'm told that when Rome and Parthia were content with merely regarding each other with hostility, there was plenty of traffic across the Euphrates. I imagine that's how we gleaned information about matters over there. Now the other side of the river might as well be the end of the world. I did send a patrol across a few days after my cohort arrived. They marched up the bank and over the low ridge on the far side, and nothing has been seen of them since. Nothing. They just disappeared. There have been sightings of the enemy, though. I know they have sent raiding parties over the Euphrates to the north of here, but they've made no attempt to cross the ford. However, any fool knows that if they do invade Syria in strength, Bactris will be where they strike first. And how long do you think me and my men will hold out?' He sighed. 'Given that your embassy is bound to be a futile waste of effort, you might as well remain here and help defend Bactris.'

'What's the point? If you're right, then I'll die either on the other side of the river or cooped up here. All that's left for me to do is choose where. If I stay here and Parthia attacks, then death is certain. If I choose to continue with the embassy, at least there is a chance, small though it might be, that King Vologases will agree to make peace. If that happens, I will survive, and so will you and your men. Think on that and wish me well.'

Clodius chewed his lip thoughtfully for a moment, and then shrugged. 'It's your funeral, brother.'

'I hope it doesn't come to that. I am not the kind of soldier who lives in search of a glorious death. I'd rather do all I can to maintain peace and live a long life. But if war comes, then of course I'll do my duty, even if that means laying down my life for Rome.'

The prefect considered this. 'For what it's worth, I hope you get the Parthians to keep the peace.'

The sound of footsteps echoed off the chamber walls, and Cato turned to see the clerk returning with bread, cheese and a shank of mutton on a large platter balanced on his forearm, a small wine jar in his other hand. Clodius indicated a clear spot at the end of one of the tables. 'Enjoy the food, Tribune Cato. It may prove to be your last supper.'

Cato exchanged a terse farewell with the prefect after he had finished eating, and then went to find the garrison's quartermaster to arrange for supplies to be provided for himself and his men. Although it was after nightfall, there were still a handful of officials hunched over their slates as they worked in the glow cast by oil lamps. Cato recognised the slim man with thinning hair working at the largest of the desks, and smiled as he approached him.

'How goes it, Graniculus?'

The quartermaster looked up and frowned for a moment before his craggy features creased into a smile. 'By the gods, Tribune Cato!'

He lowered his stylus and rose stiffly from his stool to salute. 'This is a surprise, sir. I had no idea the Praetorians had been sent back to the frontier. That'll come as a huge relief to some.' He nodded in the direction from which Cato had just come. 'Our new commander is a little jumpy. Same goes for his men.'

'Ah.' Cato clicked his tongue. 'The rest of the cohort is back in Tarsus, alas. I'm here with a small party, just for the night, before we continue on our way. We'll need supplies.'

The hopeful gleam in Graniculus's eyes faded as he digested the reason for Cato's presence. He forced a smile. 'Never mind. I'm sure we can keep the Parthian wolves from the door a while yet.'

'That's the spirit.'

'What do you need from our stores, sir?'

'Food and feed. Some items of kit. Garum, if there's any to be had, and wine to top up our waterskins.'

'Consider it done. And while you're here, I still have a few flasks of Falernian to use up. Be damned if I die and leave it for some bloody Parthian.'

Cato laughed. 'Now that is something worth drinking to.'

Graniculus dismissed the other clerks before producing a stoppered jar from beneath his desk. 'No cups, I'm afraid.'

Pulling out the stopper, he handed the jug to Cato, who lowered his head to sniff the spicy aroma of the sweet wine.

'I don't know how you do it, Graniculus. Where on earth do you come by such good wine?'

The older man tapped his nose. 'Secrets of the trade. Any half-decent quartermaster in the army can get hold of almost everything. In peacetime, at any rate.'

Cato raised the jug and took a swig, then handed it back as he swilled the liquid around in his mouth, savouring it before he swallowed.

'By Bacchus, that's good. Do you have any to spare?'

Graniculus hesitated a moment before nodding reluctantly. 'For the right price.'

They drank some more before Cato asked the quartermaster if he had heard anything about the situation in Parthia from traders passing through before Clodius had taken command.

'Not for the last month or so before the Dacian lads arrived, sir. Up to then, there was the occasional merchant's caravan. Things have been relatively quiet since the conflict kicked off last year. At first it looked like Corbulo was going to go straight in. When you and that Armenian noble set off, I thought that was only going to be the first of the columns the general sent out. As it was, he pulled all the units back from the frontier a few months later, and beyond the cohort sent to cover the crossing, we've not seen any sign of our army, or theirs.' He took another swig before he handed the jug back to Cato.

'How did things go with your Armenian lad, Rhadamistus? Did you get him back on his throne?'

Cato arched an eyebrow. 'You mean you don't know?'

'News reaches us slowly out here, sir.'

'Since you ask, it ended badly. We got him on the throne, and there he might have stayed if he hadn't turned out to be a tyrant.'

'Not Rome's finest hour.'

'Quite.'

The quartermaster regarded Cato thoughtfully. 'I dare say there were some who tried to have the blame pinned on you. That's how it usually works.'

'It may yet happen. Meanwhile, the general still needs time to prepare the army for war. And that's why he's sending an embassy to Parthia to try and persuade them to accept peace.'

Graniculus's eyes widened as he grasped the truth. 'You're leading the embassy?'

'Afraid so. Not by choice, I can assure you.'

'Sweet Jupiter! Seems to me that Corbulo's chosen you to get the shit end of the stick every time.'

Cato sighed. 'That's the way it goes, brother. Let me have some more of that wine. I'll need all the Frisian courage I can get when I lead my men across the river in the morning.'

CHAPTER ELEVEN

'What's the reason for the delay?' General Corbulo demanded as soon as he had reined in his mount in a swirl of dust and grit. Macro and the section of mounted Praetorians who served as his escort halted a short distance along the road from their commander.

Corbulo jabbed his riding crop as he continued. 'The rearguard were supposed to have crossed the bloody river hours ago.'

The centurion from the Sixth Legion who was in charge of the engineering detachment mopped his brow and pointed back down the slope to the river, where a swift current ran between the two banks and surged around the breakwaters twenty paces or so upstream from the bridge.

'They haven't been able to get over, sir. It's the centre section. It started to give when the first of the heavy wagons began to cross. I ordered the wagon to be backed up onto the far bank while we repaired the damage.'

Macro looked across the river and saw the long line of the motionless baggage train stretching back along the road that followed the river before it ran round a looping bend and disappeared from view. The mules and oxen stood in their traces, lazily flicking their tails, as the drivers sat beside their wagons and carts. The bridge had been destroyed by the rebels as soon as they were aware of the approach of the Roman column. However, there was a ford five miles downstream, where the river emerged from the hills and flowed less swiftly, and the mounted vanguard and the main column of infantry had been able to cross there. The engineers had been tasked with bridging the three piers that remained standing, using timber cut from the trees growing on the slopes above the river. The sections extending from each bank looked sturdy enough, Macro thought. The problem was the middle section, where a thirty-foot gap had to be spanned.

Breakwaters had been erected upstream and trestles had been constructed to support the section. Some large logs had been swept downstream and struck the piles of the trestles, and now several men were hanging onto the timbers as they hurriedly attached more ropes to secure the undamaged sections. Many others on both sides of the river were holding a rope across the water to try and snag the logs and pull them into the banks. Even as they watched, Macro could see another log bobbing through the rapids a quarter of a mile upstream, and it was obvious that the engineers would not be able to deal with the others in time before the fresh danger swept down on the bridge.

Corbulo took in the scene and grasped what was happening at once. 'This is the work of the rebels.'

The centurion nodded. 'The logs we've managed to land were all cut down and trimmed of branches to make sure they didn't lodge in the shallows. The enemy know what they're about, sir.'

'Then we must hunt them down and put a stop to their games.' The general turned to one of his staff officers. 'Fabius!'

'Sir?'

'Get back to the vanguard. I want the cavalry to advance along the bank and drive the rebels away.'

The junior tribune saluted and wheeled his mount round to gallop back up the road to Thapsis, while Corbulo turned his attention back to the bridge. 'Now let's see how bad the damage is.'

He gave the order to dismount and strode down towards the bridge in the company of the centurion. Macro handed the reins to one of his men as he followed. The sound of rushing water swelled as they approached, and the officers in charge of the engineers were having to shout orders as they competed with the din. The general stepped up onto the nearest section of the repaired bridge. The freshly cut corduroy of tree trunks had been packed with brush and covered in earth, and felt perfectly solid as Macro tested his weight on it. Corbulo did not hesitate as he walked up to the middle section and paused in the centre to examine the damage more closely.

'We've lost one of the upstream piles,' the centurion explained. 'The first of the logs struck it and carried it off, and both pieces struck the downstream pile before they were done. If there's another strike, I fear we'll lose that pile as well, sir.'

Corbulo grunted and stepped to the edge, gazing down for a moment before he retreated and rubbed his jaw. 'We'll try to get a wagon across.'

The centurion looked alarmed. 'It ain't safe, sir.'

'Your men seem to have done a decent job of bracing the remaining trestles,' Corbulo countered. 'Let's put them to the test. If there's no problem with the first wagon, the rest can cross one at a time. It'll take until after dark, but we should get the baggage train and the rearguard over so that we can continue the advance tomorrow. We can't be delayed any longer.'

The centurion chewed his lip. 'Sir, I must protest—'

'Your protest is noted.' Corbulo cut him short. 'Now get over there and send the first wagon across.'

The centurion gave Macro an imploring look, but the order had been given and Macro knew that the general had good reason to take the risk. The longer it took to crush the rebels, the more likely they were to inspire further uprisings amongst the tribes and towns in the mountains.

The centurion shook his head in resignation and called to the men still working on the trestles to climb up and return to the riverbank before he turned to make his way across the span to the waiting baggage train. The first cart was a heavy four-wheeled affair drawn by a team of four oxen and loaded down with a dismantled catapult. The driver and his mate were leaning against the rear wheel as the centurion strode up and issued his orders. Macro saw the driver shake his head, and there was an ill-tempered exchange before the centurion pointed back in the direction of the general to underscore his authority.

'If that can get across safely, anything can,' Corbulo mused. 'Then that driver will see there was nothing to worry about.'

Macro gave a non-committal grunt, and they moved over to the safety of the section leading from the pier to the bank to watch proceedings. He had serious misgivings about Corbulo's experiment and braced himself to address the general.

'Sir, it might be a good idea to remove the load and carry it across separately. We may need every one of the catapults if the rebels refuse to surrender and force us to besiege Thapsis.'

'Maybe, but if we unload all the wagons and carts, it'll take far too long. We're advancing too slowly and we only have ten days of rations left on the wagons. I know it's a risk, but if the bridge holds, we'll be across the river and outside the walls of

Thapsis in three days' time.' Corbulo glanced at him sternly. 'Have a little faith, Centurion, and I'd be obliged if you don't question my decisions again unless there's a more compelling reason to do so.'

'Yes, sir.'

They stood in silence as the driver climbed onto his bench and picked up his whip. Macro felt a slight tremor through his boots, and looking down, he saw the engineers working a captured log past one of the remaining trestles. A moment later, it appeared downstream, a dark, glistening length surging along with the current.

'Here we go,' Corbulo announced.

Macro turned to see the oxen shuffle forward and the wagon lurch into motion and trundle up the short rise to the first span of the repaired bridge. The driver reined back as he approached the central span, and the oxen stepped forward at a languid walk, steering away from the edge. Pair by pair the beasts moved onto the middle of the bridge, and now Macro could see the tense expression on the driver's face as he glanced down at the impacted soil on each side. The front wheels edged onto the span and the wagon rolled forward steadily towards the slight decline leading to the far bank.

'There!' Corbulo exclaimed with satisfaction. 'I told you—'

He was interrupted by a sharp splintering crack from underneath the bridge, shortly followed by a splash. The driver instinctively hesitated and pulled back on his reins again, bringing the wagon to a stop. Macro saw the earth surface tremble, then shimmer, before a section at the edge abruptly gave way and dropped out of sight.

'Keep moving, you fool!' Corbulo shouted. 'Forward!'

The driver snapped out of his brief trance and cracked his whip over the heads of the oxen as he shouted at them. 'Gerrron!'

The wagon jerked into motion, and then the surface under the rear axle shuddered and collapsed, bringing the vehicle to a halt once more. There were more crashes from beneath, and the central span lurched as one side dropped a foot, canting the wagon over and alarming the oxen, who now bellowed and strained against their traces in a futile attempt to escape.

'The wagon's going to go!' Corbulo shouted. 'Macro, with me!'

The general dropped his riding crop and ran forward, steering clear of the terrified beasts as he called out to the driver, 'We have to save the oxen!'

The driver threw his whip aside and jumped down from the bench, then turned to sprint back the way he had come, heedless of Corbulo's enraged shouts.

'Leave him, sir!' Macro said as he ran over to the heavy iron shackles that fastened the traces of the wagon. He grabbed the first pin and yanked it out savagely, calling out to the general, 'Get the yokes off 'em, sir!'

Corbulo nodded and eased his way between the first pair, fumbling for the locking bolt that secured the animals to the wagon's pole. One of the oxen handlers edged in and was caught and crushed for a moment between the leading beasts before they parted and he was able to work the bolt free and move onto the next yoke. Meanwhile Macro had ducked under the pole, keeping clear of the hoofs of the rearmost oxen, and was struggling to work the other pin free, but it was jammed. Gritting his teeth, he pulled with all his strength, but the iron pin would not budge under his straining fingers.

He released it and exhaled explosively. 'Fuck!'

Snatching out his dagger, he reversed the grip and hammered the shackle with the pommel as he growled, 'Move . . . you . . . bloody . . . little . . . bastard!'

137

Suddenly the pin shifted; a moment later, it came free and the end of the chain dropped to the ground. He turned at once and saw that the general had removed the second yoke and held the chains near the head of the right-hand leading ox.

'That's it, sir! Get 'em moving!'

With the wagon no longer anchored to the oxen, the front wheels rolled back as the timbers under the rear wheels gave way and the vehicle began to slip into the gap opening up in the central span. Corbulo had drawn his sword and now struck the rump of the leading ox hard, so that it jerked into motion and began to trot towards the safety of the next span, drawing the other beasts with it. Macro hurried after them as the air filled with further splintering crashes and splashes. Abruptly he was thrown to his knees as the surface of the bridge canted over violently, openings ripping through the central span and shattered timbers, brushwood and grit bursting into the air. With a loud rumble, the front of the wagon tilted up and disappeared and the whole of the span trembled as the ponderous vehicle crashed through what remained of the trellis beneath. There were only moments left before the whole structure gave way, Macro realised, and he launched himself to his feet and sprinted after the oxen. Behind him the collapse of the central span filled his ears with a cacophonous roar, and his heart filled with dread and desperation.

A short distance ahead, the last of the oxen had made it to safety and Corbulo was running back towards him, bellowing, 'Run, man! Run!'

Macro had barely two paces left to go when he felt the ground start to slip away beneath him. He hurled himself forward, splinters bursting around him, but he was already falling. He threw his arms out, and the fingers of his right hand caught on the edge of the end of a length of wood. Instantly he closed his grip as his left hand desperately scrabbled for purchase and clawed only air. He spun slowly on his arm, feeling the muscles stretch and burn with effort. Glancing around and down, he saw that the entire central span had gone and the last of the timbers had splashed down into the river twenty feet below. He felt his fingers starting to give way under the burden of his weight, and he knew that if he fell, he would be drowned or smashed to pieces against the boulders further downstream.

'Not yet!' he growled to himself, finding a final reserve of energy. He saw a cross beam running underneath the end of the timber he was already grasping, and snatched at it with his left hand, curling his fingers over the edge. He had won only a brief reprieve, though, as he lacked the strength to haul himself to safety.

'Here!' he shouted, straining to be heard above the rush of the current. 'Down here! Help me, for fuck's sake!'

His forearms were trembling violently, and he clenched his eyes shut to offer a last prayer before the end, the words spoken through clenched teeth. 'Jupiter, Best and Greatest, I beg you to take care of my Petronella. And Cato and his boy, and all the lads of the cohort . . .'

He felt a hand clamp round his right wrist, and then another took his left, and he blinked his eyes open to see Corbulo's face straining with effort against the clear sky beyond.

'Hold on, Macro. I've got you.'

One of the Praetorians appeared at the general's side and took Macro's left hand from the general, and a moment later, a rope flicked over the edge of the ruined bridge beside him.

'Put your foot in the loop,' Corbulo ordered.

Macro looked down and saw his boots dangling in space. He reached out and got his left foot securely into the loop.

'Haul him up!'

139

With the general and the Praetorian keeping a firm grip on Macro's wrists, he was raised over the edge of the broken timbers. He rolled away from the drop and lay there for a moment fighting for breath, limbs trembling and his heart drumming against his ribs. The general knelt beside him and placed a hand on his shoulder. 'You're still with us, Centurion. Catch your breath before you try to get up, eh?' He stood and picked up his riding crop before moving away to inspect the damage.

Macro's mouth was dry and he did not trust himself to reply coherently, so he merely nodded. After a moment, he eased himself up into a sitting position, hunched forward. He felt nauseous, and for a moment he was sure he was going to be sick. After a few deep breaths, however, the feeling began to pass, and he climbed to his feet and made his way to his commander's side.

The gap between the two remaining sections of the bridge yawned wide over the torrent below. Most of the trestles and the timbers of the roadway lay in a tangled heap on the rocks at the foot of the stone piers, along with the shattered remains of the wagon and the dismantled catapult. The centurion in charge of the engineers had rushed forward to the far side of the gap, and now cupped his hands to his mouth as he called across.

'General, sir! Are you all right?'

Corbulo nodded as he looked up from the wreckage, across the river towards the baggage train, contemplating his next steps. The failure to repair the bridge had divided his army. Although the vanguard and the bulk of the column was on the road to Thapsis, the siege train, supplies and Prefect Orfitus's Syrian cohort of auxiliaries were cut off on the far side of the river. It was a difficult situation, Macro reflected. Corbulo faced a choice between halting his advance to stop and repair the bridge, while fending off further attempts by the rebels to interfere with the work; or continuing the advance with the troops that had already crossed the river, trusting that they could find fresh supplies along the line of march. The third choice was the least palatable: taking the bulk of the army back across the ford to rejoin the baggage train before taking a much longer route through the mountains to Thapsis. He might lose as much as half a month by the time he was in a position to attack the rebels in the town. And time, as he had made clear from the outset, was not something he could afford to waste.

The general filled his lungs and called across to his chief of engineers. 'We'll continue the advance. I want you to find Prefect Orfitus. Tell him he is in command of the baggage train. He's to fall back to where the column camped last night and wait for further orders. Have you got that?'

The centurion nodded.

'Very well. Give the order for the wagons to turn round, and then find Orfitus.'

The man saluted and turned to stride back to the waiting wagons and their drivers, and the muleteers leading their small teams of animals laden down with sacks of barley and rolled-up tents. Corbulo turned his back on the gap and met Macro's gaze.

'Not a happy state of affairs, Macro.'

'No, sir.'

'Well, there's no point in wasting any more time. Get the escort mounted up; we're returning to the main column. We'll make camp as soon as we catch up with the vanguard.'

'Yes, sir,' Macro replied. Although the legionaries carried their pickaxes on their marching yokes, the tents and the stakes for the palisade were on the wagons. It was going to be an uncomfortable night and the men would have to consume what rations they had with them sparingly. The column was already divided, with two thirds of its strength lacking ready supplies as it marched into enemy territory.

He turned away and strode off to carry out his orders. General Corbulo was right: it was not a happy state of affairs. Unless their fortune changed soon, the situation had all the makings of a disaster.

CHAPTER TWELVE

They crossed the Euphrates before dawn to make sure they would not be seen by any Parthian scouts observing Bactris. Keeping close to the river, Cato led the way downstream for three miles before they came to a wadi cutting into the steep bank. They turned away from the Euphrates and followed the dried-up watercourse as it wound inland. The reeds, grass and trees that grew alongside the great river quickly gave way to a barren expanse of undulating terrain where stunted bushes dotted the rock-strewn landscape. As dawn rose over the desert, they stopped close to the edge of the wadi and dismounted. Cato took Apollonius with him to the rim and cautiously rose to inspect their surroundings.

There was no sign of life apart from a distant haze of smoke to the north, in the direction of Bactris.

'Looks like campfires,' Cato decided. 'Probably a Parthian screening force guarding their side of the ford.'

Apollonius nodded, and then pointed to the east, squinting into the rising sun as it burnished the desert with a fiery red glow. 'And that, I would say, is the road we're looking for.'

Cato shaded his eyes and saw distant movement. Straining, he could just make out a line of camels moving with their characteristic forward and backward sway. Some of the animals were mounted, and there were drovers walking amongst them to keep the caravan moving at a steady pace and avoid gaps opening up.

'How can you be certain?'

'I've travelled it before. It follows the general direction of the Euphrates all the way from Samosata to Ctesiphon. It's a well-used trade route and serves our purpose. We can ride parallel to it without drawing too much attention from those on the road. They'll assume we're a Parthian patrol covering the river. We'll be fine. As long as we don't run into a real Parthian patrol.'

'Quite,' Cato responded. 'But I want to put some distance between us and any nervous, arrow-happy Parthian war bands guarding the frontier before I reveal our presence and announce that we're an embassy sent from General Corbulo. Hopefully we'll be treated well enough while we're escorted to Ctesiphon.'

'If they don't just kill us on the spot, of course.'

Cato looked at him. 'Is that likely?'

'If I thought that, I wouldn't be here, Tribune. But I've learned never to take things for granted. From previous experience I know that the Parthians respect diplomatic niceties. Not only that, but if any harm comes to us, King Vologases will not be inclined to show mercy to those who provide Rome with one more reason to wage war on Parthia.' Apollonius nodded. 'I doubt we'll come to any harm on the way to Ctesiphon. After that, it's down to your qualities as a diplomat, and how Vologases responds to the general's terms.'

'That's not very reassuring,' said Cato. 'I'm a soldier, not a diplomat.'

'Just be yourself. Be honest and direct. And leave the deceit and back-stabbing to those who are better qualified for such things.'

'Like you?'

Apollonius grinned and nodded. 'Just like me. So what now, Tribune? Shall we get moving?'

Cato hesitated. They were in the enemy's land now and it was tempting to stay in concealment for as long as possible. But at the same time he realised that his embassy needed to make itself known in order to avoid being taken for a raiding party or a reconnaissance mission.

'We'll ride down the river, keeping between the road and the Euphrates for a few days. That should get us clear of any Parthian war bands.'

'And if we encounter any soldiers before then?'

'Then we explain our purpose here, and request that we be taken to the nearest authority.'

'If they refuse to listen?' Apollonius regarded him searchingly. 'What then?'

'Then we draw our weapons and fight our way out and make for the safety of the frontier.'

'And abandon the embassy?'

Cato nodded. 'I'll not lead my men to a pointless death if I can avoid it.'

Apollonius shrugged. 'I hope General Corbulo shares that point of view, should you live to account for the failure of the embassy.'

Cato slithered back down the slope of the wadi and gave the order to remount. Once all the men were back in their saddles, he turned his mount towards a stretch of the wadi where the slope was less steep and waved his arm forward.

The small column emerged from the wadi onto the level ground and began to head south, keeping a mile's distance from the caravan making its way along the trade route. Turning in his saddle, Cato saw the trail of dust kicked up by their horses and knew that they would easily be seen by anyone glancing in their direction. As long as they kept their distance, however, he doubted if anyone in the caravan would be curious enough to ride out and investigate the small party of men shadowing them. They might report their sighting at the next watering hole or village, but by the time the information reached anyone in authority who might be inclined to act, the embassy would have long since passed by. The real danger, Cato knew, was a chance encounter with a Parthian patrol.

They rode on as the sun climbed into a clear sky and beat down mercilessly on the parched landscape. At noon, the caravan stopped and Cato did likewise, since he needed to keep the camels in sight in order to maintain his course between the road and the river. Once the horses were tethered, the men found what shelter they could in the shade of the sparsely leaved bushes that dotted the terrain. Apollonius produced a cane from one of his saddlebags and used it like a tentpole beneath his cloak to provide shade. The horses stood, heads down, ears and tails twitching as small clouds of flies buzzed around them.

There was some muted conversation for the first hour, then only silence as the men closed their eyes against the harsh glare of sunlight and breathed softly through their mouths. Flaminius, sitting closest to Cato, kept tapping his fingers on the side of his canteen in a relentless staccato that became more and more irritating as time dragged on. Cato's exasperation grew moment by moment, and he felt an urge to shout at the slave to stop it, but refused to allow himself to relinquish the calm veneer he adopted in front of his command. It was vital, he felt, for an officer to appear imperturbable.

From time to time he opened his eyes and looked round the horizon, but the only movement he saw was a handful of buzzards inscribing languid circles high above. Then, satisfied that no one was approaching, he looked over at his men. He caught Apollonius's eye. The agent nodded towards Flaminius and rolled his eyes, then eased himself out from under his shelter and crossed over to the slave, sitting down beside him in the shade of a stunted shrub. He offered his wineskin to Flaminius and entered into a quiet exchange that Cato could not make out. Within a short space of time, however, Flaminius had stopped drumming on his canteen and was smiling and laughing with Apollonius.

It was an interesting exercise in man-management, Cato reflected as he watched them. The agent had noted Flaminius's edgy mood and the wearing effect it was having on Cato and acted to put an end to it in a way that was far more effective than Cato simply snapping an order, something that would have caused bad feeling. Once again he found himself wondering about the true nature and motivations of the general's agent. He was undeniably irritating in the way that most individuals with uncamouflaged intelligence were. At the same time, he had a keen understanding of other men and could − when he chose to − speak to them on their own terms, thereby winning their confidence and willingness to share what they knew. It was no wonder that General Corbulo prized him so highly.

On the other hand, he was elusive about his origins and unwilling to share what he was really thinking. Instinctively, Cato did not trust him. There was too much about the man that reminded him of another imperial agent, Narcissus, who had schemed his way to influence under Emperor Claudius. Before his death, Narcissus had drawn Cato and Macro into his shadowy world on a number of occasions.

Cato reached for his canteen and took a small sip of water, gently swirling it about with his tongue before he swallowed.

He put the stopper back into the canteen and lowered it to his side as his gaze returned to Apollonius.

If he was truly similar to Narcissus, then he would surely have valued his skin too highly to have embarked on this dangerous embassy. So why was he here? Cato briefly considered the possibility that Apollonius was motivated by altruistic notions of patriotism, and then dismissed the idea. From what he had revealed of himself so far, the agent seemed to be rather more of a cynic than an idealist. And such men, while agreeably open-minded, were equally disinclined to put any cause before themselves.

Cato squinted into the sky and then over towards the road, and saw the faint haze of dust that revealed the caravan was on the move. He stood up stiffly and cleared his throat.

'On your feet! Mount up.'

They kept pace with the caravan until dusk, when it halted again. As darkness fell, Cato could see the glow of campfires and gave the order for Optio Pelius and four of his men to feed the horses, then take them to the river to water them. Two men were posted to keep watch while the rest ate and prepared the bedrolls for the night. Cato had ordered that no fire be lit, even though it was cold at night in the desert. So the men huddled up in their cloaks and lay down to sleep.

Cato himself stayed awake for a while longer, his restless mind anxious about the perils that lay before them. The faint silver crescent of the moon and the bright glint of the stars provided enough illumination to see for some distance. His eyes and ears strained to detect any suspicious movement or sound. At length he heard the men returning with the horses. Once they had tethered the mounts and turned in, he waited a while longer just to make certain there was no sign of danger, and then made for the bedroll that Flaminius had prepared for him. As he did so, he spotted Apollonius slipping silently away from the others.

'Psst!' he hissed. The agent paused and turned back as Cato approached him and spoke in an undertone. 'Where are you going?'

'Where all good men go when they need a shit – away from their comrades.'

Cato was not sure he believed the man, but it seemed ridiculous to challenge him. 'Don't go far, and don't be too long.'

Apollonius's lips parted to reveal the dull gleam of his teeth as he laughed softly. 'That's a matter to take up with my bowels, Tribune. But I'll do my best, out of consideration for your concern about me.'

Cato clenched his jaw. 'Just get on with it.'

He returned to his bedroll and sat down, pulling the folds of his cloak tightly around his shoulders. After some time, Apollonius returned and settled down, and very soon Cato could hear him snoring with a steady rhythm. Satisfied that the man was asleep, he took a last look round, making sure the two men on watch were standing to, then lay on his side and closed his eyes. At first he felt the cold keenly, but soon his body warmed beneath the cloak, and he drifted into an untroubled sleep.

'Sir!'

Cato felt himself being roughly shaken, and wondered how this could be happening when he was sitting in a steam bath perched on the edge of the cliff at the palace on Capreae . . .

'Sir! Wake up!'

He was shaken again, and this time woke instantly from his

dream. He sat up, blinking. Optio Pelius stood over him. It was still night, but Cato could make out the anxious expression on the man's face.

'What's the matter?'

'It's Flaminius, sir. He's gone.'

'Gone?' Cato stood up, rubbing his face to try and clear his mind. He looked towards the place where his slave had been sleeping earlier and then quickly around the shadows that surrounded his men, but there was no sign of Flaminius. 'How in Hades did he get away without the sentries spotting him?'

'It's dark, sir. It's possible,' Pelius replied reasonably. 'The lads weren't asleep on the job. I checked 'em both just now, and when I got back here, I discovered he was gone.'

Cato looked at him. 'Just now? Then he must be close by.'

'He might be. I don't know if he was gone earlier on. I just noticed when I came back.'

'Shit . . . There's not much we can do now. If we try and find him, we'll only blunder about in the dark without doing any good.'

'Yes, sir.'

Cato thought a moment and shook his head. 'Where does he think he's going? If the Parthians catch him alone, it's likely they'll take him as a spy and execute him on the spot.'

'Perhaps he's heading for the river, sir. If he gets across and keeps going, he may make it back to Judaea.'

'What's happened?' Apollonius interrupted them. Cato turned and saw that the agent had stood up and was approaching them.

'Flaminius has gone.'

'Was he taken, or did he make off?'

Pelius shook his head. 'If there was anyone out there, the lads would have been aware of them and raised the alarm.'

'Really?' Cato muttered. 'If they didn't notice someone creeping out of the camp, it's possible they might have missed someone creeping in.'

'Maybe,' Pelius conceded reluctantly.

'Either way, he's gone.'

Apollonius cracked his knuckles. 'What do you think he's up to?'

'How in Hades should I know?' Cato replied.

'He's your slave.'

'I only bought him from the slave market a couple of days before we left Tarsus.'

'So you have no idea about where he's from? Or know much about him? He could easily be a spy.'

Cato thought about that. What if Apollonius was right? What if it was not a coincidence that Flaminius was there in the market when Cato passed by? After all, his sorry tale was bound to elicit the pity of another soldier. But it was hard to believe. How could anyone have known Cato would be there at that time? The idea that Flaminius had been planted to get the tribune to buy him was too far-fetched. Apollonius's suggestion was unlikely. In any case, thought Cato, the agent was in no position to cast doubt on others.

'Rather less easily than you could,' he countered. 'After all, I knew nothing about you until General Corbulo introduced us. I still don't know anything of significance, and your evasiveness is not helping matters. I'm not sure I can trust you any more than I can trust Flaminius.'

'Except I'm still here at your side, and he isn't,' Apollonius said pointedly. 'I don't like it. I can't believe he's taken exception to being a slave and run off to find his freedom. Not here in the dark, in enemy territory. Even if he's unhappy about being part of the embassy, he must know that he stands a better chance staying with us rather than trying to make his way back to Roman territory alone.'

'I wouldn't bet on it. He's a veteran. He knows how to look after himself.'

Apollonius looked out into the darkness briefly. 'We have to find him.'

'Be my guest,' Cato replied drily. 'You can go after him if you wish, but I'll not waste my time, nor that of my men. We'll see if we can find him at first light. He hasn't taken a horse, so he won't be able to get very far. But if we can't find him within the first hour of the day, we'll abandon the search and continue on our way.'

Apollonius looked like he might protest, but then forced himself to be still for a moment before he nodded. 'Very well, Tribune. It's a shame to lose a man, but I expect you are used to it. We'd better get back to sleep, then.'

Cato nodded, not trusting himself to respond to yet another barbed comment. He turned to Pelius. 'Tell the sentries to keep their bloody eyes and ears open before you turn in. I don't want any more surprises tonight.'

'Yes, sir.'

Cato lay still for a while, fretting over Flaminius's apparent desertion. It troubled him that he had misjudged the man's character. At the same time, he was human enough to empathise with Flaminius's predicament and understand how a proud veteran would chafe at having to live as a slave. Nevertheless, the man had lived under the strict discipline of the legions, and understood the bond between soldiers and the duty to obey the orders of a superior officer. The Praetorians who formed Cato's escort had had no choice in the matter once they were picked for the job, and none of them had deserted, so Cato could find

152

no acceptable excuse for Flaminius's action. Perhaps the man valued his freedom more than loyalty to his comrades, or perhaps he was merely a coward. Either way, he must be punished if he was caught. It was an unpleasant prospect, and some part of Cato hoped that Flaminius would make good his escape to save him giving the order to have the slave beaten.

He turned over and tried to expel all such thoughts from his mind. He envied Macro's ability to fall asleep almost at will. He forced himself to concentrate on counting each breath back from a hundred, and after a dozen slow, deep breaths he slipped into a dreamless sleep, untroubled by the cold.

Pelius woke him just before dawn, when there was enough light to clearly see the surrounding landscape. The other men stirred and rose stiffly before they began to saddle the horses and load their kit onto the sturdy horns on either side of the saddles. In Flaminius's absence, Cato was obliged to prepare his own mount, and assigned the slave's horse to one of the praetorians. The air was still cold and the breath of the men and the horses curled in thin clouds of moisture that swiftly faded. As the light grew along the eastern horizon, the last of the escort contingent was ready.

The mournful cry of a bird sounded some distance away, and Apollonius paused from adjusting his saddlebags to look in that direction. Cato saw the agent's body freeze for a few heartbeats as his keen eyes swept across the surrounding landscape.

He trod softly to the agent's side. 'What's the matter?'

Apollonius did not reply at once, but kept staring, a slight frown creasing his brow.

'I'm not sure, Tribune . . . I thought I heard something out there.'

Cato felt a chill grip the base of his neck. 'Where?'

Apollonius raised his hand and pointed towards a clump of

bushes, burnished by the rising sun, just over a hundred paces away.

'Flaminius, maybe?'

'It could be, but . . .'

Suddenly Apollonius drew his sword and went into a crouch, tightening his grip on his reins with his left hand. He thrust the sword forward. 'There!'

Cato saw the swirl of dust from behind the bushes, and a moment later heard the unmistakable soft thudding of hoofs.

'Praetorians!' he shouted to the other men. 'Mount up!'

CHAPTER THIRTEEN

'Parthians!' Apollonius cried out as he slung himself up into his saddle. Cato and his men followed suit. Grasping their reins, they looked anxiously about as horsemen burst from cover across and charged towards them.

Cato craned his neck and saw a small hillock a mile away to the south.

'Praetorians! On me!'

Pulling on his reins, he turned his horse and spurred the beast into a gallop, followed by the rest of his men, racing over the even ground as they made their desperate bid to escape the trap. Whatever Apollonius might have said about the Parthians respecting an embassy, Cato's instincts and experience had taught him to treat the approach of any enemy as a threat until proven otherwise. Glancing back over his shoulder, he saw the nearest Parthians through a cloud of dust, bent forward as they urged their mounts after their prey. There were two groups of the enemy, one directly behind them, the other a quarter of a mile to the east. Cato could just make out their dark figures against the glare of the sun as the rearmost riders threw flickering shadows on the whirling dust. With the river and more broken ground to their right, there was only one direction left to Cato and his men, and they raced towards the crest of the rise Cato had spotted a moment earlier.

He felt his heart pounding in his chest as the horse's hoofs drummed the dry ground beneath him. The keen thrill of excitement and terror coursed through his veins, and he gritted his teeth and clamped his calves against the coarse material of the saddle cloth. Another glance revealed that the Parthians to his left numbered at least fifty men, but the dust kicked up by his own men now obscured the enemy riders closest to them. There was no prospect of winning against such odds. Their only hope, however slender, was to outpace their pursuers. But already Cato could see that the leading riders of the party to his left were drawing ahead of them. He felt his spirits sink at the thought that the mission into Parthian territory was over almost as soon as it had begun.

Cato and his men were close to the hillock now, and he resolved that if it came to a fight, they would take what little advantage they could from the high ground. He pulled firmly on the reins to steer his mount towards the crest, and a moment later reached the foot of the slope. His pace slowed as the gradient quickly increased. The sides of the hillock were steeper than he had thought. He smiled grimly to himself. So much the better.

'Keep up, lads!' he called out as he urged his horse up the rock-strewn ground. His ears filled with the snorts and strained breaths of the other mounts and the grunts of his men driving them on.

When he reached the crest, he saw that there was a patch of even ground perhaps thirty feet across with several large boulders and some scrub rising from the gritty soil.

'Dismount!' he ordered as he swung his left leg over the saddle horns and braced himself to drop lightly. At once he un-slung his shield and drew his sword, stepping back from his horse as the other men followed suit. Optio Pelius ordered two of the men to hold the horses while the rest formed a loose cordon around the crest. Apollonius was standing behind one of the boulders, shield resting against his thigh as he jammed on his helmet.

'Just as well I made sure you had some kit,' Cato observed wryly.

He stood by the rock and looked back at their pursuers. The party that had been behind them had drawn up a short distance from the foot of the hillock, and their horses stamped and tossed their heads as the leader surveyed the position the Romans had taken. There were no more than thirty of them, Cato estimated. The other party had now swung in towards the rising ground, dividing into two bands to cut them off from the east and south, closing the trap. In the distance, he could see the rear of the caravan moving along the road, seemingly oblivious to the action taking place barely a mile distant. He was briefly amused by the notion that even if politics and war enveloped the soldiers of kingdoms and empires, many aspects of everyday life continued heedless of such life-and-death struggles as he and his men now found themselves in. He wondered what the merchants and camel drovers made of the horsemen dashing across the red-hued landscape. Then his mind dismissed these thoughts and he focused on the nearest of the enemy as their leader turned and bellowed orders to his men.

Apollonius cursed as his fingers fumbled at the ties of the helmet beneath his chin.

'Here,' Cato growled. He set his shield down, sheathed his blade and quickly did the job for the agent, then adjusted the helmet so that it sat firmly on the other man's head.

'Thanks.' Apollonius picked up his shield and readied his sword. 'I've never had to fight in soldier's kit before.'

'Then let's hope your first experience of it won't be your last.'

'I'd rather we didn't have to fight at all.' Apollonius looked down at the Parthians as they formed up into two lines, the first drawing their swords while the second opened their richly patterned bow cases and began to string their weapons.

'If they're out for our blood, then we'll not give up without a fight,' Cato responded. 'I'll be damned if we just throw down our weapons and beg for mercy.'

'We're on an embassy,' Apollonius said patiently. 'We're not supposed to be offering them a fight.'

'Try telling them that.'

'That's just what I had in mind, as it happens.' Apollonius looked down at the Parthians. The leading rank were edging forward towards the slope, as their comrades drew the first of their arrows and nocked them. 'If they will only give me the chance.'

He sheathed his sword and stepped into the open, raising his hand and calling out to the Parthians in their own tongue. But before he had spoken more than a handful of words, the enemy leader shouted an order and his men swiftly raised their bows and loosed a volley of arrows up towards the crest of the hillock.

'Arrows!' Cato shouted at once. 'Take cover!'

The agent hesitated, a look of shock on his face as he followed the path of the arrows.

'You too!' Cato grabbed his arm and hauled him back behind the rock.

There was a whirring in the air and then the clatter of arrows striking rock while others pierced the soil. A screeching whinny sounded, and Cato looked round to see a shaft protruding from the neck of one of the horses, its feathered flights shimmering. The beast reared up and kicked out with its front legs. The

Praetorian holding the reins tried to reach up with his spare hand, but the horse recoiled in terror and then swerved to one side, snatching the reins from his grasp. With no restraint on its movement, it bolted forward and down the slope straight towards the Parthians, tossing its head from side to side, red froth flicking from its muzzle. The enemy hurriedly opened ranks to let the maddened animal through, and then surged up the slope roaring their war cry, a shrill ululation of triumph.

'Here they come, lads!' Cato called out, then, more calmly, 'Stand by to receive cavalry!'

There was another volley of arrows, finely calculated to strike home a few heartbeats ahead of the horsemen. Another of the horses was hit in the rump and an arrow tore through the bicep of one of the Praetorians holding the reins. Before anyone could come to his aid, the Parthian horsemen reached the crest and surged in amongst the rocks and shrubs. Their raised swords glinted in the light of the rising sun, and dust and grit erupted into the cool dawn air.

'Up and at 'em!' Cato roared, raising his shield and sword. A rider reined in just beyond the rock where he and Apollonius were sheltering, and Cato sprang forward. The Parthian saw him out of the corner of his eye and began to twist in his saddle to strike out with his sword, but he was too slow. Cato thrust up, the point of his sword catching his opponent just under the ribcage, tearing through the loose cloth of his robe, then flesh and muscle, before ripping into his organs. The edge of Cato's shield struck the flank of the horse, and the animal gave a muscular flinch to the side, yanking the rider free of the blade. He let out a grunt, then clamped his knees and turned the horse, slashing wildly at his Roman attacker. The blade gave a fiery glint as it swept down, and Cato just had time to turn it aside with the flat of his own sword. For an instant the Parthian was on the cusp of losing his balance, then he steadied. But before he could recover his seat, Apollonius darted forward, grabbed at the sleeve of his sword arm and wrenched him to the side. With a shocked cry, the man released his sword and tumbled from his saddle, landing heavily at Cato's feet. Instinctively Cato raised his sword to strike at the Parthian's exposed neck, but Apollonius thrust his shield out, and the blade rang as it struck the boss before glancing aside.

'Leave him to me,' said Apollonius.

There was no time for anger at the intervention, and Cato turned aside and ran several paces towards another rider, who was engaged by Optio Pelius on his other side. One of his comrades shouted a warning, and the rider glanced round in time to see Cato charging towards him. He feinted at the optio's helmet, forcing Pelius to throw his shield up, and then pulled hard on his reins, turning his mount to face Cato. As he did so, the horse's flank crashed into the optio, knocking him down.

The horse loomed in front of Cato, its nostrils flaring as foam flicked from around the bit. Without hesitating, he struck the animal between the eyes, gashing the flesh there and jarring, but not shattering, the heavy bone of the beast's skull. Maddened with shock and pain, the animal bucked viciously, rear legs lashing out. The rider tried desperately to cling on, but was thrown forward and crashed down on top of Cato, driving him face first to the ground. At once he released his shield and thrust himself up, rolling to the side as the winded Parthian gasped for breath. Cato's sword arm was on the wrong side and he lashed out with his left fist instead, striking his foe high in the throat. There was a crunch as cartilage gave way under the blow, and the man's jaw worked furiously as he tried to draw breath.

Cato clambered back to his feet and snatched up his shield,

backing towards the rock where Apollonius had dragged the wounded man he had hauled from his saddle. He was now holding the Parthian down at sword point while he covered them both with his shield.

'What in Hades are you doing with this one?' Cato demanded. 'Finish him off and get stuck in.'

Apollonius shook his head. 'I need him if we are going to get out of this trap alive.'

Before Cato could respond, another rider burst around the side of the rock. He rose up to strike him, but the horse carried the Parthian beyond reach and the tip of Cato's sword cut into the air a moment too late. He swore with frustration as he stood in a braced crouch, weighing up the balance of the skirmish. From where he stood he could see that two of his men were down, one pinned under a crippled horse that was frantically struggling to rise. Several of the Parthians were also down in the dust, and loose horses swerved and ran across the crest. The men tasked with holding the reins had been forced to release the mounts in order to defend themselves. As Cato watched, the Praetorian with the wounded arm backed against a rock, desperately fending off two riders. A slash from the first cut deep into his wrist, and as his sword tumbled from his fingers, the second Parthian stabbed him in the throat, driving his helmet back against the rock with a dull clatter, blood spurting from the wound.

'You bastards!' Pelius bellowed as he charged forward, smashing the rim of his shield up into the face of the nearest man, crushing his nose, and then turning on the other, stabbing him in the thigh and then again in the arm. Both Parthians kicked their heels in and galloped their horses away, down the slope towards their comrades waiting at the foot of the hillock. Their flight panicked the handful of Parthians still fighting, and they hurriedly disengaged and rode off, leaving the surviving Praetorians masters of the hill.

'Pelius!' Cato called over to the optio.

'Sir?'

'Check on the men and horses and report to me.'

'Yes, sir!'

Cato's breathing was laboured and his heart was beating wildly. He inhaled deeply before he paced out from the rocks and looked over the ground around their position. The larger body of Parthians were now forming up in two groups to the east and south, already stringing their bows to rain arrows down on the crest of the hill. Elsewhere, riderless horses – wounded and unhurt alike – were galloping away in every direction. He edged back into cover and met Apollonius's enquiring gaze with a shake of the head.

'We're fucked. They're going to hit us with a barrage of arrows and then charge up and kill off any of us still left.' He pointed his sword at the Parthian who lay propped up against the rock, looking anxiously at his captors as he clasped a hand to the bloody cloth around his wound. 'Now, tell me why he's still alive.'

'Unless we can parley with them, we're dead,' Apollonius replied.

'I don't think they're in a mood to talk.'

The brief exchange was interrupted as Pelius trotted over, puffing with exertion. 'Sir, we've lost two. Two more are injured badly enough to be out of the fight. And the horses have bolted. Looks like we're stuck here.'

Cato nodded grimly. 'Better tell the others to get ready for more arrows. They'll hope to take some more of us down before they risk another charge. But the next time, they'll all be coming for us.'

The optio grasped the point immediately and responded steadily. 'Last stand, then. I'll tell our boys to make sure the enemy never forget the cost of taking on the men from the Second Praetorian Cohort, sir.'

'Very well. See to it.'

They saluted each other solemnly before Cato planted his sword in the ground and mopped his brow.

'There is another way,' said Apollonius. 'Let me speak to them.'

Cato thought for a moment. 'It'd be better if you saved your effort for the last charge.'

'Then what difference does it make? I'm dead either way.'

'Fair point . . . All right, then. For what it's worth, give it a try.'

Apollonius released his grip on the shield and let it fall aside as he grabbed the Parthian by the folds of cloth around his neck and hauled him to his feet in one powerful movement. He spoke to the man in a harsh tone, gesturing with his sword to emphasise his words. The Parthian nodded vigorously, and Apollonius paused before he slowly sheathed his sword and turned to Cato.

'Here goes.'

'Good luck,' Cato said flatly, fully expecting this to be the last exchange between them in this life.

Steering the Parthian in front of him, the agent emerged from cover and took several paces away from the rocks on the crest, so that the enemy could see him and the prisoner clearly. Some of the men from the party who had attacked them readied their bows, but a curt order from their leader caused them to lower them and ease off their bowstrings. Then he walked his mount forward and called out to Apollonius. The agent replied, and Cato caught a mention of his name and that of Corbulo, followed by a further long explanation, before the Parthian spoke again. There was no mistaking the anger in his tone.

Apollonius looked back towards Cato. 'He says he doesn't believe we're an embassy.'

'Then ask him what other reason we'd have for being on this side of the bloody frontier.'

Apollonius turned to direct the question down the slope, and there was another outburst from the Parthian.

'He says we're spies, and his men will put us to death like the dogs we are.'

Cato's gaze was drawn to two riders approaching from the other party. They were led by a man in shimmering blue robes. Behind him came a standard-bearer with a long flowing banner designed to look like a serpent. They galloped up to the man who had been addressing Apollonius, and there was a brief conversation before the new arrival waved the other man aside and trotted his horse directly up the slope, stopping no more than ten feet from the agent. He looked at Apollonius haughtily as he spoke.

'He asks what proof we have that we are an embassy.'

'That's easy enough,' Cato responded. He leaned his shield against the rock and reached into his sidebag for the document setting out his credentials, signed and sealed by General Corbulo. Holding it up, he stepped into the open and approached the rider. As he did so, he suddenly became aware that he was still holding a sword stained with Parthian blood. Realising that this might not provide a sufficiently diplomatic appearance, he slowly replaced the blade in its scabbard before he held up the scroll bearing the general's seal.

'Here's the proof. Now tell him that Emperor Nero will be angered when he hears that his embassy was attacked before we could state the purpose of our mission in these lands. Tell him

164

that I demand that we are taken to the nearest city so that our wounded can be treated and fresh horses provided in order that we might continue our embassy to King Vologases.'

Apollonius translated, and there was a brief silence as the Parthian considered Cato's demand. Then he spoke.

'He says that our credentials will be presented to his lord, who will then decide our fate.'

'Did he give the name of his lord?'

'Yes. Haghrar.'

'Haghrar?'

'He demands that we surrender our weapons to his men. He says that they will escort us to the city of Ichnae and that no harm will be done to us.'

'I see. And if we refuse to surrender our weapons?'

Apollonius relayed the question, and the Parthian's lips lifted in a sneer as he gestured to the men at the bottom of the slope and the others surrounding the hillock.

'He says that if we refuse to lay down our weapons, he will give the order for his men to unleash a blizzard of arrows against us before they come up here to take our heads as trophies.'

'Can't say I find that a terribly appealing prospect.' Cato was silent for a moment, as if reflecting on the other man's demands. But in the end, it came down to a simple choice: die under a hail of arrows, or concede to the Parthian's demands. He let out a deep sigh, then put the document back in his sidebag, slipped the leather strap over his head and folded it around the scabbard before laying it down on the ground. Then, turning back to the crest, he drew a breath and called out the order.

'Praetorians! The fight is over. Lower your weapons and come out.'

CHAPTER FOURTEEN

'I thought this was supposed to be an easy run for the troops,' Macro mused. He was standing to one side of the road, shading his eyes from the midday sun as he scrutinised the defences of Thapsis, two miles off in the middle of the small plain bordered by mountains. The modest city was built on a ridge that dominated the surrounding terrain, through which snaked a modest river. One end of the ridge rose gently from the plain, while the other, half a mile away, ended in sheer cliffs. A low wall surrounded an acropolis overlooking the city.

The only feasible approach for any attackers was the easier ground at the far end of the ridge. And here lay the bulk of the defences. Sturdy-looking towers were linked by stretches of a formidable wall, in front of which lay a wide ditch crossed by a single narrow causeway leading up to the gates of Thapsis. Beyond that there was an open patch of ground before a further sprawl of buildings, where the city's growing population had been permitted to expand the settlement. A column of tiny figures and carts was making its way up to the city, while more columns snaked away across the open countryside towards the safety of the mountains on the far side of the plain.

Two of the other centurions from the cohort stood with Macro surveying the terrain as the rest of the Praetorians marched past at the head of General Corbulo's force. The general had ridden ahead with a cavalry escort for a closer inspection of the defences, and Macro could see them where they had halted on rising ground a mile further along the road.

'I wondered why the rebels hadn't sent someone to ask for surrender terms,' Centurion Nicolis commented. 'Now I can see why. There's no chance of us overcoming those defences with a quick attack. The only hope we've got is to bottle them up in there and wait for the siege train to join us, however long that takes.'

'Even then, we've got our work cut out for us,' said Metellus. 'They have the high ground. If the rebels have any artillery, they'll easily out-range our weapons, and that's going to make life hard for the crews if they're to get close enough to batter the defences.' He sucked his cheek for a moment before concluding, 'I'd say we're going to have to starve those bastards out of their defences.'

'If we don't starve first,' Macro observed sourly.

Three days had passed since the bridge had collapsed and the bulk of Corbulo's small army had been cut off from its supplies on the baggage train. Since then, the men and horses had been living off the thin pickings to be had from the land either side of the road twisting through the mountains before it gave out onto the plain. A few herds of goats had been snapped up by the cavalry scouts before their shepherds could run them off into the hills, and the army had scavenged what little was left in the villages they passed by. Almost all the inhabitants had gone, taking with them whatever food they could carry and doing their best to destroy or spoil what they were forced to leave behind. And now, as Macro beheld the richly cultivated plain around Thapsis, he saw columns of smoke rising up from farmsteads and fields as the rebels burned most of their grain stores and homes to deny the Romans sustenance or shelter.

'And you can bet those bastards have been stocking up on supplies while they waited for us to appear,' he added.

He turned to watch the last of the Praetorians marching past, followed by the leading cohort of the detachment from the Sixth Legion. The men wore grim expressions, and there were none of the usual jocular exchanges and occasional bursts of singing that Macro had experienced on many of his previous campaigns.

'Any news about the bridge?' Nicolis asked hopefully.

Macro cleared his throat and spat to one side. 'It's still being repaired, according to the messenger who came in at noon. Two more days at the earliest, Prefect Orfitus reckons. Then four, maybe five days before the baggage train catches up with us.'

Nicolis grimaced. 'We're going to be hungry, then.'

'You said it, brother.' Macro sighed. 'I want all our men to hand over whatever they've got left to their officers. Metellus, I'm putting you in charge of rationing. Every man in the cohort gets an equal share. We've got to make it last, so half-rations it is.'

'That's going to make me a popular lad, sir.'

Macro glanced at the passing legionaries before he responded. 'I don't like the mood of the soldiers in some of the other units. I don't want that spreading to the Praetorians. Keep your ears open. Listen to the men. If they start grumbling, come down hard on them. Put 'em on fatigues. Better we keep them occupied than let them have a chance to grumble. Nicolis, your lads are going foraging as soon as we've made camp. I want them out there before the other units get their hands on whatever the rebels have left behind. But mind you make it clear to them:

anything they find is to be handed over to Metellus. Any man caught eating anything, or trying to hide food, is to be given a good hiding. Understood?'

Nicolis raised his vine cane and nodded. 'I'll make sure they do as they're told, sir.'

'Good.' Macro paused briefly. 'And see if you can find anything we can use for shelter.'

Since the cohort's tents, along with those of all the other soldiers marching with Corbulo, had been loaded on the carts of the wagon train, the men had slept in the open for the last three nights. It had rained hard the night before last and they had been forced to march in sodden kit for most of the next day, souring their mood even further. The same rain, according to the messenger sent by Orfitus, had caused a surge in the flow of the river and carried away one of the trestles at the bridge, causing yet more delay to repairs. What was supposed to be a straightforward punitive expedition was turning into a punishing trial of frustration and endurance, Macro reflected as he nodded to the other centurions.

'Right, lads, you have your orders. Let's get back on the road.'

He led the way along the column and they fell into step beside him. Once they caught up with the Praetorians, he continued to the front of the cohort and gave the command to increase the pace, so that they would set an example to the rest of the column as well as impressing the enemy with their tirelessness.

By the time they reached the general and his escort, one of the staff officers had chosen the site for the camp: a stretch of open ground at the end of the ridge, just beyond the overflow settlement. It was not far from the ford where the road crossed the river, so the men and horses would not have to go far for their water. It was also well beyond the range of any missiles that might be shot from the walls and towers of Thapsis.

The engineers were still marking the ground with tall poles as the Praetorian cohort marched up and were directed to their lines not far from the centre of the camp, where Corbulo's headquarters would be located. Macro gave the order for the men to down packs and take up their picks before the officers led their centuries to the stretch of ground assigned to them for the construction of the defence ditch and rampart. They set to work at once, breaking up the soil and digging, throwing the spoil inside the perimeter to be packed down to form firm foundations for the rampart. As the other units arrived, they joined in the work, and the sounds of the picks striking earth and stone carried across the campsite.

Satisfied with the progress his men were making, Macro made his way over to where Corbulo's headquarters staff were setting up shelters fabricated from materials looted from one of the hill villages the Romans had passed through. The general was sitting on a stool, scrutinising the approach to the gates of the town. His small group of staff officers stood behind him swapping observations about the defences. As Macro joined them, a servant came forward with a wine jar and a basket filled with bread, cheese and meat.

Corbulo glanced at the contents of the basket before turning towards the servant. 'Where did you find all this?'

'In some of those buildings, sir,' the servant explained. 'There was plenty of food left behind. Looked like they'd tried to hide it.'

'Good work,' Corbulo acknowledged. 'Now take it away.'

'Sir?'

'You heard me. I'll have the same as the men from now on, as will my officers. There's little enough to go round. Take this to the quartermaster and tell him to add it to his stocks. Then get him to send his men forward to those buildings to search for more food.'

'Yes, sir,' the servant responded, with a look of disappointment. A sentiment that was shared in the exchanged glances between the staff officers. Macro could not help smiling at the discomfort of the young men from noble families who made no secret of their sense of entitlement to the best supplies to be had. He also felt admiration for the general. Corbulo might believe in firm discipline, but he was prepared to share the privations of his men. That example would be valuable in the days to come.

Corbulo caught Macro's eye as he approached, and nodded approvingly. 'Your Praetorians looked smart as they marched up, Centurion Macro.'

'Yes, sir. Thank you, sir.'

'Once the camp's defences are ready, I'll have your century with me when we approach the gates to demand the rebels' surrender. Let them see the kind of men they'll be up against if they're thinking of fighting it out.'

'Yes, sir. I'll make sure the lads put on a good show.'

'See that they do. I want this business concluded as swiftly as possible so that we can teach any other potential rebels a lesson. And then we can get on with preparing the army for the invasion of Parthia.'

'Yes, sir.'

Corbulo turned his gaze back towards the walls of Thapsis for a moment before he continued. 'If the people up there come to their senses, we'll only have to execute a few ringleaders, take hostages and leave a small garrison behind. With luck we'll be marching back to the bridge just as the repairs are completed, and the people of Thapsis will be relieved that Rome has shown

171

them mercy. That should dampen any further appetite for rebellion.'

For a moment, no one commented, then Macro coughed gently. 'And if they don't come to their senses, sir? Given that we'll be short on supplies until the siege train arrives, we'll find taking the town a tricky prospect.'

Corbulo turned to him with a sour expression. 'You are something of a master of the art of understatement, Centurion.'

Macro shifted uncomfortably. 'Yes, sir. Sorry, sir.'

'Nevertheless, you have cut to the truth of it. We are not in a position to mount a direct assault on the town. So I must make certain that the rebels are aware that siege weapons or not, I will not permit them to defy Rome. They must be made aware of the consequences. If they refuse to submit, we'll lay siege to Thapsis until we starve them into surrender. And then we'll kill every man in the town and enslave the women and children before we burn the place to the ground.' Corbulo smiled grimly. 'When I have said my piece, they will be in no doubt as to the wisdom of putting an end to this revolt and reaffirming their loyalty to the emperor.'

It was late in the afternoon as General Corbulo gave the order for the bucinas to announce his approach. Wearing a clean cloak of dazzling scarlet over his polished breastplate, he led a small party of staff officers, equally well turned out, from the camp and up the road that passed through the settlement towards the town gates. Immediately behind him marched four men blowing a series of brassy notes on their bucinas to make sure that the rebels were made aware of their approach and to signal that no trickery was intended by the Romans. Next came the standard-bearers carrying the eagle of the Sixth Legion, the general's personal standard, an image of the emperor and the standards of the other units in the camp. Macro's century of the Second Praetorian Cohort brought up the rear, each man as neatly turned out as was possible given the limited time to prepare. Macro marched at their head, his medal harness gleaming over the dull rings of his mail vest.

The procession made its way steadily up the gentle slope and began to pass through the abandoned buildings of the lower settlement. Most of the windows and doors hung open and the roadway was strewn with abandoned baskets, broken jars and other items hastily discarded as soon as the Romans had marched into view. Scores of soldiers were foraging for food, firewood and materials to build shelters. They stood aside as Corbulo and his small column marched by, then resumed their search. On the far side of the settlement stood a loose line of pickets, keeping a watch on the town wall some three hundred paces away. There were dead dogs on either side of the road, and Macro guessed that the defenders had killed them to save having to feed them once the siege began.

Closer to, the defences of Thapsis looked more formidable than ever. As Macro marched up the road towards the gatehouse, he noticed a series of thin posts set in lines across the open ground, and realised that the defenders had placed them there to indicate the range from the wall. The furthest was no more than two hundred paces from the outer ditch; just beyond bowshot, he estimated, relieved at the prospect of the rebels having nothing more powerful than arrows to meet any attack.

Corbulo halted the column a safe distance beyond the outermost range-markers. Macro deployed his century into line just behind the colour party, and ordered them to stand to attention. A final series of notes blasted from the bucina men, and then one of the staff tribunes walked his horse towards the town. Macro could see the glint of helmets and spear points along the battlements of the gatehouse, and at the walls and towers, as the rebels watched the officer draw closer.

He reined in thirty paces from the gates and addressed the defenders in Greek.

'People of Thapsis, General Gnaeus Domitius Corbulo sends greetings in the name of Emperor Nero of Rome. The general wishes to parley with you to discuss the terms of your surrender. He offers leniency to all save those responsible for betraying the treaty with Rome through which Thapsis has enjoyed peace and prosperity. How do you respond?'

As the echo of his words died away, a figure climbed onto the battlements above the gates and sat down nonchalantly with his legs dangling over the dressed stone. From his position Macro could make out the man's green jerkin and conical helmet and the outline of a beard. He surveyed the Romans before him, then the camp, before he responded in the same tongue, calling out loudly enough that he could be clearly heard.

'I speak on behalf of the patriots of Thapsis. My name is Ordones, and I return your greetings. The treaty with Rome was agreed by the despots who ruled here before. Now the people have chosen to throw off their chains and pay no more taxes to your emperor. Send word to Nero that we are no longer his vassals. Return to Tarsus in peace.'

'Damn the man's impudence,' Corbulo snapped, and spurred his horse forward so that he might speak directly to Ordones, regardless of the risk. He checked his horse in front of the tribune and glared up at the rebel. 'I will not permit you to break the terms of the treaty. Thapsis has submitted to Rome and Rome will not relinquish her authority over this town. You will surrender or you will be obliterated, and ten years hence, no man will recall that Thapsis ever existed. I will give you until dawn to surrender. If the gates are not opened when the sun rises, there will be no further opportunity to surrender. You will die, Ordones, along with every man within the walls.'

'Before that happens, you have to take the town,' the rebel retorted. He gestured towards the Roman camp. 'I see no siege weapons. And without those, your half-starved army is never going to succeed, no matter how many men you hurl against our walls.'

'The artillery train will catch up with us soon enough. And when it does, we will bring down your precious walls in a matter of days.' Corbulo clenched his fist around the pommel of his sword in frustration. 'Don't be a fool, man! Save the lives of your people and surrender. Do it now.'

Ordones laughed. 'I think not. We have the advantage here. Our walls will hold. We have plenty of men under arms, and enough water and food to hold out for two years.'

'Then my army will take Thapsis in two years and a day. Rome never admits defeat. You know this is true. You have no choice but to surrender.'

'We have already made our choice, General Corbulo.' Ordones drew his feet up and half turned as he made a gesture with one hand to someone out of sight. 'You will not have to wait until dawn for our decision.'

With that, he climbed down behind the battlement and an order was shouted. At once, Macro saw archers appear on the towers. There was no need to warn Corbulo; the general had already sensed danger and had wheeled his mount round and started galloping back down the road, shouting at the tribune to follow him. The latter was slower to react, and had only gone a short distance before the first arrows were loosed. Macro saw the dark shafts sweeping down and then quivering as they struck the ground about the two riders. Miraculously, none of the first volley struck either man or their mounts as they raced for safety.

The second volley, more ragged than the first, sped down in a shallow arc. The tribune suddenly arched his back and flung his head back as he was struck, but managed to stay in his saddle. As he leaned forward and urged his horse on, Macro saw the shaft that had lodged in his right shoulder. A moment later, the general's horse reared up and unleashed a piercing whinny. Two arrows had plunged into its croup. The animal dropped back onto its forelegs and ran on a short distance, then stumbled as its rear legs gave out. Corbulo released the reins at the last moment and threw himself to the side as the horse collapsed and rolled over. It came to rest in a small cloud of dust, kicking its forelegs and tossing its head as it tried, and failed, to rise. Corbulo was on his feet in an instant, running down the slope as the wounded tribune galloped past him.

'Fuck,' Macro growled, dropping his vine cane and running towards the general. There was a brief respite, then more arrows rose from the town's towers. He raised his shield as he pounded up the slope, and gritted his teeth in anticipation. An instant later, the first arrow struck the shield and deflected over him. More landed on either side before he reached Corbulo and covered them both with his shield, grasping the general's arm and hauling him close.

'Let's go, sir. It's too uncomfortable to stay here.'

With Macro keeping the shield raised, they rushed past the last of the range posts. Several of the Praetorians came forward with raised shields to escort the two officers to safety. The sound of jeering came from the walls, the defenders brandishing their bows and other weapons. Macro paid no attention as he quickly examined the general for any wounds.

'You're all right, sir,' he said with relief, catching his breath.

Corbulo was breathing hard and managed a nod before he muttered, 'My thanks . . .'

'Just repaying a debt, sir.' Macro looked over to where the wounded tribune was being helped down from his nervous mount by two more of his men. 'Get him back to the camp! And you, take his horse.'

The rest of the staff officers and the colour party hurriedly retreated behind Macro's century until only Corbulo and Macro himself remained. The general was staring towards the walls of Thapsis with a look of cold fury. 'How dare they? Now they'll find out what happens to those who abuse the rules of a parley.'

Macro nodded. To his mind the rebels had committed a cowardly outrage and had therefore forfeited any chance of negotiating surrender terms. Death or slavery was the fate that awaited the people of Thapsis from this point on.

His thoughts were interrupted by the muffled sound of several cracks within the space of a heartbeat, and as he looked towards the battlements, he saw several dark dots rise up from behind the town's walls and climb swiftly into the afternoon sky. The general saw them at the same moment and turned to the waiting Praetorians.

'Get back! Get back to the camp! Go!'

The rocks hurled from the catapults inside Thapsis slowed as they reached the peak of their trajectory, then plunged downwards. Most of the Praetorians and the other men were aware of the danger and now ran to get clear of the path of the missiles. Some, however, had not seen the rocks or were too slow to react, and paid the price. The first rock struck close to Macro and his commander, and the impact made the ground shudder beneath their boots as grit and dust exploded into the air. Another struck the ground right at the feet of one of the bucina men, smashing his legs, the impetus carrying the boulder onwards to knock down the standard-bearer behind him, crashing into his hip. More of the missiles plunged down amongst the buildings a short distance further down the slope.

Macro straightened up as the last boulder landed and looked through the swirls of dust thrown up by the impacts. 'Fall back!'

The men needed little encouragement to escape from the threat of further bombardment and ran back down the street towards the camp. Amongst them were the staff officers, spurring their mounts through the fleeing crowd. Macro gave the general a gentle shove.

'Get going, sir.'

As soon as Corbulo had moved off, Macro called to survivors of the colour party to gather up the injured, while he himself recovered the standard that had fallen to the ground when its bearer had been struck down. Above the din of scrambling boots he caught the sound of more clanking as the rebels prepared to unleash a second wave of rocks. He ordered the last of the men on the slope to run, and then turned away to follow them through the abandoned settlement. As the missiles smashed through buildings and crashed into the streets and alleys, the men who had been foraging joined the retreat, desperate to get beyond the range of the rebels' artillery.

As he passed through the heart of the settlement, Macro saw the mangled bodies of two legionaries who must have been standing close together when they were crushed. One was still alive and gasping for breath as he writhed feebly. Crouching down, Macro saw that the man's jaw and throat were smashed and that he was beyond help. Macro ran on as the next volley of missiles crashed down amongst the buildings. The following volley fell some distance behind him. Realising that he was safely out of range, he slowed to a walk as his mind grasped the guile of the trick the enemy had played on them. The range posts had been set out for the archers alone. The rebels had used the dead dogs to mark the ranges for their catapults.

'Clever,' Macro muttered to himself. 'Bloody clever. Round one to you. But you'll pay for that, my friends. I swear it, by Jupiter, Best and Greatest.'

CHAPTER FIFTEEN

'What's the butcher's bill?' Corbulo asked as he stood with his staff officers and stared at the town looming over the tiled roofs and plastered walls of the settlement that lay between Thapsis and the Roman camp.

Macro consulted his tablet. 'Three Praetorians killed, five wounded, three of whom should recover. Eight legionaries killed, nineteen wounded. The surgeon reckons twelve should make a full recovery. Two mules—'

'Mules?' Corbulo turned to him.

'Yes, sir. They were harnessed to a cart being used by the foragers when the building above them took a hit and collapsed. Still, they'll make a decent stew.'

'Stew aside, that's a damned shame,' Corbulo mused. 'We need all the mules we can get.'

Macro nodded. The humble beasts of burden were vital to moving supplies. They and their drovers were almost as valuable as the men who did the fighting.

'What about Tribune Lepidus?'

'The surgeon managed to remove the arrowhead, but he says the tribune's shoulder blade was shattered. His arm will be almost useless.'

'Much like the rest of him, then,' Corbulo mused. 'I was

going to send him back to Rome when his service period was over in any case. He can take his war wound home with him to impress the plebeian voters. They appreciate that kind of thing far more than any actual competence.'

Macro tended to take a more sympathetic view of soldiers who had been crippled while serving Rome and were then forced to find whatever living they could back in civilian life. Of course it was different for the likes of Lepidus, who came from a privileged background. He would never have to perform manual labour or go hungry, and his crippled arm would serve as a badge of honour and ease the way for his political career. He would not suffer unduly, Macro reflected as he responded to his superior. 'I imagine so, sir.'

'Anything else?'

'That's all, sir.'

Corbulo gathered his thoughts. 'We'll have a funeral at dawn tomorrow for those we lost. I want every one of our men to be there to bear witness. Our comrades died as a result of the enemy's refusal to abide by the customs of war. The rebels are without honour and deserve no mercy. I want you to make that clear to your men. Our purpose here is no longer to persuade the people of Thapsis to end their rebellion and take their place amongst our allies once again. It is to destroy Thapsis and make an example of that man Ordones and all who follow him, whether they do so willingly or not. We will avenge our dead, gentlemen, in the most ruthless manner possible, so that no one doubts the consequences of betraying Rome. When we invade Parthia, as we inevitably must, it is imperative that our lines of communication are secure. We cannot afford to have any rebels threatening our rear.'

He paused to ensure that his officers understood the situation. 'In order to ensure that Thapsis is taken, there's much work to be done. I want the town sealed up so that no one can leave or enter it. Tomorrow we will begin work on earthworks to extend from the camp around the hill. I want a ditch and rampart with towers every fifty paces. That will require more men, more labour and above all, more supplies. To that end the cavalry will head out tomorrow and scour the surrounding land for food. The peasants here are no different to anywhere else; they'll have hidden the stocks they couldn't bear to destroy. We need to find those supplies. I don't care who you have to torture in order to get them to reveal where their food is hidden. Every man, woman and child of this miserable little kingdom is fair game as far as I am concerned.

'At the same time, there will be plenty of people hiding in the forests and hills. We need to round them up to work for us. That way, if the rebels feel tempted to try a few long shots to disrupt our work, they'll only be killing their own people, and giving away the range of their artillery while they are about it. We can adjust the course of the earthworks accordingly. Once our siege train arrives, we'll construct a battery to breach the wall.'

'Excuse me, sir.'

Corbulo turned towards the voice and nodded. 'What is it, Prefect Cosinus?'

'If their catapults can reach ours, they'll be able to destroy the battery long before it breaches the wall.'

Corbulo frowned. 'A good point. However, I don't expect they'll have anything on a scale to match our catapults.'

'I don't know, sir. After all, they have the high ground. Even a modest catapult might out-range anything we have in the siege train.'

'We'll discover the truth of that soon enough,' the general responded tersely. 'And if we need bigger weapons, then by all the gods, I'll have them made. Meanwhile, we'll need to fortify the river crossing as well to ensure there is no repeat of the earlier debacle, and have outposts established to guard the road to Tarsus.'

As the scale of the undertaking became apparent to the officers, Macro noticed some of them exchanging anxious looks. Their response was not lost on Corbulo either. He cleared his throat and continued in a commanding tone. 'This expedition is about to become a much more difficult operation, gentlemen. But it is necessary if we are to march into Parthia without having to worry about being stabbed in the back. It is also something of an opportunity. I was already planning to take the army into the hills for training and to toughen up the troops. Now that will be no mere exercise. They will have to face a real enemy and endure the privations and discomfort of an actual campaign. It's about time the army did some proper soldiering.'

Macro nodded his approval, along with many of the others. He felt a surge of professional excitement at the prospect, and then guilt over having to delay his return to Petronella. He had told her that Corbulo's expedition into the mountains would be a quick affair, and now it was clear that this was no longer the case. A siege could last a matter of days, months, even years. A cursory inspection of the natural defences of Thapsis and the strength of the wall and towers protecting the only feasible line of attack revealed that General Corbulo and his army faced a considerable challenge. Still, there was always the promise of loot and slaves to be had when the city was taken. If Macro was fortunate, his share of the spoils would bring a gleam to his wife's eyes, and she would find it in her heart to forgive him. But first he would have to break the news to her. His smile faded somewhat as he contemplated writing the required letter. It would need careful consideration, and he was not good with words. If only Cato were here to advise him. He'd know precisely what to say to mollify Petronella.

'Oh shit!' one of the centurions exclaimed, and pointed towards the town. In the gathering gloom of twilight, Macro saw a fiery orb rise over the wall and flare a course against the backdrop of the first stars to emerge in the night sky. There was a faint roar of flames as it plunged towards the settlement and crashed through a roof with a burst of sparks and shattered tiles. A moment later, further blazing bundles dropped amongst the buildings, and a wavering glow between a cluster of houses revealed that a fire had started.

Macro turned to the general. 'Sir, should I take some men forward to put the fire out?'

Corbulo shook his head. 'We've lost enough men today already, Centurion.'

'But there are still supplies and materials to be had in there, sir. We'll need those for the fortifications and the camp.'

'Maybe, but it's not worth the cost.' Corbulo watched as flames licked into the sky, and then added resignedly, 'Let it burn.'

As the men in the camp looked on, a steady barrage of incendiaries struck the settlement and started further fires, which steadily spread through the abandoned buildings until the settlement was ablaze from end to end and giant tongues of flame flayed the starry heavens and cast their glare across the surrounding land for over half a mile. The heat from the conflagration drove the sentries from the rampart facing the settlement, and even where he stood beside the general, Macro winced at the blistering wave that swept over the camp. His ears were assaulted by the din of the roaring flames, pierced by explosions as the timbers of the buildings burst in the heart of the inferno. The ground around the settlement shimmered with rats, dogs and cats as the fire drove them out from their hiding places and forced them to flee into the night.

For over an hour, Macro and the rest of the men in the column stood mesmerised by the spectacle. Then, at length, he turned away and made his way over to the tent lines marked out for the Praetorians, though there were no actual tents. Most of the men would have to lie on makeshift bedding composed of scrub covered with their spare cloaks. Those who had been first into the settlement had returned with an assortment of leather wagon covers and rolls of linen that could be fashioned into shelters. But most would be sleeping in the open, as they had done since crossing the river three days ago. At least tonight they'd be warmed by the fire. Macro smiled grimly to himself.

He found Centurion Metellus sitting on the back of a small wagon that had been recovered from the settlement and drawn by hand back into the camp.

'What's this for?' asked Macro.

'Supplies, sir.' Metellus lifted the leather cover to reveal bags of grain, an assortment of jars, slabs of salted mutton and rounds of cheese. 'It's what we have left from foraging on the march and what we found in the settlement. I thought it would be best to keep it all in one place and under guard.'

'Good idea. Any problems with men hoarding food?'

'No, sir. Not that I'm aware of. They're obeying your orders. Same goes for the officers.'

Macro cocked his head to one side in amusement. 'Normally, the very first person I'd suspect of helping himself to supplies would be the quartermaster, but seeing as it's you . . .'

Metellus smiled back. 'Don't worry, sir. If I catch myself sneaking anything off the wagon, I'll give myself a beating I won't forget in a hurry.'

185

'That's the spirit.' Macro clapped him on the shoulder. 'Right then, you'd better start preparing tonight's issue. I'll have the men come one century at a time. Make sure they all get a fair share; I don't want any arguments or fights breaking out. Carry on.'

He made his way to the Sixth Century and ordered Centurion Porcino to send one man from each section to collect rations, then did the rounds of the other centuries of the cohort to explain the arrangement. While the supplies were carefully measured out by Metellus, some of the men began to prepare fires using rocks and soil to provide a base for the small iron grilles they cooked their meals on. Each section had a cauldron in which they cooked up the grain and meat they had been issued into a stew, which the section leaders ladled out into mess tins. Soon the comforting odour of woodsmoke and food wafted over the tent lines and the men gathered around the fires as they waited to be fed.

Macro did the rounds, swapping jokes and pausing for brief exchanges as he gauged the mood of the cohort. Satisfied that the Praetorians were in good heart, he gave the watchword for the duty century, commanded by Porcino, and then joined the men of the headquarters section of his own century: his second in command, Optio Pantellus, the four clerks, the bucina man, the standard-bearer of the cohort's insignia and the man who carried the imperial image. A space had been left for him beside the fire, and he squatted down gratefully, warmed through by the cooking fire and the heat on his back from the burning settlement. He jerked his thumb over his shoulder.

'Better make the most of it, lads. When that lot dies down, it'll soon get cold again.'

'Something we're going to have to get used to, sir,' said Pantellus.

'Word travels fast,' Macro observed. 'But you're right. And don't tell me you really believed that nonsense about this all being over in a matter of days so we could march back to the inns and fleshpots of Tarsus.'

Pantellus shrugged. 'I'd hoped.'

'Come now, we're soldiers, this is what we're paid for. Best of all, there's going to be plenty of loot to go round once we take Thapsis. We'll all do very nicely out of it. And there's nothing a Tarsus whore likes better than a Roman soldier weighed down by silver.'

'I'll drink to that.' The standard-bearer raised his canteen and took a slug of wine. Macro caught his eye and raised a brow. The man handed the canteen to his neighbour, then watched helplessly as it was passed round the circle until it was returned to him all but empty.

The wine did not eliminate Pantellus's misgivings, and he stared at the cauldron as he addressed his companions. 'If we don't take Thapsis soon, we'll be here when winter comes. It'll get much colder very quickly up here in the mountains. Mark my words. And there'll be rain. Lots of rain.'

At that exact moment, Macro felt something strike him softly on the cheek. He blinked and looked up, and another raindrop fell on his exposed forehead. The patter of rain on the ground and the plink of drops landing on armour grew steadily into what he hoped was a passing shower.

'Now look what you've gone and done,' he said sourly as he stared at the optio. 'Tempting fate like that.'

Pantellus looked sheepishly at the others. 'I was just saying, lads . . . The gods are having a bit of fun with us.'

'Oh, piss off,' the standard-bearer growled as he gathered his cape around his shoulders and pulled the hood over his head. 'Next time, keep it to yourself, eh?'

The section leader, the senior clerk, leaned over the cauldron and gave it a brief stir with the ladle to test the stew's consistency. 'It's ready, boys. Time to tuck in.'

Macro was served first, making sure the clerk scraped the ladle along the bottom of the cauldron so that he got some chunks of the meat that lay there. He ate quickly before handing his mess tin to one of the other clerks to clean and return to his kitbag, then stood up and stretched his shoulders as he returned his attention to the burning settlement. The flames had already begun to die down before the rain started to fall, and he hoped it would douse the flames before they consumed all the remaining food and useful materials in the buildings. As if in answer to his prayers, the blaze began to shrink back and separate into a number of smaller fires. His men, however, were groaning and complaining as they did their best to cover up under their cloaks. The veterans amongst them had water-proofed their capes with applications of animal fat, and they mocked the discomfort of those companions who had not yet learned how to survive a mountain campaign.

Macro bade them goodnight and hurried over to the wagon guarded by Metellus and two of his men. Climbing into the rear of the vehicle, he eased himself under the leather cover and out of the rain. There, propped up against some sacks of grain, he let his chin sink onto his breast and quickly dropped into a deep slumber, to the accompaniment of the steady sound of rain and distant thunder as sheet lightning flickered along the mountains surrounding Thapsis.

A grey dawn sky revealed that the sprawling camp surrounding the wagon had been turned into a quagmire overnight. The lanes between the tent lines were slick with mud, and large puddles dotted the ground. Many of the men awoke to find themselves lying in icy water, their clothes drenched. A handful of small fires still burned in the settlement, and slender columns of smoke curled into the air. Most of the buildings were now blackened ruins. Beyond, the walls of Thapsis looked all but impregnable to Macro, regarding them as he climbed out of the wagon, and rubbing his back as he yawned. He was hungry and thinking about having something to eat when one of Corbulo's clerks came squelching through the mud towards him.

'Centurion Macro, sir! The general sends his compliments and wishes you to join him as soon as convenient.'

Which inevitably meant at once, Macro knew.

'Very well.' He broke off a hunk of bread from a small loaf in one of the sacks in the wagon and took a bite. The bread was stale, but the aching hunger in his stomach was such that even the simplest of food tasted delicious. Chewing, he followed the clerk back through the camp, past the sodden soldiers stirring into life under leaden clouds that threatened further rain. The air was chilly, and he prayed that the siege would not endure well into winter, as Pantellus had suggested. It did not take much effort to imagine the biting cold in the mountainous terrain that surrounded Thapsis. Any supplies brought up from Tarsus would have to struggle through the snow and ice of the mountain tracks, and while the general might consider such conditions a useful means of toughening up his army, it would not do much for morale.

Corbulo's headquarters had been much improved by the timber, furniture and leather coverings that had been recovered from the settlement before the incendiaries had set fire to the buildings. There was a cluster of crudely made tents, and boards had been laid down over the mud immediately around them, as well as within. Macro returned the salute of the two Praetorians from Nicolis's century standing guard outside the entrance of the largest tent, and ducked inside the flaps. A large pole held up the middle of the structure, and a section had been removed at the rear to provide light to work by. The general was seated at his desk writing on some waxed slates. To one side stood a cavalryman, spattered with mud.

Macro approached and coughed. 'You sent for me, sir.'

Corbulo glanced up. 'Centurion Macro, I have a job for you. This man has just brought word from Orfitus. It seems the prefect questioned one of the locals, who revealed a usable ford some miles upriver from the bridge. So he has taken it into his head to lead the baggage train and rearguard to this ford and cross the river to join us while the repairs to the bridge continue.'

'That's good news, sir.'

'Well, I hope so. But I can't help having a few misgivings about Orfitus blundering about on mountain tracks in enemy territory. I need an experienced officer to take command of the rearguard and make sure it reaches Thapsis safely. You're the best man I have to hand, so I'm sending you.'

Macro could not hide his surprise. 'But sir, Prefect Orfitus outranks me.'

Corbulo tapped the waxed tablet with the end of his stylus. 'Not any more. This is your authority to take command until the rearguard reaches the camp. Once I have set my seal to it, you will be in charge. I've also passed word to the Macedonian cohort to have one of their squadrons made ready to ride with you to ensure you get through.' He paused to indicate the man standing beside him. 'This is Optio Phocus of the Syrian cohort. He will be able to provide confirmation of the authority if that is needed. Since I have no idea about the location of this ford Orfitus claims to have found, I suggest you stick as close to the river as you can while you track down the rearguard. When you have found them, take over from Orfitus and get the baggage and siege train here as quickly as possible. We need the supplies, and I want those weapons assembled and pounding the walls of Thapsis. Don't take any risks along the way. You will construct fortified camps each night. I'd sooner a short delay in the rearguard getting here than take any chances. Is that clear?'

'Yes, sir.'

'Good. Who's the senior centurion in the Praetorian cohort after you?'

'Centurion Porcino, sir.'

'Then tell him he's in command during your absence.' Corbulo thought briefly, then nodded. 'That's all. Get whatever kit you need, and the optio here will find you a horse. I want you on the road as soon as possible.'

Corbulo hurriedly concluded writing the authority, then pressed his seal ring into the wax, snapped the tablet shut and handed it to Macro.

'There. May Fortuna ride with you, Centurion, and bring me my catapults, safe and sound.'

A light shower was falling as Macro led his small force out of the camp. The Macedonian auxiliaries had arranged their long cloaks to cover their saddlebags and slung shields as best they could while keeping themselves warm. The road, which had been worn and heavily rutted when the Romans had approached the city, was now slick with mud and strewn with puddles. Macro gave the order to move off it and advance along the more solid ground at the side.

Shortly before noon, they reached the point where the road climbed into the mountains that surrounded the plain of Thapsis. Macro looked back at the city and the outline of the Roman camp below it. If the general had misgivings about

Orfitus, then Macro had misgivings about himself. While he was perfectly confident and competent in his role as an officer fighting on the battle line, and quite capable of taking temporary command of the cohort, he felt anxious about the task now entrusted to him. The stakes were high. Without the baggage train, the general's column would have to abandon the siege and hand the rebels a victory that could well spark further uprisings and threaten the stability of the Eastern Empire at the same time as Rome faced the threat of war with Parthia. It seemed to Macro that the outcome hung on the success of Cato's embassy and his own safe shepherding of the rearguard to Thapsis. If either of them failed, a high price would be paid by the Empire.

CHAPTER SIXTEEN

'They're treating us well, all things considered,' said Apollonius as he set down his flute and reached for another fig.

'Are you ever going to play that thing?' asked Cato.

Apollonius laughed. 'One day. For now I prefer to practise in private, until I can get a decent tune out of it.'

His expression became serious. 'If anything should happen to me, I'd be grateful if you would return the flute to Corbulo for me.'

Cato frowned. 'Why?'

'It has a certain sentimental value to the general. I know he'd be grateful.'

'Oh, very well.' Cato gazed out across the flower beds and fountains to the wall that surrounded the palace of Haghrar at Ichnae.

There were slender towers at regular intervals along the wall, for decorative purposes rather than defensive, Cato reflected as he sat on the couch opposite the agent. The thin pillars supporting the roof were covered with reliefs depicting vines and small birds. They would be pulverised by the very first missile hurled from a catapult. Like much of the city, the palace had been built by those unused to the powerful siege weapons deployed by Rome, and Greece before them. Since the days of Alexander, the nature of warfare in the lands watered by the Euphrates and the Tigris had changed, and the plodding ranks of Alexander's phalanxes had largely given way to bodies of horsemen moving swiftly across the landscape. All the same, Cato mused, the walls were tall enough to serve as a prison, and the vigilant sentries patrolling between the towers discouraged any thought of escape.

Apollonius swallowed and cleared his throat. 'Wouldn't you agree, they're treating us well?'

'I suppose so,' Cato replied. While he and Apollonius were well looked after, the rest of the Praetorians were kept in one of the rooms in the barracks attached to the palace. Although they were fed and allowed out into the yard to exercise for an hour early in the morning and again in the evening, that was as far as their liberty extended. Still, Cato concluded, they were alive, and the men who had been wounded in the skirmish were recovering thanks to the skilled ministrations of the palace physician. The only man's fate he had any doubt over was Flaminius. The Parthians had not mentioned him, so Cato assumed that his slave had made good his escape. For the same reason, he had told his men not to mention Flaminius, in case he was still at large.

'I just wonder,' he continued. 'Are we guests, hostages or prisoners? Or condemned men?'

'That depends on how Vologases reacts to the news of our embassy. If he has already decided on going to war with Rome, then our little band is going to be superfluous. In which case, if the whim takes him, he might send our heads back to Corbulo as a statement of his intentions. I doubt we'd be much use to him as hostages, given that Rome has a long tradition of demanding hostages rather than providing them. The best we could hope for is to be kept alive for any future exchange of prisoners. But if Vologases has an appetite for peace, I am confident we will be accorded the treatment appropriate to our diplomatic status. In the meantime, do try one of these figs, they're quite delicious.'

Apollonius picked up the silver bowl and offered it to Cato. With a sigh, he took one and gently tore off a segment of the succulent fruit, chewing it thoughtfully. The agent was right, the fig was delicious. Just as delicious as the rest of the food they were served. In the same way that their rooms were comfortable and the clothes they were given to wear were finely made. But none of it changed the fact that they were caught in a gilded cage, awaiting the judgement of King Vologases.

Cato was restless by nature and found this enforced life of leisure something of a trial, even though it was less than a month since they had been forced to surrender to one of Haghrar's war bands. He had asked the nobleman's steward if he might be permitted something to read, but Haghrar had given strict orders that most of his library was out of bounds, lest the Romans use it to harvest intelligence about the lands of the Parthian empire. Only the shelves of poetry and philosophy were made available.

'What do you make of our host?' asked Cato.

They had encountered Haghrar on a handful of occasions since they had reached the city and been brought before him. The nobleman had far lighter skin than most Parthians Cato had seen, and had addressed them in fluent Greek. It was likely that he was directly descended from the lieutenants of Alexander the Great, who had divided their king's empire between them after his death. As their influence waned and that of Parthia grew, some of the former Greek kingdoms had fallen into the orbit of the new power in the region. Haghrar had listened to

Cato's explanation for his presence in Parthian territory and examined the document prepared by General Corbulo, before announcing that he would hold the Romans at Ichnae and send a message to King Vologases to ask for instructions. Since then, they had come across the nobleman walking through his gardens. On each occasion, Haghrar had merely asked politely after their health and comfort before moving on.

Apollonius looked round warily to make sure they would not be overheard, but there was only a slave watering some broad-leafed plants in large decorated pots fifty feet away. Reassured, he took another fig and chewed on it as he considered his response.

'Hard to say, given how little we have seen of him. But I find it interesting that he felt obliged to refer the matter to Vologases before taking any action. He is even wary of treating us too harshly or with too much cordiality. As if he knows he is being watched and reported on.' Apollonius stroked his top lip as he stared at the bowl of figs on the small table between their couches. 'I think it tells us a lot about the way Vologases rules his empire.'

Cato nodded. 'Which raises the question, are his nobles too cowed to act independently? What if they secretly wish to free themselves from such a tyrant?'

'That's two questions,' Apollonius observed flatly without looking up.

Cato had grown accustomed to some of his companion's idiosyncrasies since they had set out from Tarsus, and let the remark pass without comment.

'I wonder,' Apollonius resumed, 'if our host might be the kind of man who could be persuaded to detach himself from such a master. It would be interesting to discover what it might take to turn him against Vologases.'

'It would need more than just one noble to undermine the king.'

'True, and if our host is entertaining doubts about his loyalty to Vologases, he might well be sending feelers out to others to gauge their thoughts on the matter.' Apollonius looked up suddenly and gave Cato his habitual wry smile, which implied he was already two or three steps ahead of the tribune. 'However, that is all mere supposition. No more than wishful thinking, unless we can find out more.'

'Well, we're hardly in a position to do that, are we?' Cato pointed out.

'Not at the moment, no.'

Cato folded his hands together and leaned forward to rest his chin on them as he scrutinised the agent.

'What?' Apollonius arched an eyebrow.

'I was asking myself, once again, just what is the true purpose of your assignment to the embassy?'

'The general told you. I'm here to act as your guide and adviser. That's all.'

'I am having a hard time believing that.'

Apollonius affected an offended grimace. 'I'd hoped you would have a little more trust in me after all this time. I have not given you cause to suspect me of any wrongdoing. And it was me who saved our necks when the Parthians trapped us. A man might expect a little gratitude for that deed. I can't help your suspicious nature, Tribune Cato. But then, perhaps your cynical inclinations have served you well in the past. You strike me as the kind of man who takes very little at face value and constantly questions the actions of others, questioning himself most of all. That may well account for your success in life. There are men – rather more than is healthy for Rome – who assume they have the answers simply because they lack the intellect to ask pertinent questions. Such men are fools. As are those who crave the reassurance of blindly following such fools.' He returned Cato's stare with a shrewd expression. 'But you are different. Aren't you? I can see it, and I can see that you know it to be true. And that is why Corbulo picked you for the embassy, and why he picked me to accompany you. We are more alike than you are happy to admit.'

Cato did not reply. He did not like the idea that anyone could see into his thoughts. It made him feel vulnerable and open to being manipulated. Nor did he like the notion that he was a kindred spirit of Apollonius. And then, as if to confirm what the other man had deduced, he wondered why he might resent such a comparison. The answer that came to him, just as irritatingly, was that he disliked the man precisely because he recognised in him much of what he disliked in himself, namely that impatience with men less able than himself, and it was easier to focus that dislike on the agent instead. He sighed with frustration.

Apollonius's knowing smile appeared on his face once again. 'I'm right about you, aren't I? Don't take it too badly, Tribune. It's my job to look into the hearts and minds of men. Sometimes it's a bit of a challenge. But not in your case. You wear your integrity and intellect like medals. Which is also why Corbulo picked you. It's important that the Parthians believe what you say when you negotiate with Vologases.'

'*If* we get to negotiate with him.'

'Yes. If. And while you are doing the talking, I'll be watching the other side like a hawk and reading their reactions. Then we'll know which men stand with their king, and which men we can play to our advantage. And that's the real purpose of my being sent into Parthia with you. Happy now?'

'I am hardly in any position to be happy,' Cato replied. 'But being better informed is preferable to ignorance.'

'So it is.'

'Then let's just hope you get the chance to look into our host's heart and mind sometime soon,' Cato concluded as he rose from the couch. 'Now, I need some exercise. Enjoy the figs.'

He strode away, down one of the gravel paths that ran through the neatly kept rows of trimmed flowering shrubs and the boughs of trees that shaded stretches of the paths. When he reached the foot of the wall, he took the path that ran around the garden and increased his pace, clasping his hands behind his back in the posture he habitually adopted whenever he needed to walk and think. Brushing aside his irritation with Apollonius, he turned his mind to the possible outcomes of his mission.

If Vologases was prepared to discuss a peace treaty on terms acceptable to Rome, then the emperor might accept that as enough of a victory to cancel his plans for war with Parthia. The glory-seekers might well howl in protest, but many lives would be spared, and much silver. Cato knew just how much the last consideration weighed in the minds of those advisers closest to Nero. If, however, Vologases refused Corbulo's terms, as Cato thought more likely, given that they were the usual humiliating demands that Rome insisted on, then other factors might temper the Parthian king's reaction. Such as the ongoing war being waged far to the east against his son, Vardanes, and his Hyrcanian allies. The possibility of disaffection amongst his nobles, or even the defection of one or more of them to Rome, would make Vologases think very carefully before he refused Corbulo's demands. Particularly a man like Haghrar, who ruled over the most vital stretch of Parthia's frontier with Rome. If Ichnae and the surrounding territory came under Roman control, then even the capital at Ctesiphon would be within easy reach of the legions.

The prospect excited Cato's imagination, and while his inherent belief was that war should be avoided if possible, the chance of dealing a knockout blow to Rome's long-standing enemy was too tempting to easily ignore.

Two days later, as dusk fell on the palace and the servants began to light the torches and braziers, a Parthian officer came to find Cato in his quarters, where he was reading a volume of Greek poetry he had been allowed to borrow from Haghrar's library.

Cato lowered the scroll. 'What is the meaning of this interruption?'

The Parthian frowned at the prisoner's assertiveness. 'My lord Haghrar orders you to attend him at once.'

'I see.' Cato stood up. 'I'll need my adviser to come with me.'

'No. My lord sent for you alone.'

Cato briefly considered insisting that Apollonius be present as well, but it was clear that the Parthian officer was the kind who obeyed his orders to the letter and was not inclined to deviate.

'Very well. Take me to him.'

He followed the Parthian out of the room and into the corridor. Apollonius was already standing at the entrance to his own room. 'What's happening, sir?'

'Haghrar has sent for me.'

Apollonius stepped forward, but the Parthian thrust his hand out and pointed to the room. 'Back inside.'

Apollonius did not move, but turned his gaze on Cato. 'Well?'

'He has sent for me. Not you.'

'I don't like the sound of that. It would be helpful if I was there.'

Cato nodded lightly at the Parthian. 'His orders were specific. Just me.'

Apollonius stroked his jaw. 'Let me know what happens.'

The Parthian gestured towards the far end of the corridor. 'My lord is waiting.'

He moved off at a fast pace, and Cato followed more steadily, so that the Parthian had to slow down for him. They emerged from the wing reserved for guests and visitors and made their way past the banqueting hall and the audience chamber to Haghrar's private quarters, where they passed two pairs of guards standing at each end of another corridor.

'It seems your master fears for his safety even in his own palace,' Cato commented.

The Parthian glanced at him with a cold expression, but made no reply before they entered a modest chamber with benches at the sides.

'Wait here,' the officer ordered, and went over to the door on the far side of the chamber. He knocked twice before entering, then strode out of sight, and Cato heard a brief exchange before the Parthian reappeared on the threshold and beckoned to him urgently.

'My lord is ready to see you.'

Cato was shown into a small room, scarcely twenty feet across. Opposite him was an opening leading onto a narrow balcony overlooking the palace gardens. The walls were hung with tapestries depicting fabulous flowers and beasts of the ground and air, many of which he could not identify, such as the black and white bear-like creature chewing on bamboo. He wondered if they were mythical, or merely unknown to

Rome. Haghrar sat on a large divan to one side in a short-sleeved black silk robe and sandals. His arms were muscular, and from the breadth of his shoulders and the thickness of his neck, Cato knew that he possessed an uncommonly powerful physique. His dark eyes peered out from beneath the finely plucked brows of a broad forehead, and his curly black hair was cropped short.

He regarded Cato for a moment without speaking, and then turned and gave a curt instruction to the officer who had escorted him. The man bowed deeply and backed away towards the door, before closing it and leaving his lord alone with the Roman.

Haghrar eased his legs off the couch and leaned forward before he spoke. 'King Vologases has responded to my message.'

There was a brief silence as he watched closely for a reaction, but Cato kept his composure and did not speak.

'The king says he will receive your embassy. I am ordered to deliver you and your men safely to Ctesiphon as swiftly as possible. We will leave tomorrow and travel by river.'

Cato nodded. 'That is good news, my lord.'

'I hope so. I am not convinced that the king will be content to accept the terms demanded by your general.'

'That would be a great pity. A war between Rome and Parthia would not be in the interest of either side.'

'No?' Haghrar gave a cynical smile. 'I am not so sure I agree with you. Your emperor has only recently come to power. He needs to win himself a little glory to establish his reputation and his . . . What is the term you Romans use? Ah yes, imperium. For his part, Vologases might decide that a war would be a most useful means of uniting his nobles and allied kings against a common enemy and stop them squabbling and plotting amongst themselves.'

'And perhaps plotting against their king,' Cato suggested. 'It is no secret that his hold on power is not as firm as he might wish.'

Haghrar's smile faded. 'There are always some men whose loyalty to their sovereign is corrupted by personal ambition. That is as true in your empire as it is in ours.'

'Possibly,' Cato conceded. 'But Nero exercises far more direct control over his empire than Vologases. Is it not the case that what Parthia calls its empire is in reality more akin to a loose alliance of kingdoms? Not all of whom are content to regard Vologases as their undisputed ruler.'

'If you are referring to the Hyrcanians, they have long been resentful of Parthia's influence over their lands. They are little more than a distraction.'

Now it was Cato's turn to smile cynically. 'Rather more than a distraction, I think. Especially since the king's own son is leading their struggle to free themselves from the tyranny of Parthia.'

'A struggle that has been underwritten by Roman silver. And it is no secret that when Rome pays out in silver, she demands repayment in uncompromising loyalty and eventual surrender of sovereignty. Parthia needs no lectures from Romans on the subject of tyranny and the underhand means by which that may be imposed on others.'

Cato stood in silence as he considered the words and demeanour of his captor. It was hard to determine the extent of Haghrar's loyalty to his king. And yet it was vital to coax that out of him in order to better understand the balance of power within Parthia.

'My lord, I cannot deny the truth of what you say. Yet there is an opportunity to make peace. Rome and Parthia have been enemies for too long and enough blood has been shed on both sides. Many Romans are weary of the near-constant state of war on the eastern frontier. And I am sure the same is true in Parthia. There must be some amongst his nobles and vassal kings who fear that Vologases is leading them towards a costly war. Men who would rather have a new man on the throne in Ctesiphon rather than risk further conflict with Rome.'

'There are always malcontents in any empire,' Haghrar conceded. 'Vologases has his enemies, as does your Emperor Nero.'

'I assume these men are known to you, my lord? Do you not have some sympathy for their concerns? After all, in the event of war, your lands are closest to the frontier with the Roman Empire. It is you who will first endure the brunt of the forces unleashed against Parthia. I can imagine that such a prospect must weigh heavily on your mind.'

Haghrar chuckled drily. 'You can imagine that? I dare say you can. But if you think for an instant that I will betray my innermost thoughts to you, then you are a fool, Tribune Cato. Even if I knew which nobles are disloyal – if indeed there are any at all – I would not name them to you. Still less would I trust you in regard to my own loyalty to Vologases.'

'You have my word that what is spoken between us now will not be repeated outside this room.'

'I am unlikely to trust the word of a Roman when I can hardly trust a single man amongst my servants. For all I know, your purpose here is as much to do with spying as it is to do with making peace. In the same manner, there are many others here in my palace who claim to serve me, while feeding information back to their master in Ctesiphon. Some of them I know about, and I make sure they hear exactly what I want them to hear and pass on. But I am certain there are many others I have yet to discover. Men, and women, who are very close to me. So you will understand why I am reticent about discussing any matter pertaining to my loyalty to the king.'

'I understand perfectly, my lord,' Cato replied. 'So then, let us talk in more abstract terms. If, say, Rome was to offer an alliance with any given Parthian lord that would guarantee his position as ruler of his domain and free him from the concerns of whatever fate Vologases might intend for him, I would imagine the individual concerned might be inclined to consider such an offer very carefully.'

Haghrar met his gaze firmly for a few beats before responding deliberately, 'I imagine so.' Then he eased himself back on his divan and folded his arms. 'Now, I am tired of your games, my Roman friend. You need to leave me now. Go and tell your men to prepare for our journey to Ctesiphon.'

'Very well, my lord.' Cato wondered what Apollonius would make of Haghrar's divided loyalties when they had a chance to discuss the matter. 'I am sure there will be plenty of opportunities to resume our conversation during our journey.'

'Yes. That is more than likely.' Haghrar closed his eyes and waved a hand towards the door. 'Go, Tribune. You have taxed my patience enough for one day.'

CHAPTER SEVENTEEN

It was dawn five days later, and Cato watched from the aft deck as the crew of the flat-bottomed barge used their sweeps to thrust the craft away from the riverbank into the current. They had passed beneath the great trading city of Dura Europus the day before and were nearly halfway to the place where they would land and cross the narrowest point between the Euphrates and the Tigris before reaching the Parthian capital.

The spare hands and the passengers had all been ushered towards the stern by the captain to raise the bow and make the work easier for the men poling the ship out of the muddy bed of reeds. The slender stalks of green rustled against the timber sides, and then they were free and gliding slowly along a short distance from the bank. The captain cupped his hand to his mouth and shouted another order, and the men with the sweeps trotted to the waist and slotted the long oars into the pins on either side, straining as they rowed the ship out of the shallows towards the middle of the river.

A thick mist hung over the water so that the sun was an indistinct orange orb low to their left. A moment later, the reeds dissolved into the mist as the craft moved further out, and Cato felt the hairs on the back of his neck tickle as he looked round the smooth surface of the water stretching out around them before it merged into the haze. There was an eerie atmosphere about the scene, and it occurred to him that this was how the crossing of the Styx might look when death came for him.

He made his way forward and leaned on the bow rail, looking down at the glassy swirl of water around the stem as the sweeps propelled the ship steadily along. A lookout joined him to scan ahead for shallows and call corrections to the sailor on the steering paddle at the stern.

'It's an unworldly setting, isn't it?' Apollonius said quietly as he joined Cato and stared out at the mist.

Once again, Cato had the feeling that the man had been reading his thoughts, and he had to stifle his irritation before he could respond in a neutral tone.

'What's the matter, Apollonius? Losing your nerve?'

'Far from it. There's something quite serene about it all. As if we are cast off from reality into some timeless void, without direction, where anything is possible. If anything, I feel excited.'

'Excited?' Cato looked at him, wondering if the man had lost his mind. 'We're prisoners on a voyage into the heart of the empire of Rome's most bitter enemy. I would say that our chances of persuading Vologases to accept peace are no more than one in four. And if he chooses war, I doubt we will ever see our homes again. Even if he lets us live and keeps us as prisoners. Frankly, I don't see much scope for excitement in our situation.'

'No? I'm surprised. I'd have expected a soldier with your experience to revel in the risks we are taking. You've faced graver dangers than this, surely?'

'I've faced danger in battle. I've faced the dangers of becoming embroiled in politics. But I had a measure of control over my actions. This, though?' Cato gestured vaguely at the mist. 'I am at the mercy of events and live on the whim of these Parthians. I do not care for it. What I feel is fear, Apollonius. Fear that I may never see my son and my friends again. Fear that they will never know what has become of us if Vologases chooses to make us disappear. I imagine it's different for a man who has no family. No friends.'

It was a calculated remark to test the agent. Apollonius returned his stare coldly.

'How do you know there is no one waiting for me, Tribune?'

'I don't, but I think I know you well enough now to believe that there is no one you care about, or who cares for you. All you have to live for is the excitement of putting your life at risk, and of course the arrogant delight of counting yourself somewhat above the rest of us in terms of intelligence and calculation.'

Apollonius's lips pressed together in a tight line for a moment, and Cato nodded with satisfaction. 'It is not terribly pleasing to have someone see inside your mind, is it?'

'You think you know me? Perhaps you even think you understand me.'

'Yes, I reckon I am beginning to.'

'Then you are mistaken, Tribune. Don't fool yourself, or it will not end well for you. It is better that you do not attempt to fathom my nature or why I choose to be as I am.'

Cato frowned. 'Are you threatening me?'

'Consider it a warning. Never assume that you understand a person, no matter how close to you they are, or you will be in danger of letting your guard down just when you need it most. In the situation we are in, that could cost you your life, and the lives of your men.' He half turned to gesture towards the Praetorians clustered around the foot of the mast. Some had settled back down to sleep, while others talked quietly, as if afraid of being overheard by any dangerous creatures lurking in the mist. The two wounded men, Quintus and Grumio, lay on mats, their backs propped up against the mast. Without their sword belts or even their daggers, the soldiers looked vulnerable. Further aft stood the Parthians assigned to guard the Romans. They, by contrast, were armed with swords, and their bow cases lay at the foot of the small stern deck, close at hand.

As Cato regarded them, the door of the cabin beneath the deck opened and Haghrar emerged. He stretched his shoulders and yawned before he turned and spoke to the captain. The latter bowed his head as he replied, at some length. Seemingly satisfied with the captain's reply, Haghrar gave him a curt nod and strolled forward. His men backed out of his way as he passed by, making for the bow. The Praetorians did not stir, but merely regarded him quietly.

'Good morrow, Tribune.'

'Sir.' Cato briefly dipped his head in greeting as Haghrar glanced at Apollonius.

'And to you, Greek.'

Apollonius bowed deeply. 'My lord. I trust you slept well.'

'As well as anyone can in this mosquito-infested stretch of the river. But the captain tells me we will soon be clear of the reeds. He says we should reach our destination in three days. Sooner if there is a breeze across the river.' Haghrar looked out at the mist. 'I shan't be sorry when this voyage is over. I detest travelling over water. It's unnatural.'

'This is nothing compared to the conditions at sea,' said Cato. 'Have you ever gone to sea, my lord?'

'No.' Haghrar stroked his jaw. 'I have never seen the sea.'

Cato was surprised. 'Truly?'

'Why would I? The land I rule is far from any shore. I was raised to be its lord from youth and my duty has taken up nearly all my time and strength.' He paused. 'I would like to visit the coast once before I am taken from this world. You have travelled across the sea, Tribune?'

'Yes, sir. Many times.'

'What is it like? I have heard that it is filled with terrible beasts, and that when the gods are angry, the waters are whipped up into mountainous waves that destroy many of those who dare to set sail. Is that the truth?'

For a moment, Cato was startled by the questions. Could Haghrar really have so little idea about the sea? Perhaps it was only surprising because the extensive nature of Cato's travels had long since inured him to such novelties. The oceans held little mystery for him any more. Yet here was a chance to try and win some respect for Rome's reputation.

'It is true that there are monsters in the deep. And that there are storms that wreck many ships and drown their crews. But the sea beyond the coast of Syria is Rome's domain. Our fleets have tamed it. The writ of Rome extends even over the oceans. There is no other navy to challenge us, and every ship that crosses the sea does so under Roman protection and control. Just as our legions control the land.'

Haghrar looked at him sharply. 'Not all the land. Not Parthia. Never Parthia. Have you forgotten what happened to your General Crassus at Carrhae?'

'I have not forgotten, my lord. No Roman ever will, which is why there will always be some who yearn to avenge Crassus. And they will have their way, unless we can achieve a lasting peace.'

One of the lookouts suddenly turned and called back along the deck. The captain came forward quickly and there was a hurried exchange in low voices before the lookout thrust out his hand and pointed to the right. Both men stared intently into the mist. Then the captain turned and snapped an order to the men at the sweeps. At once they raised their blades and held them poised above the surface of the river as the ship glided on.

'What is it?' Cato asked softly.

'The lookout says he caught a glimpse of another vessel,' Haghrar replied.

'Surely that's no surprise? We've passed plenty of vessels since we left Ichnae.'

'They don't generally put out from shore when the mist is this thick. We're only here because I am anxious to get to Ctesiphon as swiftly as possible.'

'So who could be out there?' Cato nodded towards the mist.

'I don't know.'

'Shh!' the captain hissed at them, heedless of the difference in station between himself and the Parthian lord.

Everyone on deck was now keeping quite still as they stared anxiously into the surrounding milky shroud. Cato strained his eyes but could make out nothing, and all he heard was the mournful cry of some marsh bird away in the mid distance. For a while the ship drifted on the smooth water, and then he heard voices not far off. He turned quickly towards the sound, but saw only the impenetrable mist. And then, just for an instant, a skein of grey parted and he saw the outline of another craft off the starboard quarter.

It was hard to judge the precise distance, but they were close, and now he could make out the ghostly shape of figures standing on the foredeck. A tiny flickering glow of orange appeared and rose above the men, and then shot up into the air, flaring as it arced between the two ships. There was no need to shout a warning, as all on board were now looking in the direction of the other vessel. In any case, it was clear that the fire arrow was going to fall short. But not by much. It plunged into the water fifteen feet from the side with a soft splash. At once there came the sound of a horn from the other vessel, joined a moment later by another from ahead, and a third from off the port beam. Then Cato heard the oars, splashing through the water as the craft he had caught sight of surged through the mist, its features quickly becoming more distinct as it closed on them.

'Look there!' Apollonius cried out, pointing ahead as another vessel loomed out of the mist, driven against the current by rowers. 'Who in Hades are they?'

'Pirates,' Haghrar growled.

'Pirates?' Cato shook his head. 'River pirates?'

'Of course,' Haghrar responded angrily. 'Don't you have pirates on the sea?'

Before Cato could respond, Haghrar turned to bellow orders to his men. At once they snatched open their bow cases and began to string their bows. The captain was also shouting instructions, and his crew quickly shipped their oars. Those that had them readied their weapons, while the rest snatched up boathooks and belaying pins.

The third pirate boat had emerged from the mist, and all three were now closing on the barge. Cato turned to Haghrar.

'What about me and my men? You can't leave us defenceless. Give us our weapons and we can fight too.'

The Parthian nobleman hesitated, and Cato pointed towards the nearest boat, clearly visible now. Its deck was packed with men brandishing weapons and shouting war cries as they closed in on their prey. Haghrar gritted his teeth and nodded. 'Very well. Come!'

Cato and Apollonius dashed after him towards the soldiers and crew around the mast. Haghrar spoke to one of his men and pointed to the hold, and the Parthian swung himself over the open cargo hatch and scuttled between the jars of wine and garum the barge was taking down to the capital city. Cato called his men to him.

'They're going to return our swords to us, lads. Make sure we give a good account of ourselves; let's show these Parthians how real soldiers fight.'

'How about us, sir?' said Grumio. 'Me and Quintus can do our bit.'

Cato glanced at the wounded man and grinned. 'You can't keep a good Praetorian down, eh?'

The Parthian returned and heaved a small chest up onto the deck. Cato bent over it and flipped the bolt back, swinging the lid open. His sword lay on top, and he snatched it up and drew the blade before dropping the scabbard by the chest. The other men hurriedly retrieved their own swords and handed the wounded pair their weapons, then formed a loose group around the mast. Cato saw that Haghrar and his men had readied their bows and were already nocking their arrows, taking aim on the nearest pirate boat.

Even as they drew back the strings, the enemy unleashed the first volley. The shafts rattled home before there was any chance to shout a warning, whirring past, splintering wood and striking down two Parthians. One of Haghrar's men spun round, dropping his bow to the deck and clasping at the shaft that had pierced his side. A sailor was the other casualty; an arrow had torn through his left hand as he brandished it in a fist, and pinned it firmly to his chest. There was no time to look after either man, as the rest of those on deck lined the sides and prepared to defend the barge.

More arrows rained down from the archers on the boat approaching from the other side. Cato shouted to his men to take cover, and repeated the order in Greek. They ducked behind the side rail as the shafts struck the hull and whipped overhead. Cato squatted beside Apollonius and watched Haghrar and his men bravely loosing arrows as swiftly as they could. One more of the Parthians was downed as an arrow ripped open his throat; he fell onto his back and lay writhing as blood pooled on the deck around his head.

With a jarring blow that caused those standing to stumble, the first of the boats crashed against the barge's side. Unlike seagoing vessels, the river craft had low freeboards, and there was no need to climb up the sides. Instead, the pirates vaulted over the rail and landed on the deck, ready to strike down the defenders. Haghrar dropped his bow and snatched out his sword, and his men followed his lead, joining the crew as they charged at the boarders.

Cato snatched a breath and rose up, shouting, 'Up, Praetorians, and at 'em!'

With a roar, his men sprang to their feet and hurled themselves at their enemy. Cato made for a wiry man in a worn and stained linen cuirass with bronze plates stitched to front and back. The pirate carried an axe with a long haft, and he swung it back and raised a buckler in his left hand ready to parry Cato's blow. With blood pounding in his ears and every muscle and instinct tensed for instant action, Cato rushed forward, keeping his centre of balance low. Instead of making the amateur's mistake of striking out at the buckler, he twisted and grabbed at the rim with his left hand and wrenched it towards him with all his strength. At the same time he stabbed low with his sword into the pirate's guts, just above the pelvis, where there was no protection. The impact made the pirate stagger to the side and his axe arm wavered a moment, before he recovered his wits enough to try and strike back. It was an awkward angle to make a killing blow, but Cato was only wearing a tunic, and he knew that almost any blow that landed would deal a terrible wound. He braced his boots and launched himself forward, inside the reach of the axe, thrusting the man back against the ship's rail. The pirate's torso went slack, and with a final shove, Cato sent him over the side to fall back onto the deck of the attackers' boat.

Glancing quickly about him, he saw that the barge's deck had become a battlefield, as soldiers and crewmen duelled with pirates and the cool, damp air filled with the clatter of weapons and the grunts of men fighting for their lives. As bodies parted, he caught a glimpse of Grumio and Quintus slashing at the legs and groins of the nearest pirates. Then he spotted a man climbing over the side two paces away and rushed towards him, stabbing him in the ear in a burst of blood and bone. The pirate spasmed and then slumped forward across the rail, dropping his sword and a round shield. Cato snatched the latter up and covered his body as he turned to see that his men were holding their ground just forward of the mast. Haghrar and his men were fighting it out closer to the stern, while the crew were scattered across the deck, their lack of armour and swords distinguishing them from the pirates.

There was another shuddering impact as the boat coming upriver struck the bow. A handful of men went down, but the rest managed to keep their balance and resumed their struggle. Cato saw Apollonius rush to the bow, beckoning the nearest crewmen to follow him. As the first of the fresh wave of pirates swung his leg over the bowrail, the agent swept his dagger up and round so swiftly that Cato could barely follow the movement. Blood spurted from the pirate's throat, then Apollonius punched him in the jaw with his sword guard and sent him tumbling out of sight.

The bow of the pirate boat ground along the side of the

barge, and more men began to climb aboard. Cato saw at once that Apollonius needed help if he and the two crewmen who had joined him were not to be overwhelmed. Slamming his shield into bodies and thrusting with his sword, he fought his way forward. As he reached a clear space on the deck, he saw that there was only one man still aboard the first pirate boat, holding it to the side of the barge with a boathook as he stood beside a small brazier, still alight. Sheathing his sword, Cato pulled a dagger from the hand of a dead pirate on the deck, took the end of the blade between his fingers and thumb and raised it above his shoulder as he sized up the target fifteen feet away. The pirate was busy shouting encouragement to his comrades and only saw the danger at the very last moment. His eyes widened as Cato hurled the blade. It flew end over end and struck the man in the throat at an angle, scoring a flesh wound before it dropped to the deck. But the shock of the blow was enough to make the man release his grip, and the wooden shaft of the hook fell into the water between the two vessels as he stumbled back, clutching at his throat with blood-smeared fingers and knocking over the brazier. Cato drew his sword again and used the point to give the smaller craft a push, and the gap between the two vessels widened. Satisfied, he hurried forward just as a cry of alarm came from one of the pirates, who had seen the boat drifting away.

Pushing his way between Apollonius and the crewman at his side, Cato raised his shield to fend off a spear thrust and then cut down viciously on the shaft, splintering the wood so that it snapped as it smashed down on the ship's side. Just below him, he could see perhaps twenty men pressing forward as they tried to rush aboard the barge and overwhelm the defenders. The crewman to his right had armed himself with one of the sweeps and was frantically lashing out with the blade, knocking men down but without harming them. Still, Cato thought, he was disrupting the attack nicely. To his left, Apollonius was using his sword expertly, parrying attacks and striking back with quick, targeted blows, taking out the eye of a pirate who had dared to venture within reach.

Cato realised they were holding their own for the moment and took a step back to briefly survey the fight across the main deck. The pirates must have realised too late that the passengers aboard the barge presented a formidable challenge. Several of them had fallen, and more were wounded and holding back from the fight. Haghrar appeared to have lost two or three of his men, but Cato's Praetorians were standing firm in the area around the mast. Over the beam, Cato could see the third boat approaching, still nearly a hundred feet away as it powered forward under oars. There were enough men aboard to swing the fight the pirates' way.

A hoarse shout drew his attention back to the deck, and he saw a large bearded man in a gleaming breastplate and oval shield bellowing angrily at the pirates before closing on the nearest Praetorian and feinting with his sword. The Roman moved to counter the blow, but the pirate leader performed a swift undercut and then thrust home into the Praetorian's chest, driving him back and down onto his knees before kicking the blade free and rounding on the next man as the nearest of his followers cheered him on.

'Apollonius!'

The agent backed off from the side rail and glanced at Cato as the latter pointed.

'The pirate captain. See him?'

'The bearded oaf?'

'Yes. Can you get him from here?'

'Cover my position, Tribune.'

As Apollonius withdrew, Cato stepped up and slashed wildly to drive back those who had edged forward. He took a light blow from an axe on the edge of his shield and nearly lost his grip.

'Oh, you would, would you?' he snarled, and slashed his sword at the axehead, sending sparks flying.

Behind him, Apollonius wiped the blood from the blade of his dagger on the hem of his tunic before grasping the blade and raising the weapon over and behind his shoulder. He squinted along the deck towards the pirate captain, who now had his back to him as he slammed his shield into Pelius and knocked the optio to his knees. The pirate raised his arm to strike the killing blow, and Apollonius hurled his throwing knife. It flickered over and through the men fighting across the deck and struck home squarely at the base of the pirate's neck, between his shoulder blades. The captain let out an enraged roar as he let go of his shield and groped for the haft of the knife with his spare hand. Pelius reacted swiftly and slashed his sword at the captain's left knee, cutting through muscle and shattering bone. The pirate toppled to one side, close to the mast, and at once Grumio and Quintus set upon him, stabbing furiously at his head, arms and chest in a flurry of savage blows. Apollonius nodded with satisfaction and charged into the melee.

A groan rose from the remaining men of the first pirate boat as their leader went down, and Haghrar seized the chance to order his surviving soldiers and the crewmen to finish off the attackers. They surged across the deck, joined by the Praetorians, hacking at their opponents with fresh determination. Some of the pirates backed to the side, only to discover their craft had drifted some distance off. Smoke rose lazily from its deck, and there was the glint of flames from the fire started by the overturned brazier. The pirates either stood their ground until struck down, or threw aside their weapons and dived into the river. Only the strong swimmers reached their boat; the rest managed a few strokes before their kit dragged them down, arms flailing pitifully before they disappeared under the surface leaving a swirl, then ripples, before there was no trace of them.

As the last of the pirates still on the barge were finished off, Cato beckoned to Haghrar.

'My lord, bring your archers forward. Hurry!'

The Parthian shouted to his men as he raced forward and took the sailor's place at Cato's side. But just as Cato wounded another attacker in the arm, he was caught in the side by a blow from the rim of a shield and immediately felt a terrible pain across his ribs. He fell back, gasping in agony as he struggled to breathe. At once a nimble young pirate from the second boat leaped over the rail, dagger clenched in his teeth and brandishing a studded club in his right hand. He made a swing at Apollonius, and the Greek had to throw himself aside to avoid the blow, leaving room for the pirates to board the barge.

Haghrar and the remaining sailor fought to hold their ground as more pirates began to climb over the starboard bow. The man with the club turned back to Cato as he tried to rise from the deck. He took the dagger from his teeth and grinned in triumph as he raised his club to dash the Roman's brains out. Then his expression twisted into a look of shock as an arrowhead smashed into his face and punched through the back of his neck. He tottered forward before slumping down beside Cato. Even then, he still raised his dagger to strike, and Cato slashed desperately at his wrist, so that the knife dropped harmlessly to the deck as the youth rolled choking onto his side.

More arrows cut down those who had boarded, and then the archers reached the foredeck and shot down into the throng aboard the second pirate boat as fast as they could manage.

Cato pointed to the sailor with the oar, and mimed thrusting something away as he croaked, 'Fend . . . off.'

The man nodded and positioned his blade against the stem post of the pirate boat, thrusting as hard as he could so that a gap opened. One of the pirates, still bold enough to try to board the barge, was caught with a foot on both craft, and tumbled into the river with a loud splash.

The archers continued to shoot, scoring hits nearly every time, so that bodies littered the foredeck of the pirate boat as the gap between the vessels widened, but the pirates had started to shoot back at Haghrar's men, and now the first arrow struck down the soldier next to the Parthian lord. He waved his men to take cover behind the bulwark, and they bobbed up briefly to shoot before ducking down to prepare their next arrow.

Meanwhile, Cato had begun to breathe again, but each breath drawn was accompanied by an agonisingly sharp stabbing pain in his side. He stepped over bodies as he made his way towards Apollonius and the Praetorians, nodding a salute to Pelius.

'How are we doing, Optio?' he asked, wincing.

'Are you wounded?' Pelius asked anxiously.

Cato shook his head. 'Winded. The men?'

'Two wounded and another two killed, sir. Caecilius and Grumio.'

'Grumio?'

Pelius pointed his sword to where the Praetorian lay face down across the body of a pirate a short distance from the mast. Cato shook his head in pity. Then he caught sight of the third boat approaching and braced himself to cope with the pain as he pointed out the new threat. 'Praetorians, to the side!'

His men rushed to the side rail, bloodied swords held ready

as they faced the third pirate crew. Cato thrust some of the sailors after the Praetorians until men stood ready in an unbroken line. At the bows, Haghrar had also seen the fresh danger and ordered his archers to shift their aim, and now arrows sped across the narrow gap between the barge and the deck of the remaining pirate boat.

Cato clutched his ribs tenderly as he looked round. Flames were now spreading along the deck of the first attacker, and smoke billowed into the air. A shouted command caused the oars of the third boat to drop into the water, the rowers holding them in place to slow the vessel as water surged over the blades. The bow came to rest fifteen feet from the barge, and then began to ease away as the rowers reversed course. The pirates' expressions were grim as they stared towards the flames on the first boat.

'Cowards!' Pelius shouted at them, punching his sword up. 'Come and get it, you dogs!'

But the enemy's spirit had been broken, Cato realised. The boat backed away steadily until it dissolved into the mist. The pirate vessel that had attacked the bow was now wallowing off the beam, the deck littered with bodies and groans carrying across the water. Cato made his way forward to Haghrar.

'My lord, tell the captain to get us moving. Before those bastards recover and come after us.'

Haghrar called across to the barge's captain. The latter nodded and gathered several of his surviving crewmen, who took up the sweeps, and soon the barge was drawing away from the scene of the ambush. Soon all that could be seen of the pirates was the wavering glow of the burning boat accompanied by the anguished cries of those struggling to put out the blaze.

Cato eased himself down on the edge of the cargo hatch and

took shallow breaths to keep the pain from his ribs at a tolerable level. He looked over the deck as Haghrar's men moved amongst the bodies strewn across the planking, stooping to help themselves to valuables or finish off those pirates still living with a thrust of the blade under the chin and up into the skull. Some of the crewmen not working the sweeps stood or sat in a numbed state as they beheld the carnage, while others attended to those who were wounded, bandaging slashes and puncture wounds with strips of cloth torn from the clothing of the dead. Pelius ordered the Praetorians to start heaving the dead over the side while he dealt with their own wounded. There was a steady series of splashes as the corpses were dropped into the river.

Apollonius approached and looked down at Cato with a concerned expression. 'Tribune, you'd better let me have a look at you.'

'I suppose you happen to be a physician along with all your other talents,' Cato growled.

'Something like that. Stand up.'

There was authority in his tone, and Cato decided to give the agent the benefit of the doubt. After all, it was Apollonius's blade that had caused the death of the pirate captain and led to the routing of his crew. Steeling himself, he rose to his feet, undid his belt and lifted the hem of his tunic far enough to expose his ribs.

Apollonius crouched slightly as he inspected the broad stripe of red, and then glanced up at Cato. 'Brace yourself, this is going to hurt.'

Cato gritted his teeth and looked directly ahead as the agent's fingers touched his side, and then pressed more firmly, tracing the contours of his ribs. A burning sensation increased agonisingly, and Cato's jaws ached with the effort of keeping them clamped together. At last Apollonius straightened up and indicated to Cato to let the folds of the tunic fall.

'Nothing broken as far as I can tell. At worst you've suffered some badly bruised ribs. But you're in for several days of pain, and you won't find laughing much fun.'

'Just as well I'm not in a humorous mood then.' Cato reached carefully for his belt.

'I wouldn't wear that for a while,' Apollonius advised, and Cato slung it over his shoulder on the other side of his body.

'Do you think those pirates will try to come after us?' the agent asked.

'I doubt it. They lost too many men, and may lose one of their boats into the bargain. I dare say they'll return to their lair to lick their wounds, and vow to investigate their targets more thoroughly before they attack next time.'

Apollonius smiled. 'We gave them a nasty surprise all right.'

Cato regarded him silently for a moment. 'You fought well. Clearly a man to be reckoned with. I'd think twice before I tangled with you.'

'Then pray you never have reason to. I'll see what I can do for the injured amongst the crew, and our Parthian friends.'

Apollonius made his way aft, to where one of the sailors was propped up against the side, trying to tie a dressing around his wounded arm one-handed. Cato watched him speculatively, wondering just what his chances might be if they ever had cause to fight. Then he saw Haghrar approaching him. The nobleman had a strip of cloth tied round his forehead, and a dark stain was already seeping through the material over his temple. He stopped in front of Cato and bowed his head.

'I owe you and your men my thanks, Tribune. If it were not for you, we'd all be dead.'

There was no point in false modesty, so Cato nodded.

'Roman soldiers fight hard, my lord. That is why they are feared across the known world.'

Haghrar thought briefly before he conceded the point. 'Truly spoken. It is a pity they are often so poorly led.'

Cato began to chuckle, then winced painfully.

'You are injured, Tribune?'

'A few bruises, that's all, my lord.'

He realised he was still holding his sword, and that his men were still armed. He flipped the weapon, catching it by the flat of the blade and offering the handle to the Parthian noble. 'You'll be wanting this back.'

Haghrar looked down at the sword for a moment before he shook his head. 'You and your men can keep your weapons. I owe you that honour. Provided you give me your word that you will not use them unless I give the command.'

'Fair enough,' Cato agreed. He reversed his grip with both hands and let the sword hang down. 'After all, who knows what further dangers lie ahead of us?'

Haghrar stared at him intently as he replied. 'Who indeed?'

CHAPTER EIGHTEEN

As they reached the crest of the ridge overlooking the road leading down to the bridge, Macro reined in and surveyed the scene. Most of the men assigned to the engineer detachment were busy driving fresh piles into the riverbed a short distance upriver. The posts had sturdy screens fixed to them, like arrowheads, and were arranged in an overlapping chevron in order to divert any more logs away from the bridge and up against the bank, where they could be hauled out. More legionaries were deployed in forage parties, cutting down pine trees on the slopes either side of the bridge. A handful of men stood guarding the bridge itself. There was no sign of any wagons from the baggage train, nor of the Syrian auxiliaries. Macro had been half hoping that Orfitus might have abandoned his independent advance and returned to the bridge, thereby relieving him of the burden of tracking him down.

His attention shifted to the bridge itself. One of the trestles had been replaced, but the second was still missing, and the gap in the middle span had only been bridged by a narrow strip of boards with a rail on either side. Wide enough for a man or a horse perhaps, but certainly not able to bear the weight of a wagon. He sighed as he realised that it would be many days before the bridge was repaired and supplies could flow across it to reach the column besieging Thapsis.

He clicked his tongue and tapped his heels in to urge his mount to advance, then waved his arm forward to signal Decurion Spathos and his cavalry squadron to follow him. Optio Phocus edged forward to ride at his side as they descended the track to the bridge.

'I imagine it will take us two or three days to catch up with Prefect Orfitus, sir.'

'I imagine so,' Macro replied. 'Assuming we can get the horses across in one piece.'

Phocus stared at the slender walkway stretching across the current rushing beneath the bridge. 'That ain't going to be easy.'

'You think?' Macro responded wryly. 'Thank you for pointing that out, Optio.'

'Sorry, sir.'

As the slope evened out and they approached the bridge, they were greeted by the centurion commanding the detachment, who had turned away from the camp desk where he had piled the wax tablets bearing his plans and calculations.

'Centurion Macro, isn't it?'

'The same.' Macro swung his leg over the saddle and dropped to the ground, rubbing his buttocks. 'How are things going, Munius? You don't seem to have made much progress here.'

The smile faded as the other man scratched his head. 'Perhaps not. But things haven't been helped by those rebel bastards.'

'Oh? How so?'

'They're still sending logs downriver. Not all the time. A day or two can pass, and then they'll hit us with a steady flow. My guess is that they have a small group working on the job, waiting until they've cut enough timber to send a whole load down. Still, we've used the intervals to put up the screen to divert the logs away from the bridge. Once that's completed, we'll be free to work on the trestles and repair the gap over the central span.' Munius did a quick mental calculation. 'Four to five days should see it done. Provided there are no more raids, of course.'

Macro looked at him. 'Raids?'

The engineer nodded and pointed across to an open patch of ground a hundred paces from the river. Much of the ground was covered by a blackened mass of charred wood. More logs and cut timbers were stacked a short distance away. Several legionaries stood guard around the undamaged materials.

'What happened?'

'They came down from the ridge three nights back, just after Orfitus led the baggage train off and took his cohort with him. The rebels killed the sentries, set light to the timber and fled into the night. They had archers positioned on the slope to pick off the men I sent to put the fires out. After we lost the first two men, I pulled the others back and we had to let the whole lot go up in flames. Took us two days just to cut enough new timber to continue the work. I sent some patrols after the rebels at first light, but they know the mountains well and are lightly kitted out, so they gave us the slip easily enough. But now that you've brought us some cavalry, we'll be able to chase the bastards down if they try it on again.'

'We've not been sent here to reinforce you. I've got orders to find Prefect Orfitus. We'll be off just as soon as we can get across the river.' Macro pointed towards the narrow walkway. 'I hope that can take the weight of a horse. What do you reckon?'

Munius laughed nervously, and then paused when Macro failed to join in. 'Wait, are you being serious?'

'Deadly serious. I haven't got time to waste going downstream to find that ford. Besides, the water level has risen and I doubt the ford is safe any more. We have to cross here. Let's go and have a look at that walkway, shall we?'

Macro turned to order Decurion Spathos to dismount the squadron and have the men strip the horses of everything except their reins. Then he strode out onto the first span and up towards the edge of the gap where he would have fallen to his death if General Corbulo had not saved him. He slowed as he reached the end of the walkway and examined the slender structure. It was no more than a pace across, with a taut rope on either side serving as a handrail. Glancing beneath it, he saw that it was propped up at either end by wooden beams, but the ten feet in the middle had no support as the walkway crossed the raging torrent below.

He took a deep breath and stepped forward, testing his weight. There was a slight creak, but no perceptible give beneath his boots. He continued, testing the surface every few paces. As soon as he got to the unsupported stretch, he felt the boards move slowly up and down with each step he took, and suddenly the rope handrail seemed to offer no security at all. At the midpoint, he stopped and flexed his weight on bending knees. The boards shifted and creaked alarmingly, but held firm. The walkway would be fine for a man crossing by himself, or even several at a time, but Macro could well imagine the difficulty of coaxing a horse across the slender span.

'Hmm,' he mused as he turned about and returned to where Munius was waiting. 'It'll do.'

They returned to the Macedonians waiting beside the horses. Each man's saddle, bags and kit was piled at the side.

Macro jerked his thumb over his shoulder as he addressed them.

'Right, lads, that's the way across the river. And this is how we're going to do it. First man leads his horse across while the second man carries his kit over afterwards. The second man returns for his horse while the next carries his kit, and so on. I've checked the walkway and it's sound. Just make sure you keep well within the guide ropes and take it slow and gentle. Any questions?'

Spathos shook his head. 'It's madness, sir. The horses won't like it. Any of them panic, they'll go into the river and take their rider with them if he's not careful.'

'That's why I said slow and gentle, and put blinkers on the horses. That'll help.'

'There has to be another way across, sir,' Spathos protested.

'Even if there is, we can't afford to waste time finding it.' Macro sensed that any more discussion would only serve to unnerve the men. It was far better to keep them moving than give them time to think about the risk. 'We're crossing here and we're doing it now. I'll go first.'

He pointed to the nearest auxiliary. 'You carry my saddle and kit. Wait for me to get across before you come. Clear? Spathos, put the blinkers on my horse.'

While the decurion did as he was ordered, Macro stripped off his helmet, harness, mail shirt and weapons so that he was left in only his tunic and boots. If he fell, and was fortunate enough not to be dashed to pieces on a rock, he hoped he might survive the drop and swim to the bank.

Once the blinkers had been fitted, Spathos handed the reins to Macro.

'Fortuna watch over you, sir.'

'She always does, lad. She's got a thing for me.' Macro

winked and then took his position close to the head of the horse, keeping it on a short length of rein. He stroked the mare's cheek gently as he spoke in an undertone. 'Come on, my girl. Let's show these frightened streaks of piss just how it's done.'

He stepped a pace ahead, so that the mare could see him but not much else, and then clicked his tongue. 'Walk on.'

He paced in a slow, deliberate manner across the first span towards the gap and stepped onto the walkway without hesitating, keeping the horse as close as possible to the centre. The sound of the water churning beneath caused the mare's ears to prick up and twitch, and Macro spoke soothingly. 'Easy, girl. Easy there.'

They continued steadily, the horse's hoofs sounding loudly off the wooden boards. As he reached the weakest stretch in the middle, Macro felt his heart beating hard, and there was a moment's hesitation before he forced himself to go on. The mare followed, nostrils flaring, and Macro hung on tightly to the reins to stop the animal looking from side to side. The boards creaked ominously beneath them and sank with every step they took towards the centre of the walkway, and then they were past the most dangerous point and the planking was more solid. Then, just as Macro placed his leading boot on the safe ground at the far end of the walkway, the horse gave a frightened whinny and stepped slightly to one side so the rope pressed up against its flank. Macro tightened his grip on the reins and pulled gently.

'No silly buggering about, girl. Come on now.'

For a moment the horse was still, and then it stepped forward again, walking off the end of the walkway and down the span to the far bank. Macro breathed deeply as he halted and reached up to remove the blinkers. 'Thank you.'

Handing the reins to one of the legionaries, he returned to the bridge and beckoned to the auxiliary carrying his saddle and kit. 'Your turn!'

The auxiliary hefted the saddle onto his shoulder and picked up the bundle of saddlebags in the other. There was no way for him to carry the armour and weapons as well, so Macro decided to send him back for that once he had completed his first task. He could see the rest of the squadron watching fixedly as their comrade made his way up the walkway and began to cross. When he approached the centre and the boards began to bow under him, the auxiliary hesitated and looked down, but before Macro could draw breath to bellow at him to get moving, he suddenly picked up his pace and scurried forward the final few steps.

'There you go.' Macro grinned at him. 'Piece of piss, eh?'

The auxiliary smiled sheepishly. 'If you say so, sir.'

'I do. Now put that lot down and get back over there for the rest of my kit. Off you go, my lad.'

One by one the other thirty horses were led across the slender walkway, followed by one of the laden men of the squadron, before the latter turned back to fetch his own mount. The horses, trained to endure the din of battle, were calm. There was only one, more skittish than the rest, that refused to make the crossing, rearing up and lashing out with its forelegs when its rider tried to draw it closer. Macro could see that the beast was more than likely to come to grief, and ordered the auxiliary to take it to the rear and try again when all the others were across. Still the animal refused, and Macro reluctantly ordered the man to remain with Centurion Munius and his men. The rest of the squadron and Optio Phocus replaced their saddles on their mounts and loaded up their kit in readiness to follow the route taken by Orfitus and the baggage train.

As the last of the men made his preparations, Macro took Munius aside so that they would not be overheard.

'Corbulo and the lads up at Thapsis are on short rations as it is. If the line of communication back to Tarsus isn't established soon, things are going to get much worse. Especially with winter approaching. When the rains come, and then the snow, we'll have trouble getting supplies and reinforcements through.' He turned briefly towards the bridge. 'I dare say the rivers will be swollen too. So you better make sure the repairs are as sound as they can be while the water level is still low.'

'We're doing a good job,' Munius insisted. 'And we're doing it in good time, considering the circumstances.'

'I'm sure you are. But Corbulo might see things differently. He's a hard task-master and he'll brook no delay and no excuses. I'd get the job done if I were you. Just saying, brother.'

Macro strolled back to his horse and climbed into the saddle. Glancing round to make sure that the rest of the men accompanying him were ready, he raised his arm and swept it forward, and they rode out of the engineers' camp and onto the road that followed the river upstream in the direction that Orfitus had taken.

Macro was keen to catch up with the baggage train as swiftly as possible, and he drove the squadron hard, alternating a steady canter with an hour or so of the men walking the horses to rest them a little. The track ran close to the bank for several miles before the river entered a gorge and the route bent away sharply, following the floor of a valley as it rose into the mountains. By nightfall they had covered at least ten miles by Macro's reckoning, and they left the road and entered the fringe of a forest for the night in case the enemy was watching the road from the heights. He permitted no fire, and the men ate a meal of hard bread and salted mutton before they cut small boughs from the trees for their beds and covered themselves with their cloaks to sleep. The horses were tethered in a small clearing, just large enough to provide some grazing. As darkness fell, Macro took the first watch with the horses, while one of the auxiliaries stood on the treeline watching the road.

He still felt uneasy about the role the general had assigned to him. Orfitus was bound to protest, even if he could do nothing about the authority Macro held over him, and the prospect of commanding the baggage train while dealing with a resentful subordinate worried him. Worse still, once the baggage train rejoined the column, Orfitus would resume his seniority in rank and might well take advantage of that to avenge his humiliation. Perhaps not just for the duration of this campaign, but whenever their paths crossed in the future.

'Shit.' Macro pulled his cloak closer about his shoulders. It was a cold night, and the steely glow of the moonlight only served to heighten the chill. He longed to be back in a warm bed, pressed against Petronella's body, and found himself yearning for the day when he took his discharge from the army to spend the rest of his life with her.

'What the fuck am I thinking?' he muttered to himself. 'I'm a bloody soldier, not some old fart idling away what time remains to me.'

But he could not shake off the desire for the comforts and female companionship promised by a life with his new wife. Sure, he had had many friends in the army, many of whom were as close to being family as you could get, but almost all of them were dead now, or long retired. He got on well enough with the other centurions of the Praetorian cohort, but only Cato remained from the old days with the Second Legion on the frontier with Germania and the invasion of Britannia. Perhaps that salutary fact was proof that Macro had defied the odds long enough. Even Fortuna might finally grow weary of him and let him perish on the battlefield, or waste away from sickness, or simply be stabbed in the back by a footpad on some dark street in Tarsus or Rome. He felt the cold hand of mortality upon him and knew that he wanted more life, and that he wanted to spend it with Petronella.

A twig snapped somewhere in the mid-distance, and Macro was on his feet in an instant, sword drawn as his eyes searched the shadows for any sign of danger. Something moved, and he lowered himself into a crouch, muscles tensed and ready to spring into the attack. Then a deer cautiously crossed the edge of the clearing, paused and glanced directly at him before bolting out of sight. Macro let out a long sigh and sheathed his sword.

'I am definitely getting too old for this . . .'

The next morning, they were back on the road in pursuit of the baggage train. The route wound up the slope at the end of the valley as a fine rain began to fall from iron-grey clouds. Here they came across three men working to fix a wagon with a snapped axle. The solid wheels had been removed and lay at the side of the track, where unloaded nets of horse feed and sacks of grain were piled. A team of oxen chewed at the grass growing on the slope and looked up placidly at the sound of approaching riders. The rear of the wagon was propped up on stumps of wood and the replacement axle had been put in place. As Macro rode up, the men were lifting one of the wheels ready to replace it. They paused in their work, and the thick-set drover raised a hand in greeting.

'Have you been left alone to deal with this?' asked Macro.

'Aye, right enough.' The drover spoke with the hard accent of the Suburra in Rome. 'Prefect told us to sort it out and catch up as best we can.'

'Taking a bit of a risk doing that in rebel territory.'

'That's what I told 'im, sir. Leave us enough men to keep us safe, I said. But he just rides off and leaves us 'ere at the side of the road. Bastard snotty officers . . . No offence meant to you, sir.'

'None taken. I came up through the ranks. Right, let's get you sorted out.'

Macro ordered his men to dismount, and a section of the auxiliaries helped to replace the wheels and lift the cart while the drover knocked the stumps away. As the wagon was reloaded, he asked, 'How long ago were you left here?'

The drover eased his gut out and rubbed his back. 'Oh, that was about noon yesterday. Hard to tell exactly, thanks to the bloody clouds. But about then.'

Macro did a quick calculation. 'If we ride hard, we should catch up with them before dark.'

'Well, that's all very fine for you,' the drover said with a hint of bitterness. 'It'll take rather longer than that for me and my two lads. And we'll be easy pickings for any rebels.'

'No doubt.' Macro turned to Spathos. 'Decurion, have ten of your men escort the wagon. We'll ride on with the rest. Let's be off. Mount up!'

The drover stepped between Macro and his horse and took his hand. 'Thank you, sir.'

Macro responded with a curt nod. 'Just get your wagon back with the rest of the baggage train as quick as you can, eh?'

'We'll do our best, sir. May the gods bless you.'

Macro felt a touch of embarrassment at the man's cloying gratitude. 'That's enough of that sort of thing now.'

He retrieved his hand and stepped up to mount his horse before settling himself in the saddle and raking up the reins. 'Detachment! Forward!'

Breaking into an easy trot, he set off up the road, and within a short space of time they had climbed far above the wagon, which seemed to be crawling along. The rutted road soon became little more than a track as it emerged onto a plateau. In the distance, perhaps two miles ahead, Macro could make out more proof that the baggage train had come this way. A handful of individual soldiers were making their way along the track.

'Stragglers?' Decurion Spathos suggested.

'Looks like it,' Macro responded. If they were men from the Syrian cohort, it was a poor effort if they had only got this far before they fell out of the line of march. Prefect Orfitus should not have tolerated it, he mused. He certainly would not have.

As they caught up with the men, the landscape changed. There were few trees, and the even landscape was mostly dotted with scrub and rocks. A chilly wind blew across the plateau as the rain began to fall in earnest, stinging drops driven almost horizontally into exposed flesh as cloaks and the manes of the horses whipped about. Macro did not stop for the stragglers from the Syrian cohort, but gave them a withering look of contempt as he rode past, ignoring those who pleaded for help. Some, he noticed, had already abandoned part of their kit, and they would be dealt a sober lesson when they caught up with their cohort and were put on a charge. Macro resolved that he would have a private word on the matter with Orfitus when he reached the baggage train. This was not acceptable. Not even in an auxiliary unit.

When they reached the far end of the plateau, Macro saw that the track sloped down into another valley, curving gently for a few miles in the direction of the river before disappearing around the edge of some crags. And there, a mile down the slope, he saw the baggage train, standing still just past a fork in the road. The route to the left cut through a gap in the ridge that ran along the edge of the valley and, as far as Macro could work out from his recall of the terrain, seemed to be the most direct route to the river and presumably the ford Orfitus had reported. So why had the baggage train halted? More puzzling still was that there was no sign of the Syrian cohort apart from half a century guarding each end of the line of wagons, as well as the handful of stragglers doing their best to catch up. Where in Hades were the rest of the Syrians? Macro wondered.

'I thought he was supposed to be finding the quickest way to get across the river,' said Spathos.

'He was,' Macro responded before he rounded on Optio Phocus. 'That's what he told you, right?'

'Yes, sir.'

'Then why in the name of Discordia isn't he making for the bloody river?'

Phocus shook his head helplessly. 'I have no idea, sir.'

Macro puffed with frustration. 'I need to get to the bottom of this, before some fool causes any more mischief.'

As the horsemen descended into the valley, the wind died away and the rain petered out. Trees grew densely on either side and the condition of the track steadily improved. Macro felt his spirits begin to sink as they trotted along. He was relieved to have found the baggage train unharmed, but he felt certain that something was wrong. He needed to track down Orfitus as quickly as possible.

He increased the pace to a canter as he continued along the road at the head of his men. As they reached the Syrians standing guard at the rear of the baggage train, he reined in and halted, then turned to Phocus.

'What's the name of the optio in charge?'

Phocus glanced over the auxiliaries, barely thirty in number, forming a line across the road. 'Laecinus, sir.'

Macro walked his horse up to the man in question. 'Optio Laecinus?'

'Yes, sir,' said the fresh-faced junior officer.

'Why has the baggage train halted?'

'Prefect's orders, sir.'

'And where is Prefect Orfitus?' Macro demanded. 'Where's the rest of the cohort?'

The optio turned and pointed towards the crags. 'He took the rest of the men in that direction, sir.'

'Why?'

'There's a rebel camp further down the valley. Orfitus means to attack it.'

Macro groaned. 'Oh, shit.'

He closed his mouth and fixed his lips in a thin line as he thought quickly. Orfitus should not have left the baggage train so poorly protected, no matter how tempting it was to deal a blow to the enemy. His sole duty was to carry out the orders Corbulo had left him with when the main part of the column marched on Thapsis. He craned his neck and looked around the valley. That was when he saw them, a party of horsemen on the skyline, observing them. A sickening dread filled his guts and he turned quickly to Laecinus.

'We have to get the wagons across the river.'

'But the prefect's orders were that—'

'Fuck the prefect, I'm in command now. On the general's orders. I want the wagons turned round and put on the road leading towards the river. Get started with the nearest of 'em. Phocus!'

'Sir?'

'You ride up the column and tell every drover to turn his wagon and get moving down the other fork. Go!'

He pulled his reins to turn his mount to Spathos and his remaining men. 'Drop your saddlebags and ready your weapons, lads. We're in for a fight!'

CHAPTER NINETEEN

Spurring his horse forward, Macro swerved off the road and galloped along the length of the baggage train to his left while the trunks of trees flitted past some twenty feet to his right. As he rode, he noted that the supply wagons were still at the rear of the column and that the siege weapons were loaded on the wagons at the head. He also saw the wagon drivers and their teams watching as the horses thundered past, and wondered if they knew how much danger they might be in. No doubt they had believed that the expedition to Thapsis would be over quickly and they would make a tidy profit from their contracts to supply Corbulo's soldiers. Instead they had been sitting idle for many days, and now they were terribly exposed to a rebel attack. He could not help wondering whether they were more preoccupied by the prospect of fading profits than the threat posed by the enemy.

The rest of the century left behind by Orfitus was positioned at the front of the wagon train, and Macro halted the squadron again to interrogate the unit's commander.

'Your name?'

'Centurion Mardonius, Sixth Century, Fourth Syrian Aux—'

'Mardonius.' Macro cut him off. 'What's going on here?

Your optio says the prefect has taken the rest of the cohort forward to attack a rebel camp.'

'Yes, sir.' Mardonius turned and pointed towards the crags where the road turned out of sight. 'Not far beyond there, sir. Four miles or so, according to Thermon.'

'Thermon? Who's that?'

'The guide, sir. He's the one who told the prefect about the ford. He was scouting ahead when he saw a band of rebels and followed them far enough to see their camp. Then he reported back to Orfitus, and he gave the order for the cohort to advance and destroy the camp.'

'And the prefect just took him at his word, I suppose,' Macro said flatly. 'So why has the baggage train not taken the turning towards the ford? What's Orfitus up to?'

'Thermon reported the enemy camp before we got to the fork, sir. He also said there was another ford just beyond it. A safer one to cross, given the recent rains. He said it might be dangerous to use the crossing he had originally mentioned. So the prefect ordered the baggage train to stay on the same road and then halted it before we reached the crags while he took the rest of the cohort forwards,' Mardonius explained. 'He said he'd send orders to continue the advance as soon as the rebel camp was taken.'

'He's a trusting man, your prefect.'

'Didn't seem to be any reason not to trust the guide, sir. He's one of us.'

'What do you mean?'

'A veteran. Retired legionary.'

'You believed him?'

'No reason not to, sir. You can take the man out of the army, but you can't take the army out of the man, as they say.'

241

'I'll deal with this Thermon later,' said Macro. 'Meanwhile, you get these wagons turned round and head for the original ford.'

Mardonius frowned. 'That's not what the prefect ordered, sir.'

'It doesn't matter what he told you. General Corbulo has put me in command of the baggage train.'

Mardonius looked doubtful.

'For fuck's sake,' Macro growled as he flipped open his sidebag and took out Corbulo's authority, thrusting it at the other officer. 'Read this.'

Mardonius stepped forward and examined the wax tablet and the seal. 'Looks real enough. I'll get the wagons turned round.'

'Good man. Once they're on the move, drive them hard and get to the ford and across the river as quick as you can.'

'Yes, sir.' Mardonius made to turn away, but Macro called him back.

'One other thing. Have your men ready to cover the rear of the baggage train.'

Mardonius cocked an eyebrow. 'You think someone's planning to attack us?'

'Better to be safe than royally buggered up,' Macro replied. 'Get moving.'

As the centurion trotted over to the leading wagons to give the order to turn about, Macro wheeled his horse towards the crags and urged it into a canter as he ordered Spathos and his men to follow him. He looked up to the ridge where he had seen the horsemen in the distance, but they had gone, and that added to his growing unease. Following the curve of the road as it passed beneath the crags, it occurred to him that if the baggage train was going to be ambushed anywhere, here was where it would have been most vulnerable. A handful of men on the heights above would be able to roll boulders down onto it, or shoot fire arrows with impunity. Fortunately, the prefect had halted the wagons before they had entered the killing ground.

Round the corner of the crags, the valley began to open up into rolling terrain studded with copses of cedar trees and outcrops of rock through which the road snaked. From the slightly higher ground Macro could see the Syrian auxiliaries marching just over a mile ahead, and no more than half a mile further on lay the rebel camp. He had been expecting the usual makeshift affair constructed by irregular soldiers, and was surprised to see a fortified position on the crest of a small hill. A palisade surrounded the camp, where perhaps twenty or so round huts had been erected. He could even make out the figures of the defenders, too few to hold out against Orfitus and his auxiliaries. Perhaps he had misjudged the situation, thought Macro. Maybe the prospect of being responsible for the baggage train was making him unnecessarily anxious.

He continued down the road at a canter, keen to catch up with the Syrians and get the anticipated confrontation with Orfitus dealt with. He soon lost sight of the cohort and the enemy's camp, and thereafter only caught glimpses of them through the trees and when the road passed over higher ground. Then, as he rode out from a thick belt of cedar trees, he was presented with a clear view of the scene scarcely a quarter of a mile off as the cohort deployed into line just out of arrowshot of the camp. The rebels were shouting their defiance and brandishing weapons from behind the palisade. Macro estimated that there were no more than twenty of them. They could not hope to hold out for long against the auxiliaries, and would soon be paying for their defiance with their lives.

Prefect Orfitus was sitting on his horse beside the colour party as he directed the preparations for the attack, and Macro led his men over the open ground towards him. As they became aware of the riders' approach, Orfitus and his centurions turned to watch, as did some of the men, until their optios bawled at them to face front.

'Why, it's Centurion Macro.' Orfitus greeted him with a nod. 'What on earth brings you here? As it happens, you are just in time to witness the crushing of this rebel nest. I trust you will enjoy the spectacle, and Corbulo too, when you report back to him.'

Macro glanced over the men around the prefect. 'Which one of you is Thermon?'

'He's not here,' Orfitus answered. 'He's scouting further ahead, in case there are any more of the enemy skulking out there who might be tempted to intervene in our attack on their camp.'

'Scouting? I hope you're right, sir. But I'm not sure we'll be seeing Thermon again.'

'Why?' A look of suspicion appeared on the prefect's face. 'What are you implying?'

Macro did not want to be drawn on the matter. There would be time to deal with the guide later on. There was no easy way to announce the purpose of his presence, so he simply took out his authority and handed it over. 'From the general, sir.'

Orfitus opened the wax tablet and read the contents quickly, then once again at a more measured pace as his expression fixed in a frown. He closed it and looked up at Macro as he returned the document.

'You're being put in command of my cohort? You?'

'Yes, sir.'

'But you're just a bloody centurion. That's impossible.'

'Nevertheless, those are the general's orders, sir. As Optio Phocus will confirm.'

Orfitus glanced at the optio. 'Is this true?'

'Yes, sir,' Phocus replied uncomfortably. 'He asked me to confirm it in person.'

'It's a bloody outrage.' Orfitus shook his head. 'I protest. I'll report this to the emperor himself.'

'Do that if you wish, sir, but meanwhile we are both serving under the command of General Corbulo and we are obliged to obey his orders. Therefore I *am* taking over the cohort.'

'No . . . no, you are not. I refuse to accept this.'

'Sir, there is no time for this now. You can make your complaint later, but as of this moment, you and your cohort are under my command.'

Orfitus glared, and then laughed. 'Ridiculous!'

Macro cleared his throat and spoke loudly and clearly so that the entire cohort could hear him. 'I am Centurion Lucius Cornelius Macro. By the authority of General Corbulo I am now your commanding officer. Decurion Spathos!'

'Sir!'

'Have two of your men escort the prefect back to the baggage train.'

As Spathos chose his men and they trotted forward, Macro spoke quietly to Orfitus. 'Please go quietly, sir. Or I'll order them to tie your hands to the saddle and gag you.'

The prefect's jaw worked furiously for an instant before he replied through gritted teeth. 'I don't care what it takes, or how long, but you will pay for this, Macro. No one humiliates me like this and gets away with it. I swear it by Jupiter, Best and Greatest.'

Macro nodded to the two cavalrymen. 'Take him away.'

Sitting stiffly in his saddle, Orfitus tugged his reins and spurred his horse into a trot as he made for the road. His escorts hurried after him and took up station on either side. Macro let out a relieved sigh and then turned his attention to the rebel camp. The shouting had died away and there was only one man still behind the palisade. He carried a standard, which he waved slowly from side to side so that the red streamer fixed to the tail of a red lion rippled in the light breeze blowing off the hills. Then he turned and disappeared from view.

'What now?' Macro muttered.

His query was answered by the faint drumming of hoofs, and the optio on the extreme right of the auxiliary line called out, 'They're running for it!'

Macro turned to look. At first he saw nothing. Then the standard appeared beyond the slope below the camp, followed by a party of riders galloping towards the road and then making their escape along it, away from the Romans.

'Shall I chase the bastards down, sir?' Spathos asked easily.

'No,' Macro replied. 'Their mounts are fresh. You'd never catch 'em. We'll have to let them go for—'

He was interrupted by the faint sound of a horn from behind them, and tugged his reins to turn his mount towards the sound. 'That's coming from the baggage train.'

Optio Phocus looked at him. 'What is it, sir?'

'How in Hades would I know?' Macro snapped. He drew a sharp breath and bellowed his orders. 'Fourth Syrian! Form column on the road! At the double! Spathos, take your men and ride back and report on what you see. Oh, and keep Orfitus with you when you catch up with him.'

'Yes, sir!' Spathos wheeled his men around and the squadron raced back along the road towards the crags.

As the auxiliaries tramped back to the road, Macro scanned the sides of the valley and saw that they were being watched by a cluster of horsemen on the ridge, close to where he had seen the earlier group. The same men, he reasoned. But there was no one else, and the only sign of trouble was the occasional blast of a distant horn. It did not have the characteristic flat blare of a Roman instrument, and that caused him to fear the worst. When the cohort was ready, he was tempted to give the order to close up, but the need to return to the baggage train outweighed the marginal advantage of being in tight formation in the case of a sudden ambush.

'Fourth Syrian . . . at the quick step, advance!'

They set off, marching swiftly back towards the crags, with Macro at the head of the column, constantly scrutinising the treeline for any sign of danger as he fretted about the fate of the baggage train. They had gone just over a mile when he saw Spathos and his men, together with Orfitus, galloping back towards them. Beyond, a dark column of smoke smeared the grey sky beyond the crags. Any remaining doubt that Macro had entertained about the trap that had been set for Prefect Orfitus faded and died at that moment. The rebel posing as a guide had carried out his part perfectly, luring away the bulk of the cohort and leaving the wagons and their precious contents vulnerable to a surprise attack. Macro swore an oath to himself that if they ever captured the guide and it was proven that he had once genuinely been a Roman soldier, then Thermon would die the lingering death worthy of such traitors.

'Keep marching!' he shouted to the centurion leading the first century of the cohort, and then spurred his mount forward to intercept Spathos. They met on a rise in a swirl of dust kicked up by the horses. At once the decurion thrust his arm in the direction of the baggage train. 'We're under attack, sir! There's hundreds of them!'

'How many?' Macro demanded. 'Calm yourself, man! How many do you estimate?'

Spathos drew a deep breath as he thought quickly. 'No more than a thousand.'

Orfitus edged his horse forward as he addressed Macro. 'You were right, Centurion. I was tricked. I—'

'Save that for later, sir.' Macro turned back to Spathos. 'Any cavalry?'

'Some, perhaps fifty. The rest are on foot.'

'Any Parthians? Or regulars?'

Spathos shook his head. 'I didn't see any.'

'That's something to be grateful for. What's the damage so far?'

'Several of the wagons are on fire. Most of the drivers and their teams have abandoned the rest. Some of them were fighting alongside groups of auxiliaries making a stand, but not many were left as far as I could make out.'

'Right.' Macro quickly considered what he'd been told. 'Listen, you've got to go back there and do your best to disrupt the attack.'

Spathos's eyes widened in alarm. 'What? With twenty men? We'll be cut down in a heartbeat, sir.'

'Not if you keep moving. Charge up and down the wagon line. Carve up as many as you can, but don't stop and get stuck in a melee or you will be finished. You have to break them up, distract them long enough for the Syrians to arrive. Do you understand?'

It was a harsh order, and the odds against the Macedonian cavalrymen surviving were overwhelming. But it was a necessary sacrifice, and the decurion nodded grimly. 'I understand, sir.'

'Then the gods be with you, brother. Go!'

Spathos turned to his men. 'Come on, boys! Rome's been paying us for long enough. Now it's time to earn all that silver! On me!'

Orfitus hesitated a moment then turned his horse and galloped after the others. Spathos quickened his pace to a canter, and his men followed him in a ragged column, heading for a fight they could not possibly win. Macro watched them briefly, then hurried back towards the Syrians.

'Pick up the pace, lads! Our comrades' lives depend on it!'

He set his horse to advance at a brisk walk, and the auxiliaries lengthened their stride to keep up as they approached the crags. By now, several columns of smoke were rising into the sky, and a dark pall hung over the valley on the far side of the rocky cliffs. As they followed the curve around the base of the crags, they could clearly hear the sounds of the struggle: the strident blasts of horns, choruses of war cries from the rebels, and the crackle and dull roar of flames.

Ahead, the valley began to open out again, and Macro was presented with a vista of burning wagons closer to, while those further off were as yet undamaged and still in harness. Towards the rear, a gap had opened up where those wagons that had been turned round were making for the fork that led to the river crossing. And teeming around the head of the baggage train were hundreds of men clad in furs and assorted helmets, breastplates and weapons. Spathos's squadron, Orfitus amongst them, were charging back up either side of the road, still led from the front by the decurion. Macro frowned. There was no sign of the enemy horsemen that Spathos had reported shortly before.

A rumble and a loud crack followed by a cry of alarm sounded from behind, and Macro turned just as a boulder and a shower of smaller rocks and loose soil smashed down amid the ranks of the leading Syrian cohort crushing two of the auxiliaries. The nearest men stumbled aside in shock and the entire column shuffled to a halt.

'Look out!' a voice cried out as another, smaller lump of rock tumbled down from the top of the crag, and this time the men had enough warning to scatter from its path as it smashed down onto the road. As more rocks of different sizes fell down the face of the cliff, Macro strained his neck to look up, and saw a figure far above directing men out of sight. Jerking the reins, he steered his horse away from the crags and onto the open ground beside the road. Another boulder caught three men from one of the other centuries who failed to move fast enough as it deflected off an outcrop and swept them away.

'Get off the bloody road!' Macro bellowed. 'Off the road, you fools!'

The order was echoed by the centurions and optios as the auxiliaries ran from the boulders crashing down amongst them. Macro saw at least ten bodies in the eddies of dust that had been thrown up by the impact of the rocks. It was fortunate that no more men had been crushed, but the real damage had been done. The cohort had been stopped, and was now retreating from the road in a disorganised mass.

He pointed to the standard-bearer. 'You, get on me and hold that thing as high as you can . . . Fourth Syrian! Re-form! Behind the standard. Quickly, boys!'

Cajoled and sworn at by their officers, the auxiliaries began to form up in their centuries again, many men watching anxiously as more rocks were hurled down. But they were out of range now, and as soon as the rebel Macro had seen realised that no more damage was being done, he shouted an order to his men and ducked out of sight. Freed from the fear of being crushed by boulders, the auxiliaries took their places, though Macro could see that many of them were shaken by the attack.

As the last few men fell in, he calmly called out the order to resume the advance, and the column continued forward, making for the blazing wagons at the head of the baggage train. Only a handful of rebels remained close by, looting the bodies of the auxiliaries and drivers, and darting in towards the burning wagons to snatch anything that might be of value. But as soon as they became aware of the approach of the rest of the cohort, they turned and ran to catch up with their comrades attacking the other wagons and using torches to set them alight.

Macro passed the first of the bodies lying in the long grass either side of the road, rebels and auxiliaries bearing bloody wounds. Many still lived, and while the rebels tried to crawl out of the path of the oncoming cohort, the Syrian wounded begged them for help.

'Leave them!' Macro shouted as an auxiliary in the First Century broke ranks and made to help one of his comrades. 'Get back in line!'

There was no time to stop. The destruction of the baggage train had to be halted. He glanced at the nearest burning wagon and picked out the frame of a catapult amid the hungry orange flames. He felt a leaden despair weigh down his heart at the sight. There would be little, if anything, left of the siege train even if they succeeded in driving the rebels off. And that would mean that Corbulo would no longer be able to smash a breach in the walls of Thapsis for his men to assault. Instead, he would be forced to abandon the siege or spend the coming winter months starving the town into surrender.

They were drawing closer to the mass of rebels surrounding the surviving wagons, and some of the leaders were trying to arrange their men into a battle line to counter the threat. Macro closed to within a hundred paces of the enemy without any arrows or slingshot being unleashed in his direction. Then he halted the cohort and ordered them to form a line across the road as Spathos, Orfitus and the ten remaining riders charged out from the rebel swarm and galloped over to join the Syrians. Macro could see that their mounts were blown, and ordered them to form up behind the auxiliaries to act as a last reserve. The optios called the time as the centuries alternated turning to the left and right. A gap was left, wide enough to keep clear of the burning wagons. When the last man was in position, Macro took his place with the colour party. He thought of dismounting to fight with the men, but he knew that his place was in the saddle, where he had an overview of proceedings and could keep control of the auxiliaries.

'Fourth Syrian! Draw swords!'

There was a ragged din of scraping and rasping as the short swords were pulled from their scabbards and held level at waist height, points protruding ahead of the line of oval shields like steel teeth. The nearest of the rebels fell silent at the sight and a hush settled over this part of the battlefield as Macro drew his own sword and raised it high for a beat before sweeping it down to point at the enemy. 'Advance!'

The five centuries edged forward with the optios calling the time, holding their staffs out to mark the line. Four deep, it rolled onwards, and the rebel leaders shouted at their followers to make ready, shoving forward those too nervous or stupefied by battle to respond swiftly enough to their orders. Soon a rough formation stood ready to receive the Syrians.

From the saddle, Macro could see over the enemy. Nearly

a mile beyond, the rear third of the baggage train was on the move, covered by the survivors of the Sixth Century and the wagon crews, who had armed themselves with whatever weapons were at hand. In between the two Roman forces, the rebels were looting the abandoned wagons and unhitching the draught animals before driving them towards the nearest trees. Men with torches moved from wagon to wagon setting fire to the contents, and more columns of smoke curled into the air. Macro felt sickened as he watched the siege train being consumed by flames. All that could be saved now was what remained of the supplies.

The gap between the two lines closed, and he could see the auxiliaries instinctively hunching slightly lower behind their shields as they neared the enemy. One of the rebels gave a loud cry, hefted a throwing spear and hurled it at the Romans. The point glanced off a shield and sliced through the thigh of the adjacent man. He slowed briefly before continuing his advance, blood flowing down his leg. More missiles were thrown, and two of the Syrians went down, their places hurriedly taken by the men marching behind them. At the last moment, some of the more courageous rebels charged forward with wild cries and hurled themselves at the Roman shield line in a series of thuds and clatters. There was no longer any need to maintain a rigid line, nor was it possible, and the optios dropped back behind their centuries to make sure none of the men tried to retreat as the intensity of the fighting began to unnerve the more anxious amongst them.

As ever, the wild fervour of irregulars was no match for the training and battle tactics of even an auxiliary unit like the Fourth Syrian, and the short swords began their deadly work in the tight press of bodies along the battle line. The rebels' assorted spears, long swords and clubs were difficult to wield effectively, and soon the Roman line was moving steadily forward, leaving scores of fallen men in their wake, the wounded finished off by the rear ranks of auxiliaries as they passed over them. Several of the Syrians had also been killed or wounded, and those who could still walk followed on as best they could. The others had to be abandoned where they lay, hoping that their comrades might return for them after the fight was over.

It did not take long for the enemy's spirit to crumble as they were relentlessly pushed back and cut down. Macro saw the first rebels creeping away from the rear, then more turned and fell back. One man started to run, and at once others followed suit, and then whole sections of the battle line were breaking away and fleeing from the auxiliaries.

'They're bolting, lads!' Macro cried out, brandishing his sword. 'Keep going! Drive the bastards back!'

The cohort was pressing forward more quickly, and the very last of the rebels still willing to stand and fight was run through and then stabbed in the side. His body jerked as the blades were wrenched free, and he collapsed to his knees and was kicked onto his back as the Roman line passed over him. They advanced over open ground without any further resistance, passing the first of the wagons that had not yet been set on fire, though the mules had been killed in their traces as there had been no time to drive them off. Further on, Macro could see that some of the wagons were still hitched to surviving animals. He rode along the back of the cohort to the century closest to the road, then reined in and ordered the centurion to assign men to each intact wagon with harnessed animals they passed, and instruct them to turn the wagons round to follow the cohort towards the fork in the road.

The bulk of the rebel force, still reeling from their rough

handling by the auxiliaries, had fallen back to the foot of the slope leading up to the ridge. From the safety of their position they watched the Roman line pass by nearly a quarter of a mile away. The rest were taking what they could from abandoned wagons and carts before the cohort reached them, and further off, more were harassing the remnants of the baggage train still in Roman hands as they rumbled back along the road. Macro saw the rebel leaders riding along the front of the main force, rallying their men for another attack.

'Sir! Behind us!' Spathos cried out.

Macro twisted in his saddle and looked back. A large party of mounted men was picking its way down the steep slope beside the crags. The same men who had unleashed the boulders onto the Syrian cohort. There were at least fifty of them, more than enough to present a real threat to the cohort in its current formation, Macro realised. With luck they would not descend quickly enough to join the fight before Macro's men reached the safety of the defile. The line had served its purpose, and the cohort needed to move more quickly if it was to protect what was left of the baggage train.

'Fourth Syrian! Halt!' Macro barked. 'Form column!'

The officers realised the need to act swiftly, and doubled their men across the open ground as the auxiliaries re-formed behind their standards a short distance from the road. Macro ordered Spathos and the other mounted men to form up behind him, and led the way to the head of the column. As they waited for the change in formation to be completed, Orfitus edged his mount closer to Macro.

'This may go down as one of the shortest tenures of command in the history of Rome.'

Macro looked at him sharply, but noted the dark humour in the other man's expression and responded with a wry grin. 'It's early days, sir. They haven't done for us yet. Your lads are doing well.'

'They're not my lads any more,' Orfitus conceded. 'And if they're acquitting themselves well, that's down to the training you gave them back at Tarsus.'

The men were ready to move, and there was no time to continue the exchange. Macro filled his lungs and gave the order to advance at the trot. It would fatigue the men, he knew, but it was vital that they close up on the wagons making for the river crossing. The air filled with the rumble of studded boots pounding across the ground, scabbards slapping at thighs as they went. They soon left behind the last of the burning wagons, and as they passed those still intact and harnessed to teams of oxen or mules, men peeled off to get them moving again. Whips cracked as the auxiliaries urged the ponderous vehicles forward, driving the draught animals on as fast as they could go as they struggled to keep pace with the rest of the cohort.

A hundred paces from the fork, Macro ordered the men to slow to a walk as they approached Optio Laecinus and what was left of his men, who had formed a thin line across the road. Behind them the supply wagons were turning right onto the road that led to the ford. A short distance from the fork, the thickly forested slopes of the hills on either side closed in. Macro sighed with relief. It would mean that the cohort would be able to cover the rear of the baggage train more easily than over open ground.

'Good man, Laecinus,' he said. 'You've done well to save as many wagons as you have.'

The optio had sheathed his sword and was tying a strip of cloth over a wound on his thigh. He completed the knot before he saluted. 'Have you seen my centurion, sir? Mardonius?'

Macro shook his head. 'He's gone. There were no survivors at the head of the column. You're in command of the Sixth Century now.'

'Centurion, they're on the move again,' said Orfitus.

The rebels were pacing back towards the road in a loose mass. Their leaders were shouting encouragement and waving their weapons, while horns blared a challenge to the Romans. Now that he had the chance to see the entire enemy force, Macro realised that Spathos's early estimate was wrong. There were at least fifteen hundred of the rebels, possibly more. They outnumbered the men of the cohort by three to one. He looked around quickly to gauge the situation and knew that the wagons driven by the auxiliaries would not reach the fork before the enemy. The rebels would have to be held off long enough for the train to enter the defile beyond the fork.

'Fourth Syrian! Halt! Left face!'

The auxiliaries turned towards the rebels as Macro gave his orders to Spathos. 'Decurion, do what you can to cover the wagons and keep them moving.'

'Yes, sir.'

'What about me?' asked Orfitus.

'Your choice, sir. Ride with Spathos, or fight here with your men.'

'Put like that, there is no choice,' Orfitus replied. He swung his leg over the saddle horns, dropped nimbly to the ground and handed the reins to one of Spathos's men. Then, seeing a shield close to the body of a rebel nearby, he picked it up and tested its weight.

'It'll do,' he muttered, and drew his sword. He exchanged a nod with Macro, then shouldered his way through the men of the First Century and took his place in the centre of the front rank.

'Well, now,' Macro mused. 'The lad's got an iron backbone sure enough.'

A loud, long blast sounded from one of the rebel horns and the rest joined in. The enemy's individual war cries swelled into an incoherent roar as the rebels rushed over the open ground towards the Romans.

'You've seen those bastards off once already, lads!' Macro called out. 'Give 'em another taste of Roman steel to finish the job!'

The auxiliaries prepared to receive the charge: front foot forward, rear foot set at an angle to brace the body as the men crouched a little to improve their balance. Shields swung round and the gaps between them closed up so there was just enough space to advance their short swords, ready to strike at the rebels. Macro nodded with satisfaction. They would never be as good as legionaries, still less his Praetorians, but they were far better than the men he had first met on the training ground at Tarsus.

The grim silence and stillness in the Roman ranks rarely failed to have an unsettling effect on an enemy, and Macro could see some of the rebels slowing as they allowed their more bloodthirsty comrades to reach the Syrians' shield wall first. The swiftest of the rebels charged home, slamming shield to shield or striking out with their weapons. Either way, they were quickly dispatched by the auxiliaries either side of the man they had targeted. More and more of them crashed into the cohort until the battle line was continuous and the deadly business of close combat began in earnest.

Watching from his saddle, Macro felt a hot surge sweep through his veins: the urge to throw himself into the fight. If Cato had been there and in command, he would not have hesitated. But today the responsibility fell on him, and he felt an instant's empathy for his friend who was so often weighed down by the burden of command. It was one thing to be a line officer; quite another to be a commanding officer with the fate of his men resting in his hands.

Glancing round, he watched the wagons rattle past behind the cohort. Only the last four had not yet reached the fork. Spathos and his men, their work done, turned and raced towards the left flank, where the rebels were already starting to spill round the end of the Fifth Century. The sight of the frothing mounts ridden by blood-streaked men with long cavalry swords was enough to send the rebels running, and the threat to the exposed flank passed. Once he was sure that his men were holding their own, Macro cupped a hand to his mouth to ensure that he was clearly heard over the cacophony of battle.

'Fourth Syrian! Prepare to fall back on my count!' Some dust caught in his throat and he coughed, spat to clear his airway and drew a deep breath. 'One! Two!'

The first instruction was to make ready, the second to step back. As he called out, the line stepped away from the enemy, and for a moment there was a gap, before the rebels surged forward to renew the struggle, beating wildly at the auxiliaries' shields and striking at any of the Roman soldiers who exposed their bodies. As Macro called the time, the cohort steadily retreated on the fork and then backed down the route leading to the ford, the slopes of the vale closing in on either side. Too late, the enemy realised that the moment had passed to seal victory. No longer would their superior numbers count in their favour as the Roman flanks were protected by the dense undergrowth beneath the trees.

As the gap between the belts of trees narrowed Macro pulled his flank centuries in, one at a time, until only two centuries stretched between the treeline either side of the road. Keeping one of the freed-up centuries in reserve, he ordered the others to fall back half a mile before forming a new line of defence. Once they were marching off, he turned his attention to the fighting raging across the narrow strip of ground between the trees. Both sides were tiring. Their blows were struck with laboured effort, and there was a perceptible reluctance for men to step into the place of a fallen comrade, or to renew a duel once they had stepped back to avoid a thrust. Now was the time to strike a mortal blow, Macro decided.

'Fourth Syrian! Halt! Prepare to advance!'

Some of the men in the rearmost ranks looked towards him in surprise and anxiety, but obeyed the order. Already he saw the doubt in the expressions of the nearest rebels and knew that his instinct had been right.

'Advance!'

The auxiliaries took a pace forward, punching out their shields and stabbing into the enemy's tightly packed bodies. It was the work of a moment for the rebels' fear to spread through their ranks like a wave, and as if of one will, they broke contact with the Syrian cohort and drew back, rapidly widening the gap between the two sides. The auxiliaries continued to advance, stepping over the bodies sprawled across the ground before them, pausing to stab at wounded rebels. Macro let them continue for twenty paces before he called a halt and ordered the century held in reserve to turn about and march off down the road.

As the sound of their boots crunching on the grit and packed earth faded, a quiet calm fell over the two forces still facing each other across the stretch of beaten-down grass splashed with blood and littered with bodies and discarded shields. Macro fully expected the enemy to sound their horns and charge again, but they had already lost many men and there was little resolve to continue the battle.

One of their leaders, however, still had fire in his belly and strode out into the open, advancing to within fifteen paces of the Roman line. Then he spread his arms wide, spear in one hand, shield in the other, and shouted a challenge at his enemy.

'Hold your ground,' Macro warned his men. 'No one moves against that bastard unless I say so.'

The rebel thrust the point of his spear towards Macro and repeated his challenge, with unmistakable contempt in his voice, but Macro merely stared back as he growled.

'Don't tempt me . . .'

Then he cleared his throat and called out in a hoarse voice, 'Second Century, about turn and fall back!'

As they withdrew, then formed column and marched away, Macro ordered the First Century to fall back too, until the trees drew close enough on either side to cover their flanks. Then they halted again. But there was no attempt by the enemy to follow them. Not even the man who had issued the challenge to Macro moved. He simply stood glaring as his enemy moved off. Before the trees closed in, Macro took one last look along the road. Burning and abandoned wagons stood in a line reaching out towards the distant crags. The rebels might have failed in their bid to destroy the entire baggage train and its escort, but they had done great harm to General Corbulo's chances of taking Thapsis before winter came to the mountains.

'First Century, form column!'

The sixty-odd survivors of the unit moved quickly from line to column before Macro gave the order to quick-march down the road. As Orfitus passed by, the two men exchanged a glance and a brief nod of mutual respect. The prefect had shown plenty of guts, thought Macro, but that would count for very little when he had to account to General Corbulo for the loss of the siege train and many of the supply wagons, and both men knew it.

Macro remained alone for a moment, staring back at the enemy and the devastation they had wreaked. Then he tugged the reins, gently wheeled his mount around and trotted after his men.

CHAPTER TWENTY

'Wait here,' Haghrar ordered as two crewmen slid the boarding ramp out from the side of the barge and onto the quay that stretched for over two hundred paces along the bank of the Euphrates. Trading vessels of all sizes were tied up alongside as gangs of stevedores toiled to unload and load their cargoes. On the far side of the quay lay a row of warehouses backing onto the wall of the town of Tanassur, which thrived from taxing the trade that flowed up and down the Euphrates and the camel caravans that came from Seleucia on the Tigris, carrying spices and silks for the markets of the Roman Empire.

In other circumstances, the sights, sounds and scents all around him would have excited Cato's senses, but he largely ignored them as he stepped between the Parthian noble and the boarding ramp.

'Wait for what, exactly?'

'Instructions from the king. I will speak with the governor of the town. He may have received instructions from Vologases.'

'And if he hasn't? What then?'

'Then you will wait here in Tanassur while I send a messenger to Ctesiphon to ask for further instructions.'

'How long will that take?'

'Two days at the most.'

That was not as long as Cato had feared. 'Very well.'

'Do you mind?' Haghrar indicated the boarding ramp, and Cato moved aside to let the Parthian step ashore. He paused on the quay to look back. 'I have your word that you and your men will not leave the ship? Nor make any attempt at escape?'

'You have my word; besides, where would we go? It's hundreds of miles to the frontier. We wouldn't get very far even if we tried.'

'All the same, don't step off the ship. I've left orders with my men not to permit it.'

'I have given you my word,' Cato reminded him pointedly.

Haghrar nodded and then turned to stride across the quay, dodging out of the way of a string of heavily laden camels before entering the town's gate and disappearing from view.

It was approaching noon, and already the crowd along the wharf was thinning as people went to find shelter from the sun. Cato moved to the bows of the barge, where a linen awning had been erected between the mast and the stem to provide shade for the crew and passengers. Apollonius and the Praetorians were sitting against the side rail, facing the river, so that they had a good view of the wharf. The Parthians and the crew sat opposite. Despite having fought off the pirates together only a few days before, the two groups had kept to themselves and regarded each other with wary suspicion, such was the long-standing enmity between Rome and Parthia.

Cato eased himself into the middle of the deck and lay back against a large coil of rope with his hands behind his head.

'I must say, given that Haghrar may well return from the governor bearing orders to kill us, you seem very calm,'

Apollonius commented as he wiped some dust from his flute and blew an experimental note, which came out flat.

'Would it make any difference if I wasn't?' Cato responded drily. 'Our fate is in the hands of the gods. Well, Vologases at any rate. We'll know his decision soon enough.'

'And what do you think his decision will be?'

'I think he will at least want to hear what we say. He's got nothing to lose from doing that.'

'But will he think there is anything to gain after we have presented Corbulo's terms, I wonder?' Apollonius paused briefly. 'On reflection, it might be wise for you to consider what you say, as well as how you say it, if we are to have the best chance of surviving this mission.'

Cato opened his eyes and turned towards the agent. 'What are you suggesting?'

Apollonius stretched his shoulders and shuffled closer, lowering his voice. 'I am suggesting that you might want to think about tailoring what you say to suit your audience. The priority is getting a peace agreement with Parthia. We both know that the king will never concede to all of Corbulo's demands, so the solution is obvious. Only make demands you know he *will* agree to. Then we draw up and agree the treaty and take it back to Tarsus.'

'What's the point?' Cato demanded. 'You know damn well that Corbulo won't accept a treaty based on anything less than the terms he has stated. Even if he did, he would have to refer it to Rome. The Senate and Nero are even less likely to go along with it.'

'Of course, but by the time Nero responds to Corbulo and the general communicates the response from Rome to Vologases, the best part of a year will have passed. A year in which Corbulo will have had the chance to further strengthen and equip the army for war with Parthia. Tribune, you know that as long as Rome and Parthia exist, there will always be conflict between them. But if Corbulo is in a position to crush Parthia decisively, there will be peace on the eastern frontier.'

'So you think I should betray my honour and lie to King Vologases in order to get a peace agreement I know will not be accepted by Rome? Is that what you are saying?'

Apollonius gave a slight smirk. 'I would say that is a succinct summary of the situation.'

'Ye gods,' Cato muttered. 'What depths of cynicism will you not sink to? You spies are every bit as conniving as the most base politician in Rome.'

Apollonius's smirk faded. 'You soldiers really do think your shit smells better than other people's, don't you? What is politics but the continuation of war by different means? We fight with whatever weapons come to hand, but we all serve the interests of Rome. For an intelligent man, you can be woefully short-sighted at times.' He spoke with a hard-edged tone that Cato had not heard before. 'Think it through, Tribune. We cannot negotiate a peace with Parthia on Corbulo's terms. He knew that when he set them out. And he will be able to present those terms to Rome to prove that he was not being weak. So he has covered his back as far as the emperor is concerned. Your true purpose here is not to make peace but to buy time. You must keep the negotiations going as long as possible, and then agree a treaty you know will not be honoured. And if you do that, then you, I and the men of your escort get to live. If, however, you stick by the word of Corbulo's demands, the negotiations will collapse swiftly and Vologases will have our heads.'

'So you are telling me to lie.'

'Like I said, we use whatever is available. A lie is just another weapon at our disposal. You do what you must to get Vologases to agree a peace treaty, and you get us out of Parthia alive. Those are the only things that matter; that is the truth, and you know it.'

Cato gave a bitter chuckle. 'Truth? That is a word that sits very poorly in your mouth. Your kind seem to think that the truth is the same as not being caught in a lie.'

Apollonius's eyes narrowed fractionally. 'Climb down from your pedestal, Tribune. Despite what you think, you are no better than any other man if you let yourself be blinded by self-regard for whatever principles you think you stand for.'

Before Cato could respond, the agent moved back to the side of the deck and picked up his wineskin, taking a slug before lowering his head and closing his eyes, as if in rest.

As the midday sun beat down, the quay was largely deserted. On board the barge, most of the men under the awning were asleep, and the air was filled with the dull buzz of flies and the rhythmic rumble of snoring. Even though his eyes were closed, however, Cato was awake and thinking through his earlier exchange with Apollonius. Much as he hated to admit it, even to himself, there was some merit in what the agent had said. What disturbed him, however, was the feeling that the real purpose of the embassy had never been to make peace with Parthia. Corbulo's line was that it was worth making an effort to get a treaty, and Cato had believed him. Indeed, he had hoped that he might successfully appeal to whatever humanitarian instinct dwelled within the heart of King Vologases. After all, what sane man would wish a costly war with an unpredictable outcome on his empire if it could be avoided? Cato fully understood that he was something of an idealist, and that such a thought was an abstraction at best, and a dangerous delusion at worst. In real life, those men fated to rule empires did not subscribe to the same set of values as those they ruled. What did the lives of thousands of their subjects matter to the likes of Vologases or Nero? Even so, he had still believed he might win the Parthian king round to a different way of viewing relations with Rome, and persuade him that peaceful coexistence might at least be contemplated.

'What a fool I am,' he whispered to himself in a burst of shameful self-awareness.

He opened his eyes quickly to glance from side to side in case his words had been heard, but no one stirred. The only other man awake was one of the Parthians, a black-skinned man with yellow eyes who was thumbing gleaming beads along a string to help him concentrate and ward off drowsiness. He stared at Cato briefly but showed no other reaction, and Cato closed his eyes again as he continued following his train of thought.

Very well, he reflected, the embassy was little more than a ruse to buy more time for Rome to prepare for war. There had only ever been the possibility of a fragile peace. In which case it was Cato's duty to get himself and his men out of Parthia safely, however that was achieved.

The sound of approaching footsteps on the quay interrupted his rumination; a moment later, he heard boots on the gangway and sat up. Haghrar had returned at the head of a squad of spearmen dressed in flowing green robes. Their officer was armed with a sword and wore a gleaming black breastplate inlaid with silver stars and the design of a rearing horse. As the spearmen jumped down onto the deck with a series of thuds, those sleeping under the awning stirred and blinked, looking over at the men fanning out across the deck. The last of the spearmen was followed by two men in green tunics carrying a studded chest. Haghrar and the officer stepped

268

forward as Cato and the others under the awning scrambled to their feet.

'What's the meaning of this?' asked Cato, gesturing towards the soldiers. He felt a cold dread in his guts that they had been sent to kill him and his men.

'Tribune Cato, this is Ramalanes, a captain of the royal palace guard.' Haghrar gestured to the officer. 'He was waiting at the governor's palace and has been ordered to escort the embassy to the capital. There are horses being saddled to take us to the Tigris, where we will cross the river to reach Ctesiphon.'

Cato squinted out into the bright sunlight. 'What? Now?'

'At once,' Ramalanes cut in, addressing Cato in Greek. 'But first, you and your men will hand over your weapons and all your belongings. You may keep only your clothes and boots.'

Cato frowned. 'We are here on an embassy. We are not to be treated like prisoners. When Emperor Nero hears of this—'

'You are to do this at once.' Ramalanes spoke over the top of Cato's protest. 'Everything is to be placed in the chest. Do it now.'

He shouted an order to the men carrying the chest, and they set it down in front of the mast, slipping open the bolt and lifting the lid before standing erect on either side. For a moment, Cato was inclined to refuse, but his men were outnumbered and would be made short work of if the Parthians used force.

'Now,' Ramalanes insisted.

Cato sighed. 'Do as the man says, lads. All blades and other personal items in the chest. Let's be quick about it.'

The men hesitated, and Cato saw that they were looking to him for a lead on how to respond. Reaching for the scabbard and sword belt he had set down by his saddlebags close to the coiled rope, he picked up the bags in the other hand and approached the chest, laying everything inside. One by one his men followed suit, then returned to their positions under the awning. Apollonius was last, handing over his belongings, except his flute.

'I'd like to keep this,' he said.

'Everything,' Ramalanes ordered.

Apollonius reluctantly placed the flute in the chest and backed away.

Ramalanes looked them over and then pointed to Cato's equestrian ring. 'That too.'

'My ring?' Cato held up his hand. 'This is my sign of rank.'

'That is not my concern, Roman. I have my orders. A ring may conceal poison, to be used against my king or yourself. Take it off and put it in the chest.'

Cato shook his head, but did as he was told before rejoining his men. The chest was closed and the lock slid back into place, then Ramalanes shouted an order over the quay and some more of his men led a string of horses out from the shadows between two of the warehouses. He beckoned to Cato impatiently.

'Lead your men ashore, Roman.'

'My rank is Tribune, Parthian, and I am leading an embassy on behalf of Emperor Nero,' Cato blustered. 'You will treat me with the respect due to my station.'

Ramalanes looked to Haghrar, and the latter nodded delicately.

'Very well, Tribune,' he said with exaggerated deference. 'Please lead your men ashore.'

Cato turned to his men, most of who were grinning at the Parthian captain's discomfort; even those who spoke no Greek had followed the gist of the exchange. 'Let's go, boys. Back in the saddle.' He rubbed his buttocks, and the others, including

Apollonius, laughed as they stepped up onto the gangway and crossed over to the quay.

The Romans, including the wounded men, were made to mount a line of horses, with their escort positioned on each side. Haghrar took his place at the head of the column, alongside Cato and Ramalanes. The saddle on Cato's horse was not the sturdy kind used by the Roman cavalry, but a smaller, more comfortable affair, and he settled onto it gratefully. Then he saw the chest being carried from the barge.

'Where are you taking that?'

Ramalanes glanced in the direction Cato pointed. 'It will be carried behind us by mule, Tribune. Your weapons and belongings will be returned to you when my master orders it.'

'Make sure that they are. I will hold you responsible for anything that is missing.'

The Parthian captain scowled, then barked an order to his men and spurred his horse into a canter. The column clopped down the length of the quay and up the short ramp at the far end onto the riverbank. To their left, a tall wall ran around the town, while ahead lay a road striking out across a well-irrigated expanse of level ground. It was noticeably different to the mainly arid landscape of the upper Euphrates, and as they rode past numerous farms and villages, Cato began to appreciate where the wealth and power of Parthia derived from. Not only were there rich farming lands, but the revenue from the trade that passed through Vologases' realms must deliver vast sums of gold and silver. There was considerable truth to the tales of Parthian treasure that were bandied about in Rome.

Ramalanes led them on at a steady canter, mile after mile. The baking sun crossed the sky and shone behind them as the afternoon wore on. Then, as the shadows of their mounts lengthened on the road ahead, they reached a staging post with a large compound surrounded by stabling. Opposite the arched gateway was a long building constructed of mudbricks, above which was a terrace shaded by a roof made of loose palm fronds, such as Cato had seen on the banks of the Nile some years before.

As soon as they dismounted, the Romans were marched into a large room with a pile of sleeping mats in the corner; opposite, a simple bench over an open drain served as the latrine. As the last man entered, the door was closed and locked. Three windows high up on the wall provided illumination. There were no bars in the windows, and though the walls would have been easy enough to break through, Cato dismissed any thought of escape, since they would be unarmed and alone in the heart of the Parthian empire. Instead he ordered the men to get the sleeping mats out and rest. Apollonius took his to the far corner of the room, and sat hugging his knees and staring into space with an anxious expression. In all the time he had known the agent, Cato had never seen him in such a subdued mood.

After they had been brought food and water, Cato went round the men exchanging comments and jokes before he made his way over to Apollonius.

'You look worried.'

'I am worried. Much hangs on whether Vologases will negotiate with you.'

'So we agreed, back on the ship. Is there anything else that concerns you, and that I should be told about?'

'If there is, you'll find out soon enough.'

Cato squatted on his haunches. 'What in Hades is that supposed to mean? Spit it out, man, before I have to wring it out of you.'

The agent regarded him closely, then shrugged. 'It's nothing.

I just don't like being held prisoner. Bad memories. But that's a tale for another day.'

'A true tale, or a false one?'

Apollonius pushed a half-eaten bowl of stew to one side and lay down on his side. 'Get some rest, Tribune. You'll need a fresh mind when we reach Ctesiphon.'

'I swear, by all the gods, if you weren't on our side, I'd have stuck a blade between your ribs long ago,' Cato growled, then stood up and walked back to his bedroll.

After the nights sleeping on the deck of the trading vessel, the cell was stifling, and sleep did not come easily for most of the men. Cato pretended to fall asleep quickly in order to let them think he was not concerned in the least by their situation. Some of the others sat and talked for a while; they were unable to play dice, since even those had been taken from them. At length, when all the Praetorians had finally gone to sleep, Cato raised his head to look over at Apollonius, and saw by the faint glow of moonlight coming through the window that the agent was sitting up again, hugging his knees and slowly rocking.

They were woken at first light and escorted out into the yard, where flatbread and a hunk of cold mutton were pressed into each man's hands to eat while the horses were saddled. Then Ramalanes ordered the Romans and his own men to mount and led the party out of the gate and back onto the road, riding hard.

Even with a comfortable saddle, Cato's aches and sore rump from the previous day grew more disagreeable with every mile. After stopping at another station at noon, they were fed again and given water while fresh horses were made ready, and then set off again. It was at dusk that they first sighted Seleucia in the distance. A vast city spread out along the bank of the Tigris opposite, it was over half the size of Rome, Cato estimated. Beyond the city walls he could make out the outlines of the roofs of Hellenistic temples and public buildings, and in the centre of the city, a sprawling acropolis that dwarfed the one in Athens.

By the time they reached the city, night had fallen. The watchmen passed them through the gate the moment they made out the uniforms of the guards of the royal palace. There were still plenty of people and carts on the streets, and even though the main thoroughfare was fully thirty feet across, Ramalanes was forced to slow his party to a walk as they made their way across the city, past the looming mass of the acropolis, and entered the huge open space of the agora, illuminated by torches and braziers. Crowds were gathered about street performers – acrobats, mime-players, bear-baiters and musicians – while philosophers spoke to their followers and would-be prophets spouted blandishments to the more gullible and desperate inhabitants of the city. As ever, Cato noted, the crowds attracted by false prophets were far larger than those attending to the wisdom of philosophers. As the horsemen neared the far side of the agora, one of the prophets, a man with bulging eyes and a weak chin, saw them and thrust his arm out, howling at them in Greek.

'See there! Romans! Prisoners of our King Vologases' brave soldiers. It is an omen. I, Mendacem Pharageus, foresee a great victory for our king and a shining future for Parthia!'

The crowd turned and jeered at the Romans, and some stooped to find clods of filth and turds to hurl at them. Several of the palace guards were struck as well, and Ramalanes rounded on the mob and drew his sword.

'Enough, you dogs!' he yelled. 'Stop, or I'll have the head of the next fool who throws any more filth!' He turned to the prophet. 'And you, Pharageus, have spouted enough shit yourself for one day. Begone before I have you thrown into the Tigris!'

Pharageus needed no further warning. He jumped down off his stool, gathered up the coins that had been thrown at his feet and scurried off across the agora. Ramalanes sheathed his sword and steered his horse back alongside Cato's. 'My apologies, Tribune. The city is plagued by such rabble-rousers at the moment.'

'We have them in Rome as well, I am sad to say.'

They left the agora and followed the avenue down to the wharf that ran along the bank of the Tigris for over half a mile. Hundreds of ships and lesser craft were moored alongside, while beyond, the broad expanse of the Tigris flowed gently past the city. A half-moon hung low in the sky, and the ripples on the surface of the great river shimmered like a band of leaping sardines. The outline of the far bank was clearly visible in the pale light, and the flicker of torches glinted here and there along its length.

Ramalanes turned upriver, and after riding another two hundred yards, they passed through a wall stretching across the wharf and dismounted. A flight of stone steps led down to a pier jutting into the river, where a large barge was moored. A torch burned from a bracket fixed above the bow. At the sight of the horsemen, the crew stirred from where they had been sitting along the pier and took their places in the wide-beamed craft.

'Down there,' the Parthian captain instructed. 'In the boat.'

They boarded the barge, and the crew shoved off from the pier and settled to their oars as the current began to take the vessel downriver. Then, under the orders of the man at the tiller, they lowered the oars and began to row in unison, and the barge lurched away from the west bank and out across the dark water. Cato was seated next to Haghrar on a bench facing aft, so that he could see more and more of the vast expanse of Seleucia as they pulled away.

'It is a fine city, is it not?' said Haghrar. 'Even Rome cannot match such a spectacle, nor its wealth.'

Cato said nothing, but he now understood why he had been led through the city to the wharf, rather than round the wall. The route had been chosen to impress upon him the power and riches of Parthia.

The hubbub of Seleucia faded behind them, and soon there was just the creak of the oars in their rowlocks and the splash as the blades bit into the surface of the Tigris. Cato soon noticed that they were not making for the distant glimmer of Ctesiphon, but were instead steering towards what seemed to be a small town a short distance further downriver. He leaned closer to Haghrar.

'Where are we going? I thought the king was in Ctesiphon.'

'He has a palace there, but he spends most of his time at another palace on the river. That is where we are being taken.'

It took over an hour to cross the river, Cato estimated, and as they drew closer to the far bank, he began to make out some of the detail of the palace. There was a dock with several more barges, and beyond that an open pavilion where fires glittered. The sound of music and laughter carried out across the water to those on the boat. Some distance further from the bank rose the outline of a huge residence with many towers and domes, dark against the background of stars.

'Looks like quite a party going on there.' Cato pointed towards the pavilion.

Haghrar grunted. 'Our king is a man of the flesh, Tribune.

He enjoys wine and the company of women and other entertainments. But you'd do well not to underestimate him. His mind is as sharp as the edge of the finest sword.'

'I'll bear that in mind.'

The barge drew up against the dock with a light bump, and two crewmen leaped ashore to secure the bow and stern as the Romans and their Parthian escort climbed out. They were marched up from the dock onto the bank, and Cato saw that a broad path led directly towards the palace. On either side, immaculately tended gardens stretched out into the night. A hundred paces to his left was the pavilion, and now he could see the dais on one side where a golden divan overlooked the brightly illuminated guests as they feasted and enjoyed the music and entertainers. A figure was seated on the divan, gold cup balanced in hand, surveying the scene.

'I'll take my leave of you here, Tribune,' said Haghrar. 'I truly hope that we meet again one day soon. As friends.'

He held out his hand and they clasped wrists briefly.

'Perhaps I will see you in the palace over the next few days.'

'Perhaps.' Haghrar smiled quickly and then turned to stride off towards the pavilion.

'Let's move,' Ramalanes ordered, and the party tramped down the path towards the palace. A wall, fifteen feet high, emerged from the gloom, stretching out on either side of an arched gateway. As they waited to enter, Cato looked back towards the pavilion and saw a man climb the dais to bend towards the king's ear. Vologases nodded and beckoned, and then Haghrar stepped out from the crowd and bowed deeply before his master, before rising to speak and point in the direction of the palace. Vologases turned on his divan and glanced towards the party. Cato felt a thrill of excitement and anxiety about having arrived in the presence of King Vologases, the ruler of the empire that was the only remaining challenger to Rome in the known world.

The gate opened with a grating rumble, and Cato and his men were marched into the palace complex. He could see sentries patrolling the perimeter wall and there was nowhere to hide between this wall and the inner one, fifty feet away. Anyone attempting to escape across the open ground would be seen at once. Another gate stood opposite, and once they had passed through that, Ramalanes halted and pointed to Cato's men as he issued an order to the guards. They were ushered to one side amid curses and complaints from the Praetorians.

'What's going on?' Cato demanded.

'Your men are being taken to one of the barrack blocks. They will be kept there for the duration of the embassy.'

'If anything—'

Ramalanes raised a hand. 'They will be fed and well looked after, Tribune. My master has commanded it.'

Cato's anxiety eased. The command of the captain's master was a far better guarantee of the Praetorians' well-being than the warning of a tribune.

'And what of myself and my adviser?'

'I will take you to the quarters prepared for you in the palace.'

As the others were marched off, Ramalanes led Cato and Apollonius to the entrance to a long wing, where they climbed a wide flight of steps to a corridor stretching out towards the heart of the palace. Aside from guards posted at intervals along the corridor, there was no other sign of life, and the captain walked them a short distance before he stopped and indicated carved doors on either side.

'Your chambers. Your adviser to the left and you to the right, Tribune.'

He waved Apollonius towards his door and the agent opened it and paused on the threshold. 'Shall we speak later, sir?'

Cato nodded. 'After we have washed and eaten.'

'That is not permitted,' said Ramalanes. 'You are not to leave your chambers without asking for permission. That is my master's order.'

'And when do you think I may be able to have an audience with your master?'

'It is already decided, Tribune. You are to be taken before him at the second hour tomorrow morning.'

CHAPTER TWENTY-ONE

In the corner of the room stood an ivory-inlaid tub that had been filled with warm water even before he had entered. Beside it was a marble-topped stand where a brush, razor, mirror and jars of scent had been set out for him. On a shelf beneath was a neatly folded garment of finely spun wool. When Cato held it up, he saw that it was a long-sleeved tunic that dropped to his calves. A pair of sandals lay on the floor nearby. He draped the tunic on the end of the bed and looked round at the richly embroidered tapestries that hung on the walls, nodding to himself in appreciation of his surroundings. Vologases was treating him like an honoured guest for now, but there was no guarantee that such hospitality would survive Cato's attempt to negotiate a peace treaty.

As soon as he had stripped off and eased himself into the bath, a slave nipped into the room from a secret door behind one of the tapestries and picked up Cato's clothes, scurrying back the way he had come.

'Hey! You there!' Cato called after him. 'Put those down, damn you!'

He had only managed to get one leg out of the tub before the slave had disappeared behind the tapestry. It shimmered a moment, then all was still, the only sound the water slopping around inside the tub. Cato glared at the tapestry furiously for a moment before he eased himself back into the bath.

Later, as the water cooled, he got out and dried himself with a linen towel left out for him on a nearby stool, then dressed in the tunic and went through a curtained doorway to find himself on a balcony overlooking a courtyard garden washed in grey shades by the moonlight. A slight sound made him turn, and he saw a guard standing further along the balcony, watching him closely.

'So much for hospitality,' Cato muttered to himself. Vologases might well have prepared a finely gilded cage for him, but it was still a cage.

'A fine night.' Cato addressed the man in Greek, but the guard tapped his fingers against his lips and shook his head. Whether he had been ordered not to speak or had had his tongue cut out, Cato could not determine.

'Fair enough. No conversation then.'

Leaning his hands on the balustrade, he breathed in the scents rising from the garden as he examined the extent of the palace he could see. It was built on a scale that humbled the imperial palace in Rome. Having seen the streets and buildings of Seleucia, he could only guess at the wealth that poured into the coffers of King Vologases. His previous experience of Parthia had been confined to campaigns in the deserts and mountains of the disputed frontier between the two empires, and it was hard for him to equate the elusive bands of horse archers with the magnificence to be found in the heart of the empire.

The fabled wealth of Vologases was no myth, and Cato could imagine the avaricious gleam in the eyes of Rome's statesmen when he reported back after the embassy was concluded. There were riches to be won in Parthia that would dwarf those brought back by Pompey the Great and Sulla before him. But the same wealth could be used by Vologases to buy the loyalty and alliance of many kings, perhaps even those presently beholden to Rome. One thing was certain, Cato concluded. Any war with Parthia was a far greater challenge than the emperors and those who advised them could possibly imagine.

Ramalanes sent one of his men for them as the sun shone through the slats in the tall shuttered window of Cato's sleeping chamber. Cato was already awake and lying under a silk sheet on the most comfortable bed he had ever experienced. Even the bolster, also covered in silk, was of just the right softness to permit comfort while keeping his head at a comfortable angle. He stirred as the guard knocked on his door and entered the room without awaiting a reply, setting down some fresh clothes on the bench at the foot of the bed, next to Cato's own clothes, which had been washed and dried before being placed there while he slept.

'Excellency, you are to dress and accompany me at once.'

'Very well.' Cato sat up. 'Wait for me outside.'

The guard bowed and closed the door behind him. Cato swung his feet out of the bed and stared down at the clothes on the bench. The fine garments brought in by the guard made his plain army clothing look the dull, functional trappings of a peasant. And yet he sensed the shrewd manipulation of his mind that Vologases was attempting. First the display of wealth in Seleucia, and then a display of power as they were brought into the palace. Now the king was inviting him to plead his case for a treaty in the garb of a noble of the Parthian court.

He reached for his loincloth and fastened it securely before pulling his tunic over his head, then sat down to lace up his boots. A quick shave to remove several days' growth of stubble, and a brush of his hair to tame his curls, then he inspected himself in the polished bronze of the mirror. There would be no mistaking his appearance in the court of King Vologases. He was a Roman soldier through and through, and would carry himself with the self-assurance and pride that entailed.

When he stepped out into the corridor, he saw that Apollonius had chosen to wear Parthian robes. The agent shrugged. 'When in Parthia, do as Parthians do.'

They were taken to an anteroom, where they saw Haghrar sitting on one of the benches lining the walls. Opposite was a pair of doors constructed from a dark timber and inlaid with swirling flower designs of silver. Two guards armed with spears stood on either side. Haghrar looked up as they approached and raised a hand in greeting.

'I hope your accommodation was agreeable, Tribune.'

'Very, although I cannot answer for my men.'

'They have been well looked after, you have my word on it.'

Cato gestured towards the door. 'I take it that leads to the royal audience chamber?'

Haghrar nodded.

'Are we expected to see Vologases soon?'

'Hard to say. This is not the only anteroom. There are more arranged around the chamber. The king will deal with us according to the schedule determined by his chamberlain. I have no idea where we sit on that schedule.'

'Have you been summoned along with us, or separately?'

'I have no idea.'

Apollonius sat down on the bench a short distance from the

Parthian nobleman, while Cato began to pace across the room, hands clasped behind his back. Occasionally they heard voices from the far side of the door, but apart from a few snatches of Greek, the rest was in the Parthian tongue. He wondered what this delay in seeing him betokened.

An hour passed, during which the beam of light streaming through the window high up in the wall slowly angled down and bathed Cato in a golden hue. At length he stopped pacing and turned to Haghrar.

'Is it customary for embassies to be kept waiting for so long? You said there was a schedule.'

'The king keeps his own schedule,' Haghrar replied. 'All of us serve at his majesty's leisure.'

'I don't serve his majesty,' Cato pointed out.

'I don't think you understand, Tribune. Here in Parthia, the king is regarded as the absolute ruler of all men. All men. Including Romans. To Parthians, Rome is merely a land we have yet to conquer. In our eyes, that makes you a supplicant like any other.'

'Really?' Cato tugged his ear lobe. 'It's a small world indeed. That's precisely how Rome regards Parthia.'

Haghrar smiled sadly. 'Well, we can't both be right.'

'No. But if war comes, there's a chance we will find out who is.'

There was a soft scraping noise as the handle on the door turned and then it was drawn open by a guard on the far side, who spoke briefly to Haghrar.

'It's time,' Haghrar said to Cato as he rose from the bench. 'May the gods grant us the wisdom to find a way to avoid war.'

He led the way through the door into the audience chamber. A vast open space spread out before Cato, at least fifty paces long and as many across. Gilded pillars lined the walls and ran down the centre of the chamber. The high ceiling was painted deep blue and decorated with stars and a large crescent moon so that it looked like the night sky. The walls between the pillars were painted with depictions of lavish gardens and parks, as if the chamber was an open-sided pavilion set in the heart of some idyllic landscape. Palace guards were stationed around the edge of the room, and at one end was a large dais covered in furs. Upon it stood a golden throne with brilliant peacock feathers radiating out from the top. On the throne sat Vologases, in a bright green silken robe, a band of gold around his brow with a large emerald in a setting over his forehead. He appeared to be tall, and an immaculately trimmed beard outlined his strong jaw. There was an open space before the dais, around which his courtiers stood.

He did not spare a glance in their direction as Cato and the others entered the chamber, but directed his gaze at a man stripped to the waist with his arms pinioned by guards on either side. As they drew closer, Cato saw that the man's flesh was heavily bruised and scored with cuts and burns. The king spoke solemnly, and the man cried out before being silenced by a blow to the side of his head from one of the guards. Vologases continued speaking, and then waved him away contemptuously. The guards turned and dragged the man off, the courtiers parting to let them through.

A ponderous man with large jowls stepped up to the dais and read from a waxed tablet, then turned towards Cato and beckoned to him. The guard gave Cato a gentle nudge, and he stepped forward, with Apollonius at his shoulder. When Haghrar made to follow them, the official called out sharply and the nobleman stepped back. Conscious that the eyes of nearly everyone in the chamber were upon him, Cato kept his shoulders down and his back straight as he strode into the open space in front of the dais and faced Vologases. He fixed his gaze on the steady dark eyes of the king for an instant before he bowed his head.

There was silence as the Parthian ruler stared at him as in thought. It continued long enough for some of the courtiers to shuffle uncomfortably. At length Vologases leaned forward and folded his hands.

'You are Tribune Quintus Licinius Cato, are you not?' He addressed Cato in fluent, accentless Greek.

'Yes, Majesty.'

'And this is your aide, Apollonius.'

The agent bowed deeply in response before the king continued.

'You represent the embassy sent to my capital by Rome to discuss terms for a peace treaty between our two empires to put an end to the long rivalry that has existed for well over a hundred years. A rivalry that has cost Rome and Parthia much blood and treasure without any appreciable result.'

'Yes, Majesty.'

'Then I have to say I admire your ambition, Tribune.' Vologases smiled. 'And I can't help wondering what you think you can achieve when so many others have attempted and failed to negotiate a peace. You appear before me not in the finely spun toga of a Roman aristocrat, but the simple tunic of a Roman soldier. How might a simple soldier have come to possess the wisdom of a seasoned diplomat so that he should be sent on such an embassy, I wonder? I have not heard that Roman soldiers possess the temperament to carry out such a task. Tell me, Tribune, why were you chosen? Is it that men of your rank are fit for such a purpose, or are you something more than you seem? You have the look of a soldier, but maybe that is merely another Roman ploy. Well?'

'Majesty, I was chosen by General Corbulo to convey his terms. I am, as you see, just a soldier. But I am a Roman soldier and I am a tribune. I speak my mind and I keep my word. And that is why I imagine he entrusted me with this embassy.'

'So?' Vologases tilted his head. 'That is all? You were chosen for no other reason?'

'None that I know of, Majesty.'

'I see . . .' Vologases let out a long sigh as he settled back on his throne. 'Then tell us, what are the terms your general has ordered you to present?'

Cato had prepared for this moment. 'First, there is the question of Armenia, Majesty. My general says that it falls within the Roman sphere of influence. All that Rome requires is that this is acknowledged by Parthia. In return, Rome undertakes to station no garrisons on Armenian soil and only seeks to have any new Armenian ruler crowned by an official appointed by Rome. If Parthia would accept this, then the greatest contribution to the conflict between our two empires would be removed at a stroke.'

Vologases raised a hand to silence him. 'The question of Armenia has been a sore point for many years, Tribune. Before Rome involved itself in its affairs, Armenia was a long-standing ally of Parthia and would have remained so had not some wretched king appealed to your empire for assistance and drawn it into our sphere of influence. So let me make a counter-proposal. If Parthia promises not to station troops in Armenia, or to crown Armenia's kings, will Rome be content to rescind its claim to Armenia?' He paused and continued in a mocking tone. 'After all, it would remove the main source of friction between our empires at a stroke, as you say.'

'Majesty, in honesty I do not believe that would be acceptable

287

to my general or his emperor. But we are talking about substance and appearance. What would profit both empires is for Armenia to be treated as a neutral kingdom. If that is the substance of the matter, then the appearance of which empire claims that Armenia is within its sphere is immaterial.'

'So if it makes no practical difference, why should Rome not allow Parthia to appear to be in control? Let me tell you why. It comes down to stubborn Roman pride. Your people refuses to admit that it shares the world with other powers. You refuse to accept any others as equal, and once you lay claim to even a scrap of waterless desert, you will willingly sacrifice an ocean of blood just to fly your standard over it. But Armenia is ours. Parthian blood runs through the veins of its kings and nobility. It is ours by right, and Rome would steal it from us.'

Cato nodded reluctantly. 'You speak the truth, Majesty. Roman pride is a stubborn obstacle, but it can be got round.'

The Parthian ruler's brow creased into a frown. 'I am Vologases, king of kings, and I do not skulk around obstacles.'

'Pardon me, Majesty. I see things in pragmatic terms and lack the gilded tongue of a diplomat. I meant no offence.'

'Hmm.' Vologases' nostrils flared angrily for a moment before he spoke again in a calmer tone. 'What other terms does your general present to us?'

'No more than the usual formalities, Majesty.'

'Such as?'

Cato steeled himself before he replied. 'It is the custom that Rome never asks for peace, but grants it. Again, it is a matter of form, Majesty, not substance.'

'Go on. What else?'

'An exchange of hostages and a token payment of tribute.'

'What tribute can Rome afford to pay me that I do not already possess?' Vologases demanded, and many of his courtiers smiled or laughed lightly at his barbed comment before he continued, 'I assume that is what you mean, since you cannot be expecting Parthia to pay tribute to you upstart Romans, surely?'

Cato swallowed nervously. 'My general's terms are that it is for Parthia to pay the tribute, Majesty.'

The last of the laughter died away, and Cato feared that his host would be provoked into a rage at such hubris. Instead, Vologases regarded him calmly.

'Tribune, forgive me, but it seems that your embassy is no more than an empty gesture. You have been sent with terms that your general must have realised would not be acceptable. A cynic might question his motives for doing so. Is it that Corbulo hopes to lure me into negotiations he has no intention of honouring for the sake of winning himself a little time and sowing division amongst Parthia and her allies? Or did he know that I would reject his terms outright, as I do now, and there is another purpose for which you have been sent deep into Parthia?' He leaned forward again and pointed a finger at Cato. 'Well?'

'I was sent on an embassy, Majesty. That is the truth, I swear it on my honour.'

'On your honour,' Vologases repeated coldly. He turned to Ramalanes and pointed at the dais directly in front of his feet. 'Have that chest brought here.'

The captain bowed and hurried away to the rear of the hall. Cato felt an icy tingle of apprehension prick the back of his neck. He was tempted to shoot an enquiring glance at Apollonius, but the king was staring at him directly and he dared not act in any way that might be deemed suspicious. Ramalanes returned with two men carrying the chest into which the embassy's weapons and effects had been placed.

They set it in front of the throne and bowed deeply as they backed away from their master.

'You recognise this chest?' Vologases asked Cato.

'Yes, Majesty.'

The king reached for the lid and raised it before letting it drop away on its hinges. 'You recognise its contents? Come closer.'

Cato did as he was commanded, and approached the dais so that he could see inside. There were the swords and bundles of leather bags they had placed in the chest on board the barge. He wondered what could be so remarkable about them that they were being presented to the Parthian court in this dramatic manner.

'Are these your possessions?'

Cato peered closer. 'I see my sword, and my saddlebags, and the rest belong to my men, Majesty.'

'Indeed.' Vologases reached down and plucked out a flute. 'Do you recognise this?'

'Yes, Majesty.'

Taking the instrument in both hands, the king pulled it apart. The length containing the mouthpiece was in his left hand, while in the right he held the section with the finger holes. He raised this and gave it a quick flick, and a length of papyrus protruded from the broken end. Vologases plucked it out and held it up so that Cato could see that it was in fact several sheets of fine papyrus covered in tiny notations and diagrams.

'Do you know what this is, Tribune?' he demanded.

Cato shook his head, aghast.

'It is written in code,' Vologases continued. 'Fortunately, I have many scholars at court, and they were able to determine that it was a simple alphabetical replacement cipher, which they began to decode last night and finished this morning. The results make for interesting reading. Especially for a Roman general preparing to invade Parthia. There are descriptions of the terrain, estimates of distances between settlements, maps, and a diagram of the defences at Ichnae, amongst other useful intelligence.' He lowered the sheets and thrust them towards Cato accusingly. 'This is espionage, Roman! Your embassy is a sham. Your true purpose in coming here was to spy!'

As his voice echoed off the walls, there was complete silence from the rest of the chamber. Cato saw the nearest guards grasp their spears more tightly, as if in anticipation of an order from their master.

'Have you nothing to say for yourself?' Vologases demanded.

'I swear I have not seen those documents before, Majesty,' Cato said truthfully. It was all frighteningly clear to him now. He had been ordered to lead the embassy as a cover for Apollonius's spying activities. Corbulo and his agent had used him. He had been chosen for the job not because he was the most likely candidate to lead a successful embassy, but because he needed to be seen as honest. And that was why he had not been told of the real purpose of the mission, out of concern that he would not be able to lie convincingly. All this rushed through his mind in a heartbeat.

'Liar!'

'They are not mine,' he blurted out before he could stop himself. Then he clamped his jaw shut. There was no point in telling the truth and identifying the owner of the flute while claiming that he himself was innocent. Vologases would not believe him, and nor would his courtiers. And if their positions were reversed, Cato would not believe it either. It would simply make him look like a coward trying to save his own life by throwing a subordinate to the wolves. His pride would not stomach such a thing, so he kept his mouth closed.

'Not yours? You expect me to believe that?' Vologases' voice rose again. 'You had your aide there carry this for you. No doubt to allow you to deny that it was yours. Do you take me for a fool, you Roman dog? Well, do you? Answer me!'

'No, Majesty, I do not.'

'Then don't you dare lie to my face. You are a spy, and as such, your life and those of your men are forfeit. And not just *your* lives. There is one other . . .' The king raised his eyes and slowly scanned the surrounding courtiers. 'There is amongst us a man, a Parthian noble, who has so debased his honour that he has talked treason with our Roman enemies. He has claimed that there are others like him in my court who are also traitorous dogs conspiring against us. We shall discover their identities soon enough. As for the nobleman in question, he will be arrested and tortured until he gives up all the information I require. Only then will he be executed, and by such means that his torment will endure for days before he is granted the mercy of death.'

His roving gaze stopped and fixed on a face in the ranks of the assembled nobles and courtiers. 'Haghrar of the house of Attaran, step forward, traitor, and take your place alongside these Roman spies.'

Cato looked over his shoulder and saw a commotion in the throng as two guards seized Haghrar and marched him out into the open space beside Cato and Apollonius. Haghrar did not struggle and stood erect as he regarded his King. 'I am no traitor, sire. I swear it, on my honour.'

'Silence!' Vologases roared. He brandished the documents. 'These documents prove your honour is worthless. They speak of your disloyalty, and that of others. Men who would have another king of Parthia.'

'Majesty, I—'

'Not one more word, you dog!' Vologases laughed. 'You fool! Did you really think you could trust a Roman? What did the tribune promise you in exchange for turning on your king? Was it gold and silver? Or the chance to sit on my throne as one of Rome's client rulers? You would have sold your soul to Rome, and Parthia along with it. There is no shame greater than that which you have brought on yourself. Your family will perish along with you, and your name will be struck from every written record and inscription. It will be treason to even mention it aloud.'

'Majesty, my family are innocent. I beg you to spare them! For the sake of all the years I have served you, and your father before you.'

'All of which have been rendered meaningless by your treachery. Your family must perish with you. I will not leave one child alive who might one day seek revenge for his father. In any case, treachery is in your blood, and nits breed lice. All must die.'

'No!' Haghrar groaned.

'Silence!' Vologases sat back and stroked his jaw as he continued. 'It is our judgement that you, Haghrar, are guilty of high treason. And you, Tribune Cato, together with your men, are guilty of espionage.'

'Majesty, my men are merely soldiers,' Cato protested. 'They played no part in any spying.'

'They are Romans, and that is enough reason to sentence them to death. Now be silent, both of you, or I will have your tongues cut out here and now. You have been found guilty of the crimes specified, and you are sentenced to death. In two days' time, it is the feast of the god Angra Mainyu. Haghrar will be bound to stakes in the great market of Ctesiphon, and there his eyes will be plucked out and his organs cut from his living

293

body and burned as an offering to the god. As for Tribune Cato, you and your men are not worthy of such a sacrifice. You will die separately when I have decided on the nature of your execution. Guards, take them to the cells!'

CHAPTER TWENTY-TWO

General Corbulo regarded the two officers standing in front of his campaign desk with icy disdain. Rain drummed on the roof of the goatskin tent, and one side bulged where the wind was blowing in from the east. In front of him lay waxed tablets bearing the reports prepared by the two men concerning the ambush of the baggage train. They had made oral reports to him after reaching the army's camp outside Thapsis, and Corbulo had since spoken to a number of other officers and men from the Syrian cohort, the Macedonian squadron and the surviving wagon drivers in an effort to understand what had taken place. He had demanded written accounts from the two senior officers involved so that they would be available for him to use in evidence if he was called to account for the incident on returning to Rome.

He had summoned Macro and Orfitus to headquarters to inform them of his conclusions and to apportion blame for the disaster. And disaster it was, Corbulo reflected. The entire siege train had been destroyed, and half of the baggage train. The situation had been made still worse by the drivers of the surviving wagons throwing supplies from the vehicles in order to lighten them while making their escape. As for the Syrian auxiliaries escorting the train, one century had been all but annihilated and the others had lost another sixty men between them. With those still sick or recovering from wounds, the cohort had lost a third of its strength.

He cleared his throat. 'I don't imagine that I will have to labour the full extent of the unfortunate consequences of the attack on the baggage train. Suffice to say that without siege weapons, I will be forced to maintain the column outside Thapsis until further weapons can be constructed or procured, and that may set us back some months. Thanks to the rocky ground, it is not possible to dig mines under the enemy's walls, and any frontal assault has little chance of success and would cost far too many lives in any case. I cannot afford to lose men here that I will need if I take the war to Parthia in the spring. So we are stuck here until I have fresh siege weapons to breach the defences. And the responsibility for this lamentable situation lies with you, Prefect Orfitus. First, you should not have trusted this man Thermon. He may have seemed like one of us, but events proved otherwise. You showed a lack of judgement in accepting his word.'

'I was wary of him at first, sir, but there was a ford just like he said, so I had reason to trust him.'

'I'm speaking here, Prefect. Do not interrupt me again, or speak until given express permission.'

'Yes, sir, but I—'

Corbulo shot him a dark look. 'I will not warn you again.'

Orfitus nodded meekly as his superior continued. 'If the man who calls himself Thermon is captured, he will suffer death for betraying us to the enemy. Second, you failed to ascertain that the ford in question could be safely crossed by wagons at the time when Thermon told you otherwise. Your orders were to rejoin the column as quickly and directly as possible. Instead, you permitted Thermon to lure you deeper into rebel-held territory. This caused you to walk into the trap set for you by the rebels. Third, you failed to discharge your primary duty to protect the siege and baggage trains. By leaving the wagons under the protection of just one century while you took your cohort off on some adventure, you placed vital supplies and equipment in danger. We know how that worked out. Do you have anything to say in your defence?'

Orfitus swallowed nervously before he replied. 'Sir, I saw an opportunity to strike a major blow at the enemy. If we had managed to surround the camp and trap the rebels inside, we would have won a significant victory. Using my judgement, I took the initiative to take my men forward to attack the enemy camp.'

'Events have demonstrated that your judgement isn't worth the cheap wax your report is written on. As for initiative, it is my belief that you were motivated solely by the prospect of personal glory. In any case, the camp was simply used as bait to lure you away from the wagons. There was no significant victory to be had. Was there?'

'No, sir,' Orfitus replied meekly.

'No, sir,' Corbulo mimicked. He took a deep breath and exhaled impatiently through his nose before resuming in an authoritative tone, 'Prefect Orfitus, it is my finding that you imperilled the men placed under your command, as well as supplies and equipment vital to the army's performance in the present campaign. I also find that you exceeded your orders. Were it not for Centurion Macro's statement that you performed good service under him after he had taken command, and showed courage by fighting in the front line of your cohort, I would have no hesitation in stripping you of your command and dismissing you from the army. Courage and discipline are the two pillars upon which the success of the Roman military is built. You have proven yourself in one of those qualities and failed abjectly in the other, and compounded your failing by neglecting to exercise sound judgement.

'As you know, according to tradition, the failure of a unit to carry out its orders is the failure of all the men in that unit. For that reason, you and your cohort will be denied the shelter of the camp and will sleep in the open, without tents. You will also be denied any rations save barley. Your punishment will endure for a period of four months. The Fourth Syrian Cohort is to quit the camp immediately. Any of its men, including the wounded, found here after midday will be subject to death by stoning. Dismissed!'

Orfitus stiffened, saluted and then hesitated as if he was about to speak. He thought better of it, however, and turned quickly to march out of the general's tent.

Corbulo watched him go, and then turned his attention to Macro, who had been standing at ease throughout the humiliation of the prefect. 'Do you think my punishment of Orfitus and his men is too severe, Centurion?'

'It's not for me to say, sir. That's your job.'

'But you do have an opinion, don't you?'

'Of course, sir. But opinions are like arseholes – we've all got 'em. That's why I don't question your decision. It's up to the general to give the orders, and once they're given, that's the end of it as far as I am concerned.'

'And that is precisely why you were promoted to the centurionate. But you are also a man, Macro. So out of curiosity, I ask you to indulge me.'

Macro looked at him warily. 'Is that an order, sir?'

'Does it have to be?'

'It would help.'

'Then yes, it's an order. Spit it out.'

'Very well, sir. I think you did the right thing. The prefect deserved it, though it's a bit hard on his men. They fought well enough, but the centurions didn't make any attempt to question his orders. They should have said something. It will be good for the other units to see what happens to those who fuck up. The Syrian lads will be uncomfortable for a few months, but they'll learn a valuable lesson. It may even be the making of them, and the prefect. That's what I think, sir.'

Corbulo grinned. 'Then we are of one mind, Centurion Macro. Of course, we're still in a right old pickle as far as the siege is concerned. I've sent men to scour the province's arsenals for siege equipment, and requested whatever the governor of Syria can spare me.'

'Good luck with that, sir. It's no secret that Quadratus has got it in for you.'

'Quite. In the meantime, we'll need to construct what we can from local sources. The difficulty will be making up the iron components. The quartermaster says he can get a forge set up easily enough, but he'll need ingots and moulds from Tarsus. We'll also need to start foraging further afield in case there's any more delay in supplies reaching us. We've stripped the area around Thapsis, so we'll need to send columns out into the hills. I'm putting you in charge of that. As part of your duties as acting camp prefect.'

'Camp prefect?' Macro's eyebrows rose in surprise. The post was awarded to only the most senior and respected of centurions.

'Yes, sir. Thank you, sir.'

'You've proved you're up to it, Centurion. I am well aware of your record, but I reserve judgement until I have direct experience of an officer's capabilities. You did well to save what you did of the baggage train. This army will need seasoned campaigners like you in the months to come. It's going to be hard on the men. And I will make sure it is equally hard on the officers.' The general nodded to himself. 'This could turn out to be something of a blessing in disguise. The army needs a challenge. It needs discipline. It needs to toughen up for what lies ahead. There'll be no more toleration of minor infractions or regulations. Kill or cure, eh?'

Macro nodded. 'Kill or cure, sir.'

The weather began to change quickly as October gave way to November. The rain fell more frequently and the roads and the ground in the camp that had been baked hard a month previously turned into a glutinous morass. Trees were felled in the nearby forests and laboriously transported to provide log corduroys to serve as the main thoroughfares through the camp. As soon as it became clear that the army might be wintering outside Thapsis, the men began to construct more substantial shelters, using whatever materials were left from the ruins of the settlement between the camp and the town, and what could be gleaned from the surrounding landscape. Within days, the makeshift shelters of strips of cloth and leather stretched over hastily cut branches were replaced by stone windbreaks covered by wood shingle tiles held down by pine branches and small rocks. Soon the camp had taken on the appearance of a peasant village, but with a somewhat more ordered layout.

Even though the repairs on the bridge were completed and supply convoys began to reach the camp, the change of season meant that the river was becoming more swollen. The engineers were constantly having to repair further damage and attempt to strengthen the bridge at the same time. The rising waters also meant that the fords the Romans had found were no longer usable, and if the bridge collapsed again, the only alternative supply route would add nearly a hundred miles to any convoy's journey. Such a diversion caused further complications. Since the route would take the wagons through rebel-held territory, they would need a strong escort, and those men, as well as the drivers and draught animals, would require the wagons to carry their rations, thereby reducing the space for supplies needed by the army camped outside Thapsis. Even as things stood, the worsening weather was delaying supplies reaching the camp. As a result, the men in the camp were forced to go hungry, as rations were cut on the general's orders. Even Macro's forage parties were struggling to find enough to make up the shortfall.

The nearest villages and farms had been torched by the rebels before they retreated behind the walls of Thapsis, and the settlements further away from the city had had ample warning of any approaching Romans and had done their best to hide their stocks of food, or remove them, before the Romans arrived. Once in a while, Macro managed to catch the inhabitants by surprise and seize a good haul of grain, cheese, cured meat and even some wine, as well as small herds of goats and the odd pig or cow.

Those locals who failed to escape were manacled and marched back to the camp to labour on the siege works rising up around Thapsis. During daylight hours gangs of captives toiled alongside the Roman soldiers to dig a ditch extending from the main camp around the hill upon which the rebel town had been built. The spoil was heaped up to the side of the ditch and packed down to create a rampart. Sharpened stakes were driven into the top of this to form a palisade, with towers rising up every hundred paces. Two small camps were constructed a quarter of a mile either side of the main camp and garrisoned by a cohort of legionaries.

Just over a month after the arrival of the column, the town was sealed off, and there was no escape from within, nor any hope of relief from without. Now work began on the earth-works, so that the replacement siege weapons could go into action as soon as they arrived. The rebels had already revealed the range their weapons could shoot out to, so Corbulo had issued orders to his engineers to design and start construction of a more powerful catapult that would be able to hurl missiles against the walls from a safe distance.

Accordingly, a fortified enclosure was built in front of the camp, just short of the blackened ruins of the settlement. A stockpile of rocks was piled inside, with men using iron chisels and hammers to give the rocks a roughly standard shape and size.

As soon as the battery's defences were completed, the first assault trenches were dug, zigzagging round each side of the settlement, thence up the slope towards the town. When the wall was finally breached, the trenches would provide cover for the soldiers to get as close to Thapsis as possible before they rushed into the breach. Despite the rain, the ground was hard to work and the soil was filled with rocks and boulders that had to be dragged away or broken up. As the trenches climbed closer to the walls, the rebels' catapults unleashed occasional volleys of missiles to harass the work parties, but few shots ever landed in the trenches and there were no casualties.

When night drew in, the temperature dropped close to freezing and those on sentry duty were obliged to keep moving in an attempt to stave off the cold and stay awake. The general's decision to enforce strict discipline had been made known to everyone in the ranks, and the men knew that if they were discovered asleep on duty, they would face execution at the hands of their comrades according to regulations. So far there had been no executions, Macro reflected as he made the rounds of the camp one night, checking that the sentries were making the correct challenges and accepting the correct watchword. True, several men had been given a severe beating for minor infractions of regulations, such as turning up for morning assembly with incomplete kit, or failure to maintain and clean kit to an acceptable standard, or being outside of the camp without permission. The rest had swiftly learned from such examples and ensured that the offences were not repeated.

What did concern Macro was the mood of the men. There were always grumblers in the ranks, but their presence was generally leavened by the good humour of their comrades. Now, though, there was a strained atmosphere in the camp. He noticed that the men fell silent whenever officers were present, and the usual banter he enjoyed with the rankers had gone. Instead, men regarded his approach warily and did not meet his eye unless he addressed them directly. He knew from experience that prolonged hunger and cold had a bad effect on morale, but the iron discipline imposed by the general was adding to the sour atmosphere. Macro was no longer certain that Corbulo's efforts to toughen up the men were bearing fruit. Good discipline was one thing, but it was supposed to build confidence, not fear and resentment.

He reached one of the watchtowers on the side of the camp overlooking the Syrian cohort and climbed the steps. The sentry was awake, and after a brief challenge and watchword, Macro leaned on the timber rail of the tower and gazed out over the ditch. Unlike those in the camp, the Syrians had been refused permission to erect shelters and were forced to continue sleeping in the open. Five men had already died from exposure to the increasingly harsh weather, and more would be lost as winter set in. Fires flickered across the bare patch of ground on which they were eking out their punishment, and men clustered around them for warmth against the biting wind sweeping

303

down from the mountains to the north. Macro spared them a moment's pity. They were unfortunate to have been punished for what was largely the fault of Prefect Orfitus, but their suffering served as a stark warning to the men of the other units of the fate that awaited those who failed in their duty.

A sudden outburst of shouting from the heart of the camp drew his attention, and he turned away and crossed to the other side of the tower. There were pools of light around the campfires and the braziers burning close to the headquarters huts. By their glow he could see a small group of men milling around close to the quartermaster's stores. As he watched, the crowd parted to reveal two men rolling on the ground, fighting. Others flew at each other.

'Oh shit . . .'

Macro hurried down the ladder and ran towards the confrontation as fast as he could. As he approached, he could clearly hear the angry shouts carrying across the camp. Rounding a line of shelters, he saw the seething mob ahead of him, dark against the glow of the braziers. He thrust his way through the loose cluster of men at the rear of the throng.

'Make a hole there!' he bellowed. 'Officer coming through. Move yourselves!'

Some men looked back and hurriedly pulled aside as they caught sight of the crest on his helmet. Others responded more slowly, as if defying him, and Macro thrust them out of his path.

'Fucking centurions,' a voice muttered close by.

Macro drew up abruptly. 'Who said that? Which one of you bastards just signed himself up for a bloody hiding?' He slowly turned round. 'Well?'

No one dared to speak as they shuffled away from him.

'Pfft!' Macro sniffed with contempt, then continued through

304

the crowd until he emerged on open ground between the soldiers behind him and a group of Praetorians who were on guard duty. They had three legionaries on the ground in front of them beneath the tips of their spears. Centurion Ignatius stood to one side with a drawn sword in one hand and a sack in the other.

'What in Jupiter's name is going on here?' Macro demanded.

Some voices in the crowd began to call out angrily, and Macro thrust his arms into the air as he turned on them. 'Shut your bloody mouths!' he bellowed. 'Or I will come over there and rip your fucking tongues out and use them for boot leather! I'm talking to the centurion, not you cunts. Silence there!'

The crowd quietened down as he glared at them, and only when he was certain that a spoken exchange would be heard by all did he turn back to Ignatius. 'What's going on?'

Ignatius used his sword to indicate the legionaries on the ground. 'We caught these men coming out of the back of one of the store huts. They tried to run for it, but some of the men from the nearest shelters came over and caught them. As soon as they discovered they'd been looting the stores, they started beating them up and fighting over the sacks they had with 'em. I called on the headquarters guards to help me sort them out and get these three away from the mob and pinned down. Then you turned up, sir.'

Macro put his hands on his hips and turned to face the crowd. 'Get back to your lines! Right now. Move!'

There was little reaction at first; most of the men stared back defiantly from the gloom, their hostile expressions just visible in the glow cast by the braziers.

'I said move!' Macro bawled. 'The last man to turn and double back to his shelter is going to feel my cane across his shoulders! Optios! Get your men moving!'

305

His orders were picked up by the handful of junior officers in the crowd, which quickly began to disperse as the men moved off into the darkness, muttering to each other. Macro waited for a moment, then turned back to the Praetorians. 'Right, get those three up on their feet.'

The spears were reversed and the legionaries roughly hauled up from the ground to face him. By the light of the flames, he could see that their faces were bruised and bloodied. They regarded him warily.

'So you thought you'd help yourselves to some extra rations, did you?' Macro spat on the ground. 'You're in the shit now, boys. I'll have you beaten and then digging out the latrines for the rest of the bloody campaign.'

'What's all this?' a voice demanded, and he turned towards the headquarters huts to see Corbulo striding towards them wearing breeches and sandals with a cloak over his bare shoulders and chest. The Praetorians stood straight in the presence of their general, and Macro turned towards him and saluted.

'Begging your pardon, sir, but these men were found stealing supplies. They were caught by men from another cohort. Centurion Ignatius knocked a bit of sense into the mob and they're heading back to their lines now.'

'Stealing, eh?' Corbulo stood in front of the three men. 'Hungry, were we? So you thought you'd take food from the mouths of your comrades . . .'

The looters lowered their heads in shame, and the general took a step forward and slapped the man in the middle. 'Look ahead when an officer is speaking to you, damn you!'

The legionaries pushed their shoulders back and snapped their heads up, staring directly ahead as Corbulo looked hard at each of them in turn. 'Every man in this army gets the same issue from stores. Including me. No one gets special treatment. So tell me, what makes your three think you are an exception?'

The man to the left, several years older than the others, coughed. 'We're starving, sir. There's barely enough to keep up our strength. We carry on like this and we won't be able to fight. That's what I said to the boys. It was my idea, sir.'

'What's your name?'

'Legionary Gaius Selenus, sir. Second Century, Third Cohort, Sixth Legion.'

Corbulo turned to the nearest Praetorian. 'Find me the commander of the Third Cohort. I want him to report to me here at once.'

The Praetorian saluted and ran off into the darkness as Corbulo turned his attention back to the legionary. 'You look like you've served more than a few years with the eagles.'

'Yes, sir. Nine years.'

'Nine years? Then you've no excuse not to realise the importance of discipline and regulations. You also know the maximum penalty for theft while on active campaign against the enemies of Rome.'

'Yes, sir.'

'And what is the penalty?'

Selenus hesitated and then glanced at Macro. 'Please, sir, the centurion said we were to be beaten and put on fatigues.'

'Did he now?' Corbulo looked to Macro and cocked an eyebrow. 'Is this true?'

'Yes, sir.'

'Then perhaps *you* could remind me what the maximum penalty for theft is?'

'Death, sir.'

Corbulo nodded. 'That's right, death.'

'Pardon me, sir,' Selenus interrupted. 'Like I said, it was my idea. These two are from the latest intake. They're still fresh. They don't deserve to die. If you're going to execute anyone, make it me, and give these lads a thrashing.'

'Quiet. It's not for you to decide who gets punished and how. That's my duty, Legionary Selenus. You're overstepping the mark. I've made my decision. All three of you are condemned to death. Sentence to be confirmed in writing to your commanding officer and carried out by the men of your century.'

Macro saw that the bottom lip of one of the younger men was trembling, and he felt a stab of disappointment that a legionary could appear so weak. At the same time, he felt that he might have taken up Selenus's suggestion had he been the general. One death would serve as an example to discourage further theft. Executing all three was a waste of two men who might, given the chance, turn into decent soldiers once they had learned from this experience.

A figure came running up from the lines. The senior centurion of the Third Cohort. He exchanged a salute with the general before Corbulo gestured to the condemned men.

'Centurion Pullinus, do you recognise these three?'

Pullinus stepped closer and nodded. 'I do, sir. By sight. They're not from my century, though.'

'But they are from your cohort?'

'Yes, sir.'

'They were caught stealing food from the supply store. I have sentenced them to be executed.'

'Executed?' Pullinus sounded surprised, but recovered his composure in a beat. 'Yes, sir.'

'You will take them into your custody and carry out the execution at first light. They will die at the hands of their comrades, as the regulations demand.'

'Yes, sir. I'll see to it.'

'One other thing, Pullinus. Where there's one man prepared to steal, there'll be more. Since three of your men have conspired together to do so, I fear the problem may be widespread within your cohort. I put that down to poor leadership. Your leadership. Therefore you will take your cohort from this camp and set up your new lines alongside the Syrian auxiliaries. Your men will be on the same rations, and like the Syrians, you'll sleep in the open. It seems that the example of Prefect Orfitus and his men has not been sufficient for the rest of the army. Perhaps they will learn from the fate of your men. I will not have good soldiers endure having to live alongside thieves, Centurion Pullinus. Do you understand?'

The centurion seemed about to protest, but then thought better of it and nodded.

'Yes, sir. I'll give the orders at first light.'

'You'll do nothing of the sort,' Corbulo retorted haughtily. 'You'll do it now. I want your cohort out of this camp, and you will give the order immediately. And I know what the misplaced loyalty of some soldiers to their comrades can lead to. If any of these men escape before punishment is carried out, then those guarding them will take their place.'

Pullinus looked to Macro desperately, but he refused to show any reaction to the other officer's fate. The general had spoken and the matter was decided.

Pullinus swallowed and nodded. 'Yes, sir. Immediately.'

CHAPTER TWENTY-THREE

Dawn revealed a hard frost that covered the landscape in a white rime, and the first watch of the day stamped their feet and blew hard into their hands to try and keep warm in the bitter cold. Some of the men had kept their fires going, and several columns of smoke curled gently into the clear sky. Many were stirring and rising stiffly from their bedrolls, rubbing their joints, while some of their comrades yawned and coughed as they breathed too suddenly on the chilly air. The centurions and optios went from hut to hut rousing their men with harsh shouts and urging them to put on their armour and weapons for the morning assembly. Emerging from their huts, they formed up in their centuries and stood to attention as the centurions called the roll and entered the numbers on waxed tablets for the optios to take to headquarters so that the general's clerk could compile an accurate strength return for the day.

The same routine was being carried out in every cohort of the army across the Empire, Macro reflected as the Praetorians formed up in front of their shelters, a short distance from headquarters. Whether it was somewhere cold, like this mountainous region or the frontier along the Rhine, or a barren desert a thousand miles away, Rome's soldiers were all rising to carry out the same routine, just as they had for over two hundred years. It pleased him to think on this from time to time. To feel part of a brotherhood that spanned the known world and made Rome's enemies tremble at the prospect of facing them in battle. Or not, he smiled to himself. Some of those barbarian bastards just never knew when they'd been beaten, and would go down like rabid dogs rather than submit. Like those Druids in Britannia. They were all but done for now, and by the time Macro and Petronella settled in Londinium, the province would be at peace and the Druids well on their way to being a mere detail in the history of the island's conquest.

As the last of the Praetorians took his place, the centurions began the roll call, making a mark on their waxed tablets for each name answered. Once Macro had completed the count for the First Century, the other centurions came up one by one and called out their strength returns. Macro totalled them up and handed his waxed slate to Optio Marcellus. 'Take that to headquarters.'

They exchanged a salute before the optio ran off towards the general's huts, then Macro turned to face the Praetorians and sucked in a breath.

'Second Cohort of Praetorians! Attention!'

At once the men stood with their chests out, shoulders back, looking smartly to the right to dress the line before facing front. It was another good turnout, Macro nodded with approval. Although the men's faces looked a little pinched and their armour appeared to hang on them more loosely than a few months back.

'Today, there will be an execution. As you may have heard, three men were caught stealing from the stores last night. The execution will take place outside the camp, and we will be escorting the general. It's a chance for the cohort to do what it does best and look good on parade,' he added with strained

311

irony for the benefit of those who might take offence at this gibe over their performance in battle. An execution was always a grim affair, and Macro preferred to take some of the edge off the sombre mood. 'So bear in mind that we will be on show in front of those watching from the palisade and our comrades in the Syrian cohort and the Third Cohort of the Sixth Legion. Let 'em see why we're the emperor's finest. Centurion Porcino!'

'Sir?'

'Take a section and draw eighty pick handles from stores. Put them in a cart and have it ready to follow the cohort when we march out with the general.'

'Yes, sir.'

Macro paused and looked over his men again before he concluded. 'The cohort will reassemble outside headquarters when the second hour is sounded. Dismissed!'

General Corbulo stepped out of his hut and pulled on his helmet, tying the straps securely. The crest was made of stiffened horsehair rather than the feathery plume that was fashionable amongst the more ostentatious senior army officers. His silvered breastplate gleamed, and the ribbon tied across it and his military cloak had been cleaned and brushed by his body slave. His polished greaves completed his splendid appearance, but his dour expression rather undermined the effect, thought Macro.

'Let's get on with it, Centurion,' Corbulo growled as he strode to his horse and was assisted into the saddle by one of the Praetorians. He took up the reins and walked his mount out of the roped-off headquarters compound and onto the main thoroughfare running across the camp to the gate. Macro gave the order to advance, and the Praetorians, with the army's colours at the head of the column, followed the general. At the rear of the column two men pulled the cart carrying the pick handles that would be used to beat the condemned men to death. Off-duty soldiers lined the route, watching in sullen silence as the procession passed by. More stood along the rampart to bear witness to the execution. The usual hubbub of shouted orders and the clatter of tools was absent, and the quiet that hung over the camp was oppressive.

Corbulo led the Praetorians out of the gate, across the causeway over the ditch and onto the open ground to one side of the lines occupied by the Syrians and the men from the legionary cohort. The latter were already formed up in three sides of an open square. Centurion Pullinus stood in the middle with the condemned men, who were barefoot in their tunics with their hands tied behind their backs. Corbulo turned his horse towards them, while Macro led the Praetorians on to form up across the open side of the square. As soon as they were in position, he ordered the men with the cart to haul it over to Centurion Pullinus.

A hush followed, broken only by the faint jeers from the walls of Thapsis as the defenders mocked what looked like another formal parade by the Romans. Then Corbulo spoke up, loudly and clearly so that the men on the rampart would hear his words as well.

'We are here to bear witness to the punishment of three legionaries who have dishonoured themselves by stealing food from the common store. These men chose to put their appetites before the loyalty they owe to their brothers in arms. They have shamed the men of their cohort and they have shamed the legion they are privileged to serve.'

'We were starving!' Selenus shouted, and drew a swift blow across his shoulders from Centurion Pullinus's vine cane.

'You were not starving,' Corbulo called back. 'You were merely hungry, as we all are. As I am. Yet you alone chose to steal. Hunger and privation are the lot of soldiers on campaign. It is our duty to endure such conditions and get on with the job of defeating the enemies of Rome. And when we have earned our victory, we will have earned the loot we take from those enemies.' He twisted slightly in his saddle to point up at the city. 'Once Thapsis falls, you can help yourself to all the food, wine and women that lie beyond those walls. That is our prize, and until it is ours, we must accept the hunger and the cold. We must embrace it, for it will make us strong. If we can endure hardship, there is nothing we cannot achieve. That is what makes the soldiers of Rome the most feared of all men in the known world . . .'

His gaze fixed on the condemned trio. 'What we cannot tolerate, what makes us weak, is a lack of discipline. There is the discipline inflicted by military regulations, but that is only part of what makes a Roman soldier. More important is the discipline he applies to himself. A Roman soldier never puts himself before his brothers. He shares what food he has with them. He shares their discomfort, and in battle he shares their risk. He is prepared to lay down his life not just for Rome, but for the men on either side of him. And that is why we cannot tolerate those who dishonour that bond. For those who do, there is only one fate. Centurion Pullinus! Carry out the sentence.'

'Yes, sir! Second Century, down shields and javelins and step forward!'

The comrades of the condemned men did as they were ordered and stood unarmed.

'Over to the cart! One pick handle each and then form column of two, four feet apart. Move!'

The legionaries lined up at the rear of the cart, where the Praetorians issued them with the tools of execution: three-foot

314

lengths of seasoned wood that served as clubs. Once they were equipped, the men took their positions. The centurion took Selenus by the shoulder and was about to steer him towards the gap between the lines when Corbulo called out sharply.

'Not him. He goes last. If the theft was his idea, as he claims, then let him see what happens to those men he persuaded to be his partners in crime. I want him to have the chance to feel remorse for the deaths of his comrades before his turn comes.'

'Yes, sir.' Pullinus thrust the legionary to one side and grabbed one of the younger men, who allowed himself to be pushed into position without a struggle, his face numb with terror.

Pullinus addressed the two lines of men. 'If I see any of you pull your blows, you'll be on a disciplinary charge for failing to carry out your duty. Stand ready!'

The lines faced each other and the men hefted their clubs. The jeering from Thapsis had died away as the defenders realised this was no ordinary parade, and now they looked on in morbid fascination as Pullinus stood behind the first victim and gave him a sharp shove forward. The young legionary stumbled and went down on his knees between the first pair in the line, and they lashed out with their clubs, striking him on the arms, unwilling to aim for his head and take on the burden of being the ones who felled him. The youth cried out as he struggled up, then braced his feet and rushed on, head down. More blows landed as he passed between the lines. He had gone no further than ten paces when he was struck on the back of the head and went down again. As the weapons rose and fell, his skull gave way with a soft crack that reached the ears of all those gathered around. The battering continued, and Macro saw the blood dripping from the heads of the clubs as they were wielded again and again.

Pullinus, who had been tracking the victim's progress, bellowed the order to cease, and the nearest executioners drew back, chests heaving from their exertion. He bent down to prod the body with the end of his vine cane, then ordered it to be dragged aside as he made his way back to fetch the next victim. This time there was a struggle, with the condemned man writhing in the centurion's grip and pleading for mercy.

'Don't harm me, brothers!' he cried out to the men from his century. 'For pity's sake, lads! You're my mates . . . I was starving!'

'Quiet, you!' Pullinus snapped, and moved round behind him and grabbed his shoulders.

The legionary tried to push back, then turned to the general. 'You bastard!' he spat. 'You'll starve us all before this is over! I curse you!'

Pullinus thrust him between the two lines. The legionary made no attempt to run, and strode steadily forward, as if marching on parade. This time, the first pair showed no mercy, and lashed out at his head. The first blow caught him on the jaw, blood and teeth spurting from the impact. The second blow snapped his neck, and he collapsed in a heap between the two men, who made his end mercifully brief with a savage flurry of blows.

The body was dragged aside and the centurion returned for Selenus, shoving him into position. Then, at the last moment, as Pullinus braced himself to push the condemned man to his death, Corbulo's voice rang out.

'Stop!'

The first pair of legionaries were already braced to strike, and they lowered their clubs but stood ready. Pullinus released his grip and took a step back. Selenus stood trembling, his body tense with nervous energy as the general urged his horse forward. He stopped close to the legionary and pointed to him as he addressed the rest of the cohort.

'I am sparing this man, not because he deserves to live, but because he doesn't. Selenus will spend what is left of his life as an object of contempt. Every day he lives will be a reminder to him of the comrades he betrayed and led to their deaths. Every day he lives will be a reminder to the rest of you of the fate that befalls those who fail their brothers in arms. He will be the cause of your suffering the discomforts of sleeping in the open. From this day on, Selenus will endure as nothing more than a walking death sentence. His only chance of redemption will be to die in battle.'

Corbulo allowed the men a moment to reflect on his words before he turned to Pullinus and issued a quiet order. 'Get rid of the bodies. The execution parade is over.'

Then he wheeled his mount around and urged it into a trot as he rode back towards the camp gate without waiting for his Praetorian escort.

Macro stepped out and faced his men.

'Second Cohort! Right turn! Advance!'

As he marched them off, the last two Praetorians collected the pick handles and tossed them in the back of the cart to return them to stores.

Pullinus dismissed the rest of his own cohort, then cut the ropes binding Selenus before ordering the legionary to drag the battered bodies to the hole that had been dug not far from the latrine ditch, where he was forced to bury them without ceremony.

That night, the legionaries of the Third Cohort huddled around their campfires, trying to keep warm as a cold breeze swept through the valley. After the execution of their comrades, a

317

sombre mood had affected them all as they went about their duty advancing the trench that approached the city walls. Each century in turn marched up the existing trench, passing those coming back tired and grimy from their shift. Then began the weary toil of breaking up the ground and heaving the spoil up to create a berm to protect them from arrows and rocks shot at them by the defenders. On return to their lines, the rest of the day was spent scraping shelters in the ground and collecting firewood.

As dusk closed in, a cart emerged from the gate with the allocation of rations for the two cohorts banished from the camp. The half-ration of barley, together with whatever else the men had managed to forage, was added to each section's pot to produce a thin stew to be ladled out into their mess tins. The evening meal, such as it was, did little to alleviate the hunger gnawing at their guts, and the only real comfort was the temporary warmth in their bellies. Then, mess tins licked clean, they sat around their fires and tried to stay warm as they talked in muted tones or sang in an attempt to keep their spirits up.

As night fell, a figure entered the lines; a legionary carrying a large sidebag. He pushed the hood of his cloak back to reveal the felted skullcap he wore to keep his head warm, then made his way towards one of the fires, where he paused to hold his hands to the flames.

'It's a bloody cold night, brothers.'

'Aye,' one of the seated figures replied. 'But all right for those buggers inside the camp. Come out to slum it with us, have you?'

'Not at all.' Their visitor sat down, slightly apart from the others. 'I've come to show a little solidarity, that's all. And to give you this.'

He opened his sidebag to reveal that it was stuffed with

bread and cheese, and the others leaned forward hungrily. They took the food he handed out and began to tear the bread and chew voraciously on the lumps of cheese. The visitor picked out a small loaf for himself, and they all ate in silence for a while before one of the men from the Third Cohort looked up anxiously. 'Where did you get this?'

'The lads in my century chipped in with whatever they could spare. They want you to know that you're not in this alone.'

'What do you mean, brother? I don't want a part of anything that'll get us in trouble. I'm not going like those lads did this morning.' The man held up his half-eaten loaf. 'So this better not be stolen.'

'It ain't. Like I told you, it's a gift from your friends. I swear it. Now eat up.'

The man stared back for a moment. 'And what did you mean about not being in this alone? I'm not sure I like the sound of that.'

'It's nothing.' The visitor took a bite of his own bread and chewed. 'Just that there's a lot of us who think the Third Cohort got the shit end of the stick over the business about stealing from the stores. Your man Selenus was right. We're all starting to bloody well starve. And I wonder how many of us are going to end up buried with your mates before all this is over. I'll tell you something else. I've got a mate at headquarters who swears that Corbulo ain't living on the same rations as the rest of us. The general's got a personal store of the best stuff the forage parties bring in. Saves it for himself. Him and the woman he's got in his tent, keeping him nice and warm at night . . .' He paused and tore off another hunk of bread with his teeth as he looked round the faces gathered about the fire to gauge the impact of his words.

'He's got himself a woman?' One of the younger legionaries chewed his lip.

'Stuff the woman!' an older man cut in. 'What about this personal store? What's the general keeping from us, eh?'

The stranger was silent for a moment, as if trying to recall what he had been told. 'My mate said he saw hams, a haunch of venison, some pastries and honeyed cakes.'

'Honeyed cakes . . .' someone murmured.

'That's bollocks.' Another man spat into the flames. 'I don't believe a word of it. The general's one of the few aristocrats that plays straight with his men. He looks after himself no better than he looks after the rest of us.'

'Then why are we freezing our bollocks off out here while he's in his nice warm bed with some local tart?' demanded the man who had asked about the food. 'If you think he's living like one of us out here, then you're a bloody fool.'

'Brothers!' The stranger raised his hands. 'Look, I didn't come out here to cause any trouble. Just wanted to share what we can spare with you. That's all. Maybe my mate got it wrong.'

'Maybe he didn't,' a man said angrily. 'Anyway, thanks for this. We needed it. And make sure you thank your lads for helping us out. We'll return the favour if we ever get the chance.'

The others murmured their gratitude too as the stranger stood up. He smiled and nodded his head in farewell. 'Goodnight, boys. I better get off.'

'Here, if there's any more food going spare, you know where we are.'

'Sure. I'll be back.' He waved, then turned away into the darkness. As he walked, he heard the men muttering behind him, and a small smile of satisfaction lifted the corners of his mouth.

When he was a safe distance away, he changed direction and made his way down the lines until he found what he was looking for: a legionary sitting alone some distance from his comrades. He had not made himself a fire and sat hugging his knees with his cape wrapped around his shivering frame.

'Brother Selenus,' the stranger greeted him as he approached. The legionary looked round warily.

'Who the fuck are you?'

'Borenus. From the Eighth Cohort.'

'I don't recognise you.'

'Not surprised. I was transferred in just before we left Tarsus. Mind if I sit with you for a moment?'

'Why would you want to? You know who I am, and what I did.'

'I know. I've got some food to share. Compliments of the lads in my century.'

Selenus swallowed and then nodded. His visitor squatted and rummaged in his bag, then held out some cheese and a hunk of bread. 'Here.'

Selenus hesitated. 'Where did you get it?'

'It's safe. Take it.'

Selenus snatched at it eagerly and began to eat without any further questions. His visitor regarded him closely before speaking again.

'Selenus, the general was wrong to do what he did today. He as good as killed those two boys himself. Only he's like all them aristocrats and doesn't want to carry out that kind of deed in person and get blood on his hands. There's a lot of us in the camp think Corbulo's little better than a murderer. And those lads won't be the last of his victims. Listen . . .'

He leaned closer to continue talking in an undertone. Every so often Selenus would nod, or break off from his eating to make an angry comment. At length the other man patted him on the shoulder and stood up.

'I'll see you again soon, brother.'

Then he paced away into the night, making his way back between the lines before crossing over the open ground to the nearest of the Syrian cohort's campfires, where he smiled as he waved a hand in greeting.

CHAPTER TWENTY-FOUR

It was impossible to tell what time of day it was in the cell. It measured no more than eight feet by five, and the air was cool and clammy. There were no windows, and the only opening besides the low, narrow door was a foul-smelling drain that ran through the walls and across the middle of the room. Previous prisoners appeared not to have exclusively used the drain for their ablutions, and Cato had cleared away some of the soiled rushes to sit on the grimy flagstones rather than risk sitting in someone else's shit. There was a small grille in the door through which a very faint light entered the cell from the flames of a torch further along the corridor running underneath the palace's stables. The prisoners were fed twice a day, as far as Cato could estimate; he had lost feeling for the passing of time. Apollonius was in the next cell, and they were able to communicate with each other through the drain. Since there was little to say, however, and any exchange required bending over the drain and enduring the noisome stench of the effluent trickling beneath, both men preferred to limit their words.

Cato sat back against the wall and folded his arms as he thought about their situation. After Vologases had revealed his proof of the agent's spying, Haghrar was dragged off through a side door while Cato and Apollonius were escorted from the audience chamber. They were taken out of the palace to the vast complex of stabling set far enough away from the main building that the odour did not offend the noses of the king and his court. There they were shoved through a guarded doorway and down two flights of steps to the end of the long corridor before being thrust into their cells and left there.

At first he had expected their incarceration to be long enough only for Vologases to choose their method of execution. But the hours had stretched into a day, then longer, until it was hard to determine how long they had been held there. He could not believe they had been forgotten. Rather, Vologases was saving them for some public occasion to make a spectacle of their deaths so that his people could see what happened to Roman spies. He used the buckle from his belt to score a mark on the wall each time one of the guards brought him food and then swapped the empty pail of water for one filled with brackish water through a small opening at the bottom of the door. The water had caused him to suffer a bout of diarrhoea before his body became accustomed to it. He continued to score the mealtimes even after he came across a similar record. Sensing a row of notches further along the wall, he ran his fingers over them until he found the start, and then began counting. He gave up after four hundred, but continued brushing his fingertips over the notches until they finally came to an abrupt end. Apollonius had fallen silent for a long time after Cato shared his discovery and the prospect that they might be destined to eke out the rest of their lives in their grim, stinking holes far from sunlight and the attention of those going about their business in the palace.

From time to time the two men would stand at the doors and talk to each other through the grilles, but since other prisoners did the same, or shouted for the guards – who never responded – or simply babbled insanely, it was necessary to raise their voices to be heard and it was too much of a strain to keep it up for long. It suited them both to think that as long as they lived, there was hope that the Parthians might include them in a prisoner exchange, or that General Corbulo might attempt to pay a ransom for their release.

Cato clung to that thought, as he found the idea of never being able to see his son again almost impossible to bear. Even if it took years for them to be released, he might return to Rome a wasted shadow of the man he had once been, and Lucius might not recognise him. That filled his heart with grief, and there were moments when he gave in to his misery as he sat propped up in the corner of his cell. It never lasted for long; when he realised he was slipping into the mood, he forced himself to rise and exercise as best he could in the confined space. He could stretch, and do squats and press–ups and a limited number of other activities to keep his body supple and as strong as possible. But already he could feel the hunger eating away at him, and he was certain that the bones of his slender frame were becoming more and more prominent as time wore on.

He did not need to urge Apollonius to do the same, as the agent was determined to be ready to act if ever the opportunity to escape presented itself, however unlikely that might be given the regime the Parthians imposed upon their prisoners. The only time the door to a cell was opened was when the guards came to take a man to his death, or when a prisoner died and the body was removed.

The damp air affected Cato badly, and his body was racked by painful coughing fits more and more frequently. He prayed to Asclepius that he might recover and not die from a wasting illness in this terrible place. If that was to be his fate, then he hoped that he had served Rome well enough to win the right to enter the Fields of Elysium in the afterlife.

His thoughts were interrupted by the agent's voice.

'Cato . . . Cato!'

Cato stood up and rolled his shoulders to ease the stiffness that had set in from leaning against the wall. Stepping up to the door, he bent to place his mouth close to the grille. 'I'm here. What is it?'

'I need to say something to you.'

'So?'

There was a pause before Apollonius continued. 'I wanted to apologise, Tribune. It was too bad that I could not tell you the true purpose of my mission.'

'Yes. It was. You should have trusted me.'

'What difference would it have made if I had? Vologases would still have found my notes. I wonder, has it occurred to you that he might have spared us because he thought your surprise was genuine?'

'No. I hadn't thought of that. I doubt the king is troubled by the notion of whether those he condemns are innocent or not.'

Apollonius gave a dry chuckle. 'You are right. Poor Haghrar. If only I hadn't made notes on what you told me about the conversation you had with him at Ichnae he might still be alive. And, more importantly, considering plotting against his king. Speaking of Vologases, I wonder what fate he intends for us. You know, we might yet get out of this alive.'

'How so?'

'My mission was a success, as far as it got. I had made detailed notes to help Corbulo plan his campaign.'

'And they have been taken from you. I somehow doubt that Vologases will be sharing them with the general any time soon.'

'He doesn't have to. I can recall most of the details accurately enough.'

'Then why, for pity's sake, did you commit them to paper?'

'In case anything happened to me. That's why I asked you to return the flute to Corbulo.'

'Well, he's not going to be getting it back now, is he?'

'He doesn't need the flute if I am still alive. He may try to ransom me. And you too, of course,' the agent added quickly.

Cato had heard this line of reasoning from Apollonius before and wondered if the agent truly believed it, or whether he was merely clinging to the possibility to stave off despair. He coughed and cleared his throat. 'Let's hope you are right. I'm sure the general won't want to lose one of his best agents.'

'One of?' Apollonius sniffed. 'The best. By far. There's none better, and the general knows that.'

'I'm sure he does.'

A burst of shouting from further along the corridor drowned the possibility of any further discussion, and Cato slumped back down against the wall and closed his eyes. He decided to pass the time before the next issue of food and water by recalling every possible detail of their mission from the point they had crossed the frontier at Bactris. Who knew, such information might come in useful one day after all.

At about the time that the rations were usually delivered, Cato heard the clank of bolts from the door at the end of the corridor and climbed to his feet to stretch his shoulders. Footsteps echoed along the passage, pausing at each door. The orange glow of a torch gleamed off the stone wall opposite Cato's cell, and then he heard a soft voice.

'Romans . . . are you there?'

He felt his pulse quicken as he pressed himself to the grille and called out, 'Here! In here!'

'Shh! Keep quiet!'

'Who's that?' Apollonius demanded.

'Quiet, Roman. Stand back!'

Cato heard the scraping of a bolt and the squeal of hinges from the next-door cell, and a few moments later, the torch illuminated a familiar face at the grille of his own door.

'Ramalanes . . .' He felt a surge of anxiety at the thought that the time had come for them to die. 'What's happening?'

'Back,' the captain ordered.

He did as he was told as the bolt outside protested and the door lurched inwards to reveal Vologases' officer garbed in a dark cloak, torch in one hand. He gestured to Cato. 'Come out, Tribune. Now.'

Hesitantly, Cato ducked through the narrow door and stepped into the corridor, squinting at the bright flame. He saw the Parthian's nose wrinkle in disgust as the fetid odour of the cell reached him. Then Ramalanes reached past him and closed the door, slipping the bolt back into position. Cato was about to speak again when the captain gave him a gentle push towards the end of the corridor.

'Outside. Let's go.'

Apollonius led the way, with Cato following and the Parthian at the rear. There was only one face at the doors of the cells they passed: a man with bulging eyes and long locks of matted grey hair. Ramalanes swung the torch towards him and the face vanished into the gloom beyond. When they reached the door at the end and passed through, the Parthian closed and bolted it. Cato gripped his arm.

'What is going on?'

'I'm getting you out of here, Tribune. I could not say

anything in the cells in case the prisoners revealed what they had overheard.'

'I spoke your name . . .'

'Yes, you did,' Ramalanes responded with a trace of bitterness. 'I hope no one heard you. Otherwise my head will be mounted above the palace gates alongside that of Haghrar.'

'He's dead?'

'Of course he's dead. That's what happens to those who plot against Vologases.'

'And you're part of that plot?'

'I serve Prince Vardanes and his circle.'

'His circle?' Apollonius cut in. 'Are there many who are opposed to the king?'

Ramalanes turned to him. 'It is best that you do not know any more than that, in case you are captured before you reach the frontier.'

'How long were we held in the dungeons?' asked the agent.

'Nearly a month. The king was keeping you alive to sacrifice for the winter festival in two months' time.'

'Wait,' said Cato. 'How could Vardanes possibly know we are here? Hyrcania is hundreds of miles to the east of Ctesiphon. He can't have heard.'

'He hasn't. I am acting on the orders of one of his allies in the palace. Rome supports Vardanes's struggle, and so the favour is returned. If you reach safety, make sure your emperor is told that Vardanes stands by his agreement to help Rome. Understand?'

'Of course. I'll make sure his loyalty to Rome is known.'

'He is not loyal to Rome,' Ramalanes said deliberately. 'He is loyal to Parthia. He chooses to honour his arrangement with your emperor, that is all.'

Cato had the sense not to push the matter any further. 'I thank him anyway.'

'What is the escape plan?' Apollonius asked.

'There is a boat waiting at the dock. The boatman is not one of us, but he has been paid well enough to ensure he will row you across the river. From there, a cart will take you to the Euphrates, where there will be a barge to transport you all the way to Dura Europus. The captain will have coin to buy horses for you when you leave the barge, and you will ride across the desert to Palmyra. That city is allied with Rome, so you will be safe there. But first we have to get you to the boat. Come!'

'Wait!' Cato stayed his arm. 'What about my men? I cannot leave without them.'

'Your men are dead, Tribune. They were executed as soon as Vologases sent you to the dungeons.'

'Dead?'

Ramalanes nodded. 'Their heads were placed below Haghrar's on the gate. I had no chance to save them.'

Cato was not sure if the man was telling the truth, but there was no way to find out.

'We have to go, now,' Ramalanes insisted. He led the way up the stairs and out into the yard beside the largest stable block. It was night-time, and the stars glinted in a moonless sky. Two of the palace guards were propped up either side of the door, their spears resting at their feet.

'Dead?' asked Apollonius.

'Drunk,' Ramalanes replied. 'I made sure they had plenty just to make certain.'

He replaced the torch in the bracket to one side of the door and beckoned to Cato and Apollonius to follow him as he crossed the open space towards a gateway. On the far side were several carts hitched to teams of mules. Some fifty paces ahead, some slaves were loading large jars and amphorae onto the bed of the leading cart. Cato noticed that the others were already laden with more jars and other items. The rearmost, close by, was full of rolls of animal furs.

'Get in,' Ramalanes commanded. 'Then cover yourselves and wait until the carts reach the service dock. The furs are bound for the governor of Dura Europus. Wait at the dock for the boatman to come for you. He will take you across the Tigris to a quiet landing place not far from Seleucia.'

Cato took the Parthian's arm again. 'My thanks.'

'Just go. Now. Before I am discovered with you.' Ramalanes pulled his arm free.

Cato and Apollonius trotted over to the rear of the nearest cart and clambered inside, pulling furs on top of themselves and then lying still as they waited for the convoy to begin moving. Even though the night air was cool, it soon became stifling under the furs, and the tang of cured animal pelts began to catch in Cato's throat so that he feared he might have to cough. He closed his eyes and strained the muscles in his throat to keep from letting the irritation affect him too badly. At last he heard voices, and the cart shifted as the driver climbed onto his bench, cracked the whip and urged his mules into a walk.

The vehicle rumbled over the flagstones and then crunched onto gravel. Cato sensed that they were descending, and then there was the sound of wheels on wood before the cart lurched to a stop. Voices called out to each other, and he heard the thud of boots on the wharf for a while before the other carts were driven off. As the sound faded, he heard a single set of footsteps approaching, and then the furs were pulled aside by a small man, wizened like a monkey. He did not speak, but waved them off the cart, and then indicated the furs and pointed to a small craft moored nearby.

They loaded the boat, then climbed aboard, and the little man slipped the mooring ropes and poled the boat away from the bank. Then, standing on the central thwart, he took up long oars and propelled it across the current towards the western bank, downriver from the flickering lights of Seleucia. He had obviously made the crossing very many times, in darkness as well as daylight, and they soon reached the far side, grounding in some shallows just short of the river's edge, where a figure waited with a wagon drawn by the hulking shapes of oxen. Cato and Apollonius helped carry the furs from the boat to the wagon before climbing into the back. As the driver closed the flaps of the weathered goatskin covers, Cato could just make out the boatman leaning against the stem of his craft as he took a sip from a waterskin. A moment later the flap slid into place, and once again he and Apollonius were cut off from any view of the outside world.

'We need to be well down the road to the Euphrates before dawn comes,' Apollonius commented quietly as the cart jerked into motion. 'Once they find those guards outside the dungeons, it's likely that someone will check the cells and raise the alarm.'

'Let's hope they see that our doors are still closed and don't look inside.'

Apollonius sniffed doubtfully. 'They will sooner or later. Still, I'd love to see the expression on Vologases' face when he is informed that we've escaped. That'll be priceless.'

'Maybe,' Cato responded sombrely. 'However, if we don't get across the frontier, you can be sure our heads will end up along with the others on top of the palace gates. Then he'll be the one having the last laugh.'

CHAPTER TWENTY-FIVE

It was the morning after the barge sailed from Tanassur, heading upriver before tying up for the night. Cato stripped naked and waded into the river with a deck brush he had found on board. He submerged himself in the cool flow for as long as he could hold his breath, and then broke the surface with an explosive gasp and shook the water from his drenched locks of hair. He had not had it cut since leaving Tarsus, and the grime and filth of the cell had left it matted and foul-smelling. Now he brushed at his scalp until it was sore in order to get as much dirt out as possible, then proceeded to scrub his body methodically until his skin was smarting. As he emerged from the river, he saw Apollonius watching him.

'You missed a bit on your back, Tribune.'

Cato tossed him the brush and turned round as he gave the order. 'Scrub it off.'

Taking care not to work the bristles too vigorously, Apollonius cleaned the dirt from between Cato's shoulder blades and down his spine as far as his lower back. 'There. You might want to get that hair cut as well. It would be a good idea not to look like someone who has just escaped from the dungeons of the royal palace. And shave while you're at it.'

'It's a fine line between not looking like someone on the run and appearing to be a lowly member of the barge's crew. I'll keep the beard, since that makes me look less like a Roman. They're sure to be hunting for us by now. It's best we look as unobtrusive as possible.'

Apollonius shrugged. 'Then the danger will be convincing people that you are indeed a Roman if we make it back across the frontier.'

'I'll deal with that when we come to it.'

'When, you say? That's what I like about you, Tribune. Always an optimist.'

'Hmm,' Cato responded non-committally. He picked up the tunic he had been given by the barge's captain, pulled it over his head, then turned and looked at his companion. The agent's ablutions had been minimal, and his head and cheeks were covered in stubble. He had cast off the tattered remains of the clothes he had been wearing in the audience chamber and now wore a frayed tunic he had taken from the barge's slop chest. He would have little difficulty in passing as an ordinary member of the crew, Cato decided.

They made their way back along the riverbank to the barge, which had been moored to the trunk of a tree growing close to the water. The captain and the two men of his crew were huddled round a steaming pot, cooking porridge over a small fire.

'What do you make of our captain?' asked Cato as they approached.

Apollonius glanced at the man. 'I don't know how much he has been paid to take us upriver, but I hope it's enough to save Democles from being tempted by any prospect of a reward for turning us in.'

'Greeks,' Cato muttered. 'Macro's right, you can't trust

334

them any further than you can spit 'em.' He glanced at his companion. 'No offence meant.'

'None taken. But I think we should keep an eye on Captain Democles while we are on his barge.'

'Agreed.'

The captain turned and gave a gap-toothed smile as he became aware of them. 'Sit, sit, my friends! Have something to eat. You both look hungry.'

'You can't imagine,' Cato said drily as he lowered himself and sat cross-legged. Apollonius squatted the other side of the captain and took the wooden bowl and spoon offered to him by one of the crewmen. Soon all of them were eating the glutinous porridge, and Cato found it agreeable enough to have a second helping. He seemed to be permanently ravenous following his near-starvation in the cells. When he had finished, he handed the bowl over to the younger crewman, barely more than a boy, who was responsible for the menial duties aboard the barge. As the lad collected the bowls and spoons and carried them down to rinse in the river, Cato turned to Democles.

'How soon will we reach Dura Europus?'

The captain scratched his head. 'Winter's nearly on us. The mountain streams that feed into the Euphrates will be swelling the river and making it flow faster. We'll still be able to sail against the current well enough, though, so . . .' He made some mental calculations. 'Eight to ten days, I reckon. If all goes well.'

'What does that mean?' asked Apollonius.

'Depends on the wind, doesn't it? It's pretty reliable most of the time, but there are days when it fails, or blows from the wrong direction. Sometimes it brings in a sandstorm, and if that happens, we have to get to the bank and take shelter in the hold. Sand can be a bastard. Gets everywhere, and if you're out in it, it's like being scratched at by a cheap whore who's been cheated on the price.'

Apollonius arched an eyebrow. 'Sounds like you speak from experience.'

Democles looked at him and then roared with laughter. 'Oh yes. I know 'em all, from end to end of the river. If you have time, I can recommend a few places in Dura Europus.'

'Thank you,' said Cato, 'but we'll be heading off as soon as you've got hold of horses for us.'

'Me?' The captain looked surprised. 'What makes you think that's down to me? I'm only supposed to get you to Dura Europus. It's up to you after that.'

Cato shook his head. 'You've been given coin to buy the horses. Right?'

'I suppose. But what they gave me was barely enough to cover my costs on this trip. Extra mouths to feed and so on.'

'Nevertheless, you were paid to take us upriver and arrange the horses.' Cato stared at him levelly. 'And you will do precisely what you were paid to do. Understand?'

The Greek grinned. 'Of course I will. I'm a man of my word, Tribune.'

'How do you know to call me that?' Cato leaned forward.

'I overheard you and your friend here talking last night. But don't you worry, sir. I've not said anything to my boys. Your secret is safe with me. I'll get you to where you're going. I give you my word on it.'

The barge, like many such river craft, was wide-beamed and had a shallow draught, and thanks to its windage was inclined to make slow progress when obliged to tack across the broad river. It was a source of frustration for Cato, who desperately

336

wanted to reach Dura Europus and make good their escape to Palmyra as swiftly as possible. But there was nothing he could do about the pace of the vessel as it worked its way upriver. Apollonius, by contrast, accepted the situation readily, and spent most of his days sitting on the steps up to the small stern deck, trailing a hand in the water and gazing at the passing landscape of irrigated farmland broken up by outcrops of rock. Now and again they would pass a landmark familiar from their earlier journey downriver, and Cato would see the agent's expression fix in concentration as he refined his recall of the terrain.

Being of a more active and pragmatic disposition, Cato diverted himself by learning the craft of river sailing, and Democles was happy to introduce him to the rigging and steering and finding the best angle for setting the sail to make the fastest possible progress. For Cato it became an intriguing exercise in playing off the speed of the barge against pointing up to the wind as effectively as possible, and within a few days the Greek captain pronounced himself very happy with the progress his student was making.

At the end of most days, as the sun slipped towards the western horizon and the light began to fail, Democles steered the barge into a sheltered section of the bank to moor for the night. The crew and their passengers used the furs in the hold as mattresses and slept comfortably on the barge's deck, with one man keeping watch at all times for pirates, or robbers hunting for prey along the riverbank. Some nights they moored at riverside villages or small towns and went ashore to find an inn. Some establishments ran small brothels on the side, and Democles and his crew would disappear with heavily painted women into the cubicles reserved for prostitutes. Cato was uncertain of the wisdom of accompanying the crews on these visits, but he did not trust them enough to let them out of his sight for any length of time.

On the evening of the sixth day, as the sunset burnished the sky a brilliant orange that reflected off the water so that the surface looked like molten gold, the barge steered towards the wharf of a small town fringed by date palms on the eastern bank. The slender, spiky boughs swayed gently in the evening breeze as Democles ordered his two crewmen to lower and stow the sail. As ever, he judged the remaining momentum perfectly, so that the barge barely nudged the wharf as he leaned into the tiller and brought it alongside. Cato, standing in the bows with a coil of rope, jumped ashore and took a loop round the mooring post before fastening it to the cleat on the small foredeck. The stern was secured by Democles, and within moments the vessel was securely tied up for the night.

Looking along the wharf, Cato saw that there were at least twenty other river craft alongside, and most of their crews seemed to be already ashore. Several small warehouses stood opposite the barge, and further along there was a wide gap beyond which were more sheds and stores. The sounds of pipe music, drums and cymbals and raucous singing drifted over the roofs of the town's buildings. Democles turned to the younger crewman and ordered him to stand watch on the barge while the rest of them went ashore. The boy looked disappointed, but he had no choice other than to obey the order, and went to sit in the stern, radiating resentment.

'Come on, boys!' the captain said cheerily as he stepped onto the wharf. 'Sounds like there's a party going on in the marketplace. First drink is on me.'

As they followed the captain and his other crewman, Cato muttered to Apollonius, 'I wonder how much of our captain's largesse is funded by the coin he was given to buy us horses?'

338

The agent shot him a look. 'Quite.'

The small party made its way along the wharf towards what turned out to be the open side of a large square lined with shops and inns. The middle of the square was taken up by market stalls selling farm produce, clothing, pottery and cooking pots, trinkets and all the other wares that were traded up and down the length of the great river. Democles ignored the market and made straight for a particular inn on the far side of the square. A sign hung above an arched entrance to the yard within, and when Cato paused to look up, he saw a winged phallus chasing a scantily clad woman with outsize breasts and rouged cheeks above the legend in Greek: *The Cup of Eros.*

'Nice artwork.'

Democles laughed. 'Oh, there's plenty of works of art on display inside!'

He led them through into the courtyard, a large space perhaps fifteen paces across and lit by the glow of torches in brackets on three walls. At the rear was a building fronted by a counter, with jars stacked on shelves behind. Several men were busy serving customers at the bar or taking drinks to their tables. To the right of the counter was an arched doorway, the surroundings of which had been painted to look like a vulva. A trio of women stood by the door half-heartedly striking poses as they vied for clients.

'I'll be having some of that,' said the crewman.

'Easy, Patrakis. We drink first.' The captain led them to a table close to the counter and they sat on benches either side. From there Cato could see that there was a small stage in the opposite corner of the yard, where three musicians were sharing a jar of wine as they took a break between sets.

'You won't find a better place for wine this side of Dura Europus,' Democles announced. 'And I get a special rate with the women since the owner is a cousin. He used to be a mercenary fighting for the king before he was wounded in the leg and discharged. He's a good man.'

'Ah.' Apollonius nodded knowingly. 'Of all the peoples in this world, the Greeks are peculiarly blessed with the number of cousins they have.'

The captain stared at him for a moment, then shook his head. 'Right, drinks then.'

He beckoned to one of the serving men and ordered a large jug of wine for the table, slapping what looked to be a freshly minted coin into the man's hand. When the wine came, with a tray of wooden tankards, Democles poured them all a cup and then raised his for a toast.

'To our fine passengers, who have become part of the crew!'

The two boatmen drained their tankards and the captain refilled them at once. Cato had been careful to take a small mouthful and swill it around before he swallowed. It was a flavoursome wine, to which a hint of some spice had been added. Apollonius drank half his cup and smiled with approval. 'That's good. Very good.'

'I told you.' Democles beamed. 'More for you boys?'

Apollonius held out his cup, but Cato shook his head and set his own down as he leaned forward to speak with the captain.

'I take it you have coin left to pay for our horses when we reach Dura Europus?'

The captain waved a hand dismissively. 'There's plenty. Your friends paid generously for your passage . . .'

'I take it they also told you not to ask any questions about us, and the purpose of our journey,' Cato responded mildly. 'So let's just enjoy the drink and some conversation, then be on our way. We don't want any tongues wagging.'

Patrakis leered, then stuck his tongue out and licked his finger suggestively. 'That's the main reason we're here, friend. You should see the tricks those girls can do.'

A rotund man with a round, sweaty face came limping over to the table and slapped Democles on the back. 'You rogue!' he exclaimed. 'I haven't seen you for months. Nor that money you still owe me for your last visit.'

The captain turned and forced a grin. 'Why, Cousin Pericles! It's good to see you too. It has been far too long. You've met my mate Patrakis?'

The innkeeper frowned. 'I remember you. My girl couldn't sit comfortably for a week after your visit. And who are these others? I don't recognise them.'

Cato gave the captain a warning glance and the latter lied smoothly. 'Two fur merchants I'm taking up to Dura Europus with their stock.' He gestured to Cato. 'Agisthenes and his friend Alexandros.'

They exchanged a formal bow of heads before Pericles gestured to the empty space on the bench beside the captain. 'May I? It'll be good to catch up.'

'Be my guest. I'd offer you some of our wine, but alas, we only have four tankards.'

'No problem.' The innkeeper snapped his fingers at one of the serving men, and a moment later the captain was reluctantly filling the cup fetched for his cousin. 'Now then, what's the news along the river?'

Democles scratched his beard. 'Not much to tell. There's been less trouble from pirates lately. I heard that one of the pirate gangs took a good kicking a while back. If I ever meet the men responsible for that, I'll buy them drinks all night long. Other than that, there are rumours that the war against

Vardanes isn't going well, and there's word of a famine in Egypt, so the clever money is buying up surplus grain to sell to the Romans.'

'That's useful to know. Be good to get a jump on the local grain merchants. I'll make a small killing.' Pericles grinned.

'If you do, just remember who told you first, eh, cousin?' Democles tapped his finger on the table. 'So what's been happening around here of late?'

The innkeeper drained his cup and helped himself to a refill, and a pained expression crossed the captain's face. 'There's been quite a bit of excitement. Parties of palace guards racing up and down the river, and then two days ago a royal herald passed through the town. He announced that the king has posted a reward for the capture of some men who escaped from the palace dungeons in Ctesiphon. They're rumoured to be making for the frontier. And get this, the reward is fifty thousand drachma!'

Democles let out a long, low whistle and refused to meet Cato's gaze. 'Fifty thousand drachma . . . Fuck me.'

'What?' Pericles looked disgusted. 'While there are dogs still in the street?'

The captain froze for an instant, his eyes narrowing in a hostile stare, then jabbed the innkeeper in the side with his elbow. 'The old ones are the best ones . . . Still, fifty thousand. That could set a man up for life. Any news of them being captured yet?'

Pericles shook his heavy jowls. 'No, but you can bet they'll fall into some lucky bastard's lap. Ah well, back to work.' He stood up and pointed a finger at the captain. 'It's been good to see you, but mind you pay your bill in full this time before you leave.' He patted the purse at his side. 'I can always use some help for Eros.'

342

Democles pulled aside his cloak to reveal a far more heavily laden purse. 'And I am always happy to pay, cousin.'

Cato saw the innkeeper's eyes widen. He had listened to the exchange between the two Greeks with increasing anxiety, and it had taken great self-control to keep his expression neutral.

Pericles gave a farewell nod to the captain's companions, then turned to walk away stiffly across the yard, shouting to the musicians to get back to work. Cato watched Democles's face closely and saw the calculating glint in his eyes as he looked down into his tankard, swilling what was left of the wine at the bottom. The drummer and the man with the cymbal began a fast beat, and the flautist joined in with a simple melody.

Patrakis belched and stood up. 'A good drop, that. Now it's time to go and raise the mast.'

He weaved his way through the tables towards the women at the entrance to the brothel, speaking with them briefly before picking a slight, dark-haired woman with short scarred legs and following her inside. Democles, who had been following his crewman's transaction, clicked his tongue.

'Takes all sorts I guess,' he muttered.

The captain ordered another jar of wine, but Cato and Apollonius drank sparingly, not daring to indulge too much after hearing what the innkeeper had said. For his part, Democles made no mention of the reward as he delivered reminiscences about life on the river, throwing in the odd joke in an effort to keep the mood light. Cato was not fooled, and was already wondering just how much longer they would be able to trust the captain and his crew. He had hoped that word of their escape might not have spread so swiftly. And now there was this cursed reward, set at a figure that would test the loyalty of even the most principled man. And his impression was that Democles fell far short of that standard.

When Patrakis came back from the brothel, a bleary grin across his face, the captain finished his wine. 'We've got some distance to make up, so we'll cast off at first light. Best we get back to the barge and have a good night's sleep.'

Cato nodded. 'I think that would be wise.'

Pericles hobbled over at the best speed he could manage to make sure that the bill had been paid in full, and then sent them on their way with a hearty farewell and the hope that they would visit his establishment again soon. The market stalls were empty when they emerged into the square and made their way across to the wharf. Cato allowed the captain and Patrakis to pull slightly ahead as he fell into step with Apollonius.

'You saw him,' he muttered. 'I don't think we can trust him much longer.'

'I agree. What do you think we should do?'

Cato thought it through. 'We need him to get us close to Dura Europus before we cut ourselves free. And we need the coin that he was paid for the horses and supplies. I doubt he'll honour the deal he struck with Vardanes's men.'

'True.' Apollonius nodded. 'It's the deal he's thinking of with Vologases' men that worries me. It's flattering to have such a price on our heads, but it's made the situation rather uncomfortable.'

When they reached the barge, they took out some rolled furs to sleep on, and Democles declared that there was no need to set a watch, as they would be able to sleep safely alongside the wharf. Cato and Apollonius moved to the front of the barge while the crew occupied the rear deck. There was a brief conversation at the other end of the craft, but Cato could not catch any of the words that were exchanged. After a while, the five men settled down to sleep. Or pretended to. Cato was wide awake, and quietly took two of the belaying pins from their holders, pressing one into Apollonius's hand as he whispered, 'Keep your eyes and ears open. If they're going to betray us, I reckon they'll do it tonight.'

'I'll be ready.'

CHAPTER TWENTY-SIX

A s the hours of darkness passed, a thin crescent moon rose in the night sky and its reflection wavered and sparkled across the river. An owl screeched occasionally as it hunted for prey further along the bank. By and by, the sounds of music and voices from the town faded into silence and there was the odd splash of a jumping fish. In other circumstances this would have been a tranquil night, Cato thought. But his senses were alert to any potential danger, and he knew that the agent lying on the other side of the deck was equally on edge and ready for action.

Democles and his companions made their move some two hours after the town had grown silent. Cato saw their dark shapes rise up at the stern and begin to creep forward soundlessly. He tightened his grip on the belaying pin and his muscles tensed, ready to burst into action. As they drew closer, the crew spread out, the boy to the left, Democles in the middle and Patrakis to the right. Each man carried a knife as they came on in a crouch, careful not to make a sudden movement or noise to announce their treachery.

Cato waited until they were no more than two paces away, then sprang up and leaped forward with the belaying pin raised and ready to strike. Apollonius was on his feet an instant later and rushed towards Patrakis, striking his knife hand so that the blade clattered onto the deck. The crewman let out a yell of pain before it was cut off as Apollonius punched him savagely in the throat. He stumbled back, clawing at his neck and making a gurgling noise.

Cato kept the belaying pin raised as he growled, 'Drop those knives! Do it.'

'You fucking take 'em,' Democles snarled, and gave his remaining companion a shove towards Cato. 'Get him, boy!'

The youth rushed forward, knife thrust out before him. Cato leaned to one side and caught the boy's wrist with his left hand while he struck him on the side of the head with the pin. He dropped to the deck, senseless.

In the space of a few heartbeats, the captain had lost his men and now faced his two passengers alone. Patrakis had slumped to his knees and was choking on his crushed windpipe. He fell on his side and began to thrash about, emitting a dry rasping noise. Democles stepped back a couple of paces and raised his left hand, palm first.

'Steady now, boys, we didn't mean to harm you. Just wanted the reward, that's all. You can take my purse and find another boat to carry you. How's that sound?'

'It sounds like a plan,' Apollonius responded evenly. He stood erect and held out his hand. 'Give me the purse, then.'

Democles hesitated, and the agent took a step towards him. 'Now. Or else.'

'All right, friend. No need to threaten me.'

The attack was almost too quick for Cato to follow. Apollonius dropped his pin, grabbed the captain's knife hand and thrust it up so the point caught him under the chin and punched into his brain. He forced it up even further and wrenched it from side to side for good measure before releasing his grip and giving Democles a firm thrust on his chest to send him flying onto his back, his skull cracking against the deck.

Cato looked at the three bodies, and then placed his pin back in its holder.

'We can't stay here. We have to go.'

'You think so?' Apollonius responded wryly. 'We won't get far on foot, I'm thinking.'

'Then we take the barge.'

'You think you can handle this thing?'

'Yes. But we have to leave now. You cast off the mooring ropes.'

Apollonius nodded and padded forward to the bow to unfasten the rope on the foredeck cleat, then haul it in from around the mooring post on the wharf. As he hurried to the stern to release the aft mooring, Cato picked up one of the barge's sweeps and pressed the blade against the wharf, bracing his feet on the deck as he eased the vessel away. A gap opened, and then the barge pivoted slowly on the stern until Apollonius managed to release the rope, which dropped into the water with a sudden splash. Both men froze and looked around urgently in case the noise had attracted any attention, but there was no movement on the nearest boats. Cato worked his way aft, thrusting at the shaft of the oar, and the barge moved slowly out into open water.

'Get the other oar,' he said quietly. 'Put it between those two pegs. Like this.'

He demonstrated, and Apollonius followed suit on the other side. Then Cato stood on the broad bench that crossed the middle of the barge just behind the mast and took up the leather-covered handles of both sweeps. He considered having the agent row alongside him, but the thought of two landsmen clumsily attempting to coordinate their strokes and attracting

348

unwanted attention decided him against the idea.

'Get to the rear and take the tiller,' he ordered. 'Just keep us heading straight out into the river for now.'

As Apollonius hurried to the back and took up his position, Cato tested the weight and balance of the sweeps and then moved his arms forward and down so the blades swept back over the surface of the river. Then, taking every care to avoid them entering the water too loudly, he drew them back in a steady movement. The barge moved away from the other craft along the wharf at an angle, and as Cato continued rowing, Apollonius eased the tiller over so that the barge turned away gently and headed directly towards the far bank.

When they reached the middle of the river, Cato shipped the oars and wetted a finger to hold up to the faint breeze. There was just enough to get the barge under way, he judged. He undid the sail ties and then hauled on the halyard to raise the spar to which the sail was attached. The weathered linen flapped gently in the breeze before he trimmed the sail and cleated the mainsheets. With the breeze blowing steadily off the port quarter, the sail began to draw the barge upriver, and he took the tiller from Apollonius.

The sky to the east was already tinged with a paler shade of velvet that presaged dawn, and he could make out details along the river, as well as seeing more clearly the three bodies on the deck. 'We'd better get rid of them. Over the side.'

'What if they wash up close to that town? Someone is bound to recognise them, and then they'll be looking for us all along the river.'

'If we drop them here in the middle, they'll be carried some way beyond the town before they get washed up or found by another boat. But best to be sure. See if there's some ballast in the hold. Anything to weigh down the bodies.'

Apollonius nodded and stepped over to the hatch coaming. He pulled out some of the bales of fur and then some jars of wine before he located the rocks packed into the bilges. 'These will do nicely.'

There were some empty sacks in the bow locker, and he packed rocks into three of them before tying them to the feet of Democles and his two crewmen. He paused to wrench the knife out of the captain's throat and wiped it on his tunic before setting it aside and removing Democles's purse. Then, lifting the body under the armpits, he heaved it up onto the side and pushed it overboard. There was a splash and a large ripple, and Cato saw the captain's face dimly beneath the surface as he sank into the depths and disappeared. Patrakis was next, and then Apollonius went to lift the youth up. As he raised him by the shoulders, there was a groan as the boy came round, and his eyes flickered open. At once he turned his head to the side and vomited convulsively.

'Charming.' Apollonius let go and looked up at Cato. 'Well, this one's still alive. What do we do with him? We can't keep him with us. He'll give us away first chance he gets.'

'Tie him up and put him in the hold.'

Apollonius sighed. 'I don't think so.'

He picked up the knife, grasped the boy's hair and pulled his head back, cutting his throat with a firm sweep of the blade. Blood pulsed onto the deck, and the youth moaned and stared about him in panic.

'Upsy-daisy,' Apollonius muttered through gritted teeth as he lifted the writhing body and tipped it over the side. 'That's solved the problem.'

Cato glared at him. 'I told you to tie him up.'

'Yes, you did,' Apollonius said simply, then gestured at the splatters and pools of blood on the deck. 'I'd better clean this up before it gets light. Don't want us looking like a butcher's block to any boats seeing it if they pass close by.'

By the time the sun rose over the hills to the east and bathed the landscape either side of the river in a ruddy glow, the decks had been cleared of blood and Apollonius was searching for something to eat and drink. There was a locker in the deck underneath the captain's steering position, and Cato moved to one side to permit the agent to search it. He leaned in and took out two small wine jars. One was empty, so he tossed it over the side. The second was half full; he took out the cork, sniffed, winced and sent it the same way as the first.

'Water it is, then,' he muttered as he continued searching. A moment later he found a large cured sausage wrapped in a fine cloth, and a small chest. 'Aha!'

He opened the chest and held it up for Cato to see. Inside was a small fortune in silver coins.

'More than enough for our needs.' Cato nodded. 'I wonder how much of that Democles was going to spend on a couple of broken-down nags for us.'

Apollonius closed the chest and placed it back in the locker. He unwrapped the sausage and was about to cut some thick slices when he noticed the boy's blood still on the blade. Out of deference to his superior's sensitivity, he leaned over the side to wash the blood off before he proceeded. A moment later, the two men were chewing contentedly on the hunks of meat, fat and gristle as the barge maintained its course upriver with Cato resting his spare arm on the tiller.

From its position on an escarpment high above the river, the fortress city of Dura Europus commanded fine views. Cato and Apollonius gazed out over the surrounding landscape as they rested briefly after their climb from the dock far below. They had moored the barge at the far end and paid a local boy to mind it for them until they returned, so that it would not look abandoned until they were far from the city. They had taken two cloaks and spare tunics from the slop chest, and the coins Cato had divided between them were safely tucked into the bottom of the sidebags they carried. With their worn clothing and unkempt beards, they drew no attention amid the diverse range of people passing through the city. They paid the toll at the gate and walked through the gatehouse into the narrow street beyond.

The city owed its origins to a military purpose, and since the original structures had determined the layout, what was now a thriving market had once been the parade ground of the fortress. It occupied an open square bounded by the fortress's stables, which were now used as warehouses by the merchants who traded goods from the furthest corners of the known world and beyond. People of many races crowded the narrow lanes between the market stalls, dressed in clothes of every hue and style, and though most spoke in Greek or the local dialect, there were several tongues that were completely unknown to Cato.

The two Romans bought rations and spare waterskins for the journey before making their way out of the west gate of the city, which gave onto the plateau where the beast market stood. There were pens of goats and pigs, lines of mules, and corrals for the camels and horses to one side of the arena used for auctions. Cato and Apollonius approached one of the smaller dealers and examined his stock of horses. Palmyra was over a hundred miles across the desert, and it was essential to choose dependable horses for the journey along the trade route linking the two cities. They picked out three, in case one fell lame, and two saddles; then, leaving Apollonius to agree the price, Cato went to the nearest feed merchant to buy bags of grain.

As he waited for Apollonius to join him, he noticed a group of Parthian soldiers making their way through the market, stopping to question traders and random passers-by. He shifted his feed bags to the shade of an awning to one side of the thoroughfare and lay down on them pretending to be asleep. Through narrowed eyes he watched the Parthians approach. One of them passed close by and paused to glance at him. He gave a theatrical snort and yawn before picking his nose and turning on his side. The Parthian's lip curled in disgust and he continued on his way.

As soon as the soldiers were a safe distance away, Cato stood up and looked anxiously in the direction of the horse trader. To his relief, he saw Apollonius leading the three mounts. The agent gave him a cheery wave, but when he saw the serious expression on Cato's face, his smile faded.

'What's up?'

Cato pointed in the direction the Parthians had taken. 'Soldiers searching the crowd. They might not be looking for us, but I'd bet good money that they are.'

'There may be more of them on the road to Palmyra,' Apollonius said as he scanned the surrounding throng of traders and customers.

'I would imagine so.' Cato heaved the feed bags up across the back of the spare horse and tied them to the harness. 'The sooner we get going, the better.'

They led the horses to the edge of the beast market and made their way towards the area where caravans were forming up ready to begin the desert crossing. The camels and horses were drinking from a series of stone troughs fed by a channel leading back to the city, and the air was filled with the sound of voices and the deep, guttural bleating and groaning of the camels. Water splashed in a small nymphaeum set up as a grateful offering to the gods by a successful merchant, whose name was carved into its black stone base. Several men were filling waterskins there. Apollonius stayed with the horses while Cato saw to their own waterskins and made certain the stoppers were securely in place before hanging them from the saddle horns.

'Do you see?' said the agent quietly, nodding towards the Palmyra road. A short distance beyond the laden camels and their drivers, Cato could see that the Parthians had set up a checkpoint and were already scrutinising the head of the caravan moving out along the road. 'What shall we do, Tribune?'

'They're looking for two men, so we'll separate. I'll go first. If they stop me, you hold back and try and find another way. If I think they're on to me, I'll stretch out my arms. All right?'

'Why not let me go first?'

'Because you're the one with all the intelligence stored in your head. Corbulo will need that for the campaign. It's more important that you get back across the frontier safely.'

'You're right,' Apollonius conceded. 'Be careful, Tribune. For a fine soldier, you make a terrible spy.'

Cato gave a dry laugh. 'I'll do my best to keep out of trouble.'

He took the reins of one of the saddled horses and led it away from the marshalling area and onto the road behind a string of camels carrying large bales of brightly coloured cloth. He paused and lifted himself up into the saddle before he flicked the reins and continued following the camels, which swayed easily from side to side as they plodded forward on their broad padded feet. The checkpoint was just over a hundred paces away, and he felt his heart beat faster as he slowly approached the soldiers. He made his mind up that if he was challenged, he'd make a break for it. The horse was in good shape and would be able to carry him for some miles away from the road before he was obliged to rest it. Enough to outpace the Parthians, he hoped. And if they set off after him, it would give Apollonius a chance to get a fair distance along the road before they returned to their checkpoint.

The soldiers seemed to be waving camel drivers through and focusing their attention on carts and wagons and those riding horses, in groups or travelling alone. As Cato neared them, they stopped a cart and an officer questioned the driver, who looked down as he was spoken to and seemed to answer furtively. The officer snapped an order to the nearest of his men, and two of them began to search the cart while two others stood either side of the driver. The officer watched closely as the camels ahead of Cato passed by, and then stepped out in front of him and raised a hand, calling out a command.

Cato reined in but shook his head as he responded in Greek. 'I don't understand.'

'What is your name?' the Parthian demanded in accented Greek.

'Philo of Alexandria,' Cato replied.

'Where have you come from?' asked the officer. He stepped closer and patted the horse's cheek before taking hold of the bridle. 'And what's your business here?'

Cato thought quickly. He was tempted to use the fur trader cover story, but it was possible that the bodies of the barge's crew had been found and a connection made with the fugitives. 'I have come from Seleucia, where I sold my last cargo of scents from Alexandria. I am returning there now to fetch the next shipment.'

'A scent merchant.' The officer leaned closer and sniffed. 'Either you're lying, or your scents are so cheap they don't last for very long.'

Cato forced a laugh. 'Long enough for me to take the money and go, sir.'

The Parthian shook his head in disgust. 'You Greeks . . . Do you never stop cheating your customers? People like you, coming across our borders, taking our money and laughing at us behind our backs. King Vologases will see you off one day. There's a man who truly believes in Parthia for the Parthians.' He released his grip on the bridle and stepped away. 'Get out of here before I give you a good hiding.'

'Yes, sir.' Cato bowed his head obsequiously. 'Thank you, sir.'

He clicked his tongue and trotted his horse through the checkpoint without looking back, continuing for another hundred paces before slowing to a walk, fearing that he might be called back at any moment. But there was no outcry, and he sighed with relief. Half a mile down the road, he drew up and waited for Apollonius. An hour passed before he saw the agent riding towards him, leading the spare horse with his free hand. As soon as he caught sight of Cato, he slowed down, and Cato urged his mount forward and fell in alongside him.

'Any trouble?'

'No. I waited a while to give you a chance to get away if they took me.'

Cato nodded his gratitude. 'Did they stop you?'

'Briefly. Just to ask my name and a few other details.'

'What did you tell them?'

'I gave them the same story we used with Democles.'

'I see.'

Apollonius caught the strained tone in Cato's remark. 'Any problem with that?'

'Let's hope not. Come on. I want to get to the head of the caravan. Then tomorrow we'll head off on our own and ride hard for Palmyra.'

* * *

The caravan had travelled some fifteen miles along the road to Palmyra before the leading merchant and his string of animals drew up to camp for the night. The sun was still above the horizon and casting long shadows across the barren landscape. The featureless ground stretched out on all sides; sand and rocks, with stunted shrubs dotting the barely undulating desert. One by one the other merchants and their drovers moved off the road to find a patch of ground to claim for themselves. It was a long-standing convention, since only a fool would continue alone for any distance to make camp. There was safety in numbers, particularly here in the desert, where bands of brigands were often on the lookout for easy prey. The dust raised by the camels and horses hung in the evening air like a red mist, through which men and beasts moved like ghosts.

Cato and Apollonius picked their way to an area just ahead of the caravan and dismounted. They relieved the horses of their burdens and then unbuckled the saddles and heaved them off before slipping feedbags over the animals' noses. While their mounts chomped on the barley, Apollonius used his knife to cut the nearest scrub for firewood.

As the sun disappeared below the western horizon, they sat either side of the small fire the agent had prepared, propped up against their saddles. Cato shared out their rations, and they chewed on hardtack and strips of dried beef, followed by dates bought in the market at Dura Europus. As he sipped from a waterskin, Apollonius gestured towards one of the larger camp areas, where a small crowd had gathered around a fire.

'Should we join them? So that we don't stand out.'

Cato looked round before he responded. 'No one is paying us any attention. Better we stay here rather than risk being asked any awkward questions that might cause suspicion. You can be sure there are enough people in the caravan who have heard about the reward.'

'If you say so, Tribune, though I might hear something that could be useful to the general.'

Cato smiled thinly. 'Still playing your part as Corbulo's spy?'

'Of course. To the very end.'

'I hope it's worth it. Given that it has cost the lives of my men.'

'They will only have died for nothing if we don't make it to Palmyra,' Apollonius responded wearily. 'And we're not too far from there now. There's nothing between us and safety but this desert.'

'I hope you're right.' Cato was quiet for a moment as he regarded the agent. 'And what happens after we get back to Corbulo? Will you stay with the army when he begins the campaign?'

'If he pays me well enough to make it worth my while, yes.'

'If not, what will you do?'

'Why the interest in my life, Tribune?'

'You're a competent man. A quick thinker, and good in a fight. I could use someone like you in my cohort.'

Apollonius threw his head back and laughed. 'Me? Become a soldier? Why would I want to do that? It would mean obeying orders given by men I have no respect for, and giving orders to men for whom I have even less respect. All for a fraction of what I earn now. And I would have no choice in the cause I fought for. No say over whether I agreed with the purpose of a war that might claim my life. What kind of fool would sign up for that?'

'Clearly the kind you have no respect for . . .'

'I apologise, Tribune. You're a good man, and a good officer. I do respect you. Truly I do. But I have to ask you, why did you choose to be a soldier?'

'I didn't,' Cato replied simply.

'Oh?'

'I had no choice. I was my father's bequest to the army when he died. As it turned out, the army became my family. I suppose I stuck with it because it was the only family I had. The men I fight alongside are more like brothers to me than if we shared the same parents. I wish I could give you a lengthy justification that would satisfy your intellect. Some discourse on the honour of serving the emperor, defending the homeland or fighting for civilised values. But I can't. I've lived long enough to see such phrases for the hollow sham they are. I serve because the army is my family. That's how it is.'

Apollonius nodded, and stared up at the first of the evening stars. 'Some important things in life are simple, Tribune. There is no need to make excuses for them.'

'I'm not making excuses,' Cato replied sharply. 'Anyway, you've made your position clear. I won't ask you again. It's time to sleep. I want to be on the road at first light.'

He built up the fire with the rest of the wood that had been cut and then settled back against his saddle and covered himself with his cloak. He closed his eyes and breathed slowly, pretending to be asleep, and waited until he could hear Apollonius start to snore lightly. Then he opened his eyes and saw above him the full splendour of the night sky. The air was dry and clear, so that it seemed there were more stars visible than he had ever seen before, and there was something achingly beautiful about being there in the desert beneath such exquisitely serene heavens. It felt as if time itself had stopped and he was caught up in some form of eternity that granted him absolute peace of mind and soul, as though all his cares and fears were set aside for that moment of bliss. He wondered if this was proof that he was not meant to be a soldier after all. Or perhaps soldiers were not so different from other people when it came to enjoying such moments. Poets had no monopoly on the appreciation of beauty, just as soldiers had no monopoly on the exercise of violence. What would Macro make of this experience? he wondered. He realised once again how much he missed his friend. When danger threatened, there was no greater reassurance than knowing Macro was at his side, come what may, to the very end.

Cato turned on his side and closed his eyes, shifting closer to the fire to keep out the cold of the desert night. His mind cleared and he slowly drifted off to sleep.

He woke with a start as Apollonius shook his shoulder. It was still dark, and the agent loomed against the stars.

'Easy there, Tribune. We need to get ready. Dawn's not far off. Look.'

Cato turned to the east, and sure enough, he could just make out the band of lighter sky along the horizon. It was bitterly cold, and his cloak was covered with tiny ice crystals. He stood up and rubbed his hands together vigorously. The fire had died hours ago, and offered no warmth.

The two men ate some more of the hardtack and drank some water before they heaved the blankets and saddles onto the horses and fastened the straps. By the time they had loaded the feed and their rations and water, a thin light was spreading across the desert as the first camels stirred and made their characteristic groans. Then Cato looked back along the road and froze.

'What is it?' asked Apollonius.

He pointed towards a low ridge a few miles away. 'There. See the dust?'

Apollonius squinted for a moment. 'I see it now.'

The tell-tale plume rose from the edge of the ridge, barely visible to the untrained eye. A body of men, possibly on horseback.

'Trouble?' asked Apollonius. 'I don't see how they can be on to us. Otherwise they'd have stopped us at the checkpoint.'

'Maybe they've spoke to someone and found enough information to think again. Either way, we can't afford to take any risks. We have to get moving.'

'But won't they spot us riding ahead, just as we spotted them?'

'I dare say. It may give us away. But we have no choice.'

They climbed into the saddles, turned the mounts towards the road and urged them into a canter, heading towards Palmyra. Cato saw a handful of figures from the caravan rise briefly to watch them ride off, no doubt wondering at the foolishness of two men heading out on the road alone. It was a risk, but then they were beset by risks, and Cato's choice seemed the least dangerous course of action.

As they continued down the road, they looked back from time to time to track the progress of the men making for the caravan. The light strengthened, revealing that the dust was being kicked up by a party of riders coming on at a gallop. It was possible they had already seen the two men some miles ahead of them, but Cato hoped they would be delayed by stopping to ask questions of the merchants. Someone was bound to mention the two horsemen and their spare mount leaving the camp at first light. That alone would arouse enough suspicion to warrant a pursuit. The chase was on.

★ ★ ★

The road followed a course almost straight across the desert, only deviating when a steep slope or rocky escarpment broke up the undulating expanse of sand and stone. Even though it was November, the air warmed quickly as the sun climbed into the sky. At noon, they stopped by an outcrop of boulders and took shelter in the shade. Cato positioned himself to look back down the road, and as they prepared to remount, he spotted the plume of dust five or six miles back.

'Shit. I'd hoped they'd be held up at the convoy for longer.'

'It must be us they're looking for,' said Apollonius as he shaded his eyes and squinted into the distance. 'I can't think of any other reason for them being this far out along the road.'

'Then we'll have to stay ahead of them. Time to go.'

They continued to follow the road, and late in the afternoon passed a smaller caravan, ignoring the entreaties of some of the drovers to stop the night with them and sample some of their wares. As darkness fell, they took shelter in the lee of another outcrop as a biting wind blew up, carrying fine grains of sand that caught in their eyes and mouths. Once their horses were unburdened and fed, Cato climbed the rocks and saw the glow of the caravan's campfires a few miles back, and then another fire the same distance beyond, and realised that the horsemen had made up some ground.

By the end of the following day, their better-mounted pursuers were closer still, and Cato knew that if they did not find some way to throw them off, the horsemen would soon catch up with them. He confided his concern to Apollonius, who coughed to clear his throat before responding.

'If it comes to that, Tribune, I have no intention of being taken back to Ctesiphon in chains so that my head can be used to decorate the gatehouse of Vologases' palace.'

'I share the sentiment, but since the only weapon we have is your knife, the question of making a last stand is somewhat academic. If we want to avoid the fate you mention, there's only one way of going about it.'

Apollonius sighed. 'I understand . . . Do you want me to do it? I can make it quick for you.'

Cato thought for a moment. 'I'd like to say something noble about a Roman officer choosing death at his own hand, but I've seen you use a blade. Better that you make a good job of it than I foul it up.'

'All right then. I'll see to you first.'

Cato nodded. 'In the meantime, let's just do our best to get to Palmyra ahead of them. It's a day's ride from here, I estimate.'

'A day too far, then . . .'

They were back on the road as soon as there was enough light to see the way ahead. And so were their pursuers. All day they closed the gap, until they were no more than two miles away, riding towards a fold in the ground below the low ridge on which Cato and Apollonius had halted. Dusk had started to fall across the barren terrain, and it would be dark within the hour. The Parthians were close enough for Cato to count them. Twelve soldiers. There could be no thought of turning to fight them, even if they could fashion any makeshift weapons more effective than Apollonius's knife.

The horses had been pushed almost to their limit, and Apollonius dismounted to swap the saddle onto the spare mount for it to take its turn. As he worked, Cato spotted a clump of bushes with vicious-looking needles growing along the edge of an ancient wadi. He ordered the other man to give him the knife, and hurriedly began to cut some boughs from the shrubs and tie them together with rope.

'What are you doing?' asked Apollonius.

363

'You carry on with the saddling. I've got an idea that might buy us some time.'

Once Apollonius had completed his task, Cato called him over to hold the large bundle of scrub away from the unsaddled horse as he fastened the rope to each side of the harness that stretched across the animal's back. Then he took the reins and moved the beast round to face the open desert.

'Let go!'

Apollonius released his grip, and the bundle swept down and landed right by the rear hoofs of the horse, the long, thorny spikes gouging the animal's flesh all the way up its legs as far as the gaskin. At once it let out a pained whinny and lurched forward, only to be scratched and pricked yet again. Desperate to escape the pain in its legs, it kept moving, and galloped off into the desert, heading north, the brush stirring up plenty of dust as it trailed along just behind the horse's rear legs. Apollonius grasped the idea at once.

'Clever. Let's hope it works.'

'Get down into the wadi,' Cato ordered as he returned the knife and led his horse over to the edge, some thirty paces away, then down the steep slope beyond.

Apollonius followed him into the hiding place. Dust swirled about them for a moment before it settled, and they stood by their mounts' heads and stroked them in an effort to make the horses still and quiet before the Parthians approached. The light steadily faded as they waited, and then Cato's ears picked up the sound of hoofs pounding along the road, the volume swelling quickly as their pursuers galloped up to the ridge. Then there was a shout and a confusion of noises as the horsemen drew up, followed by a hurried exchange. From the tone of the voices, it sounded as if there was a difference of opinion, and Cato prayed that they would fall for his bait.

The agent looked at him anxiously as he listened.

'What are they saying?' Cato whispered.

'Shh!' Apollonius cocked his head to one side, frowning. Then there was a curt word of command, and the horsemen started moving again, drawing away from the edge of the wadi. He grinned. 'They've fallen for it!'

They waited until the sounds had faded into the distance and then climbed out of the wadi to see two clouds of dust racing away from the road. It would be dark soon, Cato realised. Before long the Parthians would not be able to see their prey and would have to slow down for fear of their mounts stumbling and breaking a leg. It might take hours for them to catch up with the horse dragging the thorny bundle of brush.

Apollonius smiled with satisfaction and relief and clapped him on the shoulder.

'Fine work.'

'I have my uses.' Cato grinned. 'We'd better make the most of it.'

They mounted and walked their horses down the far slope of the ridge, not daring to go faster in case they raised any dust that might expose their ruse. When the last of the daylight had gone, they increased their pace to a steady trot, following the road towards Palmyra and the promise of sanctuary from their Parthian pursuers. After that, it would be no more than two days before they crossed the frontier into the Roman Empire and made their way to Tarsus to report to General Corbulo. While Cato's vain attempt to win a treaty had failed, Apollonius would set down all the details of the intelligence he could recall from their journey. It might be enough, Cato hoped, to swing the delicate balance of the coming war in Rome's favour.

CHAPTER TWENTY-SEVEN

'A re you certain he's dead?' Macro asked Manlius, the centurion of the watch, as they marched through the camp towards the southern gate.

'Certain of it. The body was already cold when I was sent for.'

December had come, and the first heavy snowfall of the winter had started early the previous night and continued until a few hours before dawn. Now the camp and surrounding landscape were covered by a gleaming mantle of unblemished white. The snow had been carried on a biting gale that had howled over the ramparts, building up drifts against the windward side of the palisade. Inside the camp, the men were emerging from their shelters to prepare for morning assembly. They stamped in the snow to try to keep their feet from getting cold as they blew steamy breath into their hands and then rubbed them. There was no mistaking their surly mood as they stared at the two centurions passing by. Much as he believed in discipline, with all the fervour of a religious fanatic, Macro had some sympathy with their grievances.

They were still on half-rations and were getting thinner and weaker with every passing day. Even though the bridge had been repaired, the supply convoys from Tarsus took far longer to get through than had been anticipated, thanks to the autumn rains turning the mountain road that linked the city to Thapsis into a quagmire. Now that winter had arrived in the mountains, the snow and ice made matters even worse for the supply wagons as they struggled to get through to the siege camp, while the forage parties were finding it ever more difficult to supplement the dwindling stocks held in the supply huts close to headquarters.

Starvation might have been a grim prospect for the legionaries and auxiliaries, but it was already a daily torment for the gangs of local people toiling to complete the ditch and rampart that would surround Thapsis. Over a hundred of them had already perished, their bodies stacked in a burial pit outside the stockade where they lived when they were not labouring on the siege works alongside the Roman soldiers.

Those were not the only deaths over the month since the Third Cohort had followed the Syrians into exile outside the main camp. Eighteen men from the two units had already died from the effects of being exposed to the harsh weather that had seized the valley in its freezing grip. Prefect Orfitus and Centurion Pullinus had begged the general for another thirty to be taken back into the camp to be treated in the hospital shelters. But Corbulo had refused and told the two officers not to repeat the request on pain of a further reduction in their rations. Accordingly, more deaths had followed, as the older and weaker of the men had succumbed. While Macro could accept that the general's harsh methods might result in a tougher army, inured to suffering, he could not help wondering if the losses that entailed would be an acceptable price to pay for it.

There was, however, one development that promised hope to the men suffering outside Thapsis. Replacement siege engines had reached the army the day before and were already being assembled behind the palisade of the siege battery. Soon they would be adding their weight to the bombardment being carried out by the large catapult that the engineers had managed to construct from local resources. A section of the wall to the left of the gate had been chosen as a target, and already the battlements had been beaten down and the top eight feet or so of the wall pounded into a ruin. With the added missiles from the replacement weapons, Corbulo anticipated a practicable breach within a month. But before then, half-rations and more deaths might well prove too much for the men to endure.

Mutiny was in the air. Macro had heard rumours of men going from unit to unit to provoke dissent and hostility towards General Corbulo. He even had the name of the purported ringleader: Borenus, who claimed to be a legionary from the Eighth Cohort of the Sixth Legion. Only there was no such man in the unit. The conspirators were playing cautious, he reflected. As well they might, given that they would face the death penalty if they were identified. *When* they were identified, he corrected himself.

And now there was this new matter to take into account: the discovery of the body of one of the centurions from the same legion. It was bad enough to lose a valuable officer, but if his death proved to be suspicious, it would be infinitely worse. If he had been murdered by a disgruntled man, or men, under his command, it would set a hideous precedent across the rest of the army. When soldiers were driven to killing their officers, the collapse of discipline and the chaos that followed couldn't be far off, thought Macro as he regarded the men slowly forming up on either side as he passed by.

The body of Centurion Piso lay face down beside the drain

that passed through the latrine block on the low ground in the corner of the camp. An optio and two of his men were standing guard, while a small crowd of curious legionaries and auxiliaries had gathered around the block.

Macro turned towards them with a scowl and brandished his vine cane. 'What are you hanging around here for? Either have a piss or a shit, or fuck off out of it and get ready for morning assembly. Before I decide to pick a new team for latrine duty . . .'

The soldiers hurriedly dispersed, and he bent over the body for a closer examination. There was no sign of blood on Piso or the ground around him, and no obvious signs of stab wounds. Nor was there any snow on the body, so he had died within the last two to three hours. Macro took his arm and turned him onto his back. The centurion's eyes were wide open and his jaw hung slack, giving his face a surprised expression. Just above the fold of his neck cloth, Macro saw a patch of discoloured skin, the blue and purple of bruising. He undid the loose knot of the cloth and removed it to reveal a distinct ring of bruises around the officer's neck either side of a vivid red line.

'Strangled,' Manlius observed.

'Garrotted, more like.' Macro straightened up. 'Who found him?'

Manlius pointed out one of the legionaries standing with the optio. 'Pindarus.'

Macro looked over at the young man. He had a pimply face and a runny nose that caused him to sniff every few breaths. 'What's the story, Pindarus?'

'Story, sir?'

'Tell me how you found him, in as much detail as you can recall,' Macro said patiently.

The youngster collected his thoughts. 'I was on duty on the south tower when the change of watch was sounded. I really needed a piss and came running down here to the ditch, and that's when I found the centurion, sir.'

'What was wrong with pissing in the latrine block?'

'It's hard to see your way in the dark, sir. If you go inside.'

'Maybe, but it's against regs to take a piss or shit outside of the latrines. What if everyone did that? Imagine what the camp would be like. That's why we have rules. And that's why you're going to have a week on latrine duty. Continue.'

'I saw him lying there, sir. I thought he might be drunk. That happens sometimes, when a lad's the worse for wear. Then I realised he was an officer. I asked him if there was anything wrong, and when he didn't give me any response, I went to turn him over. But it was obvious he was dead, sir. So I went and got the optio. He saw the body and then sent for the centurion.' Pindarus shrugged. 'That's all.'

'When you found the body, was there anyone nearby?'

'No, sir.'

'Did you hear anything? Anything unusual?'

'No, sir.'

'And did you do it? Did you kill him, Pindarus?'

The youth's mouth sagged open and he shook his head. 'No, sir!'

Macro stared back for a moment and nodded. 'All right. That'll do. You and the optio keep the body under guard.'

Pindarus saluted, and Macro ordered the other legionary to report to headquarters to inform the general about the discovery. As the soldier ran off over the snow, Macro looked at the body again and gave a deep sigh.

'Corbulo's not going to like this one bit . . .'

★ ★ ★

370

'Murdered, you say?' Corbulo growled as he stared down at the body. Snow had begun to fall again, fine flakes swirling on the light breeze, and Macro had to brush off a thin layer to expose the ligature marks.

'Garrotted, sir. I imagine he had just come out of the latrine when the killer jumped him from behind. It would have been quick, and there would have been very few people about at that hour.'

'What about those on sentry duty?'

'They tend to keep an eye on the approaches to the camp, sir, rather than on what's going on inside it.'

'I'll thank you to keep your sarcastic comments to yourself, Centurion. Someone must have seen or heard something.'

'Possibly, sir. But no one's come forward with any information yet.'

Corbulo regarded the body again and then cleared his throat. 'I want to speak with Centurion Macro alone. The rest of you, leave us. And make sure we're not interrupted.'

Manlius and the others strode off to the other side of the open ground between the rampart and the lines of huts around which the men were gathering while they waited for the trumpet call to signal morning assembly.

'Who do you think did this?' Corbulo asked. 'Could it have been the rebels?' he continued in a hopeful tone. Even the thought of a rebel getting into the camp to kill Piso was preferable to the prospect of a centurion being murdered by one of his own men.

'I doubt it, sir. The only possible way in without the sentries seeing is the opening where the latrine drain passes through the rampart. But you'd have a struggle to get through that. Whoever did it was taking a risk going for a man like Piso. There's a reason why the men's nickname for him is the Beast. There are other reasons, of course.'

Corbulo arched an eyebrow. 'Other reasons?'

'From what I understand, Piso has – had – a reputation for being more than a bit free with the use of his cane. Seems the Beast was also a beater. Officers like that tend to make enemies.'

'Are you saying he was killed by one of the men?'

Macro tilted his head to one side. 'I'm saying it's likely, especially given the mood in the camp. The lads are hungry, and they're not happy about the constant punishments. Especially with regard to the men forced to camp outside the palisade.'

'Hardship's a way of life in the army, Macro. You understand that as well as any man. But murdering a centurion? That's an outrage.'

'Yes, sir. It is.'

'I will not tolerate it. The centurions are the backbone of the army. They are what holds it together through thick and thin. If the men start turning on their officers, then the army is nothing more than a mutinous rabble.' Corbulo paused and glanced round to make sure he would not be overheard. 'It looks like we may be facing the beginnings of a mutiny.'

Macro breathed deeply and nodded. 'Yes, sir. I fear so.'

'Do we know who the ringleaders are? Any names at all? Once they've spent a few hours with the torturers, we'll have the details of all those involved.'

'There is a name, sir. A rumour, at any rate. A man called Borenus. He's supposed to be a legionary from the Eighth Cohort.'

'Then arrest him.'

Macro shook his head. 'It's a false name, sir. I checked the rolls.'

'Whoever he is, do you think he's responsible for murdering Piso?'

'Maybe. Or it might just be one of Piso's men who has had enough of being beaten.' Macro cleared his throat. 'The thing that concerns me is that this might just be the start of it. Unless morale improves, it could get worse. And what with the men being on half-rations, and grumbling with it, the centurions have no choice but to go in hard to keep them doing their duty. Which only makes the men's mood worse.' Macro shrugged and made a circular gesture with his finger. 'Bit of a downward spiral, sir.'

Corbulo grimaced. 'Well, there's not much I can do about increasing the rations, as things stand. So the only way I can keep order is through maintaining an iron discipline. That's what will get them through this winter siege. They might grumble now, but they'll thank me for it later.'

Macro was doubtful. 'I hope so, sir. But I think things have gone beyond a bit of a grumble.' He gestured towards the body.

Corbulo made a face. 'Quite.'

A trumpet note sounded across the camp and the men shuffled into formation between their huts before the optios started to call their names. Corbulo regarded them for a moment before reaching a decision. 'Pass the word. I want a general assembly once the roll call is complete. It's time to nip this mutiny nonsense in the bud.'

An hour later, the modest army of some four thousand men stood formed up on the open ground outside the camp amid occasional light flurries of snow. The general regarded them from his position on the review mound in front of the standards, while the Praetorians took their station around the mound, facing the rest of the soldiers. Macro could not help feeling that the formal arrangement had something of a confrontational air about it, given the tensions in the camp. There was an unsettling quiet about the scene as well. Mostly due to the muting effect of the snow, but also in the sullen silence of the men as they waited for their commanding officer to speak. Macro stood stiffly a short distance from the general's shoulder and concentrated on trying not to shiver as Corbulo filled his lungs to begin his address.

'Last night, Centurion Piso of the Sixth Legion was murdered outside the latrine block. His killer struck from behind, like the craven coward he undoubtedly is, and garrotted him. I will have you know that Piso was a man with a long and distinguished career. He fought his way up from the ranks and was decorated for bravery on a number of occasions. It is, therefore, an outrage that his life was cut short when he had many years of service left to perform. Such men are not easily replaced. Such men are depended upon to lead from the front, to stand firm in battle and be the last to leave the field. The centurions set the standard for the common soldiers to look up to and emulate. Therefore, the murder of Piso is a loss for us all. And I will not rest until his killer is identified, arrested, tried and executed for the murder of our comrade.

'There are amongst you some who know who the guilty party is. Or who at least suspect who he may be. To them I say: it is your sacred duty to tell your superiors what you know, and to do it without delay. I have little doubt that the murderer is a man from Piso's own century, or possibly his cohort. As is the custom, in the absence of a specific guilty individual, the unit must be held accountable, and therefore I condemn the men of Piso's century to exile from the camp, effective as of this moment.'

Macro heard some faint groans from the ranks of soldiers

standing before the reviewing platform and bellowed at them, 'Silence!'

When all was quiet again, Corbulo continued. 'If I do not have the name of the killer within five days, then the rest of the cohort will share the same fate. There is no place for such a man in the Roman army, nor for those who would protect him by keeping silent.

'I am told that there is some discontent over the privations we are all forced to endure for the sake of this siege. I have heard that there are complaints about short rations and hard discipline. To those who complain about such things, I say that the choice is yours. If you are not prepared to honour your oath to serve without question the emperor and the officers he places over you, then I say you may quit this army. You may choose to turn your back on your comrades. You may choose to betray them. But if you do, you will leave behind all that the army has seen fit to equip you with. Your armour, your weapons, your clothing issue, your boots and whatever rations you may have hoarded. These things are not yours to keep. So, who here chooses to leave?'

He allowed his challenge to settle in their minds and waited for a moment before he spoke again. 'No one? None of you? Then it is settled. You choose to remain, and that means you choose to accept the discipline I impose upon you. That is the nature of the bargain between us. I have nothing to promise you but hardship and a single-minded dedication to duty. The reward for which awaits you up there!' He turned and thrust his arm towards Thapsis. 'All the food you can eat. All the loot you can carry back to Tarsus. The wine and women of Thapsis are yours. But you must earn it all. And it will not be long before those prizes are yours. Already our siege battery is beating down a section of their wall. Before long, there will be a breach, and on that day I, Gnaeus Domitius Corbulo, will lead the attack that takes the city!' He drew his sword and punched it into the air. 'Who is with me?'

Macro dutifully followed suit, as did almost all of the rest of the officers, but their cries were muffled by the snow, and their men stood in silence, unmoving and unwilling to share their commander's fervour. Corbulo slowly lowered his blade and then let his arm hang at his side as he regarded the assembled men with contempt.

'So be it. You disappoint me and shame the honour of Rome with your cowardly silence. I will not have it. And I will not allow the murderer of Piso to escape justice. Soldiers! Attention!'

The order was echoed by the centurions, and their units stamped to attention in the snow. Corbulo spared them a last withering look before he called out, 'General assembly . . . dismissed!'

As the men were marched off, one unit at a time, Corbulo turned to Macro. 'I don't like their mood one bit. They will need to be watched closely. The smallest infraction must be punished. Discipline is everything in the army, and I will see it enforced.'

Macro nodded. The general was right, to a point. But even something as essential and necessary as discipline was tested by circumstances and had its breaking point. And when it came close to snapping, a commander had but two choices: to enforce it even more rigorously to eke it out to the limit, and hope-fully beyond; or to compromise and make concessions. The problem with the latter course of action was that one com-promise inevitably led to more, which smacked of weakness. And Corbulo was not a commander who was prepared to appear weak.

'Your silence is thunderous, Centurion Macro. Do I take it that you disapprove of my firmness with the men?'

'No, sir. But it might be useful to find a way to ease some of their complaints while maintaining discipline.'

'If there is such a way, I am willing to hear suggestions.'

'They're hungry, sir. Starving, in fact.'

'As are we all,' Corbulo responded pointedly. 'Whatever scurrilous rumours may be doing the rounds about me and other senior officers. But with supply convoys struggling to get through to us and your foragers having exhausted the surrounding farms and villages, there's not much we can do about that.'

'Maybe not, but there's a forest some ten miles to the west, sir. Near the far end of the valley. I stopped close to the edge when I took a party out a few days back and saw a boar run into the treeline. As big a boar as I have ever seen, sir. I dare say there's plenty of game in there, and with the snow on the ground, it'll be easy to spot. If we mount a hunting expedition and take some wagons, and a few hundred men, we should come back with a good haul. It'll mean fresh meat to supplement the rations, and once the men catch a whiff of roasting meat, and fill their stomachs, it'll go a long way towards restoring their morale.'

Corbulo considered the prospect carefully, and then his stomach growled and both men could not help smiling. 'Very well, Macro. Make the arrangements. We'll go tomorrow. I'll lead the party. You'll remain here, in charge of the camp. It'll be good for the men to have me to thank for providing them with a fine roast.'

'Yes, sir.' Macro was disappointed not to have command of the hunting party, given that it had been his idea, but Corbulo's absence from camp for a couple of days might help reduce the tension between the general and his men.

377

Corbulo looked over his shoulder and squinted. 'Who's that?'

Macro turned and saw a small group of riders, dark against the snow, making their way along the road from Tarsus. As they drew closer, they spurred into a steady canter, their mounts kicking up snow as the riders made their way between the columns of men marching back into the camp. At their head rode an officer wrapped in a thick fur coat, and at his side a figure in a dark cloak with the hood drawn up.

Macro could not help smiling broadly. 'It's the tribune, sir. Cato's back.'

CHAPTER TWENTY-EIGHT

'The mission was something of a success, then,' Corbulo concluded once Apollonius and Cato had given their oral reports later in the day, and the general had read through the extensive notes and maps that his agent had prepared since leaving Palmyra. They were sitting around the brazier in his hut, and Corbulo reached to the side to pick up another split log to toss on the blaze before he continued. 'We may have lost the chance for a peace treaty to hold the Parthians off for a while, but I have some useful intelligence about the lie of the land, and the very satisfying bonus of having Vologases turn on one of his most powerful nobles. Haghrar's clan are not going to forgive the king for doing away with him. With luck, and a judicious bit of bribery, we might yet have another uprising to keep Vologases busy.'

'We didn't just lose the chance of a peace treaty, sir,' said Cato. 'We lost all the men of my escort. They were the pick of my cohort.'

'Fortunes of war, Tribune. Their sacrifice may well save lives when Rome invades Parthia.'

Cato's lips pressed together in a thin line and his disapproval was palpable. He swallowed his anger before he spoke. 'With respect, sir. You used me, and my men. You sent me to negotiate a deal with Vologases with no real hope of securing peace.'

'I disagree. I genuinely hoped you would make a deal, if only to delay war. I never promised it would be the easiest negotiation in history. Nor did I say we held all the bargaining chips. Any deal would have been better than no deal for the present. And now the mob back in Rome will have another war to keep them happy. It gives them an excuse to get drunk and roam around the forum boasting to any foreigners they come across about how great Rome is.' The corners of his mouth curled in contempt as he briefly considered the fickle and shallow politics of the plebs before he focused his attention on Cato again. 'I apologise if you feel I misled you. Sometimes that is necessary in the interests of the empire that we both serve. But I am delighted that you managed to escape from Parthia along with Apollonius. It would have been a sad loss for Rome if you had been executed by Vologases.'

Cato was not convinced by the general's concern. He was exhausted by the long journey from Tarsus through the snow-covered mountains to the camp outside Thapsis. Moreover, he did not trust himself not to say something indiscreet to his superior. 'Sir, you've had my report. If there's nothing else you require, might I be dismissed to find some food and get some sleep?'

Corbulo nodded. 'Good idea. It'll refresh you in time for the hunt Centurion Macro is organising for tomorrow.'

'Hunt?'

'He's found a forest he reckons may be well stocked with game. If we can bring back a few wagonloads of boar and deer, it'll fill the men's bellies and warm their hearts. We could all use a bit of cheer at the moment.' Corbulo's forehead creased into a frown. 'Given the situation.'

'What situation?'

'I'll let Centurion Macro explain. In the meantime, it's good to see you back, Cato. Truly. The way things are going, I'm going to need every good man I can find before this winter is over.'

Macro had cleared his kit out of the hut he had been using to make way for Cato.

'It's not much.' He shrugged. 'But it's dry and windproof and I'll have one of the lads get a fire going for you. It'll be as cosy as being tucked up at home. Speaking of which,' he added hopefully, 'did you happen to stop in Tarsus on your way here?'

'Briefly. I saw Lucius, Petronella and the dog.'

'How are they?'

'Cassius has refrained from eating anyone. The boy's caught a cold and is covered in snot. And Petronella sends you her love and told me to make sure you come back to her alive and well, or else she will do me great violence.'

Macro smiled happily. 'That's my girl.'

'I think she means it.'

'Of course she does,' he replied with a quick tug of his neck cloth. He gestured towards the bed made of piled pine boughs. 'Like I said, it ain't home, but it's comfortable enough, and it's as good as it gets out here in the mountains.'

Cato nodded wearily. 'My thanks, brother. Where will you be kipping down?'

'I've bumped Porcino out of his hut. He'll share with Nicolis. He's none too happy, but privileges of rank and all that. Anyway, it's good to have you back, lad. I have to admit, I wasn't too keen on the idea of you running around in Parthia. I guess things must have worked out pretty well for us, given that you're still alive.'

'I'm afraid not.' Cato described briefly what had happened to the embassy, and Macro gave a sad heave of his shoulders.

'That's a waste of good men. And no way for a soldier to die. Can't say I'm pleased with the way the general used you and the boys. You deserve to be treated better than that. He betrayed your trust.'

'There seems to be a lot of treachery of one kind or another these days.'

Macro chuckled mirthlessly. 'You don't know the half of it. We've got a camp full of starving men, a general who thinks his soldiers can fight with their stomachs backed up against their spines, just as long as they can be beaten into formation, traitors wandering around the camp stirring up mutiny, and now one of them has gone and murdered a centurion. We're sitting on a box of vipers here, lad.'

'Seems like I can't trust you on your own for a moment.' Cato smiled. 'You'd better tell me everything.'

Macro related the sorry tale of the campaign, and when he had finished, Cato shook his head at the catalogue of disasters, large and small. 'At this rate, the authority of Rome is going to be a joke the length of the eastern frontier when word gets out. The only hope for Corbulo now is that we take Thapsis before we are forced to retreat. Or before there's a mutiny, unlikely as that may be.'

'Unlikely? I wouldn't be so sure. You'll see for yourself as soon as you've had a chance to walk the lines.' Macro stepped towards the leather flap that served as a door. 'I have to go. I've got to organise tomorrow's hunt. Not that I'm going to be joining in all the fun, since Corbulo's appointed me acting camp prefect.'

'It could be a step up. A nice number to end your career on. If the promotion is confirmed.'

Macro shook his head. 'You can keep the extra pay and privileges. The paperwork and the hours dealing with everyone's requests and complaints ain't worth it. I'll be happy to revert to the centurion's beat. Anyway, the blacksmith's going to be busy knocking up boar spears all night. Which is going to add one more reason for him to feel pissed off. Can't be helped. I'll see you in the morning.'

'Make sure I'm woken at dawn.'

'Yes, sir.' Macro nodded and ducked out of the shelter, and the leather curtain slipped back into place behind him.

There was still enough daylight entering the shelter through the small gaps around the door frame and the chinks in the stone walls for Cato to see by as he removed his boots and slipped under the spare cloak and furs that Macro had left for him. He lay on his side and drew his knees up in a bid to stay as warm as possible. Outside the shelter he could hear the sounds of camp life, such as they were. It might have been the deadening effect of the snow, or the dangerous mood of the men, but there was an unusual quietness, like the prelude before a tempest. The simile was uncomfortably apposite, he thought.

The only other sounds were the occasional crack of the siege catapult's throwing arms snapping forward followed by the faint thump of a rock striking the city's defences. From what he had seen of the activity in the siege battery earlier in the day, the city wall would be under sustained bombardment by several weapons before long. Once that happened, it was only a matter of days before the wall was breached and Corbulo's men stormed the city. And then the army's problems would be resolved. Perhaps Macro's fears were less justified than the centurion thought. Cato comforted himself with that conclusion as he swiftly fell into a deep sleep.

★ ★ ★

The next day, the sun rose into a clear sky and its rays made the snow gleam with an almost dazzling intensity as Macro oversaw the final preparations for the hunt. Corbulo was taking his headquarters officers and some of the cohort commanders with him, as well as the Praetorians to provide additional manpower in case they encountered any bands of rebels. Eight wagons had been hitched up to mule teams. The first two were loaded with rations and the sturdy eight-foot spears with broad points necessary to bring down a boar. Hunting such beasts was a dangerous task. The species that roamed the hills and mountains of the region were much larger than those found in the western provinces, with lethal tusks up to a foot in length. There were bound to be some injuries, or even deaths. But the chance of providing fresh meat for the ravenous troops could not be passed up. Besides, it was good sport, and Macro was not pleased at missing out.

'We will be back by noon in two days' time,' Corbulo told him as he settled into his saddle. 'Come what may. If it's clear that there's plenty of game still to be had, we can always send the hunting party back for more.'

'I think that would be a popular move, sir.' Macro jerked his thumb over his shoulder towards the men watching the preparations around the small convoy of wagons and harnessed mules lined up facing the camp's west gate. 'The rumbling in their guts is almost deafening.'

Corbulo glanced at them and sighed. 'It will make a pleasing change for them to look at me with a grateful expression on their faces for once.' He tugged his reins and turned his horse towards the gate, giving the order for the hunting party to advance, and the wagons began to rumble through the slush and ice of the route that bisected the camp.

Cato was standing by his horse, struggling with the ties of a leather bracer, and Macro sighed and shook his head as he approached his friend. 'Here, let me help.'

Cato held out his forearms for Macro to fit and securely fasten the ties. 'Thanks.'

'You're welcome. Just take care of yourself. It would be a bloody shame for you to escape from Parthia only to let some brassed-off boar take you down.'

'I'll be fine.' Cato nodded towards the silent men watching the party making its way out of the fort. 'Keep your eyes and ears open while we're gone. I don't like the feel of things.'

Macro snorted. 'Feel of things? Jupiter's balls, you sound like some cheap soothsayer. There's nothing like the prospect of a full belly to lift a soldier's spirits. You'll see. Once you get back with those wagons laden down with fresh meat, that lot will fall into line again, meek as lambs. After that, it'll only be a matter of days before the wall is breached and the campaign can be brought to an end so we can get back to Tarsus.'

'I hope you're right.'

Cato pulled himself up on a saddle horn, swung his leg over and settled into position. He took up the reins and nodded a farewell to Macro. 'See you in two days.'

Then he trotted his mount along the side of the wagons and past the column of Praetorians to take his place with the other officers riding behind the general.

Macro watched them for a moment before he turned away and strode towards the northern gate, facing Thapsis. To the left of the snow-covered ruins of the settlement lay the siege battery. The throwing arms of the large catapult that had been constructed by the column's engineers were being ratcheted back with a steady clanking, slowing as the counterpoise lifted off the ground and the crew were forced to apply more effort. The frames of the replacement catapults brought up from Tarsus were visible above the palisade, and as Macro approached he could hear the rapping of hammers as the engineers laboured to complete their assembly.

He crossed the narrow causeway over the ditch and passed through the gate. Inside, the snow had been packed down by the constant footfall of those working on the siege weapons. The catapult's throwing arms had been drawn back far enough now for the crew to load the next rock into the large groove running along the weapon's bed. Macro paused to watch. The optio in command of the crew waited until the rock, nearly a foot across, was securely seated. Then he called out, 'Stand back! Prepare to shoot!'

The legionary standing beside the ratchet release arm attached a small iron hook on the end of a length of rope and joined his comrade standing ready for the order to unleash the throwing arms. The optio took a look round to make sure every man in his crew was a safe distance from the catapult, and then barked the order. 'Release!'

The two men grunted as they yanked the rope, pulling the ratchet arm up, and at once the throwing arms snapped forward. The rock leaped from the weapon and flew up into the sky. Macro shielded his eyes to watch as it slowed at the top of its trajectory and then plunged towards the wall, striking three courses below the ragged open space where the upper reaches had already collapsed. The impact caused a burst of dust and snow, and then a small avalanche of stones and grit tumbled onto the debris at the foot of the wall.

Macro nodded with approval, then lowered his hand and approached the observation platform in the corner of the battery. Standing there tapping his vine cane against his greaves as he watched proceedings was Tortillus, the centurion who had been given command of the siege battery.

'Looks like the rest of the weapons will be ready soon,' said Macro as he climbed the short flight of steps and indicated the men toiling over the frames, arms and torsion mechanisms of the other six catapults.

Tortillus nodded. 'At this rate, they'll be ready by dusk. Should have been ready by midday, but the work's gone slower than I'd like.'

'Trouble?'

'Not once they'd had a bit of encouragement from Lucretia.' He raised his cane. 'They know she means business. But I have to keep an eye on them all the time. The moment they think I'm not watching, they start slacking off.'

Macro gazed round the interior of the battery, observing the men at work. To a practised eye, it was clear that many of them were doing little more than going through the motions; swinging hammers half-heartedly or carrying timber and tools to and fro at a slow pace. Hunger might have weakened them, but there was more to it than that. Their demeanour was that of slaves rather than soldiers.

'Keep them busy, Tortillus. Busy enough not to cause any trouble, eh?'

They exchanged a wary glance, and Tortillus nodded. 'Too right.'

Macro turned to look out over the palisade towards Thapsis. The approach trenches had been completed, and the gangs of prisoners were at work clearing snow from them and heaping it on top of protective berms facing the city. Inevitably some soil was scraped up with the snow, and now the zigzag of the berms was marked as if by specks of soot against the white backdrop. Beyond the protective hoardings at the end of the trenches there was a strip of open ground no more than thirty paces from the ditch in front of the city wall. Macro could see that the catapult had caused considerable damage already. Below the section that had already been beaten down, a number of cracks were visible even at a distance of nearly three hundred paces. The debris had filled the ditch, and by the time there was a practicable breach, the men assaulting the city would be able to get across it without too much difficulty. The defenders might attempt a tough defence, but they would not hold out for long against the men of the legions, especially men driven on by hunger and a desire to end the siege as swiftly and ruthlessly as possible.

He stayed to watch the next shot strike the wall, then turned to Tortillus. 'Very good. Keep them at it. I want the last of the catapults assembled and in action before nightfall. Tell the men I'll buy wine for them all if they get it done. If not, it's going to be extra fatigues all round. That should do the job.'

Tortillus grinned. 'When has a soldier never worked harder at the prospect of a free drink? And I'll make sure Lucretia helps to drive home the point.'

'Perhaps we'll spare Lucretia the effort and let the wine do the talking, eh?' Macro suggested in a deliberate tone, staring at the centurion just long enough to make sure he understood.

'Yes, sir.'

'Good. Carry on, then.'

Macro returned to headquarters and spent the rest of the afternoon dealing with a succession of officers, each convinced that theirs was the most significant issue to be resolved by the acting camp prefect. First up was the quartermaster, who was adamant that the men would be forced onto quarter-rations if the next supply convoy didn't reach the camp within three days, and who suggested that perhaps it might be advisable to cut rations at once, just in case there was a further delay. Macro gently pointed out that a cut in rations might well precipitate a mutiny, in which case it really didn't matter how long it took for the next supply convoy to reach the camp. Second there was the commander of the cavalry cohort, who demanded extra feed for his mounts. Macro told him that the only feed left had to be shared with the draught animals, and if it came down to a choice, then in their present circumstances the mules came first. He sent him away with orders to kill the lame and the weakest horses at once and have the carcasses butchered and distributed to the men. Third was the priest of the imperial cult, who needed a live cockerel or piglet to sacrifice to the gods in order to gain their favour for the boar hunt. Macro suspected that the ultimate destination of any such sacrificial animal was more likely to be the priest's mess tin rather than his altar, and sent him on his way with a curt dismissal. And so it went on, until the last and most junior supplicant approached the table at which Macro was sitting, just after the sun had set and the temperature had begun to drop sharply.

'Who are you?' Macro asked wearily. 'And what do you want?'

'Martinus, sir. I'm Centurion Piso's optio. Or I was.'

'Ah, yes. Well, you're the acting centurion until Corbulo appoints a replacement, so start using the rank now.'

'Yes, sir.'

'What can I do for you, Acting Centurion Martinus?'

'It's the funeral club, sir. I asked the lads for the usual contribution from the funds to cover the cost of the tombstone, and they voted against it.'

'What?' Macro felt a spark of anger strike in his heart. It was the custom to vote for the necessary funds to pay for a comrade's tombstone. It should have been a formality. He glared at the optio and pointed a finger at him. 'Well, you go back to your men and you tell them that they will reconsider and they will vote for the necessary funds. Enough to pay for a tombstone worthy of a centurion.'

'Yes, sir.'

'You also tell them that whatever they thought of Piso, the man served Rome faithfully from a time when most of them were still sucking at their mother's tit. If they still refuse to cough up, then you tell them that I will come down there and show them exactly what happens to any man who thinks he can piss over the reputation of a good officer. Given that the murdering bastard who did for Piso is more than likely someone in his century, I'm already not well disposed towards them. The very least they can expect if they cross me is to be shovelling shit from latrine ditches for the next year. Got that?'

The optio swallowed nervously. 'Yes, sir.'

'I want you to get his funeral pyre ready to light at dawn tomorrow. If his tombstone isn't ready at the same time, then the first job of the day will be to appoint a new acting centurion, and the second will be to find a new acting optio. Now get the fuck out of my sight and go and sort it out.'

At sunset, the trumpet sounded the change of watch. The tang of woodsmoke and gruel was carried on the air across the camp as the off-duty men cooked their evening meals. From the direction of the nearest lines there came the sound of raised voices, then angry shouts. Tempers were short, and such outbursts were not unusual, so Macro ignored it and continued working. He felt his stomach growl with hunger, and as soon as he had finished drafting the orders for the next day's foraging expeditions, he laid down his brass stylus, stretched his shoulders and called for the orderly to bring him a mess tin of gruel. There was no response, so he ground his teeth and tried again.

'Orderly! Hoi! Orderly, in here!'

More shouting rose up nearby, and this time he resolved to deal with it in person. Rising swiftly from his stool, he made for the door of the shelter. But before he reached it, the leather curtain swept aside and Prefect Orfitus appeared, followed by two of his men. All three had drawn their swords, and by the glow of the brazier in the corner of the hut, Macro could see the dangerous glint in their eyes.

'What's the meaning of this?' he demanded.

Orfitus raised his sword swiftly so the point was at Macro's throat. 'Shut your mouth!'

Macro made to protest, and Orfitus shook his head.

'Don't! If you know what's good for you, you'll keep quiet.' Without taking his eyes off the centurion, he gave an order to his men. 'Bind his hands and then take him to join the others.'

A moment later, Macro was jostled out of his hut. By the light of the campfires he could see hundreds of armed men swarming about, rounding up any men who protested. Most kept quiet, and merely looked on in silent complicity as the mutineers took over the camp.

CHAPTER TWENTY-NINE

Macro stood with the officers and men herded into the corner of the camp. All had their hands tied and were guarded by as many mutineers armed with swords and spears. He could see the torches of search parties working their way through the lines as they looked for any remaining men. As far as he could make out, most of the officers had not betrayed the general; there were almost as many prefects, centurions and optios as common legionaries and auxiliaries in the crowd around him. The section of Praetorians that had remained behind to guard headquarters when the hunting party set off had remained loyal to their military oath. The only other Praetorian centurion in the camp was Nicolis, who had been ill with a fever in the shelters erected to serve as the army's hospital. He was propped up by two of his men as he tried to stay on his feet.

A big crowd was gathering outside the supply huts, and every so often there was a loud cheer as a lock gave way and the mutinous soldiers burst in to ransack what remained within.

'The fools,' Centurion Tortillus growled as he edged through the tightly packed ranks of prisoners to stand beside Macro. 'What do they think they'll do for food once they've gorged on that and drunk the last drop of wine? Once the hangover wears off, they'll have nothing left to live on. Then what?'

He drew a deep breath and shouted, 'They're eating our rations! One of you bastards go and stop them before they finish the lot off!'

'Shut your mouth!' a voice called back from the men guarding them. 'We don't obey your kind any more!'

'You will, laddie. And when this bollocks is over and done with, I'll track you down and my Lucretia will beat the living shit out of you for your cheek. This I swear, by all that's fucking holy.'

'Quiet there!' another voice cried out, and Macro saw the mutineers part to let a small group of men through, led by an auxiliary optio carrying a torch. Behind him strode Prefect Orfitus. He had sheathed his sword and now faced the prisoners and looked them over.

'You won't get away with this!' Macro challenged him. 'You know how Rome punishes mutiny. If you don't give up and release us now, you'll be signing your death warrants. Be sensible and do the right thing, and I will do what I can to persuade the general to show leniency.'

'Leniency?' Orfitus gave a bitter laugh, and many of his followers joined in. 'Corbulo hasn't a lenient bone in his body. Look how he's punished my Syrian boys and the lads from the Sixth Legion. Treated us no better than dogs when he kicked us out of the camp. We watched our comrades die because of him. Frozen to death or racked with illness until they drowned in their own blood from the coughing sickness. So spare us any promise of leniency from the general.'

Macro pushed through to the front of the crowd and stepped forward to confront Orfitus. One of the men guarding the prisoners took a pace towards him, sword raised as he looked to Orfitus for guidance. The auxiliary prefect shook his head.

'Centurion Macro, you know better than most men here that if we do as you say, Corbulo will show us no mercy. Not only would he crucify the ringleaders, he'd make the rest of us face decimation.' He turned and shouted to the men gathered about the prisoners in the darkness. 'Brothers! There is no road back from where we are now. We have cast off the chains of oppression that Corbulo forged around us. We are now free of his tyranny and we demand justice for the soldiers of this army. Corbulo has as good as murdered more than twenty men from my cohort and half as many from the legionary cohort.'

Some of the men shouted angrily, and others joined in. Orfitus waited a moment for their rage to reach fever pitch before he raised his hands and called out to them to be quiet. When they had fallen silent, he spoke again. 'Shall we do as Centurion Macro suggests? Shall we put ourselves back at the mercy of Corbulo? How many more of us will he kill before this campaign is over? Shall we surrender ourselves to the general, boys? I say no! *No!*'

The crowd roared their agreement for a moment, and then the noise subsided and Orfitus turned back to Macro. 'You see? The men no longer recognise your general as their superior. Now, Macro, step back and don't cause any more trouble. If you do, I'll have you stripped and run out of the camp. Let's see how long you last in this freezing night. Meanwhile we'll be warm in front of the fires, cooking up all the rations that bastard has been keeping from us!'

The mutineers jeered at Macro, and he snatched a deep breath of cold air. 'What do you fools think you can achieve?' he bellowed. 'What happens when you've gorged yourself on what's left of our supplies? You'll starve! At least Corbulo was keeping you alive.'

'Barely!' Orfitus shouted back. 'You call this cold and misery being alive? Some of us are already little more than walking corpses. I tell you, one more month of Corbulo in command and this entire camp will be nothing but a graveyard. Besides, we will have food. Plenty of food, brothers. The people of Thapsis have promised to feed us if we stop the bombardment of their city and dismantle our siege weapons as a sign of good faith.'

'You've been dealing with the enemy?' Macro shook his head angrily. 'You traitors! Traitors all!'

'Quiet!' Orfitus snapped. He grasped the handle of his sword and spoke softly. 'Still your tongue, or I may just cut it out myself.'

'Do your worst, you bastard—'

Without any sign of warning, Orfitus delivered a savage backhand that snapped Macro's head round and silenced him. At once he tasted blood in his mouth, and he spat to one side as his head throbbed painfully.

'Tonight we dine off the stores that Corbulo has denied us. But tomorrow, the people of Thapsis will open their granaries, and send bread, cheese, meat and wine in exchange for peace between us. One of our men has already spoken to the rebel leaders some days ago, and the deal is agreed. Tomorrow we feast!'

Orfitus's followers cheered deliriously at the prospect of filling their bellies. He called them to silence again and faced the prisoners. 'Brothers, you have a choice: join us, or be kept in binds, under guard, until our terms are met. Centurion Macro says that our cause is bound to fail and that a savage punishment will be delivered to us all. He is wrong. Corbulo has no choice but to give in to our demands. Especially when the hunting party returns to the camp and he falls into our hands. And what are those demands? First, that he grants a full pardon to every man who has sided with the mutiny. Second, that he raises the siege and marches the army back to winter quarters in Tarsus. Third, that he takes a list of our demands for full rations, full pay and fair discipline to Rome to represent our case.'

'That's a load of bollocks!' Tortillus interrupted. 'The general will never agree to it! No Roman general ever would.'

'But he will. For one very simple reason.' Orfitus half turned and point to the east. 'At the end of the valley is a road that leads to Armenia and Parthia. If Corbulo refuses to agree to our demands, we will march to the frontier and set up a new camp there. If Rome sends troops after us, we will defect to Parthia. Even if Rome leaves us alone for fear of us defecting, our presence there will serve as proof that the Empire is turning against itself, and that will only embolden the Parthians.'

'You would do that?' Tortillus asked in horror. 'You would sell us out to the enemies of Rome?'

'We won't have to. Rome will grant our demands far more readily than expose herself to the humiliation of so many of her soldiers going over to the enemy. Trust me, there is no question of Corbulo forcing us to betray Rome. We will get all that we ask for. Now then, who amongst you will join us? Speak up, and your bonds will be cut and you can take your place along with us. There will be food for you, and warm shelter. For those too foolish to accept the truth of what I say, you will continue to eke out your lives on quarter-rations until the mutiny is over. Who is with us? Speak now. This will be your only chance to choose your side. Choose wisely, my brothers.'

There was a brief hesitation before one of the legionaries close to Macro responded, 'I'm with you!' He pushed his way out into the open and crossed over to the mutineers, and Orfitus ordered one of his men to cut him free.

'And me,' said another.

More men abandoned the group of prisoners. When Macro saw Optio Martinus walk past him, he shook his head and muttered, 'Don't be a fool, lad. You join that mob and you will regret it for the rest of your life.'

The young officer paused, but could not look Macro in the eye, and then carried on towards Orfitus. There were a handful of others, and the prefect waited a beat before he nodded.

'That's it then. Martinus!'

'Sir?'

'Take thirty of your men and escort the prisoners to the latrine. Put them inside and then block up the doorway. Leave enough space to pass them food and water. Free the last man you put inside. He can untie the others. Now get these fools out of my sight.'

Throughout the next day Macro took turns with some of the other prisoners to observe what was going on outside through the gap between the lintel and the bed of the cart that had been turned on its side and pushed against the latrine doorway to block it. As far as he could see, there were six guards directly outside the entrance, with two more patrolling along its length. The guards were changed at noon, and Martinus handed over to an auxiliary officer and his men. Beyond, the camp had the atmosphere of a public holiday, as the men sat

397

around their fires eating and drinking while they laughed and sang. Sentries were stationed along the palisade, mostly on the western side of the camp, watching for any sign of the early return of the hunting party, but there was little evidence of the usual routine and no sense of the purposeful order of an army camp. Few of the soldiers were wearing their helmets or armour, and no salutes were exchanged with the handful of officers who had chosen to follow Orfitus. With the latrine block being used as a prison, the men were freely relieving themselves along the bottom of the rampart. Beyond the north wall, Macro could see the wooden limbs of the largest catapult, still against the grey sky. There was no regular trumpet call to announce the changing of the watch and the passage of the hours. No sound of hammering from the blacksmiths. The mutineers had abandoned the siege.

In contrast to the mood in the rest of the camp, the atmosphere inside the latrine block was grim indeed. The air, foul-smelling at the best of times, was now made worse by the men packed inside. It was not too cold, thanks to the heat given off by their bodies. The only seating was on the wooden boards with slots cut in them set over the drain that ran the length of the rock-walled and timber-roofed structure. Other than that, there was only the cold ground, now turned to mud by the tramping of so many boots, so most of the prisoners preferred to stay on their feet and lean against the wall while they waited for a place on the lavatory bench to become available.

The first food and drink they were given since being closed in was passed through the gap to them shortly before noon. Two baskets of bread and some jars of water. There was an immediate scramble towards the baskets before Macro took charge of distribution to ensure that every prisoner was given an equal share of the meagre rations the mutineers had allowed them. He took the last hunk of bread for himself and leaned into the corner of the building chewing disconsolately as he considered the situation. Once he had finished and found one of the jugs to slake his thirst, he sought out Tortillus.

'We have to get a warning to Corbulo,' he said quietly.

'Oh yes?' the centurion responded. 'How are we going to do that from in here, eh?'

'Get someone out of here, obviously. I'm up for it.'

'Good for you. But how?'

Macro indicated the corner of the room where the drain passed under the wall. 'Out through the drain, under the rampart, then make a bolt for the nearest cover and go and report to the general.'

Tortillus shook his head. 'You're mad. You couldn't even get a kid out through that.'

'Let's see.' Macro made his way to the corner and jerked his thumb at the optio sitting there. 'Move.'

Once the optio had reluctantly given way, he gritted his teeth and ducked his head to look through the opening. The angle was tight, but he could just make out the glimmer of daylight and its reflection in the effluent slowly running into the ditch outside. An acrid stench filled his nostrils, and he straightened up and looked along the bench towards the men sitting nearby. 'You lot, move!'

They stood, and Macro grasped the length of wood, eased it up and slid it along. Below, there was a drop of perhaps two feet into a channel a foot wide that ran towards an opening where it narrowed to half the size. Tortillus was wrong, thought Macro: not even a child could squeeze through the opening.

'See?' grunted the other centurion.

But Macro was not ready to give in. He reached down and

tested the soil and rock around the opening and found that it was not quite frozen. Leaning back against the wall, he undid the buckles of his greaves and took them off. Then, picking one up he grasped the end and used the curve that protected the knee to dig into the ground and scrape away some of the soil, pausing to pull the lumps of rock aside. Soon he had managed to hollow out enough to widen the drain beside the hole and sat back, nodding. 'We can do it. Dig out enough this side of the hole to keep our work hidden until we break out after dark.'

'What do you mean, we?' asked Tortillus as he wrinkled his nose.

Macro quietly ordered several of the other prisoners to stand by the entrance to block the view into the latrine for any guard passing by, and then handed his spare greave to the centurion.

'Let's get to work.'

For the next few hours, the two centurions and the other prisoners worked in relays to dig out enough space for a man to fit into the drain, and then carefully scooped away the foundations around the drain hole, leaving a thin shell that would look undisturbed from the outside. Then they waited for night to fall. At dusk, more bread and water was brought to them as the guard was changed. Optio Martinus approached the latrine doorway and announced a fresh offer from Orfitus to any who would join the mutiny. None did, and Martinus turned away and stood over his men as they played dice beside a brazier and drank from a jar of wine liberated from the officers' mess.

Once Macro was certain their attention was focused on the dice game, he turned to Tortillus. 'We'd better get ready. Tunics and boots only if we're going to get through the hole. And we'll need to darken up to help keep out of sight.'

He reached into the drain, scooped up a handful of filth and started to smear it on his exposed skin, including his face. Tortillus frowned with disgust before he forced himself to follow suit, and soon the rest of the prisoners were giving the two men a wide berth. Macro looked down at himself. 'Why, in the name of Jupiter, do I seem to live my life up to my neck in shit?'

Tortillus shrugged. 'Don't know, sir. Maybe there's something about you that just pisses Jupiter off.'

Macro chuckled, and then turned to one of the other officers. 'Once we are in the drain, put the board back on and start kicking off. I want their attention drawn to the front of the latrine. Got that?'

The optio nodded, and Macro took a last deep breath before climbing into the drain and lying down. Tortillus moved into place behind him, and then the board was lowered over them and several of the officers sat down on it for good measure. At once Macro felt uncomfortably closed in, and the stench was overpowering. He gripped the greave and waited. A moment later, a voice called out angrily, 'Hey, you give me that bread back, you bastard!'

'Come and get it!' came the reply. The two men started shouting at each other, and others joined in.

'Here we go,' Macro whispered over his shoulder as he drew the greave back and then punched it against what was left of the soil and stone around the drain hole. The debris collapsed into the ditch outside, and there was a swirl of effluent around him as it flowed out. Quickly he worked to enlarge the hole, and then crawled forward and eased his head outside, looking along the side of the latrine. A guard stood at the corner, leaning on his spear, but as the shouting inside grew in intensity, he picked up his weapon and moved towards the entrance and out of sight. At once Macro drew himself forward, wriggling through the hole and into the ditch, which was wide enough to lie down in and deep enough to hide him from anyone who was not close by. He crawled forward, and heard Tortillus grunt softly as he emerged from the hole and followed him.

Ahead of them, some thirty paces away, was the dark entrance to the drain that passed under the rampart into the ditch beyond. They continued crawling towards it until Macro heard voices approaching, and drunken singing. He stopped and pressed himself down, and felt Tortillus brush up against his boots before he too halted. Ten paces ahead, a soldier collapsed on his knees at the edge of the ditch and threw up, the contents of his stomach splattering and splashing down into the ditch. He paused, retched a few times, and then sat swaying from side to side. Another man appeared and slapped him on the back.

'If you can't keep your drink down, Nucer, perhaps you should have joined the Praetorians. I hear they're a bunch of lightweights. Come on. Up you get.'

He dragged the first man to his feet, threw his arm around his back and half carried him away. Macro waited a moment in case the soldier's nausea got the better of him again, then crept on, wrinkling his nose as he crawled through the vomit. Behind him, he heard Tortillus curse under his breath.

It was tempting to move faster as they neared the outer drain, but Macro managed to control the urge and kept going at a cautious pace. Then he was at the foot of the ramp and moving on into darkness. Just as he entered the covered drain, he heard the voice of the second soldier again.

'For fuck's sake, Nucer!' The sound of someone groaning with nausea seemed loud and close, and then there was a sharp exclamation. 'What the hell are you doing? Hey, you! Get up.'

'Macro!' Tortillus whispered sharply. 'He's seen me! You go. I'll deal with this.'

Before Macro could respond, Tortillus's heavy frame exploded from the ditch as he leaped out and charged towards the legionaries. 'Fucking vomit all over me, would you? You streaks of piss!'

Macro worked his elbows and knees furiously as he crawled through the rest of the drain as quickly as he could, coming out halfway up the reverse slope of the outer ditch. He slithered down over the snow into the drift at the bottom with a soft powdery crunch. This was the danger point. The filth that he had smeared over him to conceal him in the ditch now contrasted sharply with the surrounding whiteness. He swept some snow over his body, and then paused to stare up along the rampart. There was only one man in sight, standing watch in the corner tower barely twenty paces away. It had started to snow again, dull white flecks drifting down from the darkness. Tortillus's bellowing as he threw himself on the drunken soldiers and the more distant din from the latrine were clearly audible in the crisp night air, and an instant later, the sentry turned to look into the camp to observe the confrontation beside the drain.

Macro rose to a crouch and worked his way along the ditch until he was midway between the corner tower and the gatehouse, then climbed up the outer slope and ran on into the night, fearing that the alarm might be raised at any moment. But Tortillus and the other officers had done their job well, and no one saw the solitary figure racing across the smooth expanse of snow that stretched away from the camp. There was no avoiding leaving tracks behind him, but Macro hoped the snow would last long enough to obliterate them before he was missed.

All that mattered now was finding the hunting party and

reporting the mutiny to General Corbulo. He knew that the odds were against him. He had only a vague sense of where he was going. If he stopped moving, it was likely that he would freeze and be buried in the snow. And yet he knew that he must find Corbulo before the general, Cato and the men of his cohort returned to the camp to be taken by surprise. With no cloak to keep him warm, Macro folded his arms about his body and plunged on through the snowstorm into the night.

CHAPTER THIRTY

'If I ever get . . . out of this,' Macro muttered to himself, 'I swear by all . . . the gods that I will never use . . . a frigidarium again.'

As far as he could estimate, some two hours had passed since he had lost sight of the torches above the camp gates. Since then, he had pressed on through the snow, trying to keep a straight course to the west. Without reference points, it was impossible after a while to know where he was headed, but he kept going, hoping that the blizzard would pass and that the sky might clear enough for him to make out the mountains that ran along the northern and southern edges of the valley plain. It was also necessary to keep his limbs moving to stave off the cold. His tunic had become saturated from the crawl along the drain and the snow in the ditch outside, and it felt freezing against his skin. Its only benefit was to serve as a guard against the biting wind. He was starting to lose feeling in his toes and fingers, and tucked his hands into his armpits as he trudged through the ever-deepening snow.

Around midnight, the blizzard moderated and the wind dropped and the flakes no longer swirled through the air but drifted lazily to settle on the smooth mantle that stretched out ahead of him. With only the luminescence of the snow to see by, it was impossible to determine his direction, or even the distance of any snow-covered objects around him. Then the snow stopped altogether, and the sky began to clear from the west to reveal the stars and the wider landscape. Macro paused to get his bearings and saw that he was heading towards the southern range of mountains, so he turned slightly and continued, grateful that the wind had died completely and the only sound was the steady soft crunch of snow underfoot and the occasional deep exhalation of air as he forced himself on.

Ahead he saw a forest, and to the right the outline of some scattered huts and smaller structures. He made directly for them, hoping to find food and clothing. This close to the camp, it was likely that the foragers had already been through the settlement, but there was a chance that something had been missed, and that there would be no one there for Macro to have to deal with. He was unarmed and weary and had little doubt that the odds would be stacked against him if it came to a fight. As he approached the nearest hut, he paused and listened, but there was no sound until a wolf began to howl somewhere within the forest. The thought of falling prey to a pack of wild animals spurred him on, and he hurried to the low entrance of the hut, swept aside the leather curtain that hung there and stepped inside. The interior was dark, and it was only possible to make out the vaguest details, so he wrenched the leather covering from its hooks to see better.

The hut had been stripped of the most valuable items by the local people as they fled from the Romans entering the valley, and had then been looted by the foragers. All that remained was a few items of tattered clothing hanging from pegs fastened to the centre post, and scattered baskets and fragments of broken pots and jars. Macro pulled off his tunic and untied and discarded his loincloth. Then, taking a child's cloak from the post, he rubbed himself vigorously to dry his skin and remove as much of the filth from the drain and ditch as possible. He found a man's tunic and pulled that on, and then a cloak, before he tore strips of cloth from another battered cloak to wrap around his head, boots and hands.

He paused to listen again, in case his efforts had alerted anyone who might be lurking in the huts nearby, but there was no sound other than the wolf, now joined by more of the pack. He looked round and saw a small pile of staves to one side of the entrance, together with an adze. He tried a few of the wooden shafts before picking one that was sturdy and well balanced. Then, fastening his broad military belt, he tucked the adze into it and set off to search the other huts.

The foragers had been thorough, and the only food he discovered was some strips of dried beef beneath a bundle of old rags that had been overlooked by the Roman soldiers. He attempted to chew the end of one of the strips, but it was frozen hard, so he wrapped them all in cloth and tucked the bundle under his tunic against his chest in the hope that they would thaw out enough to eat.

Back in the open, he saw that more clouds were approaching from the west. He glanced at the mountains again to determine the direction the hunting party had taken, then set off once more. It occurred to him that he would miss the track entirely, since it would lie beneath the snow now, but there might be some features he recognised from the times he had led forage parties along the valley. That had been during daylight, though, he reminded himself. At night and under snow, the valley was a completely different landscape.

A fresh series of howls sounded, far closer than before, and he turned to look back towards the settlement half a mile behind. Dark shapes flitted across the snow between the huts and then gathered in a loose pack as they began to follow the trail he had left.

'Oh wonderful,' he growled. 'Thank you, gods. Why put one obstacle in a man's way when you can throw several in his path?'

He increased his pace, using the stave as a walking stick as the clouds crept towards him, slowly shrouding the stars. The ragged clothes he had taken from the hut soon proved their worth, as they trapped the heat from his body and kept out much of the cold. He was still hungry, though. He had eaten nothing apart from a hunk of stale bread since the mutineers had taken over the camp. He hoped that the strips of frozen meat inside his tunic would soon be soft enough to chew.

It did not take long for the light-footed wolves to catch up with him. Most of the pack slowed to keep pace with him thirty or forty feet behind. Far enough away to flee easily if he turned to confront them, yet close enough to spring forward and attack if he fell or faltered. A handful moved out along each side of him, at a similar distance, watching him closely as they matched his steps. They made no sound that Macro could hear above his laboured breathing and the squeaking crunch of snow underfoot. It was almost as if they were malevolent spirits rather than real beasts. He had seen wolves many times before and knew that they rarely dared to attack people. They took small children if they had the chance, but were wary of full-grown men. Yet it was not unknown for them to attack if driven by hunger, or if they sensed that their prey was weak. If they thought the latter, he was determined to prove them wrong.

For the next hour, they stayed with him and made no attempt to get any closer, and Macro's nerves were strained by the constant need to check his rear and flanks. Overhead, the stars had disappeared and darkness hung above him as it continued to devour the heavens. The ground began to slope ahead of him, and he saw a cluster of large boulders on the crest of the hill and altered course towards them. He could pause to rest with his back against a rock while he tested the meat to see if it was soft enough to eat.

As he drew closer to the boulders, the wolves began to move in. It was done so gradually that he did not notice it at first, and was then shocked when he realised they were no more than ten feet away; close enough to rush him in a heartbeat. He drew the adze with his left hand and readied the stave in his right, ready to strike at the first sign of danger.

When he reached the crest, he found himself looking down into a tree-lined vale that he recognised from some of the forage parties he had led. It was no more than ten miles to the forest and the hunting party. Almost at once, his eyes were drawn to a flicker of light close to the treeline only a couple of miles away. Then he saw another, and realised he was looking at campfires. From this distance there was no telling if they belonged to rebels, or the hunting party already making its way back to the siege camp. He must get closer to find out; if it was the enemy, then he would have to give them a wide berth and continue on his way.

There was a soft prickle on the end of his nose, and he glanced up to see that it had started to snow again. Within moments, the distant campfires were blotted out, but he was confident of the direction he must take and kept moving, sinking with each pace into snow that reached his bulky calves. Tucking the stave under his left arm, he reached for the bundle of meat strips inside the tunic and hurled it to one side. There was a pause before the first of the wolves loped over to inspect the bundle, then it tore at it ravenously as the rest of the pack dashed over to fight for their share. Macro made use of the diversion to hurry on a short distance down the slope, but there was only the briefest respite before the wolves came on again. A soft grunt sounded from his left as four of the beasts bounded forward amid sprays of snow and went a short distance ahead of him before turning to block his path. Heads lowered and legs braced, they bared their teeth in snarls. Macro continued towards them warily, poised to strike.

'Go on then, you bastards. Which one of you thinks he's hard enough?'

He heard a slight noise behind him above the snarls and instinctively stepped and leaned to the side. The wolf's body blurred past his shoulder and landed heavily in the snow just in front of where he had been an instant before. He swung the adze down viciously and the edge bit into the wolf's spine. It spasmed and dropped onto its belly, jaws snapping as blood poured from the wound, staining the snow black. At once Macro dropped into a crouch, daring the other beasts to attack. One edged closer, hindquarters swaying, and he lashed out with the stave to catch it on the snout before it could dart out of reach. It was a firm blow, and the wolf leaped back and rolled over before springing to its feet and bounding away towards the nearest treeline. Macro sensed the opportunity and rushed the other wolves, slashing out with his stave and adze as he roared at the top of his voice. They turned and ran, chasing after the beast he had struck on the snout. He pursued them for a few paces before stopping and bellowing after them.

'Who's the centurion? Eh? You gutless hairy bastards!'

The wolves continued running and disappeared between the trees. Macro straightened up, chest heaving as he breathed deeply and let the tension in his muscles ease. Then he turned back in the direction of the campfires and trudged on.

Large snowflakes drifted down around him. He kept his

course as straight as he could, but as a light breeze blew up and strengthened, the snow was driven into his face and it was almost impossible to look ahead or keep any sense of direction or of how much distance he had covered since he had caught sight of the fires.

Then, in a brief lull in the snowstorm, he caught sight of a glow to his right and he turned and quickened his pace. Drawing closer, he could see the flames clearly, and by the light they cast he could make out figures sitting nearby, and off to one side the dark outlines of wagons and mules standing with their hindquarters facing the wind. His heart warmed at the sight, before caution weighed in and made him slow down. Better to be sure than blunder into the enemy and lose his life without warning Corbulo and the others about the mutiny. Too much was at stake. So he circled round towards the wagons, their loads covered by snow, and worked his way between them until he could see the men around the campfires. One was striding towards him, a black shape against the light of the flames, and Macro ducked back behind a wagon. When there was no further sign of the man, he edged forward and saw that he had turned to urinate. As the piss arced out in a stream, the man let out a contented sigh. There was no mistaking his profile, and Macro emerged from the side of the wagon and approached him.

'General Corbulo.' He addressed his superior calmly. 'Good evening, sir.'

Corbulo turned, still urinating, and Macro stepped to the side to avoid being splashed. The general's eyes were wide with alarm, then with the shock of recognition as he made out the craggy features beneath the strip of cloth Macro had wound about his head.

'Centurion Macro . . . What in bloody Hades are you doing

411

here?' Then it dawned on the general that Macro's presence and appearance was ominous. 'What's happened back at the camp?'

After Macro had completed his account of the mutiny to Corbulo, Cato and Apollonius while he warmed himself by one of the fires, there was a brief silence as the general reflected on the perilous situation he and his army now faced.

'I should have sent Orfitus back to Tarsus in disgrace when I had the chance. Now the incompetent fool has compromised the siege of Thapsis. When word of the mutiny spreads, you can be sure the Parthians will take every advantage of our weakness. They'll be trying to stir up rebellion all along the frontier. By the gods, they may even strike first and invade the eastern provinces while I'm struggling to contain the mutiny and any more rebellions.'

Corbulo grasped his chin and gazed into the fire as one of the Praetorians added another dead pine branch fetched from the floor of the nearby forest. The dried needles flared briefly before the flames licked along the wood.

'We have to put an end to the mutiny as swiftly as possible,' he concluded. 'Much as I detest the idea, I'll have to negotiate with Orfitus and persuade him to call it off.'

'But you heard what Centurion Macro said,' Apollonius protested. 'The mutineers are demanding that you abandon the siege and retreat. If you do that, the rebels of Thapsis will claim victory. Who knows which city or province will be next?'

'Quite. Which is why there can be no question of raising the siege. I can meet most of their other demands readily enough, and then we can deal with the ringleaders when I've called up sufficient reinforcements to crush the mutiny. But for now, I

412

have to keep the men in the camp and continue the siege, whatever it takes.'

'You can be sure that Orfitus and the others will make impossible demands, sir,' Cato said. 'The kind of thing no Roman general could agree to.'

'I know. But what choice do I have? If I refuse, they will hold us all hostage along with the rest of the prisoners and take their demands to the nearest senior Roman official. And that will be Quadratus, the governor of Syria. You can be sure that bastard will use the opportunity to destroy my career for ever.'

Cato nodded. From the very first moment that Corbulo had arrived to take command of Rome's forces in the east, the governor of Syria had attempted to challenge him. He thought over what Macro had told them about events in the camp.

'You say that the mutineers opened up the supply huts?'

Macro nodded. 'Stripped them clean and stuffed their faces with everything they could find. Including what was left in the officers' mess and the general's stores.'

'Good.' Cato rubbed his hands together and then held the palms towards the fire. 'Then there'll be hardly any supplies left in the camp. It's a good thing we ended the hunt and turned back when the snow started falling, but let's not be in too much of a hurry to get back and negotiate with Orfitus. We could reach the camp by noon tomorrow. If we give it another day, the men will have started to get hungry again, with the prospect of starvation. They'll be craving food.' Cato nodded towards the wagons. 'And we have plenty of that right here, which we can choose to supply to the men, or not, as we see fit.'

'What about the supply convoy?' asked Corbulo. 'That's due to reach the camp within the next couple of days. The mutineers know it's on the way. They can easily hold out until it arrives.'

413

Cato shrugged. 'If we were to send a man to halt the convoy, with orders to burn it rather than let it fall into the hands of the mutineers, then the threat of starvation will be very real. I'd say we're in a strong position. We have control of the one thing they want more than anything else right now: food. We hold that out to them and they'll soon forget most of their other demands.'

'Aren't *you* forgetting something?' Apollonius intervened. 'Macro told us that the rebels in Thapsis have promised to feed the mutineers if they lift the siege.'

'I suspect that promise was made purely to help provoke the mutiny. Now that it's been achieved, what incentive have the rebels got to hold good to their promise? Would you, in their place?'

'I certainly wouldn't, but then I tend to take a more cynical line than most men.'

'I've noticed. Even allowing for that, I think we'll find that the rebels will put pragmatism above principle.' Cato turned to the general. 'Sir, I say we stay here for another day before we set out for the camp. If we can time our arrival for early morning, when the men will be cold, and hungry, that's when I think your offer will have the most impact.'

Corbulo thought for a moment as the other officers looked at him expectantly. Then he nodded. 'Very well. We stay here. The first order of the day is to find some food for Centurion Macro, then for us all to get some rest. I think we'll need alert bodies and minds over the next few days. The stakes are high, gentlemen. Let's be sure that we do our duty for Rome. She will never forgive us if we don't.'

Two days later, as dawn broke over the mountains to the east, the sentry on the western gate of the camp squinted into the gloom, then turned to raise the alarm. A moment later, a bucina sounded the stand-to signal and the men of the duty cohort reluctantly emerged from their huts and picked up their javelins and shields before trotting to their positions on the rampart. By the time Orfitus had been woken and had dressed and made his way to the tower above the gate, the line of wagons was clearly visible, no more than two hundred paces from the outer ditch.

Pine branches had been piled beneath and around the wagons under the cover of darkness, and now a fire had been lit behind them while Praetorians carrying torches hurried into place beside each of the vehicles. The rest of the Praetorians, under the command of Macro, formed a line in front of the wagons, shields and spears grounded in the snow. General Corbulo slowly approached the gate and halted some thirty paces away a short distance ahead of Cato, Apollonius and his staff officers. Cato looked at the faces along the rampart, then glanced to the left and saw that the siege battery appeared to be deserted, the wooden frames of the catapults rising up above the field fortifications, still and stark against the sky when they should have been battering the wall of Thapsis.

'Who claims to be in command of this mutinous rabble?' Corbulo demanded as he ran his gaze along the line of the rampart before fixing his eyes on one of the men atop the tower. 'Is it you, Orfitus?'

'Yes, General. So you know about the mutiny? I take it that Centurion Macro informed you?'

'He did. And he tells me that he is not the only officer who has refused to join your gang of traitors. Set them free and put an end to this treachery and I swear that I will hear your grievances and do what I can to address them.'

'If Macro is with you, then you already know of our

415

grievances. Agree to our demands and swear by all that you hold sacred that you will meet them, and that there will be no retribution for those involved, and we will open the gates and permit you and the wagons to enter the camp.'

'I think you overestimate your position, Orfitus. You and the rest of the men are starving. The only food directly available to you is in those wagons.' Corbulo twisted in his saddle to point back towards the Praetorians guarding the heaped carcasses of boar and deer. 'You and your fellow conspirators must surrender yourselves immediately to Centurion Macro. The rest of the men are to swear a new oath of loyalty to me, as the representative of the emperor acting for Rome. They are to march out here, one century at a time, to do so. If any of you refuse, then I will give the order to torch the wagons. The meat in them will go up in smoke, and we will all starve.'

'Burn them, General!' Orfitus responded mockingly. 'We are made of stronger stuff than you think. We can wait until the supply convoy arrives, or get the food we need from other sources.'

'The rebels, you mean?' Corbulo laughed with contempt. 'Have they given you one scrap of food yet? No? I thought not. Nor will you get anything from the supply convoy. I have given orders for them to halt and burn their wagons too if they do not receive orders to the contrary by nightfall tomorrow.' He paused, then drew a deep breath and raised his voice so that it reached as many of the men along the rampart as possible. 'The only food that can save you from starvation is in those wagons just behind me. Come now, lads. Put an end to this nonsense and we can all fill our stomachs with fresh roasted meat. I can almost smell it now.'

'Enough of your lies!' Orfitus shouted. 'You wouldn't dare burn the supplies. You would starve along with the rest of us.

416

And we all know how much the general likes his food, don't we, boys?'

Some of the men on the palisade jeered Corbulo, and then Orfitus thrust his arm out towards the general in challenge. 'You wouldn't dare burn the wagons. You wouldn't dare destroy the convoy. You are a liar!'

'A liar, you say?' Corbulo turned towards the Praetorians and raised his arm straight up in the air. 'Centurion Macro! When I lower my arm, give the order to set fire to the first wagon.'

As the men on the palisade heard his words, many let out anguished cries. Some pleaded with him not to give the order. Others turned towards Orfitus to demand that he open the gates and accept the general's terms. Cato saw the prefect look to both sides, his expression fearful as he sensed his authority beginning to melt away.

'Let's get those wagons!' he cried out. 'That meat's ours for the taking, lads! Follow me!'

He turned and disappeared from sight. A moment later, Cato saw the gates open to reveal Orfitus at the head of his auxiliary cohort.

Cato reached for his sword, but did not draw it. He was hoping desperately that the general would find the words to win over the mutineers. As the Syrians paced out of the camp towards him, Corbulo held his ground and kept his hand raised.

'This is your last warning! Halt at once, or the wagons burn!'

'Ignore him, boys!' Orfitus shouted back. 'The bastard wouldn't dare!'

The clear notes of a bucina carried across the camp, sounding the alarm, and the auxiliaries faltered and stopped just beyond the ditch. Distant shouts and cries drew Cato's attention towards Thapsis, and he saw that the city's gates had been opened and men were pouring out and rushing down the slope towards the earthworks that surrounded the siege battery. More of the rebels had reached the head of the approach trench and were already smashing down the protective hoardings and hacking the wickerwork of the fascines to pieces to let the soil and stones spill into the trench. It was clear that the rebels had seen the wagons and the ensuing confrontation and recognised the opportunity to strike a blow against their enemy. If they could destroy sections of the trenches and the siege weapons, they would set the siege back many months. With the morale of the Roman soldiers already eroded by hunger and mutiny, this might well be the decisive action that broke the spirit of Corbulo's army completely.

'Sir, it's the rebels!' Cato called out to Corbulo, loudly enough that Orfitus and the mutineers would also hear him. 'They're after the siege battery. If we can't stop them, all is lost!'

Corbulo turned to look towards the city, then back at the mutineers. Orfitus froze, not sure whether to go for the wagons or respond to the new danger. It was Cato who reacted first. He wheeled his horse about and cupped a hand to his mouth as he bellowed an order to his men.

'Praetorians! On me!'

CHAPTER THIRTY-ONE

The men by the wagons tossed their torches into the snow and snatched up their weapons, striding forward to join their commander. Cato was swiftly gauging what was unfolding and what had to be done to counter the rebels' attack. He turned to Corbulo and pointed in the direction of the latrine block as he spoke urgently.

'Sir, we have to release the prisoners. The men need their officers. You must take command here. Before Orfitus does.'

Corbulo clenched his jaw and nodded. 'I'll deal with it. Get the Praetorians to the battery and hold it at all costs. We cannot afford to lose those catapults.'

'Yes, sir. I understand.'

As Cato took a firm grip on his reins and turned his horse, he heard one last comment from Corbulo.

'Apollonius, stay close to me,' the general ordered. 'I have a special job for you . . .'

Cato spurred his mount towards the corner of the camp and drew up a short distance beyond as he saw the rebels streaming down the slope towards the battery. At their head was a band of mounted Parthians, and it was clear that they were going to reach the earthworks surrounding the catapults first. Of the handful of men that Orfitus had ordered to defend the battery, several had abandoned their post and were fleeing towards the camp. The few that remained were already closing the gate, but Cato knew there would not be enough of them to cover the length of the palisade. Under normal circumstances the battery would be adequately garrisoned and the duty cohort would be forming up to counter the threat from the rebels. But the mutiny had robbed the army of most of its officers, and without leaders, the men had no cohesion or purpose to direct their efforts. Scores of them stood by and watched anxiously from the camp's ramparts as the rebels approached.

Cato glanced round and saw that the Praetorians were doubling across the snow towards him, led by Macro. His friend was wearing a spare tunic and cloak borrowed from one of the men and holding a boar spear in his hands. Even without a helmet or armour, Macro was a force to be reckoned with, and Cato could not help grinning at the sight. Beyond, by the camp gate, the confrontation between Corbulo and the Syrian cohort appeared to have been resolved, as the general took command, issuing orders and directing the men with out-thrust hand. Orfitus stood to one side, then saluted and turned to wave his men forward to form up outside the gate. The general, with Apollonius at his shoulder, then rode into the camp and out of sight.

As Macro and the Praetorians approached, Cato swung his leg over the saddle horns and dropped down into the snow. He drew his sword, then undid the clasp at his shoulder and let his cloak fall away. There were some soldiers who believed that the heavy folds of a military cloak offered some protection from glancing blows, but Cato preferred not to be encumbered when he went into battle. Macro slowed his stride, tendrils of steamy breath swirling around his face in the bitterly cold morning air.

'We'll advance in close formation,' Cato announced. 'At the quick step.'

Macro bellowed the orders and the Praetorians closed up, shields raised as they ensured that their chilly fingers held their spears in a firm grip. Cato took his place alongside the centurion in the front rank, and as soon as the last of the men had formed up, he raised his sword and drew a deep breath.

'Second Praetorian! At the quick step . . . advance!'

The small column of two hundred and fifty men moved off through the snow, their boots kicking up a dazzling spray of white powder and clods of compacted ice. Jets of exhaled breath swirled about their helmets as their loose equipment jingled and creaked. Looking ahead, Cato saw that the battery's gate, facing the camp, was over two hundred paces away. The remaining men inside had succeeded in closing it just before the first of the Parthians reached them. Now some of the enemy had raised their bows and were shooting arrows at any Roman who dared to reveal himself above the palisade. Even as Cato watched, one of the legionaries took an arrow in the cheek and tumbled back out of sight. While their companions were busy keeping the defenders occupied, more of the Parthians had dismounted and crossed the ditch to clamber up the ramparts, turning to hoist up those behind them so that they could haul themselves over the wooden stakes and climb into the battery.

The first of the rebels on foot had now also reached the battery, and Cato could see them flowing around the sides while others raced on towards the camp. The gate facing the city was open, and a handful of legionaries had emerged to stand between the rebels and the rest of the camp. Even though the enemy could not number more than two thousand – more than the general had originally thought – they had the advantage of surprise over the mutinous Romans, and the morale of the besiegers was as brittle as thin ice. If it broke now, they would be at the mercy of the rebels and their Parthian allies.

A brassy note carried through the sharp winter dawn, clearly audible above the din of the cheering attackers. Someone had had the presence of mind to order the call to arms, and Cato fervently hoped that the training and habits of those who had served in the army for many years would govern the actions of the rest of the men. The signal sounded again, and the men lining the camp's palisade, who had been frozen by indecision a moment earlier, began to turn away and hurry back to their huts to take up their arms and form into their units.

'They're in!' said Macro.

Cato looked round and saw that the gate to the battery was starting to open. At once, the gathered Parthians surged forward, thrusting the gate aside as they burst into the fortified earthworks. Cato felt his guts lurch at the sight. The legionaries within had given their lives to buy the briefest of delays, and now the enemy were free to fall upon the catapults and do as much damage to them as possible before retiring to the safety of Thapsis.

The Praetorians had closed to within a hundred paces of the battery, and Cato drew breath to give another order.

'Second Praetorian! At the double!'

The column picked up the pace as the ground beneath them began to incline gently towards the battery. Ahead, the first of the Parthians still on horseback in front of the gate turned towards the Praetorians, raised their bows and reached for fresh arrows from their cases.

'Shields up!' Cato warned, then ordered the two men behind him and Macro to take their places at the head of the column.

The arms of the nearest Parthian bow leaped forward as the arrow was released. The dark shaft whipped through the air in a shallow arc and landed in the snow just to the right of the head of the column, quivering momentarily against the unblemished white. More arrows shot towards the Praetorians, some clattering off their shields while the points of others punched through with sharp, splintering cracks. The man directly ahead of Cato flinched and stopped as an arrowhead burst through his shield and showered his face with splinters. Cato shoved him in the back.

'Keep moving!' He raised his voice so that others might hear his command. 'Don't stop! Keep going forward!'

The mounted Parthians continued to shoot arrows at them, moving out to the flanks as the column drew closer. More archers appeared along the battery palisade to add to the steady barrage. The first of the Romans went down as a shaft struck a man in the thigh on the exposed right-hand side of the column. Gritting his teeth, he stepped aside and sank to one knee behind his shield. He shouted some final words of encouragement to his comrades before he laid his spear down to try to deal with the wound.

Two more men were lost as the cohort closed the distance to the battery. They were only some twenty paces away when the nearest of the rebel militia from Thapsis charged towards them. The enemy were equipped with an assortment of armour and weapons, some of which looked to date back to the days of Alexander the Great but were no less deadly for that. As the rebels rushed forward, the Parthians stopped shooting for fear of striking their allies and returned their bows to their cases before they drew their spears and swords.

'Second Cohort! Halt!'

The column drew up abruptly, and Cato cupped a hand to

his mouth to be heard above the din of the charging rebels.

'Face out!'

The men on either side turned to present their shields and spears, and a heartbeat later, the first of the rebels slammed against the shield wall, while others were stabbed by the Praetorians' spears. The air rang with the clatter of weapons and the thud of blows landing on shields. Cheers and war cries sounded from the rebels at the rear, while those directly struggling with the Romans fought in silence, as did their opponents, save for the grunts as they struck blows and the gasps of the wounded. Macro grasped the stout shaft of the boar spear firmly in both hands and punched it between the shields of the men in the front rank, striking one of the rebels in the stomach and tearing a gaping wound. He retrieved the blade and readied himself for the next strike.

Cato held himself back to gauge the situation. His men were holding their formation well enough.

'Second Praetorian! Advance at the slow step! One! Two!'

At each count, the men sidestepped towards the battery gate, the column moving steadily through the swirling ranks of the rebels as men continued to be cut down on both sides and bright blood splashed onto the churned snow. Cato could not see beyond the narrow confines of the fierce struggle raging around him. He had no idea if Corbulo had succeeded in persuading the mutineers to fight, or if the enemy had burst into the camp and routed the few men who had rallied to their colours when the earlier signal had sounded. All that mattered to him was saving the siege weapons.

He craned his neck to look over the front rank of the column and saw that they had almost reached the causeway across the ditch. Several Parthians stood behind the palisade on either side of the gate, taking deliberate aim as they loosed arrows into the heart of the Praetorian cohort, steadily picking off men. But there was nothing that could be done about them until the Praetorians gained the interior of the battery, Cato realised.

Even as the thought went through his mind, he saw one of the bowmen take aim at him, drawn by the sight of the crest on his helmet. In one fluid movement the Parthian drew back the arrow, squinted fractionally and released the bow-string. At the same instant, Cato ducked. He heard the hiss of the arrow and glimpsed the flicker of the passing shadow as the shaft cut by his helmet, passed between the men behind him and pierced the foot of one of the rebels beyond. Not for the first time, he rued the need for an officer to stand out from his men so he could be easily seen in battle. It might make it easier to rally soldiers, and for them to be inspired by their leaders, but equally it made the same leaders prime targets for the enemy.

'Almost there, lads!' Macro called out. 'Keep moving!'

Little by little the Praetorians edged over the causeway towards the open gate. The gap between the sturdy posts was packed with rebels keen to get at the Romans, and none of the enemy seemed to have grasped the need to close the gate. Even if they had, it would be impossible to swing it shut with the seething mass blocking the way. The column passed through the opening and the melee began to spill out over the interior of the battery. Cato saw that scores of rebels, under the direction of the Parthians, were hacking away at the cables and torsion bindings of the catapults. Others were piling combustible materials on and around the weapons, while two men were busy fanning the flames of a sentry brazier smouldering in the far corner. There was little time to spare if the siege weapons were to be saved.

'Macro, take ten men and clear the palisade. When Porcino's men are across the causeway, have him hold the gate.'

'Yes, sir.'

As Cato fed more men through the gate and into the battery, Macro gathered a small squad of Praetorians and led them up the wooden steps onto the walkway that ran behind the palisade. Ahead of him, the nearest of the Parthian bowmen turned and quickly raised his bow. Heavy as the boar spear was, it was still a spear, and Macro hurled it at his foe with all the power of his throwing arm. The blade struck the Parthian in the shoulder and spun him round so that he released the shaft out over the palisade and into the open ground beyond.

Macro bounded forward and grasped the spear as the Parthian writhed below him. He ripped it free, then levelled it again, calling out to his men behind him, 'Time to hunt some Parthians, boys!' Then he let out a roar and charged home behind his weapon. The next enemy turned to flee but collided with the man beyond, and Macro ran him through low in the back, driving both men on until they collided with more of their companions and forced him to a stop. As he twisted the boar spear from side to side to try and free it, he called over his shoulder to the Praetorians.

'Go by me, lads! Finish the job.'

One by one they shoved past and charged along the walkway, cutting the Parthians down.

As soon as Macro managed to wrench his spear free, he paused to look down over the palisade. The tail of the cohort had reached the gate, and he called to Porcino, 'Centurion Porcino! Up here!'

'Sir?'

'You and your lads are to hold the gate. Clear the bastards out and get it closed.'

426

Porcino nodded and focused his attention back on the fighting around him as Macro turned to survey the interior of the battery to see how Cato was faring.

The fight for the siege weapons was raging across the snow-covered ground inside the ramparts. Groups of rebels were clustered around the catapults, doing their best to cause as much damage as possible. Three were already alight, assisted by the jars of pitch that some of the rebels had brought with them from the city. The snow around them gleamed dully in the glow of the roaring flames as they consumed the timbers, tackle and torsion ropes. The other three weapons that had been brought up from Tarsus had been hacked about, but the Praetorians had got to them before they could be set alight. The largest of the catapults, towering above the others, was undamaged, and Cato had ordered Placinus and his century to guard it while he himself formed up the centuries of Ignatius and Metellus in a line to sweep across the interior of the battery and trap the remaining rebels and Parthians against the far rampart.

When they were ready, Cato picked up a shield from beside the body of one of the Praetorians and took his place on the right of the line. Overhead, unnoticed by the combatants, the skies had darkened and the snow had begun to fall again; large white flakes that swept through the air on a freshening breeze. Cato muttered a quick prayer of thanks to Jupiter in the hope that a heavy fall of snow would smother the flames before the three blazing catapults were damaged beyond repair. Then he raised his sword and cleared his throat.

'Second Century and Fourth Century! Advance!'

The line undulated as the men paced out, shields to the front and spears lowered and ready to strike. A handful of the more

427

enraged rebels charged the line and were quickly cut down. The rest fell back towards the rampart and braced themselves for a desperate fight. They were joined by those who had surrounded the burning catapults.

As the Praetorians approached, Cato saw that Porcino and his men had succeeded in closing the gate. The choice facing the hundred or so rebels still inside the battery was simple: fight or flee. Some chose the latter, scrambling up the low rampart and climbing over the palisade to drop into the ditch beyond. One of the Parthians called his men to form around him and then edged into a corner of the battery, not far from the nearest of the burning catapults.

Cato hurriedly ordered two sections to fall out and attempt to put out the fires, while the rest of the Praetorians closed in on the enemy. When no more than ten paces separated the two sides, he saw a commotion at the rear of the curved formation waiting for the Romans to close in. On the rampart, Macro stopped and shouted across to his comrades.

'Watch it! Fire!'

Three or four small clay pots with flaming wicks flew across the open ground between the two small forces. One of them burst on the head of a Praetorian close to Cato, showering him with an oily liquid that instantly ignited, engulfing him in flames. He staggered back, his comrades recoiling in terror, then threw himself into the snow and rolled over to put out the flames. Five more of Cato's men were alight, and presented a terrible spectacle as they staggered about like human pyres, crying in panic and beating at the flames amid the swirling snowflakes. The Praetorians wavered, and Cato realised they would only present further targets if they did not attack at once.

'Praetorians! Charge!'

He burst forward, making for the man at the end of the enemy line, a large Parthian holding a slender curved blade and a black buckler decorated with silvered designs. To his left, the rest of the Praetorians surged forward and crashed into the rebels, slamming their shields forward and stabbing with their spearpoints as their opponents tried to parry the strikes and edge close enough to use their swords, axes, clubs and spears. The Parthian raised his buckler and punched it at the side of Cato's shield to blunt the impetus of his charge, then slashed his sword down at an angle towards his neck. Cato ducked and moved into the blow so that the edge of the sword glanced off the trim of his shield. An instant later, he thrust his own sword toward the Parthian's torso, but the man made a lithe sidestep and it missed its target. The Parthian sneered and brought the edge of the buckler down hard on Cato's forearm. He snatched his hand back, only just managing to retain his grip on the sword handle.

The Parthian circled to the right, against the backdrop of the flames of the nearest catapult. Cato winced at the glare and heat of the blaze but grasped the opportunity his foe had unwittingly presented him. Swinging his shield round in front of him, he charged forward, rushing inside the reach of the Parthian's sword, throwing his weight behind the shield as it struck his opponent in the chest, then powering on and driving him back. The Parthian was trying desperately to stay on his feet and did not realise the true danger until it was too late. He slammed against the burning frame of the catapult and the flames eagerly lapped at the folds of his robes and cloak, setting them alight.

The force of Cato's charge was spent and the Parthian thrust him back two paces as he raised his buckler and sword and made ready to fight again, even as his clothes began to burn fiercely. He slashed wildly at Cato, and again, and Cato blocked with his shield before striking his own blow. The Parthian thrust his sword forward to parry it, but Cato did a quick cut-over and struck his opponent at the base of the throat. The sword point pierced flesh and cartilage and opened up a blood vessel. His opponent dropped his buckler and thrust a hand to the wound to try and staunch the flow of blood, his sword wavering in his other hand. Cato stepped up, blocked a clumsy blow and then thrust again, this time at the Parthian's groin. The man bent double as he staggered back, then stumbled over the edge of the base of the catapult and fell into the heart of the blaze with a pitiful cry of terror.

At once Cato turned, shield up, sword ready, but saw that the fight was almost over. The ground was covered with the bodies of the rebels, cut down mercilessly by the Praetorians as they pressed them back into the corner, where they had no chance to wield their weapons and could only wait for their turn to die. Now the Praetorians were picking over the heap of bodies to finish off the wounded, while their less seriously wounded comrades were helped to a safe distance from the burning catapults.

Cato turned towards the blazes and saw that there was little chance of anything useful being salvaged. But the Praetorians had saved four out of the seven weapons. Enough to continue the siege if needed. As he stood, breathing hard, he was aware of the crackle of flames and then the muffled cries of the fight still going on outside the battery. He hurried across to the steps beside the gate and climbed to the palisade.

The main force of the rebels was battling to enter the camp by the three closest gates. To Cato's right, the Syrian auxiliaries had held off the enemy attack and were now driving them back steadily along the side of the camp. The conflict on the far side was not visible from the battery, but already there was a steady stream of injured rebels, and those whose nerve had failed them, making their way back up the slope to the city. Several hundred were fighting for control of the north gate and rampart of the camp. Even as Cato watched, he saw parties of legionaries forcing their way along the rampart from each flank. He sensed that the battle was reaching its crisis. The initial advantage of surprise enjoyed by the enemy had been spent, and now the Romans were winning back ground as the rebels' morale began to crumble. He judged that they would break soon and then flee back to the safety of Thapsis. With most of the siege weapons saved, it would only be a matter of days before the wall was breached. If the mutiny was suppressed, the final assault would surely win the day. Or . . .

Cato's line of thought was interrupted by a fresh possibility, and he swiftly surveyed the ground and the relative position of the forces before smiling to himself and turning to shout an order.

'Centurions! On me.'

They came running and climbed up to join him. Ignatius had been wounded in the arm, and one of his men had followed him to dress the wound as Cato spoke to the officers.

'Ignatius, I want you and your men to guard the battery. Keep any rebels out and do what you can to extinguish the fires.'

Ignatius nodded, and then winced as the Praetorian tied the dressing off with a firm knot.

'As for the rest of you, this is the plan.' Cato grinned as he pointed towards Thapsis, now barely visible through the snowstorm. 'The Second Cohort has a chance to end this siege today, but we need to act fast. A blizzard is almost on us, and soon it'll be hard to make out friend from foe at any distance. The gates of the city are ours for the taking.'

431

He had their full attention now, and he issued his orders quickly before dismissing his officers. As they hurried back to their men and ordered them to discard their shields and helmets, Macro clicked his tongue.

'I hope you know what you're doing, sir. If this goes awry, we'll all be dead long before the general can act.'

A short while later, the man chosen to carry the message to Corbulo to inform him of Cato's plan had stripped down to his tunic. He raced off through the snow in a wide arc around the melee still being fought between the rebels and the Syrian auxiliaries. Cato watched him go, and then turned back to the men waiting behind the open gate, dressed in cloaks and furs taken from the bodies of their enemies in the battery. He removed his helmet and spoke to Macro.

'A more motley collection of vagabonds it would be hard to imagine.'

'Aye,' Macro acknowledged. 'If ever the story of this gets out to the other Praetorian cohorts, we'll never hear the end of it.'

'I think they'll forget soon enough if we succeed. Let's get moving.'

Cato gestured to the first group of men and waved them through the gate. They ran past, then rounded the corner of the battery and headed up the slope. The second group of ten or so men followed, and spread out like their comrades. Cato made ready to join the third group.

'Keep 'em coming, Macro, and I'll see you at the gate.'

'Yes, sir. May the gods go with you.'

'And you, brother.' Cato nodded and clapped his friend on the shoulder before turning away and beckoning to the group of men waiting just inside the gate, the cohort's bucina man amongst them. 'Come on, boys!'

He led them out and turned in the opposite direction to the previous group, working his way round the other side of the battery before angling across the slope, indicating to his men to break up singly and in pairs as they made their way up towards the city. The bucina man followed close behind Cato, covering up his brass instrument as best he could. Already the blizzard had blotted out the camp and the noise of battle was deadened by the falling snow. Cato could see the figures of rebels close by, many of whom had been injured, making their way to safety. But all of them were keeping their heads down as they struggled through the seething mass of white flakes.

He adjusted his pace to move just a little faster than theirs as he continued up the slope. To his right he saw the irregular shape of the ruined settlement, its blackened remains blanketed in a virginal veil of snow, and beyond it the line of the siege trench, battered down in places where the rebels had attacked the workings. He passed close to one of the wounded rebels, who held out a hand and spoke imploringly in his native tongue. Cato lowered his head and trudged on, ignoring the man's cries, which continued until they lost sight of each other. From time to time he saw other figures he felt certain were Praetorians, but did not dare take the risk of calling out to them for fear of exposing his ruse. Closer to, there was no mistaking the off-white tunics of the guardsmen under the borrowed coverings, but he hoped that a casual glance through the snow would not betray their real identity. Every so often he looked back to make sure the bucina man was still with him.

As he climbed the slope, the wind increased in strength and buffeted him, and he had to raise a hand to shield his eyes so that he could see where he was headed. At length he spotted the grey mass of the walls looming out of the blizzard and slowed his pace to allow as many of his men as possible to catch up with him. He noticed others around him halt and begin to move towards each other as the rebels continued to stagger by. He made his way over to the largest group and saw some familiar faces gathered round. There were no more than twenty of them, and he spoke as loudly as he dared. 'We'll wait just a little longer, until there are a few more of us. Then we'll strike. Make ready . . .'

More Praetorians closed up on them. But there was no sign of Macro and most of the others yet, and Cato feared that they had lost their direction in the blizzard. Then one of the rebel wounded wandered amongst them. Horrified realisation dawned on his face, and the Praetorian behind him clamped a hand over his mouth before stabbing him repeatedly in the back. He laid him down in the snow, and the rebel gasped and bled out.

More of the enemy were falling back to Thapsis, and Cato realised he must strike now while he still had the advantage of numbers, small as his group was. He indicated to his men to move out, and the party fanned out across the slope as they made for the city gates, some of them feigning injuries as they limped closer. The line of the outer ditch was all but invisible beneath the snow, and it wasn't until they were close to the bridge directly in front of the gate that Cato could clearly make it out. He drew his sword and let his arm hang at his side as he approached, hunched forward.

The gate was open, and a handful of anxious civilians looked out for familiar faces amongst those returning from battle. There were more on the battlements above. As Cato and the first of the Praetorians stumbled into the city, a woman came forward carrying a basket of dressings. Cato lowered his head and waved her away and she made for a wounded rebel instead.

Some fifteen of his men were standing around the inside of the gate when a Parthian officer emerged from the door at the bottom of the gatehouse and strode over, shouting an order at one of the Praetorians. When the man did not react, he grabbed him by the shoulders and shook him. Then froze. Cato saw a look of surprise on his face that swiftly turned to horror, and then a grimace as the Praetorian stabbed him in the guts. The Parthian let out a groan, and the nearest civilians and injured rebels turned towards him as he staggered back, his hands clasped across his stomach.

Cato threw his rebel cloak aside and straightened up. 'For Rome!' he shouted.

His men echoed the cry as loudly as they could before hurling themselves at the nearest rebels. There was no discriminating between those who were injured and those who were not, or between armed rebels and innocent civilians. The aim was to cause as much panic as possible before anybody thought to contest control of the gatehouse. The bucina man ran back through the gate, taking out his curved instrument and fitting the mouthpiece to his lips. He blew a weak note, and Cato cried out to him, 'Spit, man! Spit!'

The Praetorian nodded, cleared his mouth and tried again. This time a clear note blasted out down the slope. An instant later, figures came running forward out of the blizzard, and Cato turned to cross to the open ground just inside the city. A small mob was retreating in panic up the main thoroughfare, others fleeing into side alleys as the Praetorians struck down everyone around them, leaving bodies strewn across the slush-covered paving stones. Some of the rebels and Parthians attempted to resist, but they were too few and were quickly cut down. All the time, more Praetorians were appearing out of the swirling snow to join those already inside the gates.

Cato ordered the bucina man to follow him, and they entered the door at the foot of the gatehouse. Some palliasses lay on the floor, one occupied by a wounded man curled up on his side and moaning. They ignored him and climbed to the top, where the bucina man continued blowing the signal to summon the rest of the Praetorians and guide Corbulo's men through the snow. A brazier burned to one side of the tower, and Cato piled on more logs from the nearby stack, building the flames up so that they might act as a beacon. Then he gazed down the slope towards the camp. There were many more figures emerging from the gloom, and he realised that the rebels were in full retreat from their failed attempt to destroy the siege weapons and rout the Roman forces in the camp. It was time to close the trap on the enemy.

He crossed to the rear of the tower and looked down. Macro was grinning up at him, his barrel chest heaving from the exertion of struggling through the snow and the fighting around the gate.

'Centurion Macro, close the gate!'

Macro's grin faded. 'But sir, there's still plenty of our men out there.'

'Then they'll have to fall back on the rest of the army. We have to close the gate now, before the rebels can reach the city in force. Do it!'

Macro nodded and called out to the nearest men, and a moment later, Cato heard the grating of hinges as the massive timbered gates were pushed together and the locking bar was dragged into the iron brackets fastened to their rear. As soon as the task was complete, the centurion formed the Praetorians up to protect the gate in case any of the enemy inside Thapsis attempted to retake the gatehouse. A quick glance up the main street and at the entrances to the nearest alleys was enough to reassure Cato that there was no sign of danger from that direction.

In front of the walls, the rebel forces were still streaming up the slope. Cries of anguish rose from below as the first arrivals hammered on the timbers of the closed gate. Others stopped and turned to look fearfully back down the slope. Within a short time, the ground in front of the gate was packed with the rebels and their Parthian allies, with only a handful of stragglers and wounded still appearing through the snowflakes spinning on the wind that moaned over the ridge.

Cato strained his eyes, blinking away the flakes that blew into his face. At last he saw what he was looking for: the regular lines of the Roman cohorts as they emerged from the gloom and closed up on the enemy trapped against the defences of their own city.

'The general's here, boys!' he called down to Macro and the others. 'The general and every man in the bloody camp! We've done it!'

Cries of fear, panic and despair swelled up from the throats of the rebels as they realised that their defeat was complete. The Roman soldiers halted fifty paces away, and as the rebels turned to face them, their cries faded and the only noise was the wind. Then a figure on horseback approached. Cato saw that it was Apollonius. He stopped his mount a short distance from the enemy and called out to them in their own tongue. His announcement was brief, and there was a short pause before the first of the rebels threw his sword and shield down into the snow and stepped warily towards the Roman line. Another followed suit and then more, until the entire force had accepted that there was no choice but to surrender, or face certain death.

At the top of the tower, Cato slumped forward onto his

elbows, feeling suddenly exhausted and cold. To one side the bucina still sounded as the Praetorian continued to carry out his orders. Cato turned to him. 'That'll do, thank you. It's over now. It's all over . . .'

CHAPTER THIRTY-TWO

Two days later, General Corbulo sat warming himself in front of the fireplace in the hall of the largest house in Thapsis. It had belonged to one of the wealthiest merchants in the city, one of the leaders of the revolt against Roman authority. The merchant had paid a high price for his treachery and was manacled along with nearly two thousand others in what had been the siege camp, which now served as a pen for those who had been captured by Corbulo's army. Assuming they survived the winter, they faced a life of slavery.

Food was no longer a problem for the Romans or those they had defeated. The surrender of Thapsis had revealed vast stocks of grain and other supplies in the chambers carved into the rock beneath the city. Corbulo had permitted his men to loot the town for a day after the surrender, and his soldiers had sated their hunger and their thirst for wine, as well as their carnal appetites. The wagons from the hunt had supplied meat to roast and the aroma still hung over the city. There was even enough left over to add to the thin gruel that was prepared for the prisoners, who were nonetheless better fed than their erstwhile enemies had been for the last month of the siege.

By some divinely inspired sense of irony, the supply convoy had arrived the second morning after the battle, too late to assuage the starvation that had been a cause of the mutiny, its supplies no longer required. Their former miserable living conditions were a dim memory as the men enjoyed the comforts of being billeted in the city. Warm, dry, well fed and victorious, they had put the mutiny behind them and morale was as high as it had ever been; such was the fickle nature of soldiers, who cursed their general at dawn and acclaimed him a hero before the same day was out.

The largest proportion of the losses had been borne by the Praetorians, with scarcely a hundred and fifty men surviving from the five hundred who had left Rome with Corbulo less than two years ago. Of that number, fifteen were recovering with the other Roman wounded in one of the city's bathhouses, which now served as the army's hospital. One of the Sixth Legion's tribunes had died holding the northern gate; the only other senior casualty had been Prefect Orfitus, killed during the first evening of looting. His body had been discovered in an alley, his throat cut from ear to ear. Apollonius insisted it must have been the work of the rebels, and the body was accorded a proper funeral the very next morning.

It had been a very convenient death, as most men in the army quietly acknowledged. Even if the Syrian cohort and its commander had fought well, there was never any question of General Corbulo being able to overlook the not insignificant fact that Orfitus had instigated a mutiny and threatened to defect to Parthia should his terms be rejected. The rest of the ringleaders had been rounded up, their punishments ranging from demotion to the ranks to dishonourable discharge. Mild sentences for the crime concerned, but Corbulo had no wish to provide his men with any further cause for disgruntlement, for a while at least.

The general had every reason to be pleased with the outcome

of the siege. The rebels had been crushed and an example had been made of them that would serve as a stark warning to other frontier cities and minor kingdoms of the price that would be exacted for the betrayal of an alliance with Rome. He sighed with contentment as he stared into the fire and felt its warm glow embrace his body.

His reverie was interrupted by a knock on the door.

'Come!'

The door opened and Tribune Cato stepped into the room. 'You sent for me, sir.'

'Indeed. Come and warm yourself by the fire.'

Cato did as he was told, and the general shouted through the open door for his slave to bring them some wine. He turned back to Cato. 'You'll take a cup, I hope.'

'With pleasure, sir,' Cato replied as he pulled up a chair to join his commander.

Once he was settled and both men were nursing a cup of wine, Corbulo cleared his throat and looked up at his guest. 'I've called you here for two reasons. The first concerns a rather distasteful matter touching on the betrayal of Rome, and of yourself.'

Cato frowned. 'I'm not sure I follow, sir.'

'You will, soon enough. One of the prisoners was recognised by a legionary as having been one of the instigators of the mutiny. Apparently he was seen in the camp on a number of occasions provoking dissatisfaction amongst the men. He had given a false name. He was also seen several times in the company of Orfitus. It turns out he was in the pay of the rebels and their Parthian friends. Once he was identified, I had him questioned by Apollonius, who has a talent for knowing precisely how best to loosen the tongues of spies and traitors. Anyway, you'll find out the full details for yourself when he arrives with the prisoner. Once the man has been, ah, cleaned up and made presentable.'

Cato nodded, not yet certain what connection the prisoner had to him, although he was beginning to suspect the truth. But he was equally intrigued by the other matter the general had mentioned. 'You spoke of two reasons, sir.'

'Yes, I did,' Corbulo replied with a hint of sadness in his voice. 'There was a dispatch from Rome amongst the letters and paperwork brought from Tarsus by the supply convoy. It pains me to say it, but—'

He was interrupted by the sound of footsteps and the clink of chains outside the room. A moment later, Apollonius entered, leading another man. The prisoner was barefoot and wore a tattered tunic. There were livid bruises on his arms and legs, and an iron collar had been fastened around his neck, a length of chain fitted to it. Apollonius nodded a greeting to Cato before he indicated the prisoner, giving the chain a tug.

'You know this one well enough.'

He led the man to one side of the fireplace before he released the chain and sat on the edge of Corbulo's desk. The prisoner's head drooped as his chest rose and fell wearily.

'Look up!' Corbulo snapped, and the prisoner did as he was ordered.

'What in bloody Hades?' Cato muttered as he saw the man's face. Despite the bruises and cuts, there was no mistaking who it was. 'Flaminius . . .'

'Our good friend Flaminius,' Apollonius repeated with a slight sneer. 'Who we last saw not long after we crossed the frontier.'

'I thought he'd run off to escape slavery,' said Cato. 'How did he end up here, of all places?'

'It's quite a story.' Apollonius nodded towards the prisoner.

442

'Why don't you tell your former master what you told me earlier? You can start with your first act of betrayal. When you were caught by the Parthians shortly after you ran away from us. You told them that if they spared you, you'd tell them where we were camping. Right?'

Flaminius nodded.

Apollonius tilted his head to one side and cupped a hand to his ear. 'Sorry, I didn't catch that. Would you like me to encourage you to speak up?'

A look of terror etched itself on the man's features and he shook his head. 'No, sir! I'll tell him. I'll tell him everything.'

'Good. See that you do.'

Flaminius turned his gaze to Cato. 'Sir, you know my story. I was a good soldier. Fallen on hard times, just like I told you. I was pleased when you bought me. I would have served you loyally, in exchange for a comfortable home. Then you made me go with you into Parthia. I knew it was dangerous and I didn't want any part of it. After we crossed the frontier I decided to escape, the first chance I got. Only I ran straight into a Parthian patrol. They were all for killing me on the spot, but I traded my life for information on where to find you.'

'I wondered how they knew where we were,' Cato mused. 'Go on.'

'A group of them took me to Carrhae while the rest hunted you down. That's where a Parthian officer offered me money to serve Vologases. He told me there was a revolt brewing in Thapsis, and that he could use a man who could pass for a soldier. I said I'd take his silver and do the job.' Flaminius's head sank in shame.

'Look up!' Apollonius barked, and the prisoner flinched. 'Continue.'

'I was taken north as part of a Parthian contingent sent to

help the rebels. I advised them on how the Roman army fought. And then . . . and then . . .'

'Don't pretend you have any shame,' Apollonius said casually. 'It's far too late for that, my treacherous friend.'

Flaminius swallowed before he continued. 'It was me who led Prefect Orfitus into the trap, sir.'

'Thermon.' Corbulo sniffed. 'Just one of your roles, eh?'

'Yes, sir. And after that, they sent me into the Roman lines of the siege camp to sow dissent. When the mutiny broke out, I was instructed to broker a deal with Orfitus for food in exchange for him putting an end to the siege . . . That's all there is, sir.'

Cato felt a wave of disgust at the man's confession. At the same time, he was human enough to understand the degree to which Flaminius had resented being a slave. He knew from his own experience the stigma that attached to slavery. But betrayal on this scale was beyond any question of forgiveness. Flaminius's treachery had cost many lives. The lives of the kind of men he had once fought alongside.

'Traitor . . .'

'Quite.' Corbulo nodded. 'If there's nothing more to be confessed, you can take this scum away from us, Apollonius. I find his company disagreeable.'

'Yes, sir.' Apollonius pushed himself away from the desk and took up the end of the chain. 'Back to your cell. Last stop for you, Flaminius.'

He led the other man away, closing the door as he left.

Cato turned to Corbulo. 'What will happen to him, sir?'

'He's to be crucified outside the city gates tomorrow morning. I thought you might want to see that before you leave.'

'Leave, sir?'

Corbulo nodded. 'That's the other reason I sent for you. I've received an order from Nero that you and your men are to return to Rome. I can't delay sending you back. Not without provoking the emperor's temper. It's a pity. You're a fine officer and I would have been honoured to have you serve with me when war breaks out with Parthia. But we are servants of Nero. His will is absolute, no matter how much we would prefer not to answer to it.'

They shared a smile of complicity.

'When does my cohort leave?' Cato asked.

'At once, is what the order said. Tomorrow morning, then. Apollonius will be joining you to make my report to the emperor.'

'Ah,' Cato muttered, uncertain how much he would enjoy the agent's company on the voyage to Rome.

'Will your men be ready to march at such short notice?'

Cato considered this for a moment. He would need a couple of wagons for the wounded, and marching supplies to get them back to Tarsus. From there he could requisition three or four ships to sail to Rome. There was no reason for the cohort not to be ready to leave Thapsis the next day.

'They'll be ready. I just need to make the arrangements with Macro.' He drained his cup and stood up. 'If you'll excuse me, sir?'

'Of course. I'll have my aide draft you an authority to draw supplies and whatever else you need for the journey.'

'Thank you, sir.'

Corbulo rose to his feet and they clasped forearms. The general held his gaze, and Cato stared back unflinchingly.

'I'll say farewell tomorrow, Tribune. Of course, it is my firm hope that we will serve together again someday.'

Corbulo released his grip and they exchanged a salute, then

445

Cato turned to go in search of Macro to relay the news and give the orders for the remaining men of the cohort to make ready to march back to Tarsus.

'Back to Rome?' Macro raised an eyebrow as he pushed the half-eaten platter of cold roast boar to one side. He clicked his fingers to attract the attention of one of the serving girls of the inn he had chosen for his quarters. She cleared his plate away and gave him a shy smile before scurrying off. 'Well, I'm sure the lads will be happy to get back to their barracks. We'll be sure to get our cut from the sale of the prisoners, though?'

'I'll make certain of it,' said Cato. 'We've earned it. And the families of the men we lost will get their fair share too. It'll be a sizeable sum of money all round.'

Macro smiled happily. 'Just what I need to see me right after I apply for my discharge.'

Cato felt a nagging ache in his guts. 'You've decided, then?'

'I have. Twenty-eight years I've served. I'll be fifty in a few years. I want to grow old with my woman and enjoy life while I can. Rome owes me that. I've kept to my side of the bargain and given loyal service. It's time I was allowed to enjoy the rewards.'

'I can think of no man more deserving of a long and happy retirement, brother.'

Macro smiled. 'Thank you, sir. Coming from you, that means a lot.'

'Let's hope they approve the discharge swiftly, before someone finds you another campaign to get stuck into. You know how it goes.' Cato shook his head. 'What am I saying? I'm sure there won't be any problems.'

There was a silence before Macro scratched his nose. 'It'll be good for us all. You can take Lucius back to his home and raise

446

him in peace. I know Petronella will be pleased to see her sister again. Once my discharge comes through, we'll have more than enough from my bonus, my share of the spoils from this place and the savings held by my banker to see us through. If we stick with the plan I discussed with her, then we'll give Britannia a try. Go into business with my mother.'

'That I would like to see,' Cato laughed.

Macro's expression was serious. 'You think there'll be trouble between her and Petronella?'

'Given what I know of them both, I'd be a liar if I said I expected nothing but harmony and mutual affection. But you'll be there to keep the peace between them.'

'You make war with Parthia sound like the easy option.'

'Ah, I'm joking, brother. You'll be fine. We'll all be fine. We're going home at long last, wherever home may be. But right now, that's Rome.'

Cato picked up the wine jar, filled the cup Macro had been drinking from and then handed the jug to his friend. 'A toast. To Rome!'

Macro picked up the jar in both hands and tapped it against the side of Cato's cup as he grinned. 'To Rome!'

THE EAGLES OF THE EMPIRE SERIES

The Britannia Campaign

UNDER THE EAGLE
AD 42–43, Britannia

New recruit Cato arrives in Germany to serve under the command of Centurion Macro in the notoriously tough Second Legion. Soon the long march west for a brutal campaign in Britannia begins . . .

THE EAGLE'S CONQUEST
AD 43, Britannia

The invasion of Britannia is underway, but the Roman army is desperately outnumbered by the savage Britons. Centurion Macro and young optio Cato begin a treacherous battle against the enemy . . .

WHEN THE EAGLE HUNTS
AD 44, Britannia

Camulodunum has fallen to the Roman army, but the joy of victory is short-lived as the family of General Plautius has been captured by the vicious Druids. Cato and Macro must race against time to find them . . .

THE EAGLE AND THE WOLVES
AD 44, Britannia

As the Roman army continues its quest to conquer the ferocious Britons, it is weakened by its own split forces. The Romans must recruit native tribesmen to fight, and Macro and Cato must train them fast before they are destroyed by the enemy . . .

THE EAGLE'S PREY
AD 44, Britannia

The campaign in Britannia has been far bloodier than predicted, and Emperor Claudius needs a victory. A battle against the barbarian leader Caratacus could finally be the triumphant end that the Empire desperately need . . .

Rome and Eastern Provinces

THE EAGLE'S PROPHECY

AD 45, Rome

A band of brutal pirates have captured scrolls holding secrets that could destroy the Roman Empire. Centurions Macro and Cato must join the navy and hunt down the scrolls before the Empire falls . . .

THE EAGLE IN THE SAND

AD 46, Judaea

The eastern provinces of the Roman Empire are under threat. Centurions Macro and Cato have arrived in Judaea to regain control of the region. But the revolt is strengthening and the army must return to its full force before these provinces are lost . . .

CENTURION

AD 46, Syria

Rome's old enemy Parthia prepares to unleash its might across the border into Palmyra. Macro and Cato are posted to Syria in a desperate quest to protect the Empire . . .

The Mediterranean

THE GLADIATOR

AD 48–49, Crete

Centurions Macro and Cato are sailing home after a harrowing campaign in the east. But an earthquake forces them on to the shores of Crete, a province in chaos. The men are faced with a rebellion that could ignite a disastrous uprising across the Empire . . .

THE LEGION

AD 49, Egypt

Rebel gladiator Ajax and his crew are threatening the stability of the Roman Empire. After a series of attacks along the Egyptian coast Macro and Cato are hot on Ajax's trail, but can they defeat him?

PRAETORIAN

AD 51, Rome

A shadowy republican movement threatens Rome and the Emperor Claudius. Treachery lurks within the Praetorian Guard and Cato and Macro begin to unravel more than one conspiracy against the Emperor . . .

The Return to Britannia

THE BLOOD CROWS

AD 51, Britannia

The Roman army's fight to hold Britannia continues almost a decade after invasion. A campaign to resist the relentless natives begins, and Macro and Cato return to the perilous British shores to aid it.

BROTHERS IN BLOOD

AD 51, Britannia

Prefect Cato and Centurion Macro are pursuing barbarian leader Caratacus through the mountains of Britannia. Defeating Caratacus seems within their grasp, but the plot against the two heroes threatens their lives . . .

BRITANNIA

AD 52, Britannia

The western tribes prepare to make a stand and Centurion Macro remains behind in charge of the fort as Prefect Cato leads an invasion deep into the hills. Cato's mission: to crush the Druid stronghold. But has the enemy been underestimated?

Hispania

INVICTUS

AD 54, Hispania

Cato and Macro have been recalled to Rome, but their time in the city is short. Soon they are travelling with the Praetorian Guard to Spain, where they battle for control in a land considered unconquerable . . .

The Return to Rome

DAY OF THE CAESARS

AD 54, Rome

When Cato catches the eye of rival factions who will stop at nothing to get him on side, he must play a cunning game and enlist the help of Macro. But as the conspiracy grows, it begins to look like a civil war could be on the horizon . . .

The Eastern Campaign

THE BLOOD OF ROME

AD 55, Armenia

The wily Parthian Empire has invaded Armenia, ousting ruthless King Rhadamistus. The Romans must restore him to power, as he is vital to Rome's strategic interests, while also preparing for war with the powerful Parthian Empire. And Cato and Macro must take the lead . . .